The Last Teabag

M.G. Atkinson

First published 2019

Cover design and render by Myk.
With a very special thanks to:
My mum - Marie Shaw, my aunt - Jennifer Lemm,
The lady I made cry - Sue Drury,
and all of the readers who gave me feedback
and took the time to proof-read for me.

eMail: myk.atkinson@ntlworld.com
Facebook: http://www.facebook.com/mgatkinsonauthor

For everyone.

Prologue

What's the time?

Open O'-damn-clock, that's what! Where the hell is she?

The young man paced up and down the stretch of pavement in front of the Internet-cafe's locked, glass doors. He glanced at his watch and then looked up to see if *she* was crossing the tiled floor with the door-key's in her hand.

The sign on the door said the cafe opened at 9am.

He looked at his watch again; 9:01. *Come ON!*

His jaw clenched in frustration as he continued his pacing, his brow furrowed with anger and his eyes hard.

Life without a phone. Who could live without their phone?

He had only been without his for nine hours, and his world, the real world in front of his eyes, had become horribly stark. Without his phone he may just as well be invisible.

While Kieran, Annika and Dillon were all having *fun,* he was missing it all. All of the posts on 'Farce-book' as they called it, all of the pictures and tweets and blogs and videos and trolls and gossip and and and.

The cafe owner walked into the dining area from a door at the back and flicked on the lights.

She smiled warmly when she saw the young man at the door, and then her smile dropped when she saw he wasn't about to be polite and return it.

Fine! Bloody students!

As soon as she had turned the key and the lock had flicked back, he was pushing at the handle. What was his problem?

'Steady!' She said and frowned, stepping back as the door swung open.

'It says you open at nine!' He snapped.

She raised her eyebrow and looked at the digital-clock on the wall. It was showing 9:00 exactly. 'It *is* nine.' She replied a little icily.

The young man looked at the clock, the anger on his face and in his eyes still apparent. Arrogance rose to the front of his teenager mind. 'Not by *my* watch it isn't!' He mumbled his words and looked straight past her.

1

The woman just sighed and rolled her eyes, shaking her head. Bloody students.

After scanning his student-card and handing it back - without a thank you she noted - she watched him almost run to the nearest free booth. What was so urgent that it made him sweat?

'Just so you know,' she called over as his head disappeared behind the partition. 'If you're trying to buy drugs the university has a policy to trace suspicious Internet activity, you know?'

His head reappeared and he stared at her.

'And there's cameras in here as well.' She continued as she pointed to the small, black domes in the corners.

'I'm not buying drugs! I'm trying to locate my phone.'

Her eyes suddenly widened in surprise. 'Your phone? You're all twitchy and sweaty because of your bloomin' phone?' She shook her head and looked bewildered. 'You need to get a girlfriend, love.'

Without waiting for any kind of reply the woman turned away and began the morning coffee orders. She heard him huff though as he sat heavily back down.

The monitor in front of him snapped into cool life, slowly warming as the computer booted up.

His fingers drummed the table-top next to the mouse, itching to get clicking.

It took almost five minutes for the computer to finally give him control, but within seconds of grabbing the mouse he had several windows opened and a stream of messages waiting for him.

U left ur fone ere ya boot. Kieran's Facebook message greeted him.

He smiled and warmed up and calmed down in an instant. *Tfft!* He typed back.

The monitor chimed, it was Dillon. *Hi Gav wherv u bin? Check this out. Sum old geezer is going to top himself on the steps of parliament.* There was a video link attached to the message.

Before he had a chance to click on it the monitor chimed again. Annika joined the conversation. *Gav hav u seen this?* Another video link popped up.

The young man called Gav typed a message back. *Just lookin now.*

He clicked on the link and the window expanded as it loaded the video.

There was nothing really special to see, just an old man walking along a country lane, a dark, wooden walking staff in his right hand and a small, khaki bag over his shoulder.

He looked to be at least in his seventies, frail and doddering, but the look on his face was hard and set.

And then the vehicle carrying the person with the phone-camera passed him by and the video looped back to the beginning.

Gav typed. *Wots he doin?*

The monitor remained silent for all of three seconds before Dillon answered. *He sed hes goin to starve himself at parliament.* Another link popped up. *Read this and share it mate.*

The link took him to an almost empty Facebook page; Mathew Arnold. There was only one photo of him, and his *friends* numbered only twelve.

Gav read his latest entry.

I only have 12 followers (whatever that actually means) and I only know 3 of you in person, but I suppose it doesn't really matter, someone will eventually read this.

I've had enough now, I can't give anything else because I don't have anything left to give. How have I arrived at this point? I'm asking you seriously; how have I become so insignificant? Why am I terrified of my letterbox and knocks at the door? Why do I have to sit in the cold and dark at night because I can't afford to have the light and heating on? Why is the water-board and the electric company trying to take my things from me? Why am I always alone and hungry?

I've worked hard all my life, paid my taxes and always paid my rent and bills. I did all that because I thought it was our duty to society, our duty to keep things moving forward, keep things on the right track for a better future. For everyone. Isn't that the point? To be better and make things better? What is happening to my country?

I have 17p in my pocket as I write this on a borrowed computer, 17p until my next pension payment in ten-days. And what was I told when I pointed this out to 'them'? "There are plenty of food-banks here, Mr Arnold." Food-banks? Why does our country have the need for food-banks?

I can see there is plenty of money, I can see it in the fat of our politicians, I can see it in all of the new buildings which are going up, I can see it in the eyes of 'them'. I can see it and there is plenty of it. Why do they need every, single penny of mine as well? They are taking the food from my table and the heat from my home, the water from my taps and the light from my personal space. How is that acceptable? My neighbour's dogs eat more than I do.

Today is the first day in years that I have felt unafraid. It feels good. Just for once, I actually feel good. I feel good because I have nothing left and no alternatives, and strangely, it feels entirely liberating.

I have 10 days to go without, which I know will probably be the end of me, or if not that, I will become seriously ill first and then die. So I have decided to do it myself. Oh don't worry, I'm not going to blow my brains out or slash my wrists or anything like that. No, I'm going to take a walk I think, take a walk to parliament and give them my last 17p and then sit down on their *doorstep and go to sleep. They can have my body then as well can't they? And the clothes I am wearing just to finish off this deal they are peddling as 'life'.*

I can only wish you all, all peoples from everywhere, the very best of luck in getting through your lives. I mean that sincerely, I truly hope you have lives which are free of fear and are filled with all of the right things instead. I hope none of you ever end up like me.

Good luck,
Mathew Arnold.

Chapter One

Five-pence left in the electricity meter. The gas had run out two days ago, but he could do without gas; he could always put on another jumper if it turned too cold.

So five-pence in the meter and seventeen-pence in his pocket and he still couldn't boil the kettle to make a cup of tea.

Mathew looked down at the round, red tin in front of him, a single teabag sat at the bottom. It looked lonely he thought, sitting in that cold, little tin all by itself.

His kitchen felt like that tin; cold and empty, and cupboards bare and a silence which tried to suffocate him.

Like the teabag, all Mathew needed was a little warmth to get him going. Five pence in the meter.

He raised his rheumy, blue eyes and looked out of the window and up to a cold, blue sky.

He wouldn't get through another winter. He felt it now. The house was silent, like it was waiting for it to happen. He used to love this house.

Twenty-two years he had lived under this roof. Fifteen of those years he had shared with his wife Mary until she had suddenly passed away. Too suddenly, he thought.

It still didn't explain why he had ended up here at this point though did it? It wasn't like he had just *given up* after Mary had died. He'd found it hard, of course he had, but he didn't give up.

So *how* had he arrived here? What had happened to cause him to become so insignificant?

He felt he was just a number on a bill now, a series of digits and dashes on some computer somewhere. A cold, lifeless and harassing computer.

He couldn't remember the last time he had received a letter from an actual human being, good news or bad.

It was all printed threats nowadays; automatic demands for your money, *robots* disguised as people sitting in court-rooms signing the warrants to say it is okay for other mindless *robots* to come and drill your locks off and take your things.

How do you reason and debate with a machine? Why are the people taking orders from machines in the first place? Where have all the *real* people gone?

The silence was probably the worst of it all. The house used to have *noise* in it, house-noise; fridges clicking on and off and humming, water moving through piping, gas-boilers flaring, just the usual noises which a house made when there was life in it. Now though, the fridge was sold and the boiler was cold.

The house was telling him he was already dead wasn't it? That he was merely going through the motions of getting to the point of actually dying now.

For the past seven years Mathew had stood at this window, gripping the edge of the sink and just staring at the sky, nothing to do but worry and think, nowhere to go and no one to talk to.

Today his grip relaxed as the constant fear which he usually felt fell away with that thought; the house was telling him he was already dead.

* * *

Warm stone and the smell of hot, baking bread filled the air, an aroma which somehow seemed *thicker* in the cooling months of autumn, a comfort-blanket of taste and smell to some.

Alison crouched beneath the heat-extractor in the alleyway, back pressed firmly into the red-brick wall, and soaked up the heat through her parka while she licked the last of the cream from the éclair-wrapper. Two more, spotlessly-clean wrappers lay neatly side-by-side next to her boots.

It wasn't exactly *breakfast at Tiffany's* but it *was* breakfast.

Yesterday's éclairs were one of the main items which Alison always came across when raiding a *Gregg's* wheelie-bin.

Why did the idiots make so many if they knew they would be thrown away? And they *must* know mustn't they? There was always more éclairs than anything else in the bins wasn't there?

Her tongue finished the job of getting the last of the cream and chocolate from the creases in the waxy wrapper - every calorie she could get inside her - and then she dropped it to the ground to join its brothers.

The shop would be opening for breakfast in an hour. Rag would probably be on his way here to go through the bins before it did.

She had to keep well away from Rag, he'd already had his shovel-hands on her once.

"If you look afta' me, I'll look afta' you, if ya know wha' a mean?"

His breath stank. Alison felt sick when she thought of his brown-black teeth and the grey, yellowing, dead thing residing in his flabby mouth which he called a tongue.

He'd tried to kiss her while groping her behind, trying his damnedest to lift her from the ground and embrace her in his thick, greasy arms.

Luckily for Alison, Rag had swilled down a two-litre bottle of *White Lightning* for breakfast that day, and she had managed to slip out of his fumbling grasp and get away.

She was well aware of his reputation though; there were some, it was said, who hadn't been so lucky.

She sniffed and wiped the end of her nose with her gloved palm, her ice-blue eyes constantly on the move, unconsciously looking for trouble.

Adjusting to life on the street hadn't been too difficult for her, two years now and she could easily have passed for a *lifer*. If it hadn't been for her small frame and tight, fresh skin - although occasionally a little grimed - she would have as well; but Alison was only one week away from her fifteenth birthday and looked even younger.

The few homeless who knew her and saw her regularly, the ones who didn't carry huge chips on their shoulders and were happy getting on in the world, had nicknamed her *Nippy*, because she was surprisingly agile and fast on her feet.

At first Alison had worn the name with a kind of ego-boosting pride, but soon came to realise that most of the others were very *long in the tooth* and didn't do much *nipping* about like she did anyway. She would seem like a cheetah to them.

The novelty had soon worn off with that particular enlightenment and she had quickly stopped trying to be everywhere at the same time just to impress them.

Back in the alley and her thoughts were suddenly plucked away by the very beginnings of a noise. If she had been a sprinter in the blocks this would have been the *B* of the *BANG!* moment, as they called it.

'OI!'

The nasty bark of Rag, boomed down the closed alleyway, and even as the echoes were dying away, *Nippy* was up on top of the wheelie-bins and over the wall, sprinting across the car-park with her little heart hammering in her ears.

* * *

Polished glass windows looked in on neat, tidy offices, lining neat and tidy corridors, with tidy, neat men and women clacking away at computers or listening at switchboards or watching banks of tiny images on monitors. Neat and tidy information gathering.

And then the clacking of one particular *drone* ceased and he sat back and stared at his monitor through his round, polished spectacles.

The words *suicide* and *parliament* were flashing up on his screen.

He'd only been in the job for seven weeks and this was his first *hit* and it looked to be a biggie.

Stay cool Roger, remember your training, do it by the numbers.

He leaned forward again and clacked away professionally.

A long stream of information began to gather on the screen; IP addresses, subnet masks, bank account details, medical records, telephone numbers - hundreds of the things, dating back for at least five years - emails and their addresses, television licensing information, car tax, council tax, income tax, utility bills, catalogue accounts, shop accounts and eventually a Facebook page.

Roger the neat and tidy *drone* read the last entry of Mathew Arnold, and then picked up his telephone and dialled. It was answered almost immediately.

'*Donagle.*'

'Agent 3646 Barden, sir. I think I might have picked something up.'

'*You think?*'

'Well, um, it's a little tricky, sir.'

The silence which met Roger was prompt enough to get on with it. 'A- a man has published his intentions to commit suicide at parliament, sir.' He said, only just avoiding blustering it out.

'*Our parliament?*'

'Um. Yes sir.'

'*Do we have a timescale and do we know what his intended method of destruction will be?*' The voice calling himself Donagle asked impatiently.

'Um. Yes sir. I-I mean sort of, sir.' The bluster wasn't that far away now.

'*Well spit it out, man!* When *is he going to do it and* how *is he going to do it? It's pretty, damned-well straightforward enough!*'

It seemed the blustering was contagious; one borne of anger and frustration and the other of quickly-diminishing decorum and professionalism.

'I-I-I think it will be in a week or so,' Roger answered with an unintentional gulp. 'And it looks like he's going to starve himself or-or-or walk himself to death, sir.'

The line remained silent again for a few seconds, then came a very tiny click and then a louder thudding and scraping followed by a diminishing tapping.

Silence again for a few more seconds and then the door to Rogers shared office was thrown open and a short, wiry man in a suit came hurrying up to the startled Roger's workstation.

He stood motionless and stared at the screen, the pale skin under his left eye twitched along as he read the Facebook entry.

He didn't blink once, Roger noticed.

Donagle continued to stare, reading the entry for the third time, his mind trying to find a sensible hand-hold on the situation. A *finger*-hold would do. What kind of terrorist was this? A suicide-walker-*slash*-starver?

'Sir?' Roger said quietly. His boss hadn't blinked or taken a breath for nearly a minute.

Donagle pointed at the screen and opened his mouth to speak but didn't.

He remained poised like that for at least another ten seconds before releasing his breath and lowering his arm. 'Well. That's different.' He eventually said, blinking rapidly now.

Normally the security filters employed by the various Internet-service providers caught *domestic* suicide notes and simply left them alone - it was generally thought it was best to not interfere, as well as not giving away the fact that someone was always watching. Or as in this case, *listening in* as the *Ears* were doing.

The Ears - *Electronic, Anti-terrorist Reconnaissance and Surveillance* - were a branch-off from the security services; a fifty strong army of listeners, watchers and professional keyboard clackers, of which Jeremy Donagle was the head.

Smooth and neat was his motto, *keep the lines of information straight and you will always have a straight answer*. This was neither smooth nor neat.

'We can't send a team out after him.' Donagle crisply said, suddenly standing up straight but keeping his eyes firmly fixed on the last entry. 'He hasn't actually broken any laws by *saying* he's going to starve himself to death has he?'

Roger had the uncomfortable feeling that his boss wasn't actually speaking to him.

'And because he's not threatening *immediate* suicide,' Donagle continued, 'we can't just have him picked up and placed under section. No, no, that wouldn't do at all.'

He rubbed his clean-shaven chin and frowned. 'He doesn't actually say that he's going to die by walking, so-.' He suddenly turned his eyes on the startled Roger. 'What made you say he was either going to starve himself or *walk* himself to death?'

Roger quickly pushed his spectacles back up his nose and whipped up the mouse. He expertly clicked away and opened the video-file of Mathew Arnold walking along a country road. 'He-he's very old, sir.'

Donagle leaned closer and watched the video play its loop. As it began the fifth run he straightened up and smiled; suicide by walking was definitely *not* a thing. Smooth and neat.

'Delete it.' He said. 'Delete it and forget it; he can do as he pleases. We are here to make sure that our citizens and their liberties are not put in jeopardy by terrorists; this man is one of our citizens.'

And the wheel of fate dealt a strange hand that day for Jeremy Donagle; he was the only human-being on or off the planet that could have stopped Mathew Arnold's march to London before it had even really begun.

'But, sir, are-are you certain?' Roger asked, just giving fate another nudge, another lifeline for Donagle to take, another opportunity to stop Mathew in his tracks.

Donagle stared for a few seconds more at the still-running video.

Fate held its breath.

And then he said; 'Quite certain, agent Barden, delete it.'

'Yes sir.' Roger answered, and he took up his mouse once more.

While somewhere in the Universe, this thing called *fate* chuckled gleefully.

Chapter Two

Strange to be outside at this time, under the pale glare of the new LED streetlights. Usually by now he would be under the blankets on the sofa, reading by candlelight before sleeping.

Mathew squinted at his watch; almost half-past nine. He felt like he should be sleeping, his body-clock seemed to be nagging at him to stop and sit and sleep.

He'd been going for eight hours and was tired but not too footsore. His feet seemed to want to go on forever. He'd intended to do just that; keep walking until he either dropped or reached parliament, but now? Now he wanted to sleep.

What if I don't wake up? That'd be a waste; I could just as easily do that back at home.

What home? Whose home?

His step first faltered and then slowed and finally halted at the very edge of the cold circle of light coming from the last streetlight along this back-road.

He sniffed and blinked his eyes, looking deeply into the darkness laying in wait in front of him.

The stars were out and the pale light of the sickle moon promised to light the way ahead.

What home?

He took a step into the faded gloom. The stars twinkled, waking memories from happier, freer times.

This *is my home.*

And he took another step and then another and another.

When did my home get taken from me?

His eyes adjusted to the darkness very quickly, the moon and the stars both fulfilling their promise to light his way.

They seemed to blaze in the dark did his eyes, as they caught the faint light, a determination forging ahead of him under his hard-set brow.

The fatigue seemed to slip away, relegated to a corner of his mind as he thought of that simple but terrifying truth; his home had been taken away from him and he couldn't remember when it had happened, or how. Not the house he had lived in, but the country, the world even, this was all his home and somehow it had been slowly stolen away.

Who is to blame then? Who are the thieves and what are they doing with all that 'swag'?

While he tried to put faces to the *thieves* his ears picked up the distant hum of an engine coming toward him from the dark road ahead. He stepped onto the grass verge and pressed his back into the hawthorn hedge to wait.

He could feel the thick, needle-sharp thorns trying to press themselves through his borrowed, Belstaff jacket, and smiled inwardly; it would take more than a few thorns to pierce a Belstaff.

His heart ached for a moment as he thought of his dear friend Derek, who had given him the use of his computer to write the Facebook message.

A good man was Derek, another victim who also lived right on the edge.

'Flipping heck, Matty.' Derek muttered after reading the entry for the second time.

He turned around on his swivel-chair to face Mathew sitting next him. 'It really has got that bad, hasn't it?' His eyes were brimming and shining.

Mathew remained silent.

'I'd go with you if I could, you know? But,' he patted his legs, 'these old things won't even get me down the street now.'

'I know you would, you're a good man, Derek.' Mathew took his friend's hand in his own and clasped it tightly. 'You've always been a good friend to both of us.'

Derek nodded slowly and returned Mathew's handshake. The pair of them sat in silence for a few moments.

An air of revelation and inevitability hung over their resigned heads, they both felt it; the game was in its final stages now, this game they had been playing called living, *and it was an endgame which had been forced upon them.*

Derek sat back first, a conflicting mixture of anger and pity etched into his face. 'I can't be on the road with you, Mat, but by God, I won't just sit here and let you feel alone while you're out there.'

He reached for his walking sticks and eased himself painfully up onto his feet. 'I'll let people know, I promise, but before all that we'll have lunch and I'll get you some things to take with you.'

Mathew stood up and helped his friend to find his balance. 'You don't have to do that, Derek, it's enough that you-'

'Please don't do that, Mat,' Derek cut in, standing as straight and as proud as he could. 'This-this is different, this is like-like one of those "defining moments" you hear about, this is bigger than me or you, Mat, much bigger.'

Mathew stared at him and frowned, uncomprehending.

'I-I know I don't have that gentle touch with certain situations, Mat, but this? I can sense a change in the wind, a change for the hundreds of thousands of people who are heading to the very place you are now. Me included.'

He lowered his gaze, sudden feelings of guilt at unloading such a burden on Mathew spilled from his eyes. 'I'm really sorry, Matty,' he sobbed, 'I really am. Nobody should get to this point, nobody.'

Mathew reached out and embraced his friend gently.

Derek was right; whether he wanted the burden or not it was his now, he had somehow found himself at the head of the queue that was all. 'You don't have to be sorry, Derek, I understand.' He replied. 'You're right, if I manage to actually do this then it won't be for me, will it? Whether I want it to or not it will be for everyone who is going through what we are.'

Mathew stood back again.

Derek sniffed and sighed. 'I-I'm sorry you have this burden though, Mat, but if I know you,' he looked Mathew straight in the eye and stood up straight again. 'You will make it, I've never met a more stubborn man in my life, you just don't give up when everyone else normally does.'

Mathew smiled. 'I think that was something Mary must have beat into me over the years.'

They both laughed then; Mary was the most unassuming, caring and honest woman one could ever meet, she wouldn't even beat a fly out of the house. "Everything has a reason and a right to their lives." She would often say when carting off the captured spider or two to the garden shed.

The two friends had eaten as large a lunch as Derek could provide, sitting in a deferential and humble silence around the small dining table in Derek's kitchen.

Once they had finished and the tea was poured, Mathew's long-time friend had limped off and gathered together some essentials for Mathew to take with him. A penknife, a wind-up torch, two cigarette lighters, some cooked meat and some cheese and bread.

'I haven't any money to give you, but I've got these.' He handed Mathew a pair of walking boots and a hardwood staff. 'I don't have use for 'em anymore, or my Belstaff.' He pointed at the jacket hanging up in the hallway. 'It's like wearing a waterproof bed on your back is that thing.'

'You're a good friend, Derek,' Mathew smiled and took his hand again. 'Thank you.'

He then spent the next fifteen minutes lacing up the leather boots while he sipped at his tea before standing up and putting the jacket on. Both were a good fit.

He stamped his feet, testing the thick, rubber soles; they could have got him to London at least ten times, he thought. Once would be enough though.

'Well,' Mathew began, standing by the front door and turning to Derek. '"I am just going outside and may be some time."' He winked.

Derek chuckled and shook his head. 'You can't have those last words, they've already been taken.'

He shuffled forward on his walking sticks and then propped himself up on the door-frame. Taking the walking staff from the corner he held it out to Mathew. 'Good luck, Matty.' He said, as Mathew took the staff. 'I would say God bless, but right now I don't think He's listening to us. I don't think anyone is.'

Mathew shrugged. 'He hasn't been listening to us for years, Derek, we just didn't notice.'

'And there's your last words.'

The pair of them laughed as only doomed men could when the odds were stacked so ridiculously high against them.

Mathew opened the door and stood on the step, looking out at the familiar street he had lived on for all these years. It was a good street with good people, decent people for the most part. He would be walking for them as soon as his foot touched the path outside the gate.

His heart lurched in his chest. 'I don't know what's going to happen, Derek.' His voice was quiet with subtle dread.

Then the reassuring hand of his friend squeezed his shoulder lightly.

'Me neither, Matty, me neither.'

Bright sparks suddenly popped before his glazed eyes as the truck Mathew had heard coming down the road in the darkness brought him shuddering back to the present.

He raised his arm and shielded his brow from the overpowering glare of the headlights.

It roared past him angrily, trailing a smell of diesel exhaust and hot engine-metal behind it.

He watched as the red glow of its tail-lights faded into the night and then suddenly disappear as the truck curved its way around a dark corner.

His hammering heart slowed down and he breathed a sigh of relief, extracting himself from the hawthorn hedge. He hadn't noticed how deeply he had pushed himself into it until he popped free. The Belstaff was untouched.

Like a waterproof bed on your back, the echo of his friend's words made him smile proudly.

Mathew continued to smile as he turned back to face the darkened road. The hedges and tree-line were all speckled with damp, blue-white hues; the glow of the open sky and faded moon.

He pulled up his hood and began walking again.

The minutes and hours ticked by, Mathew's pace never faltered and the rhythm of his boots and staff were constant. But he knew he was on auto-pilot now, knew that his mind wanted to sleep.

A check of his watch showed him it was almost two in the morning.

He instinctively knew that if he stopped now and sat down he would fall asleep and most certainly wouldn't wake up. He wasn't about to be found dead in a ditch. Not on his first blooming day he wasn't.

He walked on wishing he could sleep a little.

As if the Universe had been listening in on his thoughts and wishes, Mathew heard the sudden sound of sloshing water coming from somewhere over on his right as the well-worn, rubber seal attached to a water-pipe finally split with a hiss and gurgle.

He crossed the road and followed the sound for a few feet more before coming to a gated opening in the tall hedgerow.

Walking right up to the cold, metal gate, he peered into the gloom.

A small silhouette stood a few feet inside the entrance to this open field, a square-shaped building by the looks of it, and the sound was coming from somewhere inside.

After a little effort and a careful climb over the steel gate, Mathew gingerly crossed the muddied path to the building.

He could just make out a small, wooden door on one side. It looked and sounded like it was a pump-house, part of the drainage system for these fields probably.

He reached out and tried the handle, it was more than likely going to be locked, but he tried it anyway.

It squeaked quietly and then popped open with a sudden, satisfying, surprising snap and click.

Mathew pushed the door back on grinding, unused hinges and then simply stood looking inside.

It was dry and warm and he had a waterproof bed on his back.

Chapter Three

Just as Mathew was making himself comfortable in his quietly discovered shelter, Alison was just waking up from the usual nightmares in hers.

She sat trembling beneath her cardboard *blankets*, the last of her whimpering still faintly sounding in her head.

'Y'awhite, Niffy?'

Alison gasped and spun around to face Jolly on her right, propping himself up on his elbow beneath his own blankets and peering at her through the dim candlelight.

'Y'bin to'kin' in y'sheep agin.' The old tramp said.

He chomped and smacked his toothless mouth unconsciously while he looked at her sympathetically. 'Y'neeb a shwig ov ol' nashchy?'

Alison shook her head.

It had taken weeks for her to decipher and understand what Jolly was saying when he spoke to her, and it didn't help that he spoke so quickly either.

She'd had days of frowning in concentration as he repeated his words slowly, looking at her as though he were speaking the Queen's English most perfectly while she must be a simpleton or something.

"*I shed; y'berry niffy omn y'feech. Omn. Ya. - Wasch m'lipsh - Omn. Ya. Feech.*" That particular lesson had gone on for almost an hour before Alison had finally understood; *You're very nippy on your feet.* "*Oh! Riiight. Thanks, Jolly.*"

He held up the bottle for her to see. A murky, yellow-ish liquid sloshed around inside. 'Y'shor? 'Elp y'sheep?'

'I'm okay, Jolly, I'm not that desperate.' She answered and smiled weakly.

Old Nasty, as it was affectionately known down here amongst the inhabitants of this small, secluded bridge, was an evil brew made with the carefully acquired fruits from local orchards and allotments.

Merylin, the snoring figure laid on the other side of Alison's sleeping place, was the brewer of this distinctive, mind-bending cider.

The earth could move beneath her and Merylin wouldn't wake, but put a hand near her brew and she'd be up on her feet and attacking you like a ninja bag-lady before you could get the cork out of the bottle.

There were six people living under this small bridge on the outskirts of town. It was a well secluded spot and the design of the bridge made a hollow alcove which was protected from the elements all around.

The concrete struts which held the bridge up had bubble-like indentations at their bases. When a small fire was lit in one of the indents it warmed up the whole, back wall of this little bridge-hovel, making it dry, warm and rainproof.

Jolly tucked his bottle of *Old Nasty* away and then pulled his blankets over his head, shuffling and turning for a few moments before settling down again.

Alison lay with her back propped against the warm, concrete wall and stared out into the night. The stars were bright tonight.

She liked to watch the stars, imagining herself exploring new worlds where the stars always looked different but were always *home,* her home, wherever she lay beneath them.

She'd lived in a house once, a farmhouse, and children's-homes twice.

The house had been a home once and then had become a cold and loveless place, while the *homes* had been sterile and pitiful. In the house she had a cloak of anxiety always draped around her, and in the *homes* she simply had nothing.

Alison shuddered with unconscious dread at her earlier memories, involuntarily stiffening herself, bracing herself for...

She gasped as the breath she had been holding forced it's way out of her small, tensed chest, and then she sobbed and gasped again, hardening her gaze upon the stars, concentrating on their soothing pulses and driving away the darkness from her mind with their sheer expanse. Her home.

Merylin coughed and snorted in her sleep.

Alison relaxed and lay back down. She *was* home.

When she opened her eyes again the sun had just risen, all but Merylin were still snoring.

'Good morning, my little dove.' She said to Alison.

She stood outside in the first rays of the sun, just stretching herself and enjoying the new morning. 'Come and get some sunshine, it's going to rain later; might as well get it in now.'

Now in her mid-fifties, Merylin spoke with a very clear middle-class accent. She never swore - savagely berating those who did - she was always as clean as was humanely possible under the circumstances and her eloquence with a pen, or word when reading to them all, was reminiscent of the public school governess days. She was definitely well educated, but no one knew what her story was.

Merylin was very touchy on the subject of her background. All anyone could really make of it was she was from an affluent if not wealthy family and she once let it slip that she had been a chemist. What kind of chemist, no one knew, but she certainly could make a potent cider.

Alison pushed her covers and cardboard over to one side and then slipped out to stand next to the older woman.

Merylin looked down into Alison's small, pale face, noting the darkened tracks of her night time tears.

Draping her arm around the young girl's shoulder, she pulled her close to her side and they stood facing the still rising sun.

'The night and the peace that comes with it,' Merylin murmured, 'is no place for tears.'

She stroked Alison's hair and then stooped to kiss the top of her head. 'I'm glad you didn't take Jolly's offer of a *nightcap* though.'

Alison giggled a little. 'Y' 'eard tha'?'

Merylin chuckled but didn't say anything.

They stood for awhile, holding onto each other and connecting with the new day. The sun was unusually bright and hot for September.

The canal which the tiny bridge spanned slid past quickly and quietly behind them. It was Merylin's main source of water, both for her brewing and her *essentials* as she called it.

Her brewing-kit consisted of a crude alembic made from two stainless-steel cooking pots - one sitting inside the other - and the shiny, plastic top from a flour bin.

She purified the water through her system, but by the time it was *bottled* and ready for drinking it was now full of a different kind of deadliness altogether.

She pulled a small, flat, deep-blue bottle from her pocket, flipped the pewter lid and took a mouthful.

Alison watched while the older woman shuddered and quivered as the burning alcohol ran down her throat and into her chest and finally her stomach.

Merylin caught her look. 'What!? Don't look at me like that.'

'Like wha'?' Alison asked, innocently widening her eyes.

'Like that.' Merylin snapped back, pointing at Alison's face.

'It's m' normal look.'

The older woman stuttered; how do you argue with a teenager? She hadn't been given the opportunity to get that far with her own child.

And with that thought she simply sagged and sighed, lowered her arm and her eyes and pushed those thoughts back to the forgetfulness which they belonged to.

'You must think me a total hypocrite.' She quietly spoke, embarrassed.

'Why? 'Cos y' tell me t' stay off booze an' then y'do it yasen?' Alison asked.

Without waiting for a reply she continued. 'I wish y' wouldn't, bu' I get why y'do.' She took a step closer to Merylin and touched her arm gently. 'I drink t' stars t' forge'.' She whispered.

Merylin nodded slowly and raised her eyes again. 'We shouldn't have to forget, though, should we?' She said. 'Especially you, my little dove.'

Alison shrugged. 'Shit 'app- er, I mean stuff 'appens, dunnit?' She shrugged again. 'Maybe am suppose' t' be 'ere.'

Merylin looked at her young companion, a puzzled expression of respect on her lined features, and then she smiled and raised an eyebrow. 'Happens.' She said, firmly emphasising the H.

'Wha'?'

'Shit. Happens. Pronounce your H, little dove.'

Alison covered her giggle with her hands.

Merylin turned away, smiling, and nodded for Alison to follow her.

They walked along the grassy slope of the canal-bank until they came to a spot where the tall weeds and brush had been cleared back a little. Four, wooden planks were laid out next to each other leading up to the water's edge, creating a small platform to stand on.

The pair of them washed their hands and faces in the cold, flowing water and then they pulled out their toothbrushes and stood one hand on hip as they cleaned the night from their mouths.

Once they were brushed, Merylin produced a half-filled, plastic bottle of purified water from her pocket to rinse out the foam.

'D' ya wanna come inta town wi' me?' Alison asked after wiping her mouth on her sleeve. 'Seef we can ge' some bre'kfast?'

She knew Merylin didn't often go into the town centre, she seemed quite content to just barter her brew for food or money, and use the small corner-shop a mile or so away down the road.

'Um. No. Thank you for asking though.' Merylin replied, smiling weakly.

Her mind flashed briefly to memories of the horrors of the fleeing crowd, but she quickly threw them back into well practised oblivion, showing no outwardly sign she was fighting her demon. Only her eyes could still give her away.

Alison's mind may have still been young and developing, but her time living outside, on the edge, had furnished her with a quick and subtle wisdom. There was no need for inquisitive, probing, teenager questions; pain was apparent in any language.

'I'll bring summert back f' ya.' She smiled at Merylin like a concerned aunt.

Merylin returned the smile. 'You really are a little dove, aren't you?' And stroked the girl's cheek with the back of her hand.

Taking Alison's arm and linking it through her own, the older woman steered them away from the water and they slowly strolled along the bank back to the bridge.

They were met by the smell of toasting bread.

Jolly and Peach were sitting around the tiny gas-stove, an open loaf by their feet and a slice held out in front of them on their *toasting* sticks.

Peach was the eldest of this *family* and had lived under the sky for much longer than the others. Even though she didn't know it for certain, she was eighty-six years old and was probably one of the most natural human-beings a person could ever meet.

Her life outside may have been hard on her body, but it had only succeeded in feeding her unyielding constitution. She was very able-bodied and had all of her mind, and was adamant that she wasn't going *anywhere* soon.

The other two members of this tiny clique of disowned people, Hamish and Puddle, were busy tidying away all of the bedding and making their little *bridge-home* ready for the day.

They worked with a well-practised precision, shaking out the bedding and blankets and then folding them all away between the top layers of cardboard and plastic sheeting.

Once the bedding was neatly packed, the pair of them uncovered and erected the *settee*; nine, plastic beer-crates upended and topped with more cardboard.

Of the six of them who were living here, Puddle was the silent peacekeeper, particularly protective of Peach, and also the main reason why people like Rag didn't bother them.

He was a tall, bulky man in his early-sixties, with a full-faced beard and tied-back, dark-brown hair.

Puddle rarely spoke and almost never added to a conversation, answering any questions aimed his way with a single word or sometimes just a look.

Hamish stepped out into the sunshine and waved when he saw Merylin and Alison returning from the canal.

He raised the steel kettle he was holding. 'Tea up!' He called out, cheerfully.

He was tall and a little gaunt, with sandy, shaggy hair. The scars on his face and the look in his eye told the tale of an ex-servicemen.

"Went to Kuwait hoping to get a medal and a tan and all I came back with was a bad case of SCM."

"What's SCM?" Someone would always ask.

"Shrapnel in the face, Chemicals in the blood and Madness in the head!"

He would laugh at that point, as if the punch line were an hilarious joke. He laughed because he knew that if he didn't he would probably never laugh again.

His audience, after listening and watching him tell his *joke*, were always left with an uneasy feeling in their stomachs at the *Madness in the head* part and the howling laughter.

Not the people down here under the bridge though.

Merylin cast Hamish a lingering glance.

She loved the people she lived with, loved them all dearly and fiercely, but she and Hamish had an unspoken bond of mutual affection and feeling between them.

She loved the presence of him sleeping by her side, sitting with her in front of the fire, or just sitting watching her as she made her cider. She loved the man and it somehow felt wrong. Like she shouldn't be feeling that sort of thing now, not after her demon had taken control of her life. They weren't allowed now. Were they?

Hamish returned her gaze.

She could see that he knew exactly what she was going through, knew these feelings of guilt intimately himself; you're not allowed to take anyone else into your madness with you, are you? Not allowed to be happy with someone else.

Jolly turned around on his tree-stump seat and surveyed the pair with his sunken eyes in his *Seven-dwarfs* face, and broke the saddening spell the only way he knew how. 'Wan' shum choashch?'

Chapter Four

Drip-drip-drip hiss. Pause. Drip-drip-drip hiss. Pause. Drip-drip-hissplop DONG!

Mathew sat bolt upright, his hood stuck to his face and one eye closed. 'Eh? What?'

The leaking pipe had been at it all night, but he'd been far too tired to let it keep him from sleeping.

The damaged seal had bravely hung on for almost five hours, gradually worsening until finally the initial split had become a significant tear and it had burst free altogether.

Drip-drip-hissplop DONG!

He looked around like a man who didn't know where he was or why he wasn't waking in his usual room. Then the flood of panic which his brain sent out cleared his sleep away in an instant, bringing him to the memory of his walk in the night. His legs then gave him their own reminder.

After fifteen, painful minutes of rubbing his complaining thighs and buttocks - groaning like he was a teenager in heat, he might have added - Mathew crawled up the wall and onto his feet.

'Oh! Bloody-nora!' He groaned as his spine tried to remain stooped forward while he begged and pushed the muscles to straighten it out.

The needles of sharp, nameless agonies shot up and down his back and legs as his spine finally gave up its resistance. 'Oh! God! Oh, oh!'

He stood for a minute more, slowly uncoiling and flexing his back and legs, and then turned to survey the spot he had been sleeping on. It was just a concrete floor.

He laughed and his back twanged, but he laughed anyway. Whoever it was that had said "sleeping on a hard surface is good for your back" is a complete IDIOT!

Drip-drip-hissplop DONG!

The pipe ended his thought perfectly with an almost classic, vaudeville finish.

It also reminded him it was time to go; wouldn't do to be discovered and then blamed for breaking something. Something other than his back at any rate.

A quick mouthful of food and a drop of water from his hip-flask, and Mathew was ready to be off.

It was coming up to seven-forty when he climbed the gate and began walking back up the road. 'I think I might die if I have to do that again.' He mumbled to himself.

He was still quite stunned at what it was he was actually doing and that he had already done a day and a night. Had slept rough!

'Astonishing! I hated camping.' He turned his gaze to the skies. 'I'm outside, Mary, you'd be proud of me.' He laughed.

His legs and back quickly settled into his slow pace again and Mathew was soon comfortably walking along.

He wasn't entirely sure how far he had already travelled, but thought he could have actually walked about fifteen miles. Maybe a little more.

The road he was following began a long, slow climb to the top of a steep hill. At its crest he could just make out the slender post of a road-sign. That would give him a better idea of how far he had come.

Halfway up the torturously steep hill and Mathew had to stop and sit on the stump of a felled tree by the roadside.

He pulled his hip-flask free and swilled down the remaining contents, gasping for breath between gulps because of his crawl up the damned hill.

He wiped his mouth and then looked at the empty flask, breathing heavily, his heart galloping. 'Probably shouldn't have drunk it all.' He muttered and shrugged his shoulders. 'Spilt milk and all that though, eh?'

He would have to keep a sharp eye out for a public lavatory or something, he thought. And then wished he hadn't.

So this was life on the road; backache and sore feet and public toilets for water. What next? Hiding outside restaurants and raiding the bins? What will I eat to keep me on the road?

He looked around himself. There was a lot of grass. He raised an eyebrow, unimpressed.

He looked behind. There was a fence with a standpipe and tap attached to it.

He turned back to face the front and sniffed and then rubbed the end of his nose nonchalantly. His mind was thinking of absolutely nothing at that moment.

He turned around and took in the standpipe and tap again. It was definitely there and there was definitely water coming through because there was a drip and small puddle beneath it.

Mathew turned back again. 'Someone's pulling my chain aren't they?' He scoffed and shook his head slowly.

Groggily he stood up with a tight groan, pulling himself to his feet with the help of his staff, and then a few minutes later he was back on the hill and carrying a full flask of fresh water. Not from a toilet thank you.

His eyes met the sky again. 'I'm still outside, Mary, and I'm not drinking toilet-water yet.' He couldn't help but laugh when he heard himself say it out loud.

By the time he had reached the signpost he was completely done in. Mostly because of laughing so much.

It had been years since he had laughed like that. Almost like the backlog of missing laughs had come out all at once.

He sat with his back to the sign and breathed in heavily while he wiped his eyes. 'Got to be more sensible, Mathew.' He cajoled himself. 'There's plenty of ways to end up dead in a ditch, not just falling asleep in one.' And then he broke out laughing again.

It took him fifteen minutes more to gather himself together. The laughing had done him more good than he realised.

It wasn't just his mood which benefited from the guffawing releases, his whole body was invigorated and fed by the massive rise in oxygen intake. He was in the mood for some serious walking.

Back on his feet and he stretched his back as he read the sign: Lincoln 18 miles, one arrow pointed. The other said; Doncaster 14 miles, the way he had come.

'Fourteen miles?' He muttered, eyes astonished. 'That's not bad is it?'

He felt a little proud that he had come so far on his first day. He knew his body, he knew what it was capable of and he knew he would be in for the long, slow walk. 'How about that then, eh? Fourteen miles.'

He turned away and headed off in the direction of Lincoln, smiling happily and still shaking his head at the miles he had come.

The hill wasn't as steep going down on this side as it had been coming up from the other. Once it had more or less flattened out, Mathew set his pace and dug in with both boots and staff.

An hour went by, the sun was strong and the open fields of gathered rapeseed or wheat or corn, shone brightly under its glare.

Behind him Mathew heard the sound of a car approaching, the first vehicle he had heard along this small, country road since he had begun again.

He concentrated on the way ahead, following the dark, grey road with his eyes as it wound along for miles in front of him.

He could hear the car getting quickly louder and took a step to the right, off the road and onto the rough, grass verge, but he didn't stop. He used his staff to navigate his way across the rough ridges and stoically pressed on.

The car was almost on top of him now, but instead of the roar and whoosh of a quickly-passing engine, he heard the volume drop a little as it seemed to slow down instead. The road was quite narrow after all, maybe they were just being cautious while they passed him.

A red bonnet came slowly into his peripheral vision, moving only a little faster than he was.

He glanced at it as the driver's, open window came into the same view and then he quickly looked away again and frowned as it slowly - irritatingly slowly - slid past and he was watching the back of it receding at a little over old-man per hour. There was a hand shoved out, holding a mobile phone pointed his way.

The hand and phone eventually disappeared back inside the car and after an almost fleeting moment more - to e-post to some blooming my-twitter-blog or something were Mathew's immediate thoughts, and he was right - the car geared up and sped off down the road, disappearing after only a few minutes.

'I hope you bloody crash and you break your phone.' He said, angrily.

Then; 'No. No I don't.' He shook his head, banishing the thought. 'I hope you never crash and you always get safely to where you want to be.'

He let the anger just drop away with any embarrassment he had suddenly felt at being scrutinised so blatantly and rudely.

It was far too small-minded to judge like that; a knee-jerk response. Society, not parents, seem to be the nurturers of the young nowadays, they can't be blamed for their behaviour when it's all they have ever known.

'I hope you drop your phone in a toilet though.' He added, smiling slyly to himself.

Whether he did ever drop his phone down a toilet or not made no difference; Kevin Vickers' small detour to work that morning had paid off and he had now posted the video which would fast become known as *The Freedom Walker* onto all of his social-media pages.

Kevin's mother worked behind the till at their local Coop. She had heard from one of the regular customers, "*Margaret from the Cromwell OAP flats, you remember Margaret?*" who had been "*down the W.I. I was, with Katherine and Brian.*" They had told her; "*Can you remember Mary? Mary Arnold? Died a few year back? Well, her old man...*"

True to his word, Mathew's dear friend Derek had let people know almost straight away what was happening in their world. He knew exactly who to tell to get the message spread through the pipeline and grapevine.

Of course, Mathew knew nothing of Margaret or the grapevine, he simply marched on toward Lincoln with nothing more in mind than getting to another watershed in a field somewhere.

He still had a little food left. He couldn't see clearly just yet how he would get more to keep him on the road, but he had enough sense to at least make his way to cities where he knew there would be shelters or hostels of some kind. And food-banks of course.

He didn't let it bother him, the day was just too beautiful for any of that nonsense.

The world was so amazingly different when you had woken up on the road, a journey still ahead.

He could see the subtle changes in the pastel colours of the blurring sky and horizon as the sun crept higher and higher overhead. He'd never noticed that before; how the colours changed as the sun changed its height.

He jolted to a stop in his tracks as a shadow from the sky on his left suddenly flashed overhead.

He looked up just in time to see an adult red-kite glide straight over him, not more than fifteen feet from his head.

It landed with a slow, even *whoosh-whoosh* on top of a fencepost on the same side of the road as Mathew.

Where's the bloody phone-stalker when you need one?

He had heard that red-kites had moved up from Northamptonshire somewhere and were now nesting around Lincolnshire. Seeing one for himself and so close up was nothing short of spectacular.

He raised his eyes. 'Why didn't I do this a long time ago?' He whispered. Not to be dramatic, but because he was a little afraid that he might scare the kite into flying away. Or flying right at him and maybe tearing his eyes out or some other terrifying maiming.

Mary would know what to do, she would have loved standing here.

The kite cocked its head and watched him.

If Mathew had known what it was thinking he might have crossed the road right there and then. He might even have turned around and walked back for a mile or four, but fortunately for him and his legs he didn't, and the kite just carried on looking at this strange prey.

Not prey in the sense of eating it, but prey in the sense of maybe mugging it; plenty of others like it had thrown bits of food at him before, why not it?

Birds: not as stupid as they look. Mary used to say, *very clever when it comes to getting food, you know?*

Although Mathew remembered Mary's helpful words with fondness, he still didn't realise he was being mugged as he pulled open his bag and tore off a small piece of ham from the stash Derek had given him.

He took a tentative step forward, carefully putting heel to toe slowly and gingerly, like a man testing for mines.

He took another similar step and then two more and then another and slowly stopped, his jaw dropping involuntarily.

He was suddenly within six feet of this enormous, bird of prey. So much bigger at this range and WELL within his focused vision, whereas before it hadn't been quite as stark and as vivid as it was right now.

The claws and the beak and the golden-brown eye which blinked casually as it appraised him were very, very real and enormous. But mainly real, like suddenly realising that the man in the alleyway *really* is holding a gun kind of real.

Mathew was convinced that he most certainly would get some kind of molesting if he turned his back on it now.

While the kite was convinced it was going to get a scrap of meat it could smell and see. The thing holding it was of no interest to it at all.

Carefully raising his hand, Mathew flicked the meat high into the air. It sailed over the head of the kite and landed in the field behind it.

Well what was clever about that? He cajoled. Not because the bird had done nothing, but because of his own stupidity at assuming the bird would just suddenly leap into the air and snatch the food before it hit the ground.

But then, with the satisfying breeze of the huge, flapping wings on his face, Mathew watched as the kite leaped from the post and flapped to the ground beyond the hedge.

What an amazing day today is becoming.

He stood grinning stupidly for a few minutes, waiting to see if the kite would jump back onto the post and eat the meat in front of him.

And then a little voice in his head piped up; *get moving, stupid! Before it comes back!*

Chapter Five

Streaming carpets of moving light rolled along and between more lights which were motionless, filling Alison's bright, gazing eyes with tiny starlight pricks of orange and red and white.

The city looked better from up here than it did being down inside it. Being inside it was like being inside the stone-maze innards of a giant, cold, dead animal.

It was easy to see how people could mistake the city as being alive when they were crawling all over it, running to and from everywhere; delivering, buying, moving, supplying.

The life of the city was an illusion created by them, while the *real* city lay *behind* the gilded masks of their shop-fronts which they had stuck upon it, the place where the people like Alison could be often found. Here the dead animal's rot could be seen clear as daylight.

Every high street and main road had dozens of food caterers dotted along each side. Everything from bakeries, cafes and bars to take-aways, restaurants and supermarkets plied their trades.

There was a mountain of wasted food simply because people were, well, just people; they always made too much or made mistakes.

The *real* rot lies in the hearts of the people who vehemently guarded these *stocks* of wasted food, had them under lock and key and camera surveillance in some instances. What did they think would happen if they simply left the bins unlocked?

Alison had tried to put herself in the shoes of someone who felt they had no choice but to lock the trash up so it couldn't be *stolen* - *not* the right choice of word to use it was generally felt amongst most of the homeless population.

She simply couldn't arrive at any other conclusion other than that they were idiots, greedy idiots who didn't really care whether the homeless population raided their bins or not.

No, this particular breed of idiot must think that all of the *normal*, paying customers would wait until dark and then raid the bins themselves instead of buying the stuff during the day. What other reason was there to deny a hungry citizen of food which was going to end up on a landfill anyway?

'Idiots.' Alison whispered.

In her young mind, Alison had seen the answer as clear as she could see the stars at night.

It made more sense to her to have a healthy, well-fed and well-groomed population of homeless people rather than to have them as a sickly, degenerative one which everyone else was afraid of and repulsed by.

'Greedy idiots.'

She heard the church-clock chime six, time to go into the bowels of the beast and see what she could find.

This time of evening was crossover time as Alison had come to know it; the time when the daytime bakeries and coffee-shops closed and swapped over the responsibility of feeding the population to the fish and chip shops and countless pizza parlours, kebab houses, burger bars, Chinese, Indian, Thai, Greek, Spanish and Italian restaurants, and all of the rest stuck somewhere in between.

Her favourite Gregg's was first on the list. Easy to get into from the supermarket's car-park and the bins were only locked with a triangle wheel-lock, for which she already had two keys.

The manager of this particular Gregg's wasn't small-minded and petty like most other managers were. He didn't *smush* the food together into sloppy messes of meat and potato, jam-tart and cheese for a start, and very rarely did he just throw the food straight into the bin, it was always usually boxed or wrapped.

Whether he did that because he knew his bins were being raided or because he was keeping his bins as clean as possible, Alison neither knew nor cared, she silently thanked him anyway.

She slid down the steep, grassy hill on her haunches, the slick soles of her well-worn trainers sliding like skis over the damp grass.

She hit the bottom and jumped up, sprinting to catch up with her head, and then slowed herself down.

Once she had reached the main road she followed it for a few yards before crossing over and walking down the back-alleys toward the tiny scrap-yard where she could take a shortcut to the car-park.

Raised voices met her as she approached the darkened corner at the end of the alley. One of them was Rag's. The other she didn't recognise but he sounded angry.

'Just what the hell do you think you're doing!?' Mathew shouted. 'Get your damn hands off me!'

Alison peeped around the corner. Rag was trying to pull a bag from the grasp of an old man with a stick.

'Jus' gimme the flamin' bag, you daf', ol' sod!'

Mathew raised his walking staff as high as he could and brought it down with a crack on Rag's skull.

The force wasn't enough to do any serious damage, but it hurt like hell.

With one hand clutching the spot where Mathew's stick had clouted him, the bulky Rag punched him in the left eye, knocking him to the ground.

'You ol' bastar'! Al kill ya f' tha'!' He growled.

He took a step closer and kicked Mathew hard in the stomach and then again in the face for spite. 'Kill ya! D' ya flamin' 'ere mi?' He shouted nastily.

He closed his fist around the stunned Mathew's collar and grabbed the bag.

'Animal!' Mathew hissed, and raised his stick again.

If he was going to die on the road it wasn't going to be at the hands of this stinking lout and not without a fight.

Just as he was bringing the staff down again with as much feeble force as he could muster, it was yanked from his grasp.

He continued to grapple with the heavy man who had him pinned.

Well that's it then; there's two of them and I can't fight them bo-.

Swish-WHACK!

Rag howled and flinched and rolled off to the side, trying his damnedest to see what was happening while trying to cover his head at the same time.

Swish-WHACK! WHACK! WHACK!

But the bullying Rag didn't stand a chance and fell to the ground with another *WHACK! WHACK! THUMP!*

His rump stood in the air while his face lay flat to the dirty road, eyes closed.

Mathew raised himself up, holding his winded stomach and wincing as his head began to spin and throb.

Standing in front of him, surrounded by the halo of the orange streetlights behind, stood a ferocious-looking, fiery, dwarf wielding his staff and panting hard.

Mathew jumped out of his skin when it spoke.

'Nasty bugger, 'im, we'd bes' no' be 'ere wen 'e weks up.'

Alison stepped closer and held out her hand for Mathew to grasp.

He just looked at her astonished, oblivious to the blood running down his head and chin and the fact he didn't understand all of the words she had just said.

'You're-you're just a child!' He managed to say.

And then he did wince and threw his hand to his cut lip.

The small girl flicked her hand for him to take it, indicating he should get on with it and get up. 'No one's a child owt 'ere.' She said, and stared at him hard.

Mathew blinked and stared back for a second or two more and then took her hand, groaning and creaking as he was helped back onto his feet.

'Thank you.' He puffed. 'You're very brave, you know?'

She handed the staff back and shrugged. 'Wirr'all brave.'

'What?'

'I said-' she stopped and her eyes suddenly widened. *I shed - wasch m'lipsh.* 'Oh, God! Am turnin' inta Jolly!'

'Um. What?' Mathew asked, and then added to himself; *Maybe she's a bit simple, poor girl.*

Alison shook her head and went back to the problem in hand. 'Look. I 'av t' go and so should you.'

Mathew understood. 'Yes, yes you're right.' He threw a glance at the motionless bulk of his attacker before adding; 'Thank you again for your help.'

He turned away and walked toward Rag.

'Wot y' doin'!?' Alison hissed, alarm smoothing her features.

Mathew pointed at the unconscious thug. 'Well I can't just leave the poor man like that, can I?' He answered, as if it were the most obvious thing in the world.

He bent down and took a firm hold of Rag's coat and then rolled him over onto his side.

The lout's eyes flickered and he grumbled loudly.

Mathew squeaked and jumped back, turned on his heels and began legging it as fast as his tired feet and walking-staff would allow.

Alison was almost at the end of the road already.

Living your life outside, finding shelter and a warm place to sleep wherever you can, shapes a person in a certain way. Your senses are sharpened somewhat to expect danger at any time, and your status amongst the people who all lived with safe and secure walls around them makes you feel *less* in some ways and thus expected to be treated *less* in all ways.

Being violently evicted from your *home* was one of those things which were always expected.

Puddle's senses told him that something was approaching them in the dark; heavy footsteps and what he immediately discerned to be Nippy's quiet patter.

He stood up and walked outside, standing between the others behind him and the approaching, booted footfalls in front.

Hamish followed him and stood by his side. 'What's up?'

'Someone's coming.'

Hamish looked up at his big friend's, bearded face. 'I guessed that, Pud'

Puddle ignored him; if he knew someone was coming, why did he ask?

A few minutes later and they both heard Alison's voice.

'Mind ya foot j-.'

And then the sound of bushes being flattened came to their waiting ears, followed by a thud and a loud groan.

'Jus' 'ere.' Alison lamely finished. 'Y'arite?' They heard her ask.

'Not really.' A strained, gasping voice replied. 'I think I've got stinging nettles in my ear.'

The pair of *doormen* just looked at each other. Hamish shrugged.

After a minute more listening to the bushes creaking and rustling, accompanied by someone's huffing and puffing and much groaning, the footsteps took up again.

Alison stepped into the dim light. 'Arite Puddle, 'Amish?' She turned and pointed to Mathew. 'This is Mat. 'E ran inta Rag.' She told them as she pulled Mathew along behind her, leading him under the bridge.

Puddle and Hamish looked at one another again, Puddle shrugged this time, and then they both followed Alison back inside.

Mathew stood at the entrance to the warm *room* of beer-crates and concrete, his mind flitting between pity and fear as he took in the faces of the other three sitting inside. Whose world had he just stepped into?

The room was cosy and well lit, the faces staring back at him seemed to be friendly - all were smiling at the least - but that feeling that he had just stepped off his own planet and right onto another's nagged away at him.

He felt there was a difference in the rules here; a shady deal behind a genuine smile, a den of treasures gilded with a pauper's facade.

Alison repeated what she had just told Puddle and Hamish, and then sat down next to Merylin.

The two men followed her and sat back down in their own seats.

The illusion was suddenly complete as the tiny waif who had saved him joined her companions; Mathew almost expected one of them to be called, *Fagin*.

And then Merylin spoke, shattering that illusion entirely. 'I'm so sorry you were unfortunate enough to fall prey to that disgusting man.' She said and stood up. She held out her hand. 'My name is Merylin, and you are safe here, Mathew.'

His heart hammered as he looked around at the faces watching him, all warm and smiling and concerned and welcoming, but until this one had spoken and offered him her hand, Mathew hadn't noticed the uniquely humbling depths to the humanity in their eyes.

He turned back to Merylin, shakily taking her hand. 'Thank you.' Was all he managed to say.

Chapter Six

After Mathew's cuts had been cleaned and sterilised with a milky, yellowish-looking liquid - which hurt considerably enough to make him think it must be a genuine medical salve or disinfectant or something - he sat back in quiet, wide-eyed amazement and watched the chap called Jolly take a hefty mouthful of the stuff and then magically make the bottle disappear into the folds of his black, woollen jacket.

A plate of rabbit stew and two slices of bread appeared on his lap next, startling him from thoughts of what he'd just had dabbed all over his face.

The ancient woman named Peach handed him a spoon.

He took it and then sat holding it like it was a stick he'd just found, the stew still steaming on his lap.

'Heesh imn sshock.' Jolly said.

Mathew looked at him, his eyes still wide but uncomprehending.

'Ee sed urin shock.' Alison translated.

Mathew turned to her, his face unchanged. Before he could say *what*, Merylin chuckled.

'They think you are in shock, Mathew. They take it for granted that once back home, here,' she said, indicating the space around them, 'that everyone speaks the same language.'

Jolly shook his head in disgust; some people just didn't know how to talk!

Alison's eyes widened; *wasch m'lipsh*. I can't turn into Jolly!

Mathew relaxed a little. 'I suppose they are right. I mean I *am* in shock. This-this,' he looked around at them all, 'all of you and this place, I mean, I-I-.' He just didn't really know what he was trying to say or how to say it.

He dropped his gaze to the food on his knee. 'I thought I'd nothing left.' He said quietly, and then looked back up. 'And I was right; I've been stripped of everything because of bills and rent and tax, given everything - every penny - to stop strange people from coming into my house and taking my things away from me.'

He shook his head sadly. 'We used to call that burglary, now it's called *Debt Recovery*.'

The others looked at him sympathetically, allowing him to the time to cast out his demon and bare it for all to see.

'And then I somehow find myself in the company of the very people who, for years, I have been afraid of turning into, and you turn out to be more content and in tune than anyone I have ever met.'

He threw his hands out in submission still holding his spoon. 'How has it all ended up so backward?' He asked them all. 'The wrong way round?' He almost pleaded. 'And when the *HECK* did someone turn me into a number? When did that happen and how didn't I see it?'

He slumped back and sighed. 'A machine has been harassing me for God knows how long and I let it.'

Jolly leaned over and placed a hand on Mathew's knee.

'M'sheensh'll tek owt an do owt fo' a mashter.' He looked at Mathew seriously. 'Allus 'member, vairzh a mashter b'yind a m'sheen.'

Mathew blinked quickly, trying his damnedest to decipher what the old, toothless man was telling him, and then just couldn't help himself and began to laugh until he wheezed, mouth open wide and eyes screwed shut. The second time that day.

It was contagious, the others weren't far behind him.

He still held the spoon which was jerking to and fro while they all laughed. He looked like a lunatic conductor waving out a melody of hilarity for his insane orchestra to follow.

And they were; six instruments and a conductor all wheezing and gasping and gagging in various tones and differing beats.

Alison's laugh was like a high-pitched hiccough which interspersed the heaving bass of Hamish and Puddle's barrel-chested laughs in a strangely harmonious *four-three* beat.

Peach had a fast *a-a-a-a-ah* beat going on, like a sheep having a fit, while Jolly wheezed in and out slowly and donkey-like, sawing his breath and flapping his flaccid lips wetly.

Merylin's laugh was like a deep, debauched chuckle, a noise which the Devil's mistress might make, weaving in and out between all of the other voices.

All of them could hear it, they had stopped laughing at Mathew's initial outburst at not understanding Jolly's words of wisdom minutes ago. They were laughing at the laughter now.

Mathew wondered if it was possible to die from laughing. The muscles in his abdomen were saying *yes Mathew, it is quite possible*.

His face hurt, his ear was red and stinging-nettle blistered, his mouth was swollen and his cheeks and ribs were bruised and aching, but he was as free and as happy at that moment as he had been for a long, long time. Happy and sharing it with others.

It took at least ten minutes for them to come back down again, mainly because their bodies were sending them threats of being sick or fainting.

They all sat around quietly now and ate their stews or drank their brews, or a bit of both.

'This daft 'ed,' Alison began, chewing her food and pointing at Mathew, 'was gunna 'elp Rag afta we bashed 'im.' She laughed at that.

The others didn't laugh, but they did smile.

'Is that right?' Merylin asked, impressed. 'Why were you helping the man who had just attacked you?'

Mathew finished chewing the bread and stew in his mouth and swallowed it hastily. 'It's quite acceptable to put a man down if he is a threat and a menace,' he answered. 'But you don't then kick that man when he is down. Never. Not in my book anyway.' He sat up straight, a little stiffly. 'I couldn't leave him without first making sure he wasn't seriously injured, you know?'

Puddle leaned over and filled Mathew's bowl back up with more stew and gave him a slice of bread from his own plate. He nodded once and then sat back down silently as he always did, but the message was clear.

Jolly pulled a small, glass tumbler from beneath the crate he was sitting on and filled it with the yellow liquid from the bottle in his jacket.

'Will' all jrink t' vach.' He passed the glass to Mathew.

One by one they all filled a cup or mug or glass with Merylin's cider, Alison had only a teaspoon of the stuff in a glass filled to the top with a flat lemonade.

Merylin raised her glass. 'To fighting, and knowing when not to.' She toasted, bringing it to her mouth and then drinking the lot down in one go.

The others followed suit, keeping their eyes subtly on Mathew as he downed his first taste of a cider which was brewed by a chemist with deep knowledge and dark skills bordering on moonshine-alchemy.

Now, Mathew was acquainted with the world of spirits, had drunk many a whiskey and dry ginger in his day, even a glass or two of *Courvoisier* at the work's do, but the stuff he gulped down like water just then was something his mind was insisting couldn't possibly exist.

He truly believed, *believed*, he had drunk acid and somehow it had ignited in his mouth and then hideously had turned very, very thick and refused to leave his mouth and throat, insisting instead that it slowly - ever so lava-slowly - devour his chest and lungs and melt his bones.

He began to cry. 'Oh! Mother of heaven, help me!' He squeaked. '*What is this*? What maniac do you buy this from?'

All eyes turned to Merylin but no one said anything. They just smiled without moving their faces and looked at her.

'You?' Mathew squeaked again and then coughed. 'You make this?' That was almost as stunning as the drink itself.

'She's a chemist.' Hamish said, mildly proud.

'A chemist? More like a witch!' Mathew quickly replied, shaking himself with the aftershock. 'And I say that with the greatest respect; my wife was a witch too, in her own *gardeny*-rescuer-of-small-things-and-brewer-of-flower-wines kind of way, she was.'

Merylin's glass had been refilled and she and the others raised them again. 'To your wife-witch,' she said, and chuckled. 'She sounds like someone who cared.'

Her tot disappeared, the others quickly following her.

Mathew looked down at his half-filled glass in fear, but he raised it anyway and took another mouthful to the memory of his dear Mary.

And immediately wished he hadn't.

He had to admit though, that after a few minutes of having the molten liquid inside him he felt warm throughout, glowing almost, and his aches had been relegated to a dull, occasional reminder instead of a constant prodding. And most of all he felt his spirits were genuinely lifted and he actually felt safe, properly safe. Something he had almost forgotten.

'What were you doing down by the scrap-yard?' Hamish asked him.

Mathew thought for a moment, but Alison spoke up first.

''E's off t' London.' She said, looking round at them all. ''E's gunna see th' pry'minister.' Her voice lowered conspiratorially.

All eyes turned to Mathew.

He shuffled uncomfortably. 'That's, err, correct, I am going to London. Whether I get to see the prime minister or not,' he shrugged and sat back. 'We'll have to see.'

Silence hung heavily around them while they all puzzled out what Mathew was telling them.

Merylin studied his soft, lined face and hard-set eyes. 'What do you plan on saying to her if you do get to see her?' She asked, cocking her head to one side.

Mathew sniffed and rubbed at his sore ear. 'I'm going to give her my last teabag,' he casually answered, 'and the 17p I have in my pocket; everything I had left when I woke up yesterday morning.'

He took another sip of his *witches-brew*, gasping before quietly adding; 'They've had everything else off me.'

Quietly it sank into Alison's mind what Mathew was intending to do. Her heart almost missed a beat. 'So y' gunna *walk* there!?' Her voice was raised and tight. 'Y'll fu-'

Merylin shot her a baleful glance.

'Y'll flippin' die walkin' t' London!' She quickly amended, flinching under the older woman's stare.

Mathew smiled at his young saviour. *Just a child.* 'I've been dead for years now, I just didn't notice until yesterday.'

36

The others were nodding their heads slowly, all of them understanding exactly what Mathew meant by that.

Alison on the other hand was having none of it. 'Well tha's jus' sad talk innit?' She said harshly and folded her arms, looking at Mathew as though he were a silly, little boy. 'Givin' up talk tha' is.'

Well that's a little disconcerting, he thought, *Mary used to tick me off like that when she thought I was being stupid, and now I have a child doing it. A child!*

'What makes you so sure I'll die?' His eyebrows raised. 'And if you say it's because I am old-'

She cut him short. 'It's not cos yer' owd, it's cos y' soft!'

Mathew felt slapped by that.

He looked around at the others for some support, but they were all giving him a look which said that this was his battle and so far Alison was right.

Another sip passed his lips and then he sat back in a huff, folding his own arms. 'I'm doing alright up to now.' He mumbled. The drink was giving him a little Dutch-courage.

Alison scoffed. 'A dayanarf an' yev bin mugged, hadda figh', bin rescued by a girl an' fell in nettles.'

She leaned closer to him and peered deeply into his watery eyes, one of them half-closed and bruised. 'Y' gunna die, Mathew.' She sounded serious, but also somehow a little cocky as well Mathew was thinking. Like a challenge, a challenge not to die. Clever, thoughtful girl.

He sat back up and met her gaze. 'You've got such a long life ahead of you, I understand and appreciate your concern I really do, but when you get as old as I am you'll see for yourself why I'm doing what I am doing.'

He had expected her reaction to be more inclined to just accepting what her elder was telling her and trust him. He didn't count on her almost exploding.

'Don' you *dare*-' She stopped and quickly turned to Merylin, lowering her voice a little. 'Wossat word f' wot 'ee's jus' dun t' me?'

'Patronise.' Merylin responded.

Mathew glanced at her; *why are you helping her!?*

'Don' you dare *parternise* me wi' tha' *gerenation*-gap crap!' Alison angrily continued. 'Wisdom dunt come cos ov age, it comes cos ov experience and I've 'ad a lo' more experience down 'ere than you av!'

Jolly leaned in then, a natural at absorbing tempers and changing moods.

He flashed his bottle around and topped-up everyone's drink.

'Niffy's righ' y'kno?' He said as he filled Mathew's glass.

'I know she is.' He raised his glass to Alison. 'I didn't mean to be patronising, honestly, and I'm sorry, but really? What other options do I have but to carry on and get it all over and done with?'

'You could stay here and brew that teabag?' Hamish offered.

Mathew smiled weakly. 'I suppose I could.'

He stared deeply into his glass, looking for something, but it was just a drink and there were no answers there.

Something had already begun which he had no control of now, so in fact there were no questions anymore either, only his last actions.

The people sitting around him were all a part of it as well, although they didn't quite seem to know it. He had unwittingly become a messenger for them as well now.

It didn't matter, they were no more of a burden than his friend Derek and all of the others were. If anything, these people had given him a new strength of mind to see it through.

'But you're not going to are you?' It was Merylin who brought him out of his gazing thoughts.

He shook his head. 'I can't. I'm not going to just take it lying down.'

Something connected in Alison's young mind when hearing that; she understood the importance of being heard, being seen and recognised as a person and how important it was to always fight for that.

She looked at him a little sullenly but didn't argue. She could only hope that he would change his mind once he had slept on it and Merylin's brew had worn off.

Chapter Seven

Lavender; what a bloody awful colour for a kitchen. For anywhere as far as Diane Jones was concerned.

She stirred her coffee and grimaced at the sickly walls, freshly decorated.

How does lavender fit in with the fast-paced world of a newsroom? Just the word made her think of blue rinses and powdered knickers.

Her latest assignment lay beneath her cup, happily catching the splashes of her spiteful stirring and forming a perfect, brown halo on the freshly printed sheet.

She was to report on the Facebook video which had popped up on their radar of someone nicknamed *The Freedom Walker*; some old man who was going to walk to London and then was going to starve himself to death.

It had sounded peculiarly interesting right up until the point she had actually seen him doddering along in the video.

"You're joking aren't you?"

Her editor had remained silent and folded his arms.

"For God's sake, Edmund! He's a million years old, he'll never get anywhere near *London! Send Gary!"*

Diane Jones was a pretty good reporter when it came to getting the *juice*, but taking her turn and reporting the *tattle* to fill the columns turned her into a petulant, teenage, tantrum thrower - even though she was twenty-six - and the most dreaded of the *tattle* jobs was the *elder-flower*; anything to do with the elderly and flowers.

After her spiteful stirring, Diane took an equally spiteful sip of her hot coffee and tried to ignore the feeling of being thoroughly told off.

The walls weren't about to let her though, they were mocking her now with their powdery *lavenderness*.

She tried to stare them down through watery eyes - a result of the spitefully hot coffee - and then gave up and turned away. Lavender 1, Diane 0.

She walked back to her tiny office and threw the news-sheet onto her cluttered desk, throwing herself into her chair with a huff even as the sheet settled.

The video of Mathew was still playing on her screen.

If he was heading to Lincoln, as they were guessing he was, then she would start her search there, but with any luck he might have keeled over already.

"*Don't be so damn churlish, Jones!*" Her editor's voice stung her again and she kicked herself 'God.'

She took a deep breath and then sighed heavily. Bloody lavender.

***

CLUMP-CLU-click-UMP.

Boots and walking staff were the only sounds which Mathew was really listening to now, a rhythm of slow pace and easy peace.

The day had dripped by as slowly as Newark had approached and eventually gone past.

The signs telling him how many miles before he reached it were an annoyance and a tiring reminder. They made him feel like he was moving at inches-per-hour rather than miles. He stopped looking altogether after a few hours of feeling deceived by the distance he thought he'd made and the actual distance.

CLUMP-CLU-click-UMP.

Alison hadn't been very happy about him carrying on, but she'd seen him off with some food for his bag and fresh water for his flask and plenty of words of caution for his ears; "*Stay away from t' main roads. Don' stop 'til y' 'av got a shelter ova' ya 'ed an' the wind int blowin' on ya'. If y' 'ear water check it owt but don't kip down next'oo it.*" At that point she had stepped closer and gripped him by his lapels and pulled him down to meet nose to nose. "*An' if y' see anyone 'oo looks like Rag, GO. THEE. OTHER. WAY!*" Her eyes had been anything but that of a child's when she had said that.

He felt a small, guilty weight in the pit of his stomach when he thought of the young girl who had saved him. Not just because he had, had to say goodbye and she had been genuinely concerned and sad, but because she was who she was; a child living on the street.

It hurt terribly to think of her young mind missing all of the childish wonder and beauty which comes with growing up, being forced instead to grow up instantly and get on with the hard part; fending for oneself and surviving.

Another message for him to carry and deliver.

He heard the drone of a car-engine coming up behind him, only the second vehicle that morning.

And at that very thought the driver decided to pass by and toot the horn, sending Mathew a few inches into the air and almost out of his skin.

He stopped in his tracks, breathing hard as he held his thumping chest, and just watched the small, red car getting smaller as it drove away.

Where in their stupid mind, does a person find it acceptable to just frighten people like that? There was no reason for the driver to toot at him, he was walking well off the road and on the verge. What the heck is wrong with people?

Oblivious to Mathew's stress which she had just caused, the driver truly wished *The Freedom Walker* all the best luck in the world and couldn't wait to get home and tell everyone that she had actually seen him.

Just as oblivious as the young woman had been to the shocking effect of the supportive toot of her horn, Mathew was equally oblivious to the people behind him who were looking for him. Looking in the wrong places.

The minds of these modern techno*philes*, with their hand-held computers disguised as mobile phones and their constant heads-down view of a world on a screen, had made the error of assuming Mathew would be using a similar system and thus would be using the satellite maps which told everyone else where to go.

His watch told him it was after four now, he'd been walking for almost nine hours. Hamish had advised him to begin looking for a place to bed down for the night while there was still at least a couple of hours of daylight left.

"Try not to get caught out in the open while it's dark." The burly ex-soldier had told him. *"Find a decent shelter while it's still light if you can."*

Hamish's parting gift felt reassuringly heavy in his bag; a five hundred-page book entitled, *The Park*.

"You'll be bored when you stop, that'll help pass the time before you sleep."

They had all given him good advice for the road, but he had to question Peach's offering of a long, nasty-looking bowie-knife. It didn't comfort him much either, thinking that there had been a need to offer the thing in the first place, but then she had said; *"F' rabbits an' that."*

He had still declined it; a rabbit would probably just take it off him anyway even if he *did* happen to come across one unawares.

It itched away at him thinking of those six people under the bridge.

In his own, small life under roof and behind doors, *homeless* was a fearful place to end up. It was a word which instantly painted a picture of a violent world of alcoholics and drug-users, gangs of thieves disguised as beggars.

When he really thought about it he came to the conclusion that being homeless and the constant reminder of it was one of *the* culprits behind his slow descent into insignificance.

It was almost as if he had been guided along a path which had been planned out for him decades ago, a road which made sure he constantly, blindly emptied his pockets out on to.

Never enough to have savings, but always enough - just - to keep the lights on, and then a tiered system of thinly veiled threats to constantly lash him with fear into paying or have something taken away from him if he didn't.

The six under the bridge had seen through the illusion and decided to step off the path, but why was that wrong? Why were they being punished the way they were?

Rag, the thug who had tried to take his bag, how had *he* ended up like that? Did *he* deserve to be there?

Mathew thought not. Human-beings were not born bad and mean, they had to be *made* that way. What had pushed that man so far over his edge that it made him become so *every-man-for-himself*-ish? Could Alison end up like that?

That frightening thought made him stop in his tracks, immediately making him wish he hadn't as his legs began to first buzz and thrum and then tremble quite badly.

He stepped right up to the hedge and leaned back into it, his buttocks finding a miraculously placed nesting of twigs and branches which made an excellent seat.

He glanced back the way he had come.

Was it really possible for that poor girl to end up like the lost and repudiated Rag?

When comparing the two it was easy to shake ones head and say *no, of course she wouldn't, they're nothing alike*. But the reality was; Rag had once been a small child himself, a being of chaotic innocence who had found the world the way it had been presented to him and had grown accordingly.

Somewhere along that line he had stepped off the path. Not to the place where the others had stepped off to, but somewhere far over into no-mans land.

Should the dice fall right - or wrong in this case - then Alison could find herself with no more choices than the unfortunate Rag had been given.

Mathew's heart hurt thinking of that. Such a brave and caring soul shouldn't be exposed to that kind of treachery. She deserved her chance, her right to have a life free of fear and worry, the right which was hers from the minute she drew breath for herself; *I am here, I might change the world, just give me a fair crack at it*. Wasn't that the right of everything which was born into this Universe? To simply have the chance to live freely and make a difference?

His hand dipped into the deep pockets of his coat and met Jolly's parting gift. "*Keef y' wa'm an' 'elp y' sheep.*" He pulled it out and poured a small tot into the metal screw-cap, and without giving himself the chance to back down, chugged the lot back and swallowed it.

It did its job of mugging his senses perfectly and he wheezed and let out a long groan of hateful appreciation.

Immediately the warm liquid spread its numbing venom around his chest and stomach, slowly seeping into his aching and tired legs. They stopped quivering and were reduced to a mild vibration instead.

'Hideously marvellous.' He wheezed and coughed.

Tolkien himself would have been proud of Merylin's brew; it was exactly as he imagined the Orc *medicine* which Merry and Pippin were forced to drink would taste like.

He slipped the bottle back into his pocket and then began the shuffle out of his hedge-seat. It was more difficult than it had been getting in. Mainly because his body was trying to resist and just get him to sit back down for a bit longer.

Gripping his staff with both hands he made the final lift and groggily, creakily straightened his back and knees. His boots felt heavy and his feet ached.

After a minute to gather himself he dolefully looked back, wishing he could do something absolute and final which would prevent Alison from ever falling down into that bottomless, inhuman well.

A vast bank of dark cloud stained the horizon over Lincoln right then, an ominous omen of something coming, something big and dangerous.

'Not for her.' He whispered. 'Please, not for her.' He repeated and then turned away and carried on with his march to London.

CLUMP-CLU-click-UMP.

The sky flashed behind him and then a minute later it grumbled heavily.

Chapter Eight

Burning, burning, burning! His world was nothing but conflagration all around.

The houses on his street cracked and crumbled and crashed to the ground while he stood powerless to do anything other than watch.

Voices were calling from those houses, shouting out words which he couldn't understand, voices of people he knew and had known. What were they saying?

He looked at his hands, they were burning too from the inside; a bright orange flare beneath his skin with scarlet rivulets of molten veins pulsing even deeper still.

He felt its power and its pain, this fire beneath his flesh which writhed in torment, trying to break free. And then his blazing eyes lifted and watched as flame turned to smoke and smoke turned to shape and shape to form. His walking staff stood planted in the ashes before him.

'Y' gunna die, Mathew.' It seemed to be whispering to him.

Fiery fingers reached out to grasp it, but the more he tried the further away it seemed to be.

Frustrated he began to shuffle his feet and lean closer, but the staff merely stayed exactly where it was. He tried walking with his hand outstretched and then he began to trot and run and then sprint.

The distance between his fingers and the staff was closing, but slowly, too slowly, like he was pushing through molten glass, thick and clinging.

He looked on in horror as the staff began to crack, showing veins of splintered wood, ageing before his burning eyes. He had to reach it, must catch hold of it before it shattered.

With an effort which tore him from his own, flaming skin, his hand touched the now grizzling wood and he felt the decay beneath his fingers. Wood fossilised to stone and then with a terrific, rolling rumble it cracked and tumbled like a mountain landslide.

The noise carried on for eons and then with a searing flash the rumble expanded violently and a noise of thunder exploded…

Mathew jerked from his sleep and cried out as the storm he had seen gathering over Lincoln crashed down from the skies right above him. The rain was lashing the opened truck-trailer he had hurriedly dashed into when the downpour had begun, creating a cacophony which sounded like a thousand hands beating on the canvas sides.

He sat up and shivered with the sound, pulling his hood up and fastening it tightly around his face.

After dragging the oily tarpaulin over his legs and back up to his chin, Mathew sat in the pitch-dark and looked out at the pouring rain through the opened door.

Lightning flashed again, a million, million raindrops shattered under the sear, creating a white sheet of dazzling wetness. And then the thunder rolled in from behind, galloping up and crashing over, rattling canvas, metal and bones alike.

It went dark again, dark with white phantoms popping in front of his eyes.

Once they were gone Mathew felt utterly alone once more and detached from his place in the world.

And then suddenly he didn't feel quite so alone. In fact, right at that very moment, he only felt his terror which was wishing he was alone as someone laying next to him groaned and coughed and then sat up.

'Y' arite, Mathew?' Alison's sleepy voice said. Without waiting for any kind of response, she added; 'It's still nigh', go back t' sleep.'

He listened wide-eared and wide-eyed in the dark as she rolled back over and pulled the tarpaulin over her head.

If blinking could have been heard then Mathew's lashes were flicking out a strange, erratic Morse-code of shock, bewilderment, relief and just a touch of fear. The fear was there because he wondered if he was actually still dreaming.

He sat completely still and remained almost silent, trying his damnedest to keep his breathing as quiet as possible. Which was pointless really as the racket the rain was making on the sides of the trailer was drowning out all of the usual small noises of the night anyway. Including breathing.

Maybe he had dreamt that had just happened and he was now actually awake. Maybe it was much simpler than that and he was going mental.

'Um.' He began.

'Go t' sleep!' Alison's muffled voice responded before he could say anything else.

Mathew's eyebrows raised and he smiled to himself in the dark.

When or how or why she was there he didn't care; someone had been listening when he had wished there was some way he could keep his eye on her, look out for her and keep her away from that soulless place where the horrible Rag had ended up.

Still smiling he shuffled his way back down under the tarp and was fast asleep within minutes.

When the morning came, bringing with it a damp chill on the air, Mathew sat up and immediately looked over to where Alison's sleepy voice had come from. The tarpaulin was flat and there was no sign that the young girl had ever been there.

No sound came from outside and the sun had only just risen, its first rays streaking down the wet road and across the tops of the sodden hedges.

He took a moment to stretch and yawn and then stood up, stretching and yawning some more.

Taking up his staff and his bag, he walked to the door.

Looking around he listened for any signs of anyone else being close by; a bird or two were twittering somewhere, but other than that it was almost silent.

After a minute or two more of muddling through his bewildered thoughts - mainly about his own sanity - he turned around and clambered down the frame and to the ground.

'Got y' sum bre'kfast.'

He jumped a foot in the air and then whirled around. 'AH!' The noise he made was like a loud squeak. 'I w-wish you wouldn't keep doing that! Can't you make some noise or whistle or something?'

Alison grinned; nippy *and* silent. She never tired of impressing a stranger with her stealth skills and speed.

She held out two red apples and a half loaf of brown bread.

Mathew just stared at them and then looked around; they were in the middle of nowhere. 'Where did you get those?'

Alison cocked her head to one side and frowned. 'Apples from orchards an' bread from bakeries.' She said, and held each up as though she were teaching a five year-old.

He took an apple and bit into it. 'Yes, but where from? Whose orchard? Whose bakery?' He asked, relishing the sweet taste of breakfast.

The young girl stepped closer, her frown deepening. He hadn't said it, but his question was loaded; where did she steal the apples and bread from.

'Are you enjoying that?'

'Mm. Yes, it's very good.' Mathew answered, unaware of his peril.

'An' if I sed I 'ad t' climb ova a wall t' get it, would it still tas'e good?'

She took another step and stood almost right below him, looking up - quite menacingly, he thought - into his slowly comprehending face.

He stopped chewing. 'Sorry, I-I wasn't thinking-, I didn't mea-' he looked past her angry face and down to his feet. 'Sorry.' He mumbled again.

Her face softened a little, at least he had realised quickly. That was something.

'We don' steal, Mathew. When someone teks all t' apples an' puts a wall round 'em, that's stealin'. When someone chucks food int' bin 'cos thev med too much, that's stealin'.'

She stepped back. 'It's stealin' from people who don't 'av, it's that simple.' She finished, her voice quiet but firm.

Mathew nodded his head, feeling his shame burning in his face. 'I wasn't thinking like I was here,' he said, meeting her eyes again. 'I was thinking like I used to back there.' He nodded behind him.

She felt a sliver of guilt herself then. Mathew was a very good man, she had taken to that part of him quite quickly. Adjusting to the sudden change in his late life must be terrifying for him. For anyone.

'S'arite.' She said. She tore the loaf in half. 'Let's f' get it, yea?' And held half out to Mathew, a kind of peace offering.

They ate while they walked.

'Why are you here, Alison?'

'Wha' d' ya mean?'

'Why did you come all the way out here and why are you walking this way and not back?'

Alison wrinkled her nose and sniffed. Why was she here? It was because of Rag wasn't it? It was because she had saved him from Rag - and by that she meant properly saved him; Rag would have hurt him, hurt him badly before his journey had even begun.

She looked up at him. 'Cos y' soft.' She finally answered, cheekily.

Mathew scoffed and then chuckled. 'I am a bit I suppose.'

He looked down at her delicate, grinning face. 'And you're going to toughen me up are you?'

'Well y' 'ere arn' ya?'

It only took Mathew five seconds that time to translate what she had said.

He chuckled again. 'Yes, I am aren't I?' He said, clearly emphasising the *aren't*.

'Why'd ya say it like tha'?'

'Let's just say that the way you talk hurts my dainty, old ears.'

It was his turn to turn on the cheek. He grinned perfectly as she had done.

Alison tutted and rolled her eyes. 'God! *Aunt*.' She mimicked.

They looked at each other for a second and then guffawed together.

'Almost perfect I would say.' He laughed. 'Perhaps there is hope for you after all.'

* * *

47

Twelve miles away, driving erratically while slurping her roadside coffee and trying to check her phone at the same time, Diane Jones was feeling anything but hope.

Lincoln had been a dead-end; either she had missed him as he had passed through or he hadn't come that way after all.

She scowled at her mobile phone and the red line it was telling her to follow. This was the third time that morning she had driven up and down this bloody road.

The line followed a straight route almost, from Lincoln to London without using the main A1, sticking to the B-roads which ran almost parallel to it instead.

'Where the hell are you!?'

Her front wheel dipped violently into a sizable pothole she wasn't paying attention to and the steering wheel snatched to the left.

Coffee sloshed over the top of the cup and onto her lap, her phone dropped into the foot-well.

'OH! GOD! SHIT-BOLLOCKS!'

She slapped the steering wheel angrily and sloshed more coffee onto her knee and down her leg. 'Shit! Shit! Shit!' Slap! Slap! Slap!

A lay-by approached. She pulled into it and turned the engine off, sighed deeply and then began counting to ten. She'd arrived at seven when her phone rang.

She fished it from the floor and swiped the screen to life. It was her boss, Edmund.

'If you say good-morning I think I shall scream.' She huffed.

'*You sound like you've had a rough night, Jones, please tell me you haven't slept in your car again?*'

'I haven't slept in my car again.'

She waited.

'*Fine,*' he eventually said, sharply, '*I won't bother to lecture you on the dangers of sleeping in ones vehicle during the cold months then.*'

'No, you won't.' She glibly answered.

Apart from the cold, sleeping in ones car - during what felt like the storm to end all storms - also had the effect of making one bloody obnoxious first thing in the morning.

'*Fine!*' Edmund pouted.

'Fine!' Diane pouted right back.

There was another short pause.

'*You know? I've half a mind to not give you this little bit of information which just came up about your Freedom Walker.*'

God! She hated it when he played chess with his words and pushed her into checkmate like that. But she also knew Edmund; if she remained quiet and let him think that she was hanging her head in defeat he would get on with it anyway.

'*You haven't found him have you?*' He said, right on cue. '*That's because you've been looking in the wrong place.*' He didn't sound smug, but instead had lapsed into his old-teacher mode; a little pious with his delivery, flavoured with an edge of condescension just for her.

Diane still didn't speak, but then again she didn't have to.

'*A young woman posted a comment on the video saying how proud she had been to actually see him.*'

'Really? When was this?' She couldn't stay quiet at hearing that. Sounded quite eager in fact.

And Edmund instantly picked up on that eagerness. '*Yesterday, early evening sometime.*' Short and to the point and without any real information given.

The git was going to make her pull it from him wasn't he?

She dug in and bit the bullet, swallowed the pride and all of that nonsense people seem to put themselves through unnecessarily to get what they want. 'Well? Where did she see him?'

She knew he was going to pause for effect even before she'd finished the question. Which made it just that much more stinging when he did.

'Oh! Come on, Edmund, just tell me. *Please!*'

'*Promise me, Jones, that you won't sleep in your car. We do have a budget for these things as you well know?*'

She sighed, checkmate it was then. 'I promise I won't sleep in my car.'

'*Thank you. I'm going to hold you to that promise.*'

She was sure he was actually wagging his finger at the phone when he said that.

'*Now. Our, young woman, a Miss Lucy Burton, said that she saw Mathew Arnold while she was driving home from her nightshift. She doesn't mention the exact road, but her profile-page shows that she works and lives in or near the village of Gelston.*'

'Gelston? Gelston?' Muttered Diane. 'I've seen a signpost for that somewhere, I'm sure I have.'

'*Where are you now?*' She heard him sit down at his desk and tap his keyboard.

'I've just driven through a small village called Dry Doddington.'

She heard more tapping before he spoke again.

'*Right. You're about ten miles away from Gelston, you need to head south-eastward. And Jones?*'

'I know, I know; I won't sleep in my car.'

'*Good. Call in when you have anything.*'

'Okay, see you later, Edmund, and thanks.' She said, and meant it.

'*You're welcome, see you soon.*'

She swiped at her phone, disconnecting the call, and then again to bring up the map to find Gelston.

'No wonder I couldn't find you. What are you doing all the way over there?'

Chapter Nine

Still slightly damp from the night time downpour the pine-needles felt soft and made no sound, while the aroma of the small forest cleared the mind.

Mathew and Alison sat around a small camp-fire with their backs leaning against the bird-watching hut they had discovered. The night had now fully encroached and was pitch beyond the edge of the small, glowing ring of orange.

Another fifteen or sixteen miles had passed beneath their feet today, Mathew setting the pace to his steady, tired stride.

Only once the day had worn on and the sun was clearly on its way down had Alison pulled his coat and turned them to a cut-in between the hedgerows.

He'd resisted at first, insisting that they shouldn't go trespassing on other people's property, but Alison had soon turned her *angry-wisdom* on him once again and here they were.

'A person can't own t' earth under y' feet, Mathew.'

'But we have laws that say otherwise, for goodness sake!'

'Yea, an' those laws a' written by t' people 'oo wan' t' own t' earth under y' feet, arn' they?'

She had done that thing where she stepped right up to him and looked up into his eyes; a menacing, fiery, fearless dwarf. *'Some laws, Mathew, 'av bin jus' chucked in there wi' all th' good laws so that you can't see 'em for wha' the' really are; laws for th' rich only.'*

He had given in at that point. Mainly because he could see it was pointless arguing with her while she was in her own territory, but a little of him had almost understood exactly how she saw it. He thought he'd had a clear glimpse for just a moment and it had given him enough pause to think about it.

Regardless of the law and whether he trusted it or not, looking around at their tiny camp made him feel glad that he had listened to the young girl's wisdom; he would probably be sleeping under a bush or something by now.

He watched her as she sat staring into the fire, her brow knitted and her eyes full of light and deep thought.

How dare the world do that to a child? Mathew thought. How dare it furnish her with the stare of a veteran and forego the magic of growing up?

She should be sat in a bedroom somewhere, mooning over the latest boy-bands, not sitting in the dark with an old man.

He pulled out his bottle of *Old Nasty* and filled the cap. ''Elp y' sheep?' He said and held the tot out to Alison.

She couldn't help herself and laughed at Mathew's imitation of Jolly. Laughed without thinking. Like a child.

She took it and drank half of it, her face screwed up as she swallowed it shuddering. 'Ex'lent!' She gasped and handed the rest back to Mathew. 'Keep th' cold outta ar' bones.'

'Bottoms up.' Mathew raised the cap to his lips.

He sat gasping as Alison had done for a few seconds and then returned the *potion* to his pocket. 'I don't think it would win any awards but it certainly hits the spot, doesn't it?'

'Better 'an drinkin' petrol.'

Mathew chuckled for a moment and then frowned. 'You-you haven't drunk petrol have you?'

She returned his frown. 'Yea,' she nodded seriously, 'ev'ryone 'oo's lived on t' streets 'as drunk petrol at least once.'

Mathew just looked puzzled and remained frowning.

'It keeps y' warm when it's righ' cold,' she explained. 'Stops y' from freezin' t' death.'

He blinked, astonished. A connection between the homeless and alcohol suddenly took on another shade, one even less savoury than just simple alcoholism.

'I-I didn't know that.' He nodded his head, smiling weakly. 'There's a lot of things I don't know, isn't there?'

Alison looked at him like a teacher appraising an apprentice. 'Down 'ere, y' like a child,' she said, not unkindly. 'I see ya lookin' round at fings li-'

'*Th*ings.' He interrupted.

She stared at him. Still not unkindly, but a tiny bit fiercely he thought.

'Up here,' he explained, '*you* are like a child to me, we should help each other should we not?'

He could see she was trying to work out what kind of *help* his side of the bargain could possibly hold.

Eventually she relaxed a little, she wasn't a stupid girl, she could learn a lot from Mathew as well as keep him safe. She *had* to keep him safe.

She still gave a small, exasperated huff though, because it was expected. 'Fine. *Thhh*-ings.' She shrugged and theatrically held her hands out in front of her in submission. '*THHH*-ings! Y'look round at *thhh*-ings like y'ant ever seen *thhh*-ings b'fore. Loadsa *thhh*-ings! Loads!'

Mathew scoffed and then chuckled and then couldn't help himself and laughed. '*Thhh*-ings!' He mimicked.

Together they laughed again until a minute later Alison's frown slowly returned and then she suddenly looked alert and ready to run.

'Shh!' She hissed and grabbed Mathew by the arm.

She didn't need to ask him twice; just the look on her face had snapped his mouth closed and his eyes and ears open.

Alison flicked her head to look behind them through the wall of the hut. 'Summerts walkin' be'ind us!' She mouthed.

Mathew shook his head. 'What?' He mouthed back. It was difficult enough when he could *hear* her words let alone when she just moved her mouth.

She elbowed him and then pointed to her ears, indicating he should listen behind the hut.

He cocked an ear and sure enough he heard it, a light footfall of someone or something moving around on the other side.

It moved stealthily and then stopped and then moved again, slowly making its way to the left as though it were creeping around the edge of the small hut.

It stopped again for a moment, right where he guessed the far corner was. And then it began again, only this time it was getting closer as it worked its way down toward the corner where Mathew sat.

He pointed. 'It's coming.' He mouthed silently and turned to Alison.

She was holding the horrible bowie-knife which Peach had offered to him, clasping it tightly in both hands and crouching on her haunches ready to spring.

'What are you doing!?' Mathew silently said.

His eyes were ready to leap out and snatch the knife themselves when he saw it.

He reached out to take it, or at least get her to lower it, but she whipped it away and kept her eye on the corner.

The footsteps had begun again, whoever it was would be stepping out any second.

He looked at the knife and the steady hand which was holding it. She knew exactly what she was doing, but it didn't help thinking she could leap up and actually use it on someone.

'Don't, Alison, just wait!' He mimed frantically.

Just as he leaned closer to her and reached out for the knife again a furry head appeared almost at his side.

Alison's face turned from fiery-fighter to mooning-angel in the blink of an eye, while Mathew turned and faced the big, brown eye of a small, munching deer.

'Agh!' He squeaked. The sound didn't actually come out but the intention was clear.

The deer just looked at him and then dipped its head and pulled up some of the long-bladed grass which surrounded the bird-watching hut. It chewed silently.

As usual, when presented with something *wildlife-ish*, Mathew thought of his wife Mary. She probably would have been able to tell him what kind of deer it was and how old and what sex; she was a walking book of countryside-lore was Mary.

''Mazing!' Alison whispered. 'Int sh'cute, eh? Tha's a Muntjac deer. Like a dwarf deer.'

Mathew was flabbergasted; how did she know that?

'The's loads ov 'em round 'ere. Usually the' really shy tho'.'

She dropped the bowie-knife and then pulled a piece of apple from a paper-wrapping in her pocket. She leaned forward holding the browning fruit out at arms length.

To her beaming delight the little deer stepped forward and sniffed at it and then took it from the palm of her hand. It stood up and chewed happily right next Mathew's face.

A little apple-spray hit him on the forehead and just a little dribble fell to his trousers, but his eye was locked with the deer's and he barely noticed.

The corner of his mouth raised slowly and his eyes shone brightly. ''Mazing.'

The deer's pelage was already turning to winter grey and clumps of her deep-brown coat were hanging about her underside.

Alison held out more apple and inched closer to the animal. Once she was close enough and the deer had taken more of her peace-offering, she slowly raised her hand and placed it on the deer's flank and began to stroke downward gently.

Another piece of apple appeared and then disappeared while Alison continued to draw the loose, fluffy fur out of the coat, allowing it to drop to the ground around the deer's slender hooves.

She worked serenely and happily, slowly making her way all around the animal which was content to be groomed while it stood nibbling on apple and grass.

Mathew sat silently watching the whole thing. He had never witnessed anything quite like it before.

It was like the young girl had spent her whole life living with deer, she looked like she was some kind of fairy-of-the-forest now and not the fiery, angry dwarf-warrior she had been before.

The transformation in her was quite astonishing at first, but the more he watched her, the more he came to realise that all she was, was a normal, human-being.

His world was a world where you were perpetually conditioned to be helpers and healers and carers and sympathisers, but never fighters, not injustice fighters at any rate.

Alison's world had that *fighter* in it, *she* had it in her and she was only fifteen.

She cared deeply and could show it at all levels, as she had done when she had rescued him, as she was doing now with the deer, but she also had the ability and courage to actually take the fight back to its source if necessary. Just now she had been prepared to jump out at any would-be attacker and take them on if she'd had to.

Rebel was the name which Mathew's world would label her with. But she simply wasn't a rebel, was she? She was something else, something which was kept hidden, something which was made to seem to be less when it was in fact much, much more, something which had a voice, a voice which most of us were afraid to use - had been *made* afraid to use.

It made him suddenly feel like he had been paying *protection*-money to live his miserable life. *Keep quiet, pay-up and be a good citizen. Or else!* The *or else's* were numerous and long-worded and usually very costly.

Alison looked up and saw him watching her. Her eyes glinted with hidden mischief. 'Look at all tha' luverly, soft fur.' She pointed to the pile on the ground. 'It'll look ace as an 'ood linin' around t' skin. Pass us m' knife an' summert t' catch t' blood in.' She said seriously, and pointed to the bowie-knife on the ground next to Mathew's legs.

His faced drained of all colour and he took back every word he had just said to himself, rolling them all up into a tight ball and throwing them so far, far away.

And then he suddenly pursed and tightened his lips, narrowed his eyes and pointed at her. 'Oo! You-you-' his finger wagged with the *you's*. 'I thought you were serious then! Oo! You-you-you evil, little dwarf.'

He sagged back and guffawed. 'If that's what drink does to you then you're not having any more, young lady.'

Alison scratched behind the ears of the silent deer. Laughing she said; 'I wun't do tha', wud a?'

The deer nudged her face.

Alison giggled. 'No I wun't, wud a?' Her voice had raised a couple of octaves, like she knew a kind of squeaky deer-language. 'No' unless I really 'ad to. Then I'd chop y' 'ed off real quick, wun't a, eh? I wud wun' a?' She continued, using the same squeaky deer-language.

Mathew carefully moved the knife to the other side of the camp and pulled the bottle out again.

Chapter Ten

Lincoln's high-street was the usual, busy bustle and shove of a late, Saturday afternoon.

Hamish hurried along wishing he had taken the long way home now. He usually did, but was later than usual tonight.

He stayed close to the buildings and kept his eyes in front, concentrating on ignoring the blind doorways and shadowed corners; there was nothing there that could harm him. *No terries down there. No terries down there.* He reminded himself over and over that there were no *terries* - terrorists - hiding in these buildings.

It wasn't the buildings themselves which turned on his fear, it was the bustle, the people milling up and down, in and out.

At night he could walk the almost empty streets and feel like any ordinary man in any ordinary city, his fears not quite gone but left in standby mode, blinking somewhere in a remote part of his mind.

It didn't help that the bag he was carrying had a collection of raided fruit, veg and a big pike inside. It was the pike's fault he was so late.

After spinning the banks of the canal on the eastern outskirts of the city all afternoon and with no luck, Hamish was drawing his lure back in for the last time before calling it a day.

As was superstitiously typical amongst fishermen, his line was snapped tight and a nine-and-a-half pound pike put his fishing skills to the test.

It was thirty-five minutes before he managed to land it; the crafty fish knew its domain well and had pushed itself in behind a small, toppled tree. Nothing he could do would draw it out. The tighter he pulled, the more it dug in.

And then, as he was beginning to think about actually wading into the water with his landing-net and just fishing it out, the pike had zipped back into the main flow.

Hamish was fast on the uptake and began reeling it in quickly, eventually smiling as he watched it breach twelve-inches out of the water in an attempt to twist the line into its razored mouth.

He silently thanked the gods of steel leader-line as it splashed down for the third and final time, line still intact.

Once he had it in the net and then up onto the bank, he pulled out his long, slender blade and delivered a single, killing stab to the brain pan. An instantaneous and painless kill.

After a further ten minutes to gut and clean it before removing the scales and filleting it, he wrapped it all up in brown paper and hid it in his bag full of pears and potatoes.

He lifted the bag now and sniffed at it while he walked. Potatoes, it only smelled of potatoes. Wouldn't do to be nicked for taking a fish. Apart from the hefty fine, the fish would be thrown away and wasted.

There wasn't much further to go now before he made it to the end of the busiest part of the high street. Another walk of two hundred yards or so would see him turning off the main road altogether.

He stood at the road-crossing, willing the lights to change for the milling pedestrians to cross, and when they finally did change he watched despondent as the alarm from the signal-box flashed and whistled and the railway-gates dropped down to stop the traffic.

He sighed and stood back again; he couldn't stand in the middle of all those people waiting to cross the train-lines, he just couldn't.

The shop-window behind him caught his attention as it flashed and flickered.

Turning around he was met by a large TV screen on display. He stood and watched it while he waited for the train to pass and the gates to open again.

An advertisement for fish-fingers was playing. He used to love fish-fingers when he was a kid. Fish-fingers and tomato-ketchup. He wondered if you could make fish-fingers from pike.

The advert finished and the news came back on from the break.

A young, smartly dressed woman casually sat at the side of her desk talking, reading from her auto-cue, but the volume on the television was set to mute and Hamish didn't know what she was saying.

A picture appeared over the presenters left shoulder with the words *Freedom Walker* written across the middle.

As she finished saying her line, the image behind her moved closer until it filled the screen. The lettering slid away and Hamish's jaw fell down as his brow shot up.

The still-image, taken from a security camera on the outside of a pub, suddenly came to life, and there was Nippy and Mat right in the middle of a fight in the car-park.

A group of men were battling it out for whatever stupid reasons, and Mat seemed to be just walking in amongst them and - Hamish had to rub his eyes - and he was talking to them.

And Alison looked like she was acting as his-his - another eye-rubbing - his bodyguard. A tiny, fairy-like bodyguard following Mat around.

The crossing-alarm stopped and the barrier rose, but Hamish stayed glued to the unfolding drama on the TV.

* * *

'We didn't have an extravagant wedding though,' Mathew was telling Alison. 'Mary liked the peace of countryside and forest, so we just had a small ceremony in Buxton.'

Alison looked up at him. 'A kno' Buxton, Abra'm's 'ites an' th' cable-car t' top.'

'Abra*ham's*.'

'Abra*ham's*.' Alison repeated, shaking her head but smiling.

'It's a beautiful part of the country,' Mathew remarked, 'over-popular now though.'

'Me nan used t' tek us in t' summer.' Alison casually said.

Mathew took his usual moment to work out what she was saying; she had just told him that her grandmother had taken her to Buxton. He had never heard her speak of family before.

She looked quite happy thinking about her grandmother, it was like a veil of grey-seriousness had been drawn away with the memories of her, revealing a happier soul beneath.

'I used t' like sittin' in a row-boat an' eatin' ice-cream wi' nan while Dale did all t' rowin'.' She sniggered. Her eyes were focusing somewhere a few feet in front of her as she remembered.

'Who's Dale?' Mathew asked.

Alison turned to look up at him and the veil dropped back in place. 'He's m' brother.' She answered. Not exactly darkly, but close to.

Mathew just nodded and didn't question her further. Whatever pain was attached to her brother she would tell him whenever she was ready and *only* if she wanted to.

The narrow lane they were walking along had high hedges and tall trees on one side and small, red-brick houses on the other.

As they came to the corner of the last building, which turned out to be the village pub, a shout of "*BASTARDS!*" made them both whirl around to see seven, young men wade into each other in the small car-park.

Alison leaped in front of Mathew and stood facing the fighters just waiting for any of them to spill over anywhere near them.

And then she gawped. 'Eh!? W-Wot!?'

Mathew ambled around her and clicked his way with his staff to the waiting maul of the fight.

'Shit!' She hissed to herself. 'Wot ya doin', Mathew?' She then called after him.

He didn't reply, just carried on toward the men.

'Oh! Shit!' She jumped up and followed him, trying her hardest to cover all sides of him at once.

She didn't think it was very likely that any of the men would purposely attack either of them, but fights didn't stay still, they moved and rolled and fell and flopped; punches were thrown regardless of who was standing in the way.

One of the men on the edge of the fray, a very large man in his late-thirties and grappling with two men in front of him, flicked a glance at the two figures walking up to them.

A sloppily-aimed fist slipped off his frowning brow, but he didn't flinch. Was that old-geezer going to ask them for directions or something? What?

The two men he had a hold of slowly stopped their flailing fists and looked over their respective shoulders, both of them thinking almost the exact same thought as their large opponent.

Mathew held his staff up in a kind of greeting. 'Eh! Now then, fellas.'

'It's bloody Gandalf.' One of the men being held by his shirt lapels muttered.

Mathew had reached the first three men now. Two of the seven, at the back, were still at it, but the other two were also coming to a halt as he stopped in front of them.

He looked at the big man first and then at the other two in his hands.

'Eh? What's all this then?' He asked.

'What's it got t' do wi-.' The younger of the two men being held by the bigger man was cut short as he was shaken into silence and then hushed by his comrade being held in the other fist.

Mathew sniffed. 'You're right; personal privacy is of paramount importance in any civilised society, I agree.'

He took a step closer, addressing the younger man directly. 'When you *act* civilly. Otherwise it becomes a moral obligation to *everyone* to make sure that we *do* act civilly.'

Another man in his late-twenties scoffed as he dropped his fists. 'So this is a citizen's-arrest is it?'

Mathew frowned and tutted. 'No! This is a citizen's-bollocking!' He shook his head. 'You've lost all sense of direction when you can start laying about each other in a pub car-park.' He threw his arm out and looked around. 'It's not a blooming gym now is it?' He pointed out, sounding genuinely flabbergasted.

The two men who had ended their little battle lastly, walked up and around to their respective friend's sides, effectively flanking Mathew now.

Mathew didn't really notice, but Alison zipped straight in front of him and glared at them all.

The big man looked down at her, gob-smacked, as he would later tell it, at what he saw; she was up for it, by God, she was really up for having a go at all of them.

He slowly released the two men he had been holding throughout the exchange and took a step back, looking Mathew up and down. And then he chuckled and pointed straight at him. 'You know who that is don't you?' He said to them all.

'Gandalf?' The other man repeated.

'It's *The Freedom Walker*, lads.' And he laughed whole-heartedly.

Both Mathew and Alison came to the same conclusion that they were being ridiculed now. Unable to actually bring themselves to push a little girl and an old man around, they were doing the next best thing and trying to bully them with scorn and derision instead.

'Come on, Mathew, th' bein' dick 'eds.' Alison said angrily.

'That's it!' The big man pointed again. 'Mathew Arnold! It *is* him!'

'What? H-how do you know my name?'

The men crowded round him, all smiling and genuinely believing they knew him.

'Ya famous, mate.' One of them said.

A mobile-phone appeared in front of his face.

Alison stood on tiptoe to have a look.

There he was, walking along a country road being filmed by someone from their car.

Mathew's heart skipped a beat when he remembered the slowly-passing car and then the enormous kite on the fencepost.

'Y'av 'ad twenty-two thousand views, mate.' The same voice said.

Mathew blinked and looked down into Alison's eyes which were also blinking, round, wide and shining.

'Blimey.' He said. 'How did that happen?'

All feelings of animosity were made redundant in that moment; all of these men had read and had remarked, discussed and approved of what Mathew was doing. And now they felt that they were a small part of it, touched by his final resolution and courageous strength in a very unique and personal way.

The older, bigger man held out his hand for Mathew. 'I'd have a whip-round and give you some money, but I know you wouldn't take it would you?'

Mathew grasped the shovel-sized hand and shook it firmly. 'No, we wouldn't.'

A ripple of approving laughter went around them all.

Alison just frowned.

'Then in that case,' the man continued, 'let us at least buy you both a pint and dinner to see you back on the road?' He nodded to the pub behind them. 'Our local chippy has been trying to get Agatha's batter recipe for years, you'll never have a better plate of fish and chips anywhere else.' He teased.

The rest of the young men were all encouraging them to come and join them.

Mathew looked to Alison, he would leave it to her expert judgement in this matter; she had been right about everything else so far.

Her frown slowly disappeared. 'I think th' las' time I 'ad fish'n'chips was in Buxton.'

Chapter Eleven

Toilet-water. In any toilet you would expect the presence of toilet-water and that's fine, it's arguably the only place for it really, isn't it? But *public-toilet* toilet-water, now *that* is a different kettle of turds entirely.

The thing with public-toilet toilet-water was it came with its very own, special building filled with its own unique, decorative stains and aromas.

Take urinal-cakes for instance; a marvellous attempt to bring a thousand Scandinavian forests and waterfalls, condensed into a little blue block, straight to your nostrils, along with the millions of urine samples peed onto said forest and into said waterfalls. The blue's quite striking though isn't it?

The very fact that she was even looking at urinal-cakes was a sign that she had hit a record low.

Two more days of sleeping in her car had gone by, always sure she was just about to stumble across her target, but every time she had arrived at one place a video or comment had popped up from somewhere else. Everyone but Diane Jones was bloody seeing *The Freedom Walker*.

And now, standing in the doorway of the men's public lavatory - because the ladies was locked - in the small village of Essendine, smelling like her car - which now smelled of a concoction of spicy take-aways and diesel, mixed with deodorant and just a touch of the BO it was trying to mask - Diane seriously questioned her motives and drive for the story.

The covered bulb flickered happily along, adding to her annoyance. Well, she had better get it over with hadn't she?

She stepped all the way inside and walked to the nearest sink.

The door squeaked and clicked and popped violently as the worn closing mechanism rustily tackled it. It stopped about halfway and just gave up.

Diane sighed and ignored it and filled a sink with cold water instead.

She pulled out a small bar of soap rolled inside a pink face-cloth which she carried in a small travel-bag. Sleeping in her car had enlightened her in the fine art of *roadside hygiene*; soap, face-cloth, toothpaste and brush and two pairs of clean knickers.

She unbuttoned her blouse and began washing her armpits and neck with the soapy cloth, inwardly cringing at the thought of the icy water and then sucking her breath in as it dribbled down her bare ribs and stomach.

Her knickers dropped to the floor next and she stepped out of them, picked them up and stuffed them in a pocket.

More cringing awaited her but she just bloody got on with it anyway.

After refilling the sink with clean water she began washing her face, running her wet fingers through her hair and drawing it out until it was quite lank.

And finally out came the toothbrush and she stood feeling much better as she brushed her teeth. Cleaner, calmer and ready for-

She froze mid-brush and stood like a caught-in-the-act thief staring at the door, blouse open, dribble and froth around her mouth and her knickers hanging out of her pocket. Someone was walking down the road.

Her heart pounded as the footsteps drew closer, her eyes stared unblinking, and the minty dribble now dangled a good inch from her chin.

And then she sighed as the sound began to move away again as the person outside passed by.

And then she violently reversed the sigh and sucked her breath back in as someone spoke. The long minty dribble shot straight back up.

'Will ge' off down 'ere, the'll be a gate or summert ova them fields.' A girl's voice spoke.

'Something.' A man's voice said.

'Eh?'

'There will be a gate or *something*.'

The voices were getting quieter by the second as they moved away but Diane could still hear the next words very clearly.

'*Something*! God! A' we gunna do this all t' way t' London, Mathew!?'
What!? No! How? Why now? Eh? How?

Those and many, many other questions of the very same ilk were splashed all around the public lavatory as Diane coughed and sputtered out her over-salivated toothpaste-froth.

She ran to the door and dragged it open, and stepped outside to see the two people who had been talking, the two people she had been stalking, standing across the road.

'Maffu? Maffu Arnol'?' She called, sputtering white foam and waving her toothbrush around.

Mathew and Alison both turned around to stare. Alison stood defensively in front of Mathew again; mad people were much worse than thugs.

'It's okay, Alison.' He said, and placed a hand on her shoulder.

'She's foamin' a' t' mouth, 'er shirts open an' her knickers ar' 'anging out of her pocket, Mathew. A don' think the's owt really okay abou' tha'.'

Diane crossed the road and tried to sidestep the young, serious-looking girl in front of her.

Alison nipped to the side and blocked her again.

She stopped and frowned at the mousy, little thing for a second and then looked back up at Mathew.

'Um. Are you Mathew Arnold?' She asked, ignoring Alison and talking over the top of her head.

'Yes, yes I am he. Um, can-can I help you in any way?' He asked, looking her up and down and making a point of ignoring the pink, lacy knickers which were so vying for attention. He settled his gaze on her face instead. 'A handkerchief perhaps?'

Alison giggled as quietly and as politely as she could.

On the trail of a story a journalist's personal decorum and appearance can and often does meld in with the war-torn background or the high-seas shipping disaster or the record breaking, goal-scoring sports event etc, the reporter always looking like he or she *belonged* to the scene and the story.

Diane looked down at herself; she looked like she'd been reporting on *doggers* or *swingers* or something in public-toilets.

'Oh! God.' She muttered and stuffed her knickers down into her pocket and out of sight while dragging her blouse closed. 'Oh! God.' She repeated.

It was bad enough that they had seen her underwear in the first place, but standing in front of them knowing that they *knew* she didn't have any knickers on was definitely much, much worse.

She took a small step to run away and then stopped. 'Don't go away.' She said, not meeting their eyes with her blushing face and then carried on running away.

Mathew and Alison remained still and just watched the froth-mouthed woman as she ran back into the lavatory.

'Dya kno' 'er?' Alison asked, sniffing and rubbing her nose.

'No, I don't think so, but if we are on the Internet tube-thing we can assume that she has seen it.'

Alison turned around and began walking again. 'She'll prob'ly jus' wan' a selfie wi' ya.'

Mathew turned around too and followed slowly behind. '*Probably*. She'll *probably* just want a selfie.'

'A cud jus' go 'ome y'kno?'

'And then you would learn nothing and I would get lost and learn nothing.' Mathew paused and shrugged. 'Seems like a whole lot of nothing to me?'

Alison sighed deeply and counted to ten. '*Probably*. She'll *probably* just wan*ts* a selfie.' Her young eyes widened in surprise; she actually thought that sounded quite good.

'Wonderful! Much better. Now,' Mathew began, 'what's a *selfie*? Sounds a little bit, um, sexual to me.'

Alison guffawed and then fell into a fit of giggles.

And that's how Diane saw them as she stepped back out into the daylight. Hadn't waited for her though, had they?

She trotted off toward them with a shout and a wave, and they turned to wait for her to catch up.

She stood in front of them and caught her breath.

Alison remained by Mathew's side this time; the mad woman had somehow miraculously turned into a *business*-woman, hair tied back and clothing neatly in place.

'Sorry about that,' Diane said. 'Diane Jones,' she held her hand out to Mathew, 'I'm a reporter for the *London Globe*.'

Mathew took her hand and shook it. 'Can't say that I've heard of it I'm afraid.'

'Well *we* have heard of you.' She beamed, taking her hand back and looking as though she had just told him he had won first-prize in the lottery.

Mathew just stared at her cheerfully, unimpressed.

Alison glared though.

Unfazed, Diane continued. 'I've been assigned-,' it always sounded more important if you've been *assigned*. '-to report on *The Freedom Walker*; you, Mister Arnold.'

Mathew raised an eyebrow; there was that title again; *Freedom Walker*. It made him sound like some kind of *Marathon Man* or *Olympian* or something. He'd only done about seventy miles of slow, country walking, it wasn't like he'd crossed the Gobi, was it?

He looked down at Alison. She just shrugged; she still didn't know why he'd been called that either.

Diane's reporter's nose told her that neither of them understood what was happening out *there* in the coat-pockets and handbags world of the Internet. The videos were getting more views every day, over sixty thousand at her last look, and people were talking about *The Freedom Walker* all over the social-networks.

And not a single reporter had managed to get near them until now.

'It seems to me that both of us ha-,' Diane stopped mid-sentence as Alison cleared her throat noisily.

She stared down at the angry-looking *mouse*. 'All *three* of us have questions.' She amended, tutting. 'Who are you exactly?' She then quickly asked the young girl.

'Nippy.' Alison fired back.

Mathew sighed and placed a hand on Alison's shoulder. 'This charming, young lady is Alison, and she is with me and under my care.' He said.

Alison scoffed. '*I'm* unda *your* care!?' She shrugged his hand off and walked away disgusted, muttering under her breath.

Diane could see there was a strange bond between these two. The young girl seemed to think she was looking after the old man at least and not the other way round.

The story had suddenly, subtly shifted and wasn't just the simple *elder-flower* job anymore was it?

Mathew nodded over his shoulder to the huffing Alison. 'She's a real marvel is that one.'

Diane looked past him to the girl who was now kicking the dust with the toe of her plimsolls, her hands stuffed deep in her pockets. *I'll take your word for it.* She thought. 'Yes, I can see.' She said. 'Do you think it would be okay if we had a chat and I asked you some questions?'

'I don't see why not, but Alison and I have to get off the road now so you will have to walk with us, if that's alright?'

Diane thought for a moment and looked around at where they would be *getting off the road.* It was just fields and trees lying ahead. 'Well I could do that, or you could both jump in my car and I'll drive you to where you want to be and we can talk as we drive?'

Alison stepped back up. 'Yea, le's do tha'.'

Mathew was surprised. 'Yes, like the boss says, let's do that.'

The three of them walked the few yards back to Diane's car, the journalist rubbing her mental hands together at the thought of finally getting the interview and then getting back home to wine, baths, hot food and warm beds.

They set off down the road.

'So, tell me what it is that you are doing, Mister Arnold? She asked.

Mathew, sitting in the front seat, turned to face her. 'Please call me Mathew or Mat.'

'Okay, Mat, so what exactly are you do-.'

'Jus' 'ere.' Alison interrupted, and leaned between them, pointing to a stile in the hedge through the windscreen. They had only travelled around seventy-five yards.

Diane pulled over onto the grass verge and stopped, glaring daggers at the innocently-smiling Alison who was already getting out of the car.

Mathew just sat for an embarrassed moment.

'Um.' He pointed lamely outside and then equally lamely opened the door and followed Alison.

The tiny frame of the young girl stood outlined against the background of a sun-yellow sky, triumphantly standing on the top step of the wooden stile.

Diane bubbled; the little cow-bag knew she was wearing heeled shoes and wouldn't be able to tackle wild, open fields. But she hadn't reckoned on her carrying an anorak and wellies in the boot though, had she?

She exited her car and marched with her chin held high to the rear.

Keeping her eyes on Alison, she opened the boot and delved inside. It was satisfying to see the shrimp's smile drop at the sight of her green wellington-boots. Very satisfying.

'I'll be just a minute changing my shoes.' She glibly called.

Mathew just stood and looked between the two and kept himself silent and unnoticed.

After the said minute had passed, the car-boot slammed closed and a well-clad and booted Diane Jones, reporter for the *London Globe*, stood ready to carry on.

Alison just sniffed haughtily and then climbed down the stile to the other side.

'Um, after you?' Mathew said, smiling weakly and holding his palm open to show the way.

Chapter Twelve

The lights on the night time motorway were dazzling compared to the dark country roads she had been driving along for the past three days. They were like a beacon for civilisation, *follow the lights to life* they said.

Diane's thoughts stuttered; *follow the lights to life and leave the forgotten behind in the dark.*

Her story wasn't turning out to be what she had expected it to be, and if she were absolutely honest with herself, she was still uncertain what it was that she actually had. But one thing she was certain of; Mathew Arnold was a very strange, old man.

Sitting with him and the girl around a campfire in the woods, she had experienced something. Something which seemed to be around them all but was definitely coming from Mathew Arnold. And it troubled her that she didn't know what it was.

Diane was a born and bred, big-city girl and only knew life as it *whizzed* around in front of her. Always in the now, always moving forward into the next step without really seeing what was there, while all of the other things which went on around her were blocked out by her automatic city-life filters.

Why hadn't he been angry for a start? Angry at what had happened to him, angry at everything he had lost, why not? Anyone else would have been. He'd stayed calm and almost placid when telling his story, like, like? Like what?

Her inner-voice prodded her. Like that was *all* it was, a story, something done and remembered and then told; he hadn't cared about what had happened to him by this point. But why? What had changed since he had first written his message on Facebook?

She had never been in the presence of a priest or a vicar, hell, she hadn't even been in a church before, nor had she met any Buddhists or shaman or the like, but if she *had* she would probably say that Mathew reminded her of something like that. Along with a mousy, little side-kick, not to mention walking-staff and big coat and boots.

She shook her head and scoffed. *Who the hell are you?*

A service-station appeared up ahead. Coffee and something from the cake-tray would help get her head straight.

She took the exit and pulled into a parking-space almost in front of the door. The place looked empty apart from the three, young men behind the counter.

She walked straight in and ordered her coffee and took a side order of two, large jam-doughnuts.

'Late night?' The cashier asked politely while he dug out her change from the till.

'Hm mm. Isn't it always?' Diane replied.

The young man - or was it a boy? He couldn't have been older than seventeen - handed her the change. 'It is for me.' He answered cheerfully. 'I'm always on night-shift.'

'Permanent graveyard duties, eh?' She picked her tray up.

'What?' He asked and frownd.

'Graveyard-shift, dude.' Said another young man-boy standing by the milkshake pumps. He had his head down, eyes on his phone as he flicked away expertly with his bionic thumbs. 'It means bein' on the night shift.'

'Oh, right. That's cool,' the first man-boy beamed stupidly and nodded at Diane, 'I like it.'

She pointed a finger-pistol at him and wink-*chk'd* before leaving the men-boys to their mobiles and taking a seat at the first table she came to.

The coffee was pretty good and the doughnuts were still pretty fresh considering they had been on the cool-shelf all day and night. She just might have to try one of those Danish slices as well though.

She looked up from her cup. The boys were standing around a single mobile, unblinking like silent statues or phone-zombies. Even the screen lent a hand to painting a picture of the undead-veneer with its bright, pasty glow.

'Where's he now?' She heard one of them say.

'Dunno, 'ang on.' Another replied.

She couldn't see who was speaking because all of their mouths were hidden beneath their tilted heads, but she knew who they were speaking about.

'Right. That's miles up north somewhere, near Peterborough, look?'

Diane sipped her coffee and watched them; she wanted to know what *they* thought about *The Freedom Walker*, the common man. Or boys, whichever. They were working for the *Man* so it was probably fair to call them men she supposed.

'He's just like Gandalf, ain' he?' The first man said, seriously.

The others nodded approvingly and Diane changed her mind; men-boys it was.

'God, I 'ope he makes it.' He carried on.

The others agree and nodded again.

'Why do you hope he makes it?' She asked.

All three looked up.

'Because it'd be a righteous middle-finger salute to those bastards-!'

He threw his hand to his mouth, guiltily blushing at having cursed in front of a customer. 'Oh! God! I'm so sorry!'

Diane waved her hands indifferently. '*Bastard* away, my young friend.'

The boys laughed and did a little nodding thing then which sort of made their legs bend at the knees; a bob-nodding dance which had a stupid grin as part of its uniform. 'Cool.' They were saying.

'Do you think he'll make it?' She asked.

'I don't see why not.' Man-boy two answered. 'But he does look a bit frail, don' he? A fall could do 'im in?'

He shrugged then, like he was stating the obvious. 'If they wanna stop 'im, all they'd 'av to do is send a car his way, if you know what I mean?' He winked. 'Give 'im a little *nudge.*'

Give him a little nudge? Diane frowned. 'What do you mean? Who would give him a *little nudge*?'

'Anyone who wouldn't want to be embarrassed by him.' The third man-boy said. '*Them.*' He pointed to the ceiling.

Diane continued to frown and thought about it. Not so much about the prime minister sending out *hit-men* and assassins to *eliminate the problem*, but more about how these people were perceiving Mathew's *quest*. To them it was serious enough for someone to send out hit-men and assassins to remove an old man.

'So you agree with what he's doing and what he's going to do?' She asked them.

'Yea, definitely. Maybe not the starvin' to death part so much, but I don't think anyone will let him starve anyway, d' you? There'll be loads of people down there to watch him, loads of people will feed him now.' Third man-boy answered.

'Duzn't matter 'ow ya look at it really, duz it?' Man-boy two put in. 'Cos even if 'e did stop eatin' they'd only send out PC Plod wiv a tazer-sarni anyway.'

'And the riots would ensue.' The third said. 'Guarantee it; if anyone did anything to hurt him once he had a crowd around him,' he slowly shook his head. 'It'd be bad, very bad.'

The three of them nodded slowly in unison and stared into the space directly in front of themselves.

Diane sat and waited for one of them to say something like *righteous*.

They didn't, for which she was really thankful.

She stood up. 'How about a refill and a Danish slice, the almond-topped one please?'

Man-boy one made more coffee while number two delivered the Danish.

'Coffee's on the house.' Number one said, and handed her a fresh cup. 'Night-driving policy; free refill when you're in after 11pm.'

'Great. Thanks.'

'Two-fifty.' Two said, handing her the plate and pastry.

'No night-driving pastry-policy?' She cheekily asked.

The young-man smiled and turned away for a second. When he turned back there were two Danish pastries on the plate. 'Two-fifty.' He said. 'Night-driving pastry-policy.'

Diane chuckled. 'Righteous.'

And the three began their bob-nodding again. 'Cool.'

* * *

A glass of lousy, four-day-refrigerated wine and a 3:30am hot bath; heaven.

Diane lay with her eyes closed and thought about Mathew Arnold, *The Freedom Walker.*

"I've only had to do two things in my life; work - I was an engineer on the railways for thirty-seven years - and love my wife, and I believe I have done both of those things satisfactorily and to the best of my abilities. Now I have a third thing to do and I will do that to the best of my abilities as well.

"There is no real choice about anything, Miss Jones; you either do it the easy way or the right *way, everything else is just a distraction to help you along the road to making the easy choices which are, more often than not, the wrong choices. Before you know it you're up to your neck in wrong choices."*

A long working-life as a railway engineer, a man who used his hands and his brains to do his job. A faithful and caring husband, nursing his wife through sickness until it had finally beaten her and she had died.

Strength. A strength built upon his life's experience; labour, love and loss; a triad of strength.

Peaceful resignation was close to what she felt when she sat with him, but not quite right. He didn't come across as being resigned to his lot at all, if anything it was more like he was doing a job. But that wasn't quite right either.

She flicked the hot tap back on with her foot and sipped at her wine, grimacing a little.

And then there was the girl, Alison. Fifteen years-old, a runaway at thirteen - who or what had she run away from?

Diane had found her to be quite unnerving once they had stopped trying to outwit each other. She held a cold wisdom which one could clearly see once past her *scrappy* facade.

"Guv'ments don' work right when businessmen a' polytishuns. Businessmen allus look up at wot they c'n build and never look down at wot they already done. If the' did, the'd see all of us down 'ere clingin' on f' dear life."

The perpetual frown she wore only made her look angry all of the time, but sitting round the fire, Diane saw that it wasn't an angry frown at all, it was a thoughtful frown, as though the girl were constantly trying to puzzle something out.

In Diane's world a girl like Alison would have come across as *clingy* by the way she stuck to Mathew's side, but that was as far from the truth as you could possibly get. Over-protective wasn't even the right word.

She was more like a professional body-guard cum guide, exposing herself to any dangers before Mathew did and keeping him expertly on the road while she did it.

Or maybe she was a true follower? Like a disciple? Well that was taking it a bit too far but she was on the right lines, she knew it.

She flicked the tap back off and refilled her glass.

The angle to this story was all wrong. She had been sent to report on a *protest-walk* sort of thing originally, but now Diane felt that this was becoming something much bigger. He wasn't simply the grumpy, old man having a senior tantrum, he really meant to do what he said he was going to do; give the Prime minister his last seventeen pence and then simply sit down and starve himself.

The wine disappeared in one gulp.

When she thought of it like that it made it sound so petty and petulant, an over-dramatic *look-at-what-you-made-me-do* gesture. She just couldn't write it up like that, she just couldn't.

She filled her glass again and then dropped the empty bottle to the floor beside her, laying back again to stare at the ceiling.

She needed to talk to Edmund about this.

Or did she? What if he wanted that dramatic sensationalism, that flavour of human suffering?

"I suddenly found out my life was being threatened by a machine, a computer. When or how that happened I don't know, but I really think someone has lost their way when they turn individual human-beings into numbers and then hand them over to machines to be processed."

Mathew's words continued to ring in her mind.

He deserved to have his story told properly and she was in the driving seat for pretty much all of the mainstream-media at the moment; if she could just set the *flavour* now. Or better still, keep his whereabouts out of the report entirely and then carry on with follow-ups over the days of his entire march.

She knew the other media agents would eventually work out where he was and pounce on him, but by then she would have a well-documented head-start on them all, as well as a more trusting relationship with Mathew himself.

Edmund might try to make her settle for a *bigger* story, but she knew he would eventually see that she was right; Mathew Arnold was doing something for everybody, and everybody was watching. They couldn't afford to be on the wrong side of that now could they, Edmund dear?

Chapter Thirteen

Water hushed alongside them and the air was damp and fresh while the sunshine was still unusually bright for this end of September. The storm of a few days ago had done a grand job of clearing the air.

The banks of the Great Ouse were vibrant and lush and there were plenty of birds and other wildlife hiding in and amongst the tall reeds and river-grass.

Mathew plodded on in the tiny wake which Alison was making. The ground hardly seemed to notice where she trod, she was like an elf walking nimbly along the tops of the grass.

Peaceful whispers of reed and river soothed his tired mind as he walked and thought.

Tall, large-girthed and long-armed trees looked down on them, watching them pass, sighing appreciatively with the lambent breeze running through their high, canopied boughs.

He'd never really understood trees, not until he had freed himself he hadn't.

He watched them now and smiled at them; the things they must have witnessed over the span of their far-reaching lives, the changes to land and life which they could tell a tale or two about if they could speak. Or as his dear Mary would have said; *if we could understand.*

His chest was aching again, a dull pain beneath his ribs. So he smiled again, to himself this time; the things *he* had witnessed and the tales which *he* could tell were in that ache, it was all in there, right where it should be.

'Y'arite, Mathew?'

He looked up and noticed Alison had stopped walking and was watching him keenly.

'Yes, yes I'm fine. Let's have a sit here for a minute and catch our breath.'

He ambled over to a log bench and sat down with a creak and a huff. Alison sat next to him, her toes only just touching the ground.

He could feel her eyes on him, scrutinising, looking for his pain.

'I really am alright you know? Just a bit short of breath.'

She pulled a bottle of water from her coat-pocket and handed it to him. 'Y' tired an' y' breavins tight an' av' seen ya rubbin' y' chest.' She looked at him levelly.

'Brea*th*ing.' He said.

'Brea*th*ing.' She repeated automatically. 'We'll hav' a two-night stop an' y'can get some rest.'

He saluted weakly. 'Ma'am.' He wouldn't argue with her, she had a sharp eye, it would be pointless to try and hide anything from her anyway.

They sat and watched the river-flow, the snow-white foam-sprites leaped joyously along the top of the rushing wash as it rolled past.

Over the past few days the feeling he had set out with, that feeling of total abandonment and freedom, had slowly faded and was replaced by something else now; a simple peace. He didn't even really feel burdened anymore, just resolute and peaceful.

'D' ya like eel?' Alison asked and sniffed like she often did, rubbing the end of her nose with her sleeve.

'Eel? You mean the fish and not the thing on your shoe?' He grinned.

She grinned back. 'Va fing on me shew is called a *hhh*eel.' She said, dropping as many letters as she could except for the *h*.

He chuckled. 'I can't say I've ever had eel so I wouldn't know. Why? Have you got some?'

'No, but a will 'av before we ge' off again.' She answered and jumped to her feet.

She produced a bright-orange reel from within the folds of her jacket - one of Jolly's tricks, Mathew remembered - and unwound a few inches until she had the hook showing.

Squatting down on her haunches, she picked up a stumpy twig and began digging into the grass with it, cutting out a crude circle of earth.

She lifted the sod-plug out and checked underneath. Nothing there. She replaced the plug and tried again. Still nothing, but on the third attempt she found a big, red worm.

'A-ha!' She shouted triumphantly.

She held the squirming worm up for Mathew to see. 'I will now turn this worm into an eel?' She said, in her poshest voice. 'Abracadabra!' And then impaled the unfortunate worm onto her hook, expertly double-hooking it so that it covered most of the metal and hid the snag completely.

She jogged to the riverside and threw the line out, reeling off more slack as it sank. Once she was sure it had hit the bottom she crouched back down and waited like a tiny hunter.

Her delicate fingers held the line tight with one hand while the other played it and felt the movement of the water, reading the bottom through touch. She could feel a thin line of weed and a shallow, gravely dip.

Her fingers lightly pulled the line through the dip and then allowed it to be snapped back again by the current, teasing the edge of the weeds which she knew were growing there.

The line banged and then tugged, Alison snapped it upward quickly. She stood up and began drawing it in with long sweeps of her small arms, winding it into the crooks of her elbows.

Mathew watched as the orange line was twanged and snagged backward and forward, vibrating madly as the fish on the end did its damnedest to spit the hook out. But by the looks of Alison's over-arm, winding technique, he guessed the thing didn't stand a chance against the *master*.

He chuckled to himself as he watched the small girl winding the line onto her arms. He had done that exact movement when he had been helping Mary to ball-up her knitting wool.

Alison turned around and blew her fringe out of her face. 'Tha's one.' She beamed and held the squirming black and grey eel up for him to see.

It made him feel warm and altogether much better just watching her smile like that. She looked just like the child she had missed being, like the child who had gone to Buxton perhaps.

'Well done, young lady, very well done.' He called proudly and gave her an appreciative applause.

Alison felt giddy with happiness for a moment, genuine happiness, a feeling which didn't come often enough nor stay for very long.

The world she had come from fell away like the drawing off of shadows as the sun came up when she saw the genuine approval and mutual happiness on Mathew's face.

'So? How do you cook eel then?' He called over.

Alison's eyes twinkled. 'Y' don', y' eat 'em live.'

Mathew gulped. 'Okay. You first.' And then winked and leaned forward ready for a spectacle.

The delicate, pale features of the fearless *Nippy,* hardened and her eyes impossibly twinkled more brightly still.

She held the twisting eel up by the tail and threw her head back, opening her mouth wide.

Mathew sat back up, his mouth dropped slowly from its smile as his brow raised into its frown. He thought she was just being her dark, humorous self.

The eel had calmed down a little now and Alison had begun to slowly lower its head into her waiting mouth.

A small, tight knot in his stomach reached violently up into his throat and he gagged at the thought of what he was about to see. *Look away then! Can't! I'll hear it! Oh! God, I'll hear its head crunching off!*

'Um. Okay, you win; I'm thoroughly, thoroughly disgusted, believe me.' He almost pleaded.

Alison pretended she hadn't heard him and continued lowering the eel, which was now just passing the threshold of her lips.

'Oh! God! No, please, Alison, don't-'

And then she suddenly threw the eel onto the grass and began spitting. 'Oh! Ah! It's gone in me mowf!'

Mathew just blinked. What had just happened? Wasn't the whole idea that it was to go in her mouth?

'Oh!' She gagged and wretched and spat. 'A big bit o' slime went right in m' throat!'

And then he had it and slapped his thighs, the beginnings of a long, wheezy laugh erupting as his face screwed up. She had pushed her bluff too far. He croaked and gasped even louder.

'Oh! Ah! Agh! It's 'orrible! Ah!' He could hear her gagging voice shouting.

Holding his aching belly with one hand, Mathew pulled out his bottle of *Old Nasty* with the other, weakly holding it out in her direction.

He only caught a blurry glimpse of her speeding form whizzing in and snatching the bottle from his trembling hand.

The taste of eel-slime must have addled her usually sharp mind because she unscrewed the cap and took a *swig* of the stuff straight from the bottle, forcing herself to swallow it.

A tiny sound came from her mouth, nothing discernible or really emotionally coherent, just a primal squeak.

Her eyes widened involuntarily as a world of disgusting taste was washed away by a world of flame-thrower pain.

Mathew took one, blurry look at her and thought he might just die right there and then if he laughed any more.

Stunned, Alison slowly screwed the cap back on and then turned around and walked back to the eel.

Slowly she bent down and brained it with a single crack of *Old Nasty* then walked back to Mathew and held the bloodied and slimed bottle out to him, still struggling to catch a proper breath.

He took it without seeing it properly or fully comprehending what she had done with it at first, but as soon as his fingers had touched it a picture had quickly formed in his head which brought his laughter sharply back down a notch. Thankfully, his aching stomach might have added, but didn't because of the eel slime on his hands.

Alison took her place on the bench again and stared straight ahead. 'I miss Merylin an' tha' lot.' She wheezed.

Mathew looked across at her. 'Me too.' He said. 'You'll see them again though, I'm sure of it.'

'A kno'. Still miss 'em tho'.' She sniffed.

He nodded. 'I know.' He said gently, and then draped his arm over her shoulder.

She sniffed again. 'Did y' just wipe eel-slime on me shoulder?'

'Yes, yes I did.' Mathew answered and nodded. 'Did you kill the eel with my bottle of *Old Nasty*?'

Alison nodded in return. 'Yea. Yea a did.'

Mathew smiled and pulled her closer to him.

The pair of them sat like that for awhile, just watching the river again.

They heard a cyclist go past on the track behind them, suddenly reminding them that they weren't the only people on the planet.

Alison shuffled herself off the bench.

'Two more an' we can go find somewhere t' camp up.'

She ambled back to the first eel, the stunning effect of Merylin's brew now wearing off and the warm, numbing effect kicking in.

She removed the hook and the still-living bait from the dead fish and held it up. 'Fancy a crack?'

Mathew's eyes rapidly blinked as he thought about it then he shrugged.

He opened the bottle of *Old Nasty* again and poured a cap-full. 'Okay.' He nodded and raised the cap to his lips. He took a deep breath and then threw the lot into his mouth and swallowed.

A few shakes and gasps later and he was kneeling by the waterside with the line firmly in his grasp. 'If I catch one you'll have to kill it you know?'

Alison snickered. 'Soft. I said y' wa' soft dint a?'

'I'm not *soft*, I just don't like killing things, that's all.' He argued.

'Yea, soft. What would y' do if I want 'ere, eh?' She flicked her penknife into the ground by her side.

Mathew tutted. 'Well that's obvious isn't it?' He said, shaking his head. 'I wouldn't *be* here would I? I'd be dead somewhere back there.' He raised his arm an pointed back the way they had come.

The line, being attached to his hand, tightened and dragged the bait through the water.

SNAP!

It suddenly shot off, startling Mathew as it pulled him forward.

Alison grabbed hold of his jacket and pulled him back.

'Keep ya eye on t' line, watch 'ow it sways an' drops.' She coached, coaxing his arm around to follow the flow of the running line.

'It feels like a big dog on the end of it!' Mathew's voice was raised an octave; he had never been fishing in his life before. Mary forbade it.

'Keep calm, Mathew. A don' kno' wot's on t' end ov it, but I can tell you it's not an eel.'

'It's a big dog I tell you!'

'Right; when it comes back in t'wards ya, wind t' line ova y' arms.'

Wide-eyed and thrilled - not to mention a little fuzzy from the brew - Mathew did as he was told. Arm over arm three times and then it was snapped tight again viciously.

'Oh! God! What is it!?' He squeaked.

'It's a fish. A fu-' She stopped as Mathew threw her hard, albeit awkward, glance.

'I'll tell Merylin.' He managed to say.

'It's a *flippin'* big fish.'

The line suddenly went slack as the fish swam toward them.

'Quick! It's tryin' t'spit 'uck owt!' Alison shouted and pointed at the slack line.

Mathew quickly wound in arm-full's of the stuff before it went tight again, almost right in front of them now.

'It's sittin' on t' bottom. Lets pull it up t'gether. Slowly.'

Hand over hand they both drew the line and fish up to the surface.

'Wow! Look at tha'!' Alison looked to be extremely impressed. 'Tha's a zander tha' is.'

Mathew looked down at the long, silvery fish. 'A w-what?'

'A zander. Predator like a pike. Big teeth.'

Her bottom jaw stood out when she said big teeth, her own bottom teeth showing like a bulldog's.

'B-big teeth?' He blinked and leaned away from the edge in case the fish leaped out and latched onto his face with its fangs or something.

He looked back to Alison. 'Y-you just said tee*th* instead of tee*f*.'

She shrugged. 'I 'ant noticed.' She said innocently. 'Shall we pull us dinna' owt o' t' water?'

Chapter Fourteen

Just as Diane had predicted, Edmund had resisted her initial attempt of *under*-playing the story a little and setting the flavour to something less *suicidal-protest*.

"*But he says he's going to kill himself.*"

"*I know.*"

"*So why aren't we saying he's going to kill himself?*"

"*Because it's more than just about suicide.*"

"*But he <u>says</u> he's going to kill himself!*"

"*I know.*"

"*So? You haven't mentioned it once in this report.*"

"*I know.*"

"*Jones?*"

"Yes?"

And it was right here, while lowering his voice in frustrated exasperation, that Edmund had suddenly folded.

It had nothing to do with the information she had written in her report - which was next to nothing - or the answers to his questions - which came to less than nothing. No, it was for the simple fact that Diane wasn't arguing. At all. Not a single harsh word, petulant huff or snippy comment.

He knew she had a good nose for the job and story. She was still young and fiery and usually approached all of her reports the same way; storming a path to the truth and bugger everyone - including her chief - who got in her way.

What he saw now was something like the *next-level* of her hidden, journalistic talents being revealed, a seriousness which made her eyes hard but kept her mouth closed. It had made him shiver if he were to be completely honest.

And so he had taken the report back and promised her a quarter-page column before allowing her to leave and *get on with it*.

"*And, Jones?*"

"*Mm?*"

"*DON'T sleep in your car.*"

* * *

Oh, how he loved to walk along these polished floors with their polished wood-panel walls and the paintings of stern-faced men - and a few women - watching him parading proudly past them.

This hall was his, Crispin Wells. Anyone else using it were almost always accompanied by him from his little office at one end, down to the prime minister's large office at the other.

His office, as personal as it was, was still on the *outside* he felt, while the corridor was intimately connected straight to the power-centre, his own, personal umbilical to the inside.

He rapped twice on the heavy door and waited.

'*Come.*' A woman's voice called.

He pressed down on the large, brass door-handle and went in. 'Sorry to interrupt, Prime Minister.' He said and closed the door behind him. 'There's a small matter which you should be made aware of.'

She narrowed her eyes, he knew how delicate the situation was at the minute and also knew not to bother her with trivia. Saying the words *small matter* and then bothering her with it really meant something *big* and urgent.

He handed her a newspaper, the London Globe, it was opened at page two and a column had been ringed in red marker.

She scanned the article and then pursed her lips tightly. 'And the point of showing me this is?' Her words were sharpened on those tight lips.

'Well, it may be nothing,' he answered, and actually gulped. 'But I have been following that story for a few days now, online, and *that* story,' he pointed at the paper, 'has failed to mention quite a vital point of what Mr Arnold plans to do.' He let those words sink in.

The prime minister read the article again. 'And what might that be?' She asked, looking up and lowering her glasses.

'He says that once he has handed over his last, few pence, he means to sit down and starve himself to death.'

The prime minister's eyes widened. 'Really? That *is* interesting, Crispin.' She snapped the paper up again. 'And the *Globe* didn't mention it? In fact it looks like this,' she peered closely at the column, 'Diane Jones has given it quite the *soft-touch*, wouldn't you agree?'

'My thoughts exactly, Prime Minister; underplayed to keep it quiet for as long as possible, giving him the chance to actually get here.'

She sat back in her high-backed, red-leather chair. This was a disaster in the making, he had to be *appeased* somehow. The whole world was watching the country at the moment, this kind of *social-protest* was the very last thing the government needed while they were dealing with the tricky situation in Europe.

'What do we know about Mister Arnold?' She asked.

'I've already looked into all of the social responses we possibly could have employed, Prime Minister, if that's what you are thinking?

'Mathew Arnold is an upstanding, hard-working citizen. He has no mental health issues, he's never had a serious illness and has a no criminal-record. Not even a parking-ticket'

She just nodded and sighed, crossing her legs and sitting with her arms folded. She looked like she was about to curl up for the evening in front of the TV.

A small, white pawn from a chess-set sat under a glass dome on her desk, a gift from her one-time lover and mentor. *"Never forget, Eliza, there are more pawns on the board than any other piece. Together they are a formidable force, but they are always drawn together by just one of them, the* fire-starter. *Beware the* fire-starter, *Eliza."*

She stared into the globe at the bone-white pawn. Mathew Arnold was a naked-flame and this Jones woman was attempting to fan his fire.

'Suggestions?' She asked.

'Two options are viable.' Crispin replied automatically. 'A: Send in Palmerson to locate him and have him brought here, directly to you and a waiting news-crew. It's an opportunity to turn it to your advantage if we can show that you are not only caring enough to listen to him, but also show that you are still in control of the deeper, social issues.'

She nodded. 'And B?'

'We have him sectioned and placed into care. Once he is in the system we can keep him there indefinitely. Our *affiliates* at the press will cover it as the concerned act of a caring prime minister. Again, we can use the story throughout his incarceration and *treatment*, keeping up your appearance as a *matronly carer*.'

They were both good and viable options.

'Have you actually seen pictures of him?'

'Yes, I've seen video of him.'

'Does he look as though he could actually walk all the way here?' She asked hopefully.

The other question, *would it be possible for him to just drop dead on the way*, remained unsaid by both of them.

'He's old and slow, but he also looks determined, so I would say yes, there is the possibility of him getting here, but also there is the possibility that he won't.' He shrugged slightly.

The prime minister stood up, picked the chess-piece up from the desk and studied it closely. A *fire-starter*, now of all times.

She fidgeted with the pawn, turning it slowly around so she could look at all of it. How should she control it? With the fireman or the hose?

Placing the chess-piece back on the desk she sat back down. It would have to be the fireman, plan B could always be put into action if all else failed.

'Call Palmerson,' she eventually said. 'Tell him I want to see him first thing in the morning.'

'Of course, Prime Minister, I'll get right onto it.'

The hallway seemed brighter and the paintings seemed to be smiling down at him as he walked back on air to his office.

His hallway, Crispin Wells, aide to the prime minister of Great Britain and the man who had no idea at all that his boss should have, in fact, chosen option B right from the very start.

Jeremy Donagle's old friend, that chuckling, silent watcher called fate, scoffed just a little as Crispin briskly walked his hallway, oblivious.

* * *

A break in the clouds allowed the moon to show its full, bright face, bathing Mathew's sleeping form in a cool, blue light.

Alison sat by the fire and watched him as he snored. He was frowning in his sleep and his eyes were rolling.

She had made him take another cap-full of Merylin's brew before he lay down to sleep. The air was getting damper and more cool by the day, the last thing Mathew needed was to catch a chill.

She looked away and into the fire.

It was more than a chill she was worried about, who was she trying to kid? She had seen him rubbing at a pain in his chest. Not often, but he had done it.

Her nan had done that, *exactly* that. And then she had died. Mathew mustn't die.

They had a ways to go yet, at least another seventy or eighty miles. They could reach London in little under a week at the pace Mathew walked.

Alison had been keeping them well away from the major roads, sticking to the deeper countryside instead, the place she knew the best.

It was easy for her to mark out the land and find the best places to spend the night and she always had a knack of getting plenty of food, usually from the land itself. But not always.

She dropped her hand inside her coat and laid her fingers on the money which she had secreted in there.

The big man, the one who had been fighting in the pub car-park and had bought them dinner, had quietly slipped her fifty pound. *"He hasn't took it if I give it to you has he?"*

She hadn't used much of it, there was still at least forty-four pound left. She just might have to use more as they got closer to the city though.

A shudder from darker memories ran through her tiny frame causing her to pull her legs up to her chin and huddle her arms around her knees.

London was no place for the homeless, even though it was full of them.

All big cities were a dangerous place to be living on the streets, but London was a heartless, soulless place, a place where your very essence was sucked right from your being until there was nothing left but an empty gaze and a lifeless void. You didn't die in London, you were absorbed.

Mathew grunted and stirred in his sleep again, muttering unintelligibly.

He wouldn't make it in London, she thought. She knew. He would be swallowed up and spat out onto the already stories-high pile of lost people; passed by, passed on and then passed out and forgotten.

She had lost count of the times she had wanted to plead with him to turn around and just go back with her, knowing what lay ahead and how futile it seemed to be. But every time she had turned to him to speak the words, she found that she just couldn't.

Looking at him you just saw an old man, a little stooped in the shoulder and a little frail and thin, but when *he* looked at you, you felt his keen determination staring right inside you through his cool, blue eyes.

It was like looking into a star-filled pool of peaceful courage and conviction, making all possibilities of changing their sway seem futile and pointless. His quest was quite simply resistless.

The reporter had worried her a little at first, but after spending an hour around the campfire with them, Alison could see that she also was moved in some way by Mathew. She had been much gentler with her questioning at least. It wouldn't stop her from doing her job though, and that still worried away at Alison's shrewd mind.

People were already on the lookout for him, all trying to get their pictures taken with him and have their little bit of *story* listened to. And all of them could be used as *markers* and have their dots joined up which would draw a path straight to Mathew.

Someone would surely come, someone with the mind to stop him. Not hurt him necessarily but bring an end to his march, his message. Someone would definitely come.

The fire was getting low, the amber glow had faded to red now.

Alison poked at it and threw on more wood before settling herself on the ground under the wrap of her coat.

Everything she knew about living outside was going to be tested over the next week or so. Someone would come and soon, and when they did, *Nippy* would show them what the land was really made for.

Chapter Fifteen

Were his boots walking more slowly? He studied them as they slipped into view, plopped down and slid away again. They seemed to be slower today. Not that they moved very quickly anyway, but they were definitely slower today.

He watched the smaller shadow sliding along at the side of his own. Where would he be now without her? If not dead already then waiting to die in some hospital bed probably. Or ditch.

He'd said it before and he would probably say it again; she was simply a marvel. Even now she just stuck by his side, casually keeping with his slow pace instead of being the impatient fifteen year-old that she could - should - have been.

He felt a small, guilty knot in the pit of his stomach when he thought of Alison's lost childhood. And now these precious teenage-years, which she had only just entered, were seeing her care for an old man on the road instead of caring about nothing but the latest music and boys.

'I'm fifteen t' day.' She suddenly said.

Mathew's heart skipped a few dozen beats at the unexpected and abrupt change in volume.

He stopped walking and turned to face her. 'Are you really?' He beamed at her. 'Well happy birthday, Alison.' He leaned forward to hug her.

'Thanks.'

'I think we need to get a cake.' He said and clapped his hands together.

He was rather fond of cake, Mary had, had a magical touch with sponge and cream and jam and and, 'yes, we definitely need a cake.' He repeated.

Alison just laughed. 'Where a' we gunna ge' a cake?'

Mathew laughed along. 'A *cake* shop, where else?'

Another girly-giggle. 'Yea, but 'ow we gunna ge' it? Wi' wot?'

'Wi*th* what.'

'Wi*th* what.' She replied almost automatically. They were both still chortling along.

'With some of the money which that big chap gave you.' Mathew laughed a little louder.

Alison's face fell and her laugh died quickly in her throat. He knew? How did he know that? ''Ow did y' kno' tha'?' As much as she tried, she just couldn't stop her face from blushing hotly. 'Y' wer' in t' toilet.'

'I'm old not daft, I knew those lads would have palmed it off to you.' He looked down at her seriously. 'And I'm really glad they did, Alison, and that you took it.'

He leaned closer and his grin broadened again. 'Because it means we can have a cake on this special day.'

Her guilt at her subterfuge quickly faded away and she blushed with another kind of embarrassment now. 'I ant 'ad a birthday cake since I wa' little.' Her voice was small and a little tight.

'We should get candles as well.' Mathew added excitedly, 'and maybe go to a burger-*joint* and then find a camp for a couple of days rest and *birthdaying*. How does that sound for a plan?'

Alison thought about it, it did sound great, but they had to be careful where they went, now more than ever; she was almost certain that someone had been sent out to find Mathew.

'I-I don't know.' She said, looking off into the distance. 'It could b' dangerous t' go inta towns an' tha'.'

Mathew just frowned. 'Dangerous? Dangerous how?'

'The'll b' lookin' f' ya by now.' Was all she said, as if everything should be made clear by that one, simple statement.

'Looking for me? Who will be looking for me?'

She wasn't impressed by his naiveté at all. 'Oo d' ya fi- *th*ink?'

Mathew turned around on the spot and scanned the horizons all around. The countryside was vast and open and had not a hint of a city or major road.

He faced her again. 'I-I'm not following, Alison.'

She huffed and folded her arms. 'This is *exackly* wot a meant when a sed y' wer soft.'

Mathew looked down at his boots, ticked off.

'If y' mek it t' London, y'll embarrass 'em in front o' t' whole world.' She carried on. 'The' can't have tha' can the'? No, the' don't like it when one o' t'' sheep bleats righ' in the' faces. The'll send someone t' stop ya.'

Hearing it put like that made Mathew feel like he was *on the run*. 'But I haven't done anything wrong, they can't just come and stop me from walking.'

She continued to look at him levelly. 'The' stopped y' from livin' in ya 'ouse dint the'?'

His chest panged when he heard her say that. She was right; they had put so much pressure on him that his life in the home he had lived in for twenty-two years had become unbearable.

He walked to the verge and sat down. Alison sat next to him.

'How am I supposed to reach London if they are only going to find me and stop me?' He shook his head. 'Seems so pointless. I-I mean *I* don't know the rules of *cloak and dagger* do I? I was an engineer for goodness sake!'

Alison scoffed. 'The' mekkin y' fink-' she shook her head in annoyance. '*Th*ink th' way the' want you t' think; like a sheep.'

She looked up at him. 'The' want ya t' think tha' ya 'av t' play by *their* rules, cos then y' gunna lose before y' 'av even started.'

She leaned a little closer and nudged him, conspiratorially lowering her voice. 'But y' 'av go' me.' She said and winked. 'W'll mek 'em play by *my* rules.'

If he hadn't experienced Alison's indomitable determination first hand - not to mention her uncanny skills for living and moving around outside - Mathew would probably have just laughed at the *little girl's* boasting. But the memory of the *fiery-dwarf* knew better.

'So you have a plan?' He asked her.

'Av 'ad a plan since a thumped Rag's 'ed.' She answered and patted him on the arm. 'Cummon, le's ge' back on wi ' it.'

She rose to her feet and held her hand out for Mathew.

He took it and pulled himself up, using his staff to balance. 'We can still have cake though can't we?' He asked hopefully.

They set off back along the road.

'W'll find a shop or summert in a bi'.'

'What kind of cake do you like?'

'Choc'late.'

'Oh, good choice. With iced sprinkles on the top.'

'A y' gunna sing me *'appy birfday*?'

'Bir*th*day and no, am I heck!'

They continued chatting happily as they walked beneath the lemon-white sun, the day was perfectly still.

Alison, whether she knew it or not, had lowered her frown and guard somewhat and the peace of the countryside, mingled with her quietly growing bond to Mathew, had brought the young girl that she was back a step toward the happier girl she had once been.

Almost four hours later and the road led them down a sharp hill and into the small village of *Great Gransden*.

A few pebble-dashed houses went by first and then, as they turned the corner at the bottom of the hill, they were met by another row of houses which ended at a small shop and a take-away.

The pair of them looked at each other.

'A shop *and* a take-away.' Mathew said happily. 'Who needs a burger-joint?'

After visiting the shop and choosing the best chocolate cake it had to offer, Mathew and Alison walked into *The Ming Palace* and ordered the *Ming-feast special* for two.

They sat now, on the red, comfy seats, and waited for their food to arrive.

'You know? I do believe that chappie,' Mathew subtly nodded his head toward the door with a porthole window leading to the kitchen, 'thinks we're about to run off with his menus and chairs or something.'

Alison looked up from the comic she was reading which she had taken from the table of papers and magazines in the corner.

A head bobbed into view from the side of the door and then disappeared again, only to reappear and have a look at them both again.

She turned her attention to the ceiling corners of the waiting area. Cameras were placed in two of them.

The head popped back into view for a moment, this time smiling.

'The' kno' 'oo y' are.' She told him quietly.

Mathew looked up at the man whose grin immediately widened. He waved enthusiastically through the small, round window.

Mathew lamely smiled and waved back. 'I think you're right. Well at least they haven't asked for one of those *selfies*.'

'The'v got cameras in t' corners though.'

Another head appeared, an elderly woman this time. She also smiled and waved and - Mathew blinked - did she just flutter her eyelashes at him?

He heard Alison chuckling softly beside him.

'You can shut up as well.' He huffed.

'I do believe someone has an admirer.' She said, absolutely perfectly and much to his annoyance. 'Tha's two now and one ov them was chuckin' her knickers at ya.' She continued.

'What!? She was no- I-I, she *didn't* chuck them at me!' He blustered. The uncomfortable memory of Diane Jones standing in front of him without her panties in the right place made his face turn hot and red.

'She dint mind y' seein' 'er boobs either did she?' Alison was loving it.

'Eh!? Now then! She-she. What!? No, no, no,' he shook his head and chuckled, not meeting her gaze and trying to set the facts dead, damn straight. 'No, she wasn't doing, I-I mean she didn't *show* me! I mean, they were there and-and-she didn't know did she?' He finished and threw his hands out in submission.

'I think if my boobs wer' showin' I'd definly kno' about it.' Alison mused, squeezing every ounce of *tease* right out of Mathew that she could.

'I-' He held his finger up to make a point but didn't know what to actually say, his face remained frozen with his mouth opened ready to say the next word.

The door leading to the kitchen suddenly opened and saved him.

'Two Ming-specials.' The smiling man called and placed a brown-paper carrier-bag on top of the counter.

He bent down and opened the till. 'On the house.' And held out the cash for Alison to take back.

She took it and watched the man then bow to them both.

'Um. Thank you.' She said and woodenly returned his bow, her face complimenting the scarlet wall-hangings absolutely perfectly.

Mathew did the same, feeling the same wooden awkwardness which Alison was feeling. What had just happened?

The door swung open again and the old lady stepped out followed by two young men and a young girl no more than Alison's age. All of them were beaming.

The first man produced a camera and held it up for Mathew to see, looking at him expectantly but not asking the question.

'Um. Okay.' Was all he could say really.

The old woman began pulling the others around to the front of the counter, telling them in Chinese where to stand for the picture. She sounded quite bossy, Mathew and Alison both thought.

Once the scene was set and everyone were in their places around the *intrepid pair*, the first man set the camera on the counter and pressed a button.

A red LED flashed at the front, counting down the seconds before the camera would activate.

The man ran around to his place in the crowd. 'Say *freedom*!' He called out.

They all said the word and the Chinese family all raised their right arms, fist-pumping the air as the flash went.

White nymphs popped before their eyes and everyone laughed and blinked furiously.

'Thank you.' The man said to Mathew, and took his hand, shaking it.

'You are very welcome.' He replied, and returned the handshake.

And then, quite astonishingly, each member of this family took it in turns to shake Mathew and Alison's hands and bow to them, speaking their Chinese good wishes of luck and prosperity for travellers on long journeys.

They were both equally humbled and slightly embarrassed by the gesture, but at the same time, in a strange way, they were both strengthened by it as well. It was a good feeling to find such a diverse culture humbly showing their respect for their cause.

The family had stayed by the door, peering out and watching Mathew and Alison walk all the way down to the end of the road, waving at them if they should look back.

'Ar' the' still there?' She asked him, and then saw him wave and knew the answer.

'Yes.' He replied, turning back. 'It's a peculiarly long road is this, isn't it?'

The urge to turn and look back was a continuing itch for both of them.

Somehow it felt rude *not* to turn around and acknowledge that they were there and wave back. And so they did and so they had been doing for the last eight minutes. Eight minutes which felt like twenty.

The turn in the road couldn't come quick enough, but they were soon stood waving for the last time.

'Do you think they will put that picture on the Internet?' Mathew asked casually as he waved.

'Oh, yea, definly.' Alison replied, also still waving.

'Def*initely*.' He corrected.

'Def*initely*.'

Chapter Sixteen

Do this, Palmerson, do that, Palmerson, go find an old man, Palmerson. He was sick of it. Sixty-bloody-seven and they wouldn't let him retire.

After almost forty years in the service, Cecil Palmerson began to understand what it must feel like to be a cow; his orders felt like they were delivered with a cattle-prod.

So here he was, *cattle-prodded* to the top of a hill in the middle of bloody nowhere, with his two pillocks of helpers standing behind him licking the ice-cream from their cornetto wrappers.

You'd never have guessed he held a licence to kill would you? Had been on dark-ops missions through four, different wars and had been shot seven times altogether. Oh! No, you wouldn't have bloody guessed that.

He pulled his cigarettes from his breast-pocket and lit one up.

The surrounding greens and yellows of the fields and forests soothed his annoyance a little, and playing the waiting game was what he did best, so he relaxed back on the bonnet of the car and smoked.

Still, it was a royal pain in the neck being all the way out here when he could have been back in London with Crystal. Worth every damn penny that woman.

One of his men came up and joined him.

'What is it, Dixon?' He asked the tall, stocky man.

'Latest report, sir. There's been a sighting in *Great Gransden*, a Chinese take-away.'

'When was that?'

'As far as I can tell they were in there late, yesterday afternoon, between five and six.'

Palmerson flicked open his phone and checked the map. 'They haven't come as far south as we anticipated.'

He checked his notebook next. As much as he found technology very useful he couldn't do without a notebook and pencil for jotting down his thoughts and calculations. 'Hmm. They've travelled between fifteen and eighteen mile per-day. Except for the day before yesterday. They must have had a two-night stop somewhere back near Stamford.'

He checked his phone-map again. 'Here,' he said and pointed to a place on the map. 'If they are still moving south then they will be coming down this way somewhere.'

He put his phone and notebook back in his pocket and then took a last drag of his cigarette. 'Let's head back to the cars, we can make our way north and then split up as we approach the area.'

The three men slipped back into their seats in Palmerson's Range-Rover, and he drove them all drove back down the grassy hill to the other two waiting cars at the bottom.

'They won't be anywhere near the rendezvous point by the time we get there,' Palmerson said as the other two were getting out. 'So Dixon? You take a ten mile drive east and then cut back in to target. Singh, you do the same in a westerly direction.'

The two men stood by his door and just looked at each other, puzzled.

'First one to spot a pub which is still five miles out is to call in and we'll meet there.' Palmerson explained.

They both smiled, comprehending, and relaxed.

'Might as well wait with a drink in our hands and food in front of us. We'll gather them up easily enough when they take one of the target roads.' He continued confidently and flipped the car into gear. 'Mines a double whiskey.'

He nodded once, seriously, and then drove away, leaving Dixon and Singh to watch his dust.

'Nice of him to wait for us to tell him what *our* drinks were.' Singh said.

Dixon nodded, agreeing, and then turned to his partner. 'You drink alcohol then?'

'Yea, why wouldn't I?' Singh answered.

'Well, because you're Sikh.'

'That's a bit racist innit?' Singh said as he made his way to his own car.

'How is that racist, ya gonk?' Dixon protested on the way to his.

'Well you're assuming that all Sikhs don't drink aren't you? That's a whole culture you're labelling there, mate.' He sat in the driver's seat and closed the door.

Dixon did the same and then picked up his radio. 'I'm just saying that the Sikh religion forbids the use of alcohol doesn't it?'

Singh picked up his own mic. 'You're a Catholic right?'

'Yea.'

'Well I bet that doesn't stop you from masturbating though does it?'

'You could have just stuck with drinking and gambling as a good enough example, you know, mate?'

'Yea, I know, mate, I know.'

The pair of black BMW's drove off down the road, the two men behind the wheels jibing each other over the radio all the way.

* * *

While Palmerson and his two men were heading to their *hot-spot*, Mathew and Alison were absolutely nowhere near the place, sitting instead around a small fire, eating the remains of last night's cake and drinking a proper brew of tea.

The day had been spent just resting and replenishing themselves, the plan was to stay for another night before moving on in the morning.

'I don't think there is anything much better than a cup of excellent tea and a big slice of cake.' Mathew said, chomping down and then taking a sip of tea.

'W'can get anuv- another on our way owt.' Alison bit into her own cake enthusiastically. 'O' wuneesh.' She said, her cheeks stuffed with cake and her mouth covered in chocolate crumbs and filling.

'Guv ithea.' Mathew answered, his cheeks equally stuffed.

It was still quite early, but Mathew produced the bottle of *Old Nasty* and poured them both a tot straight into the tea. '*Keef ush warm.*'

Alison laughed and little bits of cake flew out of her mouth. Mathew's impression of Jolly was just the best, he had it down perfectly.

The old Alison, the girl with the deep, furrowed brow, hadn't been seen for the past twenty-four hours. Even if she hadn't noticed, Mathew had. It gave him such an immense feeling of happiness to see her like that, just a happy, normal young girl.

He kicked himself; what was *normal*? No, not a normal young girl, just a happy, young human-being, that was it, and she was in the *right* place.

And then he said something and instantly wished he hadn't, thinking it would immediately bring back her frown.

'Did your grandmother bake cakes?'

But surprisingly it didn't and Alison just nodded as she swallowed.

'Oh! Yea,! She were allus bakin' cakes were nan.' She finished swallowing. 'She never missed a birthday or christmas an' tha'.'

'My wife Mary was a good cake maker, brilliant in fact.' Mathew said a little wistfully. 'She was very fond of faeries and made an excellent honey-cake she said came from a secret recipe given to her by a fairy princess. To die for they were.'

Alison giggled. 'Me nan used t'mek this cake she called *inside-out trifle-cake.*' She laughed loudly when she said the title.

'That sounds delicious! What was in it?'

'Y' kno' 'ow trifle's made? Sponge a' bottom, jelly an' custard nex' an' then cream wi' 'undreds an' thousan's sprinkled on t' top?'

Mathew's mouth watered. He nodded and bit into more cake with a mouthful of *Nasty*-laced tea to follow. 'Yes?'

'Well me nan baked a big, round sponge an' then cut t' middle owt, filled it wi' strawberry jelly an' le' it set.'

Mathew's eyes were wide with fascination; what a great idea; jelly inside cake!

'Then, when t' jelly wer' set, she scooped owt t' middle and filled it wi' custard an' cream an' sprinkles.'

She sat back, leaning against the walls of the wooden windbreak they were camping beneath. 'Y' can imagine what it looked like when y' cut it inta slices can't ya?'

Mathew nodded eagerly. 'Oh, yes! I can see that. I think I'd give just about anything right now to try some of that.'

Alison giggled again and raised her cup. ''Ere's to *inside-out trifle-cakes* an' *fairy honey-cakes*.' She took a big sip of her brew.

Mathew returned the toast and finished his tea in one go.

He leaned over to the fire and picked up the pot of tea they had left warming at its edge, pouring himself another cup and then offering some to Alison.

She held her cup out.

'Y' drink tea like me mam did.' She said. 'Two cups or none.'

Mathew carried on pouring but remained quiet. This was the first time she had referred to her mother and it was in the past-tense.

'Thanks.' She said, taking her cup back and filling it with milk.

She poured some into Mathew's cup. 'She din't tek sugar either, said y'might as well jus' shoot t' teabag right now an' don't bother killin' it in t' cup.' She smiled remembering.

Mathew nodded in agreement. 'She had that right; sugar for cakes and only a drop of milk for tea.' He sipped and waited.

'Yea.' Alison nodded then. 'Y'ad of liked me mam, y'ad of got on well.'

'I would *have*.' He said.

She remained quiet.

'I was correcting you there you know?'

'Oh, wer' ya? Sorry; wud *'av.*'

Mathew just laughed and shook his head. She was doing alright. At least she was trying to learn and didn't moan about him correcting her all the time.

'She wer' a good person wa' me mam. They all were.' She said, quietly.

His heart ached when he heard her say *were*, all of them gone she was saying. She was more like himself than he had imagined; completely alone, the last of a line.

She had to be given a better chance, especially her, Mathew thought. The last of a line at fifteen was simply *not* on, damn everything. Damn the stupid world and its stupid damn rules.

He added another tot to his cup and took a hefty swig.

'Y'arite?'

He coughed and wiped his mouth. 'Yes, yes I'm fine. Sorry.'

'Y'av gone a bit pale, a' ya sure ya feelin' arite?'

'No- I mean yes, I'm okay, just having a senior moment.' He laughed lamely.

Alison peered at him, watching the colour slowly return to his cheeks. He'd suddenly looked quite angry if she hadn't known better, but it had quickly passed and she was wondering if she had actually seen it at all.

She shrugged. 'Okay.' Was all she said.

She leaned across to him and picked up Jolly's bottle, adding a small tot to her tea.

She sipped at it and watched Mathew, trying to read his eyes as they stared into the fire.

'M' dad stared intut fire like that,' she muttered, startling him a little. 'Right after me mam an' Dale died.'

Mathew looked up at her, expecting to see the return of her frown, but instead she had remained the same, only understandably a little sadder.

'I'm sorry to hear that, Alison.' He said quietly. 'What happened to them?'

She sniffed and rubbed at her nose and then stood up.

'It'll b' gettin' dark in a bit. I'm gunna go ge' sumore wood f' t'night.' She said, scanning her surroundings.

She turned back to face Mathew again. 'I'll tell y'all abou' wha' 'appened when a ge' back.' She looked sincerely into his blue eyes. 'I 'ant ever told anyone before.'

And before she could change her mind she turned and quickly walked away into the deeper wood.

Mathew's eyes brimmed with admiration for the young girl's bravery; how difficult it must have been - must *be* - to lose your whole family and never speak about it? Her tiny frame didn't look like it could carry such a huge burden.

He flipped the cap on the bottle and added another tot to his tea. Be damned with the stupid world, be damned with it.

Chapter Seventeen

Eight years ago.

The red and white weather-vane whizzed around in the wind, buzzing and clicking. Alison and Dale had made it, a couple of years ago now. A day spent in the shed with hammer and nails and bits of wood and plenty of paint.

Alison stood at the side of the house and watched it while she tended her own, little patch of garden.

Peas and runner-beans grew at one side, tomatoes and carrots in the middle, and onions and potatoes at the other end, with a single row of pumpkins at the very end.

She heard the front door open. Dropping her little trowel to the ground, she wiped her hands on her dungarees and then pelted along in her wellies to the front of the house.

'We won't be long, see you later, love.' She heard her mother, Jill, say.

She turned the corner, Dale was walking down the porch-steps and her mother was kissing her father goodbye.

'Can I come?' She shouted, pushing past Dale in her rush up the steps to get to her mother and plead. 'Please!'

'Oh! Darling thing!' Her mother said, as though she were talking to an infant.

She picked her up and planted kiss after kiss on her giggling face. 'I could just eat you up; you look so cute in your wellies and dungarees.' She went for ears and neck kisses next. Alison squealed and giggled even louder.

She plopped the squirming girl to the floor and then crouched down in front of her. 'You can't really leave your dad to do all of those hay-bales now can you?'

'But, mum!'

Her dad sidled up to them. 'Y'gunna really go t'town instead o' driving t' tractor wi' me?' He folded his arms and sniffed. 'Looks like I only need t' take one shake an' cake then.'

Driving the tractor was one thing, but strawberry milkshakes and cake AND driving in the tractor was too much temptation to resist. Even if she *did* know she had been hoodwinked.

She sighed and put on her resigned face. 'Sorry Dale, a can't come wi' ya, av got to 'elp dad wi' t' hay-bales.'

'With *the* hay-bales, Ali.' Her mother said.

'With the hay-bales.' Alison dutifully repeated.

Dale pointed at her. 'Well make sure you don't eat all o' t' cake, fatty.'

Alison's giggling took up again. 'Okay, stinky.' She covered her mouth and laughed cheekily.

'We'll be back in time for dinner, Ian.' Jill said, turning and kissing her husband again. 'Just make sure you remember to turn the oven on at half-four.'

'I will, drive careful, love.'

Alison and her father stood on the steps and waved as the land-rover slowly turned down the long track and out onto the main road.

'Right, bugger-lugs, y'ready for some 'ard graft, lass?' He picked her up by the front of her dungarees in his fist and brought her up to eye-height. 'What d'ya say, squirt?' He asked and then kissed her on the forehead.

'Shall we 'av some cake first?' She suggested, grinning.

Ian laughed and pulled her into one of his bear-hug embraces, kissing her head again. 'You do mek me laugh, little lamb.'

He put her down and aimed her through the front door. 'Go on then, cut me a slice as well. I'll bring t' tractor round.'

The afternoon easily slipped by as the hay-bales in the field slowly disappeared and the cake was fervently eaten.

After returning the tractor to its shed and cleaning themselves up, half-past four came and the oven, loaded with casserole, was dutifully switched on.

At half-past five it was switched off again, casserole cooked.

Half-past six, and Alison sat at the table eating by herself while her father sat in his chair and stared at the clock.

Half-past seven, there was a knock at the door, and five minutes later Alison's father began screaming.

Over the next, few weeks Alison spent her time sitting on the steps of the porch and staring at the gate, waiting for her mum and Dale to come home.

Dad had told her they wouldn't be coming home again, but she had to sit and wait and see for herself. Dad had also told her that they had died, but she couldn't believe that, didn't want to believe it; they wouldn't just go and die, not mum, not Dale.

Her father walked around like an automaton, his eyes looking somewhere far ahead into a place she couldn't see. He hardly said a word to her, hardly noticed she was even there.

A month later and Ian's mother came to stay with them, bringing a little order back into the home-life and a little light into Alison's young, broken heart. She could do nothing for her own son though, and Ian seemed to be on a downward spiral into depressive oblivion.

'Wot 'appened to me mam and Dale?' Alison asked her one evening while they were eating supper.

'You kno' what 'appened, lass, finish your toast.'

'A don't kno' wot 'appened, dad 'ant told me owt.' She fired back, angrily.

Her grandmother turned to look at Ian who was asleep in his chair in the living-room, an empty glass in his hand and a bottle of vodka by his side.

She turned back to Alison. 'I'm sure 'e 'ad 'is reasons, Alis-'

'Tell me!' Alison stood up and shouted. 'Tell me! She wa' *my* mam, Dale wa' *my* brother! Y'can't keep it all to yasens!' Tears of frustration streamed down her cheeks and spilled over her trembling mouth. 'Tell me, nan!'

Her grandmother opened her arms. 'Oh, Alison. Come 'ere, love.'

Alison fell into her grandmother's arms, her weeping increasing. 'T-tell m-me, nan. J-jus' tell me.'

Her grandmother rocked her to and fro, holding her tightly. 'Hush now, little lamb.' She said. 'It were an accident, Ali, a stupid car-accident.'

Without giving her any unnecessary, painful details, Alison's grandmother told her how the land-rover had swerved to avoid a child on a bicycle and had crashed through the wall and rolled down the embankment into the river.

Somehow hearing the full story finally released Alison from her childish uncertainty; mum and Dale had died and they were never coming home.

Those first months after the accident had been the hardest for seven year-old Alison, but slowly she began to do the things which she loved to do.

Her small patch of garden, which had been neglected and had become overgrown, was one of the first things she put to rights.

She clung fiercely to her grandmother while slowly becoming more and more afraid of her father.

After six months, Ian was still drinking heavily and now prone to bouts of drunken rage.

Alison couldn't help him, his mother couldn't help him, only the vodka was his maleficent friend.

Almost two years passed, Alison's grandmother had all but moved in with them.

Alison herself had adjusted to life without her mother and brother; her grandmother doting on her and giving her all of the love and attention which she needed.

But time can be a fickle thing, giving healing on the one hand while carrying misery on the other.

Less than a month away from the second anniversary of the accident, Alison's grandmother passed away quietly in her sleep at the age of eighty-seven.

She had been suffering quietly with chest pains for months and knew her time was almost up. All she could do was prepare her sweet, little lamb the best way she could.

It was a week or so after the funeral that the darkness began to creep back into Alison's life. Slowly at first, as slow as hair grows, but after a few months it was definitely clouding the horizons once more.

Her father had never recovered anything of himself after his wife and son's deaths, but what little he still retained went up in smoke along with his mother's ashes.

The farm fell into a state of neglect, only Alison's little corner stayed vibrant and well cared for. A nook of escape from the dark anger inside the house.

She had become very good at avoiding her father when he was drunk - which was almost all the time now - but a day came when her luck had run out and that dark horizon spilled over to smother everything.

She stood in front of the mirror and looked at herself. She didn't recognise the girl in the reflection with the swollen eye and red hand-mark on her puffy cheek. Where had she come from? What had she done to deserve that?

Weeks and months went by, Alison's tenth birthday came and went unmarked. The girl in the mirror made more and more appearances until finally she and Alison were one and the same.

The house became a lair where a beast slept, a fearful, roaring beast who was supposed to have cared for her, looked after her and loved her the way she loved him. But he wasn't there anymore and Alison's loyalty and love cost her dearly.

It was nothing short of miraculous that she had never ended up in hospital, but a dark, horrible miracle that was; should a nurse or doctor get a look at her tiny, bruised body, they would have immediately called the authorities and the nightmare would have ended. Who knows, they both may have been saved in the end?

It was a cold, miserable December morning when Alison's father looked at her for the last time. In that brief instance before he walked out of the door, his eyes seemed to be clearer than they had been for a long time.

Alison stood at the cooker on her tip-toes, frying bacon for breakfast and just looked back fearfully.

He didn't speak, just looked at her as though he were trying to remember. And then he had smiled the faintest of smiles and walked out of the door into the cold morning air.

A single tear ran down her face; he had looked at her the way he used to look at her; like she was his daughter and he loved her. Looked at her like her dad had always done.

She sat and slept and ate in his chair in the living-room, waiting for him to come back, but somewhere at the corner of her thoughts she knew he wouldn't be.

Four days she waited, until finally the knock came at the door. She looked up into the faces of two police officers, a man and a woman.

'Hello.' The woman had said. 'Is your mother in, love?'

Alison stood barefoot and grimed, bruised and bedraggled in front of them and just began to cry pitifully.

Chapter Eighteen

Night had fully closed by the time Alison had finished her story. Mathew had remained silent throughout.

He sat now and wondered at the human world. How did that happen to a family? A child? Where in the *rules* of humanity did it provide for that kind of extreme loss?

He thought back to his own childhood; the closest he had come to being violently abused was when PC Harvest caught him and his friends *scrumping* the orchards.

A clip round the ear-hole and a promise of certain imprisonment for life if he caught them again, never failing to send them frantically running for the safety of home.

He leaned across and took Alison's hand in his own, squeezing it tightly.

'I'm really sorry about your family, Alison. I-I can't begin to imagine what you must have gone through.'

Alison nodded and dropped her gaze, remaining silent for a moment.

'He wer' a good man, me dad.' She eventually said and looked up. 'He wer' lost an' cudn't find 'is way back.'

She gave a small shrug. 'Tha' 'appens t' people sumtimes, the' jus' get lost an' can' find the' way back.'

He understood that, only last week he had been teetering on that very edge of oblivion himself, lost in his own world. It was a lonely place to stare into was no-mans land, that place where everything was shaded by unrecognisable familiarity.

'Like that poor man, Rag.' He muttered.

Alison scowled for a moment, but it quickly disappeared. 'Yea,' she conceded, 'I s'pose y' right.'

It was hard for her to reconcile the image she had of her father with the one of the despicable Rag, but she thought Mathew was right; Rag couldn't have always been like that, something bad must have happened to him which he hadn't coped with.

'Why did you run away from the children's homes?' Mathew asked. He filled both of their cups with the remaining hot-chocolate still warming by the fire. 'Were they unkind to you?'

'No,' she shook her head, 'no, the' wa' nice t' me an' very understandin', but,' she shrugged, 'it want an 'ome, not like wi' me mam an' dad. It felt '*ollow*.' She shook her head again. 'I don' kno', it's 'ard to explain. It felt like I wa' livin' in a big, empty box full of empty things. Empty kids, empty carers, all set int' a sort of *pose*.'

Mathew sipped at his drink. 'A pose? Like statues?'

'Sort of. More like robots.' She said.

'I 'ad this game once, it wa' like a little suitcase that opened up,' she made the universal *opening book* gesture with her hands. 'An' inside wer' a little village wi' little people on it. The' wer' held on by magnets an' y'cud move 'em around t' streets an' that wi' buttons an' switches. But there wa' only one path in a circle.'

She paused to let Mathew think about that and then added; 'Well, it felt a bit like tha'; everyone stuck on a round path an' doin' t' same thing over an' over again in a big, empty box.'

He couldn't work his mind around that at all, he had no experience of his own which he could compare it to. But when he stood back and looked at his whole life, he could see the similarity with Alison's round, magnetic road. The orbit of life passing by, everything you do, you do over and over again.

The homes she had spent some time in were like a precursor to that same system, honing her and teaching her until she could live on the *outside* and do it for real.

'Was it easy?' He asked. 'To escape, I mean?'

Alison laughed a little. 'I dint afta *escape*, it wan' like I wer' in prison or owt. But yea, it wer' easy; I just gev a note t' one o' t' other kids t' give t' one o' t' carers, tellin' 'em tha' I'd 'ad enough an' I 'ad t' go 'ome.'

'And so you went back to the farm?'

'No, I went in t' opposite direction.'

Mathew laughed then. 'Of course you did.' He raised his cup and silently toasted her cheeky cunning. 'So where did you sleep for that first night? I can't imagine how you must have felt, being so young at the time.'

'I curled up in a church doorway f' tha' first night. I'd go' a blanket wi' me bu' it wer' cold tha' night. It want really scary though.'

'No? I think I would have been terrified.' Mathew said truthfully.

'I'd 'ad worse.' She replied.

He nodded slowly. 'Yes, yes I suppose you have really.'

'I wer' more worried about keepin' warm than owt else.' She continued. 'First week wer' 'ard an' I wer' cold at nigh', but I found a beater's hut in t' woods an' the'd left some blankets and a sleepin'-bag inside.' She shrugged her shoulders as if to say *what else could I do?* 'So I took t' sleeping bag an' I ant looked back since.'

It was like he was looking at a fifteen year-old girl and listening to a forty year-old woman. The matter-of-fact way in which she told her remarkably, courageous story was like listening to a veteran talking about the *job*.

'When did you meet Merylin and the others?'

''Bout a year ago. Longest av ever stayed wi' anyone else.'

She settled back and pushed her feet out in front of the fire. 'I travelled wi' a lass last year forra bit. Lyndsey she wer' called, but normally am on mi own.'

Mathew stretched himself out at the other side of the fire, propping himself up on his elbow. 'How did you end up travelling with her?'

Alison smiled as she remembered. 'I shared a pie wi' 'er.'

'With *her.*'

'With *her.*' She rolled her eyes but continued to smile.

'I wa' somewhere near Swindon, I'd jus' got mesen sum breakfast from a little bakery in this village - I can' remember where - an' I went to a park t' eat. She wa' just sittin' there, starin' at nowt.

'Anyway, I jus walked normally, like I allus do-'

'You mean really fast and quiet?' Mathew asked, grinning.

Alison sniggered. 'Yea, an' when I got right close to 'er she jumped a mile in t' air and screamed, which med *me* jump owt o' me skin and chuck me pie at 'er!'

Mathew slapped his thigh and laughed his wheezy laugh.

'An' we jus' both stood there lookin' at each other and holdin' ar' chests and breathin' really 'eavy. Then after a minute she says; "*A' ya gunna eat that?*"'

They both laughed then, Mathew still slapping his thigh.

'Brilliant!' He said, wiping the tears from his eyes.

'She wa' nice wa' Lyndsey. She wer' only nineteen, came from Sco'land. She'd 'ad it rough though; she wer' runnin' away from drugs.'

Mathew nodded again. 'I see. Heroin?' He asked.

'Yea, smack. She'd 'ad a baby tekken off 'er cos of it. Ended up on t' streets cos of it. Prostituted herself cos of it.' She shook her head sadly. ''Orrible, evil stuff is smack.'

Mathew stared into the fire, his cool, blue eyes flared with bright orange flecks.

He had *heard* how devastating heroin was, who hadn't? But listening to Alison say it like that, a first-hand account so simply said but more *real* than any of the stories he had heard.

It shattered his crude understanding and filled over it with a picture which was both more vivid and vibrant, but at the same time more ugly and base.

'What happened to her? How long did you travel together?' He asked.

'A few weeks, seven or eight mebe. She wer' allus sayi-'

Mathew cleared his throat noisily.

'*Always.*' Alison said firmly.

Mathew smiled. 'Thank you. You were saying; she was always?'

'She wer always sayin' that she 'ad t keep movin', cos if she dint-' Her eyes locked with Mathews.

He hadn't moved or said a word, he'd only blinked but she knew what he was thinking.

Her eyes narrowed. 'Cos if she *didn't* the smack would find 'er again.'

She sighed and sniffed and wiped the end of her nose. 'She allu- always 'ad this look in her eye, like she wer' seein' somethin' that wer' a million-miles away.'

'Ten thousand-yard stare.' Mathew remarked.

'Eh?'

'*The ten thousand-yard stare,*' he repeated, 'it's something which servicemen who have seen battle do. I've read about it.'

'Wha' is it? Like a disease or sumert- something?' She said, automatically correcting herself.

Mathew thought about it; it *was* a sort of disease he supposed, whose carrier was conflict and war.

'Sort of,' he said, 'but it isn't like a disease which you can look at under a microscope, it's more like a state of mind which comes with experiencing prolonged and horrifying conflict.'

'Conflict.' Alison repeated. 'Yea, tha' sounds abou' right; she wer' really tryin' to stay ahead of it. Tha's why she din- didn't stay in one place f' too long; so she didn't hav' t' fight it all ot time.'

He couldn't imagine a battle more frightening than one which you had with your own self, a war in your mind which could easily be lost if you let your guard down even for a moment.

'Poor girl.' He muttered.

Alison scoffed. 'If she 'eard you say tha' she'd 'av slapped ya face an' told ya to wek up.'

Mathew just looked at her, puzzled.

'She didn't feel sorry for her sen',' she explained, 'she said tha' if ya bring shit t' yer own door then y' 'av got t' clean it up ya'sen an' not look 'round f' someone t' blame.'

She sniffed and shrugged. 'She's no' wrong is she?'

'No. No she's not.' He replied thoughtfully.

That crude, uneducated view he had once held regarding addicts and addiction shifted yet again.

He sat back up and threw some wood on the fire and then sat with his arms around his raised knees, eyes staring into the rising flames as he wondered what *else* about the world he was ignorant of.

An owl hooted close by making him jump and look up into the depths of the darkened tree-tops.

A few seconds later another hoot returned the call from somewhere deeper inside the wood.

'Pair of owls.' Alison said, following his gaze. 'Goin' 'untin' t'gether.'

'Can you tell what kind?'

'No, not really but more 'an likely the'll b' barn-owls.'

'Right.' He said.

Alison noticed his furtive looks into the tree-tops. 'Don' worry, the' don' ea' old man.' She giggled.

'That's reassuring.' He said, continuing his vigil into the darkness of the wood nonetheless.

'The' won' come near t' fire anyway, too bright for 'em.'

He put another branch on. A big one.

Alison's eyes did that twinkling, mischievous thing. 'No, *they* won't come near t' fire, but all o' t' *other* things tha' the' 'unt, like t' snakes an' rats an' that, the'll come and hide in t' safety o' light.'

Mathew whipped his coat tightly around himself and jerked around on the spot looking for that slithering, creeping thing which might be coming up behind him.

Alison laughed and rapped her hands on her legs.

He turned to face her. 'Oh! You, you,' he pointed his finger at her, jabbing it to emphasise his words. 'You blooming *arse-tit*!' He blustered. 'You could have given me a coronary!'

Alison laughed at being called an *arse-tit*.

'Am gunna tell Merylin you said tha'.' She said and giggled again. '*Arse-tit!*' She repeated and almost fell over laughing.

Mathew relaxed and then sniggered. 'You really do have an evil streak in you, young lady.'

They sat and talked and laughed for awhile longer before finally bedding down and going to sleep.

For as long as she lived, Alison never forgot those two days spent celebrating her fifteenth birthday in that little wood. Two of the happiest days she had ever had, the days when the birthday-cakes had begun again.

Chapter Nineteen

Phone? Check. Pen and pad? Check. Knickers? Check. She was ready.

Diane ran around the large double-bed in her hotel room and quickly chugged down the last of her coffee before departing. A good coffee should never be left to go cold, it should always be chugged.

She was on her way to see a Chinese family now after seeing their *selfie* on the *Freedom Walker* website.

Yep, he now had a website, created and donated by a person whom she had already tracked down and had, had comments from.

Lars Forsberg, a quiet, Swedish businessman and unsung philanthropist in his late thirties. He had donated unlimited space on his own business servers and had employed an outside company to build and administer the website.

When Diane had asked him why, he had simply replied; "*Mister Arnold is a champion for humanity, he has asked for nothing and yet he is undertaking a great task in this day and age; he is going to confront the* dragon *in its cave.*"

Confronting the dragon in its cave. She liked that, she would be using it as one of the headlines she thought.

"*There is something sick, deep inside your country, Miss Jones, and Mathew Arnold is going to draw it out, mark my words.*"

She wasn't entirely certain what he meant exactly when he said *draw it out*, but it had an ominous ring to it. Whatever it was it was highlighted by the sheer number of subscribers, worldwide, to the website - a little under eighty thousand now and counting.

Diane herself could feel something on the air, something *was* coming, but something always came didn't it? So why did she feel more *wired* than usual, more alert?

He hadn't really become national news just yet, not in the mainstream media at least, only her small piece from a couple of days ago.

He'd been on the road for a week already and the social-media network was alive with the chatter of his name and yet he was still not under a great deal of scrutiny.

She unlocked her car and dropped into the driver's seat, just sitting motionless as she frowned for a few moments, thinking about Mathew Arnold's quietly growing popularity.

A movement was silently building around him wasn't it? That's what was bothering her; it felt like there was a great wave building up slowly and silently. And miraculously, somehow, Mathew Arnold was completely unaware of it all.

Diane turned the key, and the car revved to life. She took it out into the morning traffic and made her way north to the village and the take-away.

It was the girl wasn't it? She was somehow managing to keep him away from *civilisation*, clever girl. The straighter route would almost certainly lead to a huge media outbreak and the young girl, Alison, must instinctively realise that.

How long could she keep it up for though? How much time could she gain for the *wave* to build its power and eventual momentum? Why am I even thinking like that? It's just another report isn't it?

But it was more than just another report, her heart was telling her, it was more like a *quest* and she was part of it now, part of the plan to ensure Mathew Arnold arrived at his intended destination.

Her job had already begun when she had underplayed the initial article, even if she wasn't completely aware of it. Now she had to follow the story as closely as she could and record the journey as it happened.

Her phone kept her up to date with the latest sightings. Her plan was simple; follow the selfies.

* * *

Some sixty miles north, Cecil Palmerson and his two-man team were once again sitting in a pub.

'Magnificent Sunday lunch, don't you agree lads?' Palmerson said, munching his way through a mouthful of chicken and mashed-potato.

They both nodded and *mm'ed* through their own mouthfuls.

'And it's good to know that the target is still in front of us.'

He leaned over and tapped at a spot on the map they had open in front of them with his knife. 'I'm more convinced that they went this way, into this region.' The gravy from his knife left a small, round blob over a wooded area, fifteen miles away to the east.

'What makes you so sure, sir?' Singh asked.

Palmerson tapped his nose and smiled; it never failed to please him to have a *junior* ask about his *wisdom*.

'If you take a close look,' he said, tapping the map again, 'these two roads are the only way in or out of the village where they were last spotted.'

Both men leaned closer and nodded.

'To the west of us,' he continued, 'is another wooded area and it is quite possible that they went that way but-' he held his dripping knife up for emphasis, 'they would find themselves very close to the motorway, and as we already know, they have been avoiding all of the major roads.'

He looked at them both carefully.

'So they have been *purposely* making an effort to evade-' Dixon paused looking for the right word, 'someone?'

'Not someone, Dixon, *us*.'

Dixon and Singh both looked at one another and then back to Palmerson, puzzled.

Palmerson scoffed. 'These *tree-huggers* and their little protests are all the same; they run about trying to push the governments buttons, pretending they're smart and can outwit any pursuit because they taught themselves some *survival* on the Internet. And they all run to the same places.'

He tapped the woods in the east on the map again, adding to the small gravy-pool already there. 'They're in there, they've had a plan from the start and if we join the dots we can clearly see that they have been moving in a certain *way*.'

He turned his attention to his food again 'Mark my words; they won't be coming up behind us anytime soon.'

He flicked a nod with his head through the window they were all sitting with their backs to, indicating the road outside.

Dixon and Singh nodded, casually agreeing with their superior but not fully understanding his reasoning.

In any case, none of them turned and looked through the window though, because if they had they would have seen Mathew and Alison stop right outside and begin a debate about whether they should stop for some lunch or not.

'It might be the last place we where we can get a decent meal.' Mathew said, hopefully.

Alison tutted and rolled her eyes. 'We're in England no' t' Sahara, Mathew. Besides tha' though, we've go' a lot o' stuff wi' us; if we eat 'ere we'll waste some o' this.'

Mathew looked wistfully through the window at the three, lucky gentlemen who had large, Sunday roasts in front of them. 'But-' he began.

Alison folded her arms and just gave him a hard stare.

He wilted. 'Oh! Fine,' he said and threw his arms up, 'let's get on with it then. Blooming slave-driver.'

The road ahead stopped at a t-junction.

Alison pointed at the iron gate across the main road. 'Straigh' on.'

Mathew stopped in front of the gate and stared at the spread of cows grazing in the field. 'B-but there's cows in that field.'

Alison dropped to the other side of the gate. 'Yea?'

'Well-well they're *cows*.' He tried again.

Alison turned to study the scattered black and white beasts. 'Ya sure?' Her sarcasm was unmistakable. 'I thought tha' the' wer' fat zebras or summert.'

'*Something*.' Mathew said, sharply. 'Fat zebras or *something*.' He huffed, never taking his eyes off the nearest cow.

It had raised its head and stood staring at them, its jaw slowly rotating as it chewed. Contemplatively, Mathew might have added.

'Are-aren't they dangerous though? I mean I thought they charged at you and stampeded.' He pointed lamely. 'There is rather a lot of them isn't there?'

She stepped back up to the gate. 'The' jus' cows. Would I be in 'ere if the' wer' dangerous? Or would I bring you in 'ere if the' wer' dangerous?' She asked sincerely.

He sniffed. 'Just making sure.'

He stepped onto the iron gate and lifted himself up. The top hinge on the left suddenly popped and the gate squealed as it was pulled back from its housing.

Mathew dropped back down. 'Oh! Blooming heck!'

He removed his bag and threw it over into the field and then took off his Belstaff coat and draped it over the gate. 'Give us a hand with this.' He said and grabbed a hold of the gate, making ready to lift it back into the slot where the iron hinge sat. 'You guide it back and I'll lift it up.'

While Mathew and Alison tackled the heavy, metal gate, Palmerson, Dixon and Singh walked out of the pub and stood on the pavement, tapping their respective stomachs appreciatively.

Palmerson took out his cigarettes and looked around; it was quite a beautiful day, unnaturally warm for September he thought.

His eyes followed a phalanx of geese high in the air and flying south. And then he dropped his gaze to watch the cows in the fields and the farmer fixing his gate. There was always a gate to be fixed somewhere wasn't there?

He drew heavily on his cigarette and blew the smoke out, keeping his eyes on the struggling farmer. *I wish I'd become a bloody farmer.*

He took another long drag and then flicked the cigarette away into the gutter before turning back to Dixon and Singh. 'Come on then, lads, let's have at it.'

The three of them turned the corner and walked into the car-park, and a minute later, three, black cars drove out onto the road and away, heading north and making for the road which would take them to the woods in the east.

Clang! Clang-pop-squeal! Clang-clang-clang!

''Ittin' it won' 'elp, Mathew.' Alison said, standing back and giving him a bemused look.

He stood back panting and rubbing at his burning palm.

'Well the blooming thing's almost in, just another quarter-inch and we'd have had it.'

Alison delved into her pockets and produced four foot of thin, nylon rope. 'We jus' need t' use ar' brains.'

She draped the rope over the post where the hinges were welded and then handed Mathew one end. 'Lift wi' one 'and an' pull t' post wi' t' other. Ready?'

He nodded and braced himself on his back-foot. 'Ready.' He replied.

'One, two, three.' Alison counted.

They pulled the post inward and lifted the gate at the same time. The steel hinge-pin flipped straight into its socket and dropped down with a satisfying *screeek*.

Mathew stood back and looked at Alison proudly. Then his brow knitted and he said; 'I would have suggested that, you know? If I'd known we had a bit of rope.'

He sniffed and rubbed his nose the way he had often seen Alison do.

She laughed. 'Yea, course ya would 'av.'

She picked his bag and coat up and waited for him to climb over the gate.

'I was an engineer on the railways, I'll have you know.' He told her as he dropped to the ground. 'A simple problem to solve once you have a bit of old rope.'

He took his coat and bag, and began walking again. 'Shall we go?' He coolly finished.

Alison just continued laughing and jogged up to his side, walking along the inner-hedgerow.

She watched him as he shot glance after furtive glance in the direction of the grazing cows.

'Y' kno'? Cows used t' be 'unted by wolves an' that?' She casually mused.

'No, no I didn't know that.'

'Yea, in t' ancient days the' were.'

She looked right at him to make sure he was paying attention. 'The's a sound tha' the' react to, cos it's in the' genes an' tha'.'

Mathew quickly looked down at her and then returned his watch to the grazers.

'Yea,' she continued, 'if the' 'ear a wolf sound the'll all run away.'

That sounded hopeful Mathew was thinking.

'Bu' tha' same gene thing works opposi' way if ya mek a calf sound.' She then said innocently.

He shot a glance at her again.

'Like this.'

Cupping her hands around her mouth like a trumpet, she took a deep breath and made her *calf-call*. The sound which came out sounded quite distressing.

Mathew spun around on the spot and watched in horror as the cows began to raise their heads from the grass and look in his direction.

'Ohbloomingheck!' He muttered.

She did it again and some of them took a step or two toward them.

His stomach dropped away. 'Great demonstration on how to speak *cow*, but can you stop now please? I'm thoroughly impressed, honestly, you can stop now.'

And then she did stop, rather abruptly.

He looked at her, she had gone quite pale.

'Oh! Bugger.' Was all she managed to quietly say.

He followed her line of sight.

In amongst the black and white cows stood another cow, but this one was almost all black. Very dark-brown at least.

He turned back to her. 'If you're going to tell me that's some kind of special, killer cow-'

'It's t' bull.' She hissed.

He laughed and scoffed. 'I'm not falling for th-!' And then watched, slack-jawed, as Alison began sprinting back to the gate.

'Okay, I'll fall for that.' He whimpered to himself, and nodded and then began legging it back as well.

Chapter Twenty

Mother-nature loves her home, she knows exactly where to put things so that they are in perfect harmony with their surroundings.

This includes all of the life too, everything from the lowest worm to the tallest man. Or men as in this case. Three of them. Up to their ankles in thick, black mud and absolutely giving mother-nature the finger by being in the middle of a swamp-forest in the dark, dressed in black suits and designer shoes.

Mother-nature returned the compliment by filling said shoes with *ten different kinds of shit* as Dixon put it.

'My grandparents live by a swamp like this one.' Singh remarked. 'In India. I remember playing there when we visited. It's quite a nice part of the world. Well, apart from the giant snakes and crocodiles and tigers it is.'

Palmerson and Dixon both stopped and turned around to stare at the smiling Singh.

Palmerson raised his torch and shone it straight into the young man's face.

'You'll be getting a bloody closer look at *this* swamp if you say another word, Singh.' He hissed, his shoes sucking at the mud as he tried to keep his balance.

He turned away again and began squelching along. 'Have you found a signal yet, Dixon?' He asked without turning around.

Dixon took out his muddied phone - he'd dropped it twice - and swiped the mud-smeared screen. 'No, sir, no signal at all under here.'

Palmerson grunted and continued his slow, sucking walk through the mud.

He knew they hadn't bloody come this way. *No one* would *ever* come this way! Why would they?

Singh didn't help. 'If these swamps are deep enough, Arnold and the girl could have stumbled into a bad patch and just drowned. We could have just walked right over them and not known it.'

Palmerson stopped again, and again his torchlight found Singh's squinting face. 'Do you really think they've come this way, Singh?'

'Err-'

'OF COURSE THEY HAVEN'T! NO ONE COMES OUT HERE! IT'S A FU-'

Palmerson's angry rant was cut short when a dozen or more torches were suddenly switched on, bathing the area in a tepid, white glow.

One of the torches bobbed toward them.

It wobbled to a halt and a boot-blacked face frowned down at Palmerson.

'Just who in the hell are you and what are you doing on D.O.D property?' It growled.

'D.O.D?' Palmerson's mind whirled. Bloody inter-*bloody*-net phones! Don't tell you that do they? Oh, no!

'Yes, D.O.D.' The tall, camouflage-clad man replied. 'So I ask you again, who are you and what are you doing here?'

He looked at all three of them. One of them was smiling like a stupid schoolboy.

Singh looked around proudly at the surrounding torches; what stealth, what cunning, what-

'Is he on drugs or something?' The soldier asked.

'What?' Singh snapped to attention. 'Sorry. Sorry, I was just having a *wow* moment you know, that's all.' He said.

Palmerson and the soldier stood side by side and just looked on, bemused.

Singh saluted lamely. 'Carry on.'

The pair turned to face each other again.

'Would it be easy to hide his body here if I were to just shoot him right now?' Palmerson asked.

'Oh, yes,' the soldier replied, 'easily, but that would imply that you are carrying a firearm.'

Palmerson smiled smugly. 'Yes it would, wouldn't it?'

He slid his jacket open for the soldier to see his pistol under his arm.

From somewhere behind one of the surrounding torches, a single weapon suddenly *clicked* and *clacked* as it was loaded.

The soldier standing with Palmerson sighed and looked down at the mud. 'Was that you, Berry?'

The soldier called Berry shuffled his feet uncomfortably, his boots belching in the ooze. 'Um, yes sir.'

Palmerson smiled; looked like this lad had a *Singh* all of his own.

The soldier sighed and shook his head. 'Expel the round, Berry, and don't you damn well drop it, lad!'

He looked back up at Palmerson. 'Now, you were telling me who you are, why you are here, and now also why you are carrying a firearm?'

Palmerson pulled open his jacket again, casting a wry look at the torch where he thought Berry stood. He pulled out his identification wallet and passed it to the soldier.

After checking the photograph against the man standing in front of him, he gave it back. 'Captain Hawkins, sir.'

He shone his torch up and down the length of Palmerson's muddied legs. 'So what does Mi6 need out here then, sir?'

Palmerson told the captain of his orders to locate and bring in Mathew Arnold as they casually walked through the mud, the good captain leading the way.

'I see. That's a very interesting story.' He said, once Palmerson had finished.

The older, Mi6 man frowned. 'You say that like you haven't heard of the man.'

'Oh, we haven't,' Hawkins replied, 'not out here.'

Palmerson's brow furrowed; they hadn't had news of *The Freedom Walker* and it sounded like the captain was telling him they *didn't* get news out here. That was quite disconcerting, it could only mean one thing.

He cleared his throat. 'Are you telling me that we are on a *shadow* base?'

Captain Hawkins nodded curtly. 'We certainly are, sir.'

'Oh good, God.' Palmerson mumbled. 'You're taking us straight to the bloody brig aren't you?'

'Unfortunately, yes, sir, I am taking you straight to the brig.' He turned and smiled, his teeth and eyes glowing wolfishly-white behind his blackened face. 'Not to worry though, sir, I'm sure they'll have you sorted out as soon as they've run you through security.'

'Look, Captain, is all that really necessary? Couldn't you just escort us back the way we came?'

'I'm afraid it is absolutely necessary, sir; I have my orders.'

'Oh come on now-'

'And to be absolutely clear, sir,' the captain interrupted, 'a *shadow* base has *full* clearance to use lethal force should the need arise.'

Palmerson shook his head. 'I know all of that, but surely *you* are satisfied that we are who we say we are and can make that decision?'

'Yes, sir, I *am* satisfied you are who you say you are,' Hawkins replied. 'But you shouldn't *be* here, so my orders are clear.'

'You realise,' Palmerson said, lowering his tone to a little above menacing, 'that you are obstructing a matter of national importance?'

Captain Hawkins didn't falter his step or even flinch. 'No, sir, I didn't know that; we don't get news out here, we get orders and *my* orders are to escort intruders to the brig.'

'You're an idiot.'

'And you're going to the brig.'

While Palmerson marched begrudgingly onward at the front, Dixon and Singh were further back along the column.

Singh was being escorted by the soldier called Berry.

'And this,' the young soldier said, opening one of his *utility* pockets, 'is a high-protein food made from suet and some other *secret* ingredients.'

Singh took the small, plastic tube, rolling it around and scrutinising it, his eyes open in that boyish wonder which he often had. 'What does it do?'

Berry's eyes widened excitedly. 'Amazing stuff that is, I'm tellin' ya. It's like one of them *way-breads* of the elves is that.' He said proudly.

'No way.' Singh breathed, looking at the small, white, plastic tube like it was a proper, magically-endowed thing.

He handed it back. 'What else have you got?'

Berry shoved the food-tube back into his pocket and then looked at Singh, smugly. 'Have you seen *Rambo*?'

'Yea?'

'Remember his big knife?'

'Yea, the one with the sewing kit in the handle. Great.' Singh replied enthusiastically.

The young soldier unclipped his knife holster on his hip and pulled the blade free. 'Well this is *nothing* like that.' He said, his smile broadening.

Berry held the knife in his palm. It was a good-sized Bowie-knife, Singh thought, but other than that it was quite unremarkable.

And then the soldier pushed two, raised rivets together and the knife became anything *but* unremarkable.

The handle split apart and dropped down like wings on either side. The two, small compartments which were revealed, held three, deep purple bullets, each about the size of a garden pea.

'Woah! What are those?' Singh's eyes shone with wonder.

Berry pointed to the inner section of the compartment. 'They're *special* tranquilisers.' He answered. 'That's where you load 'em and this,' he pointed to the thumb-guard, 'is the trigger.'

Singh's eyes were now almost popping out of his head. 'Tranquiliser-bullets!'

He reached for the weapon but Berry clicked the compartments closed and returned it to its sheath.

'Better not.' He said. 'It's strong stuff is that, can't be 'avin an accident. Again.'

Singh looked a little disappointed. But only a little. 'Why do you need tranquiliser-bullets?' He then asked enthusiastically.

The young soldier stared straight ahead.

Even though Singh didn't know it, Berry was mentally reciting his rank and serial number like a captured man under interrogation.

'It's okay if you don't know,' said Singh sympathetically. 'There's loads of things they don't tell me.'

'I *do* know, I just can't say, that's all. It's all *top-secret* and that.' Berry replied.

Singh nodded in agreement. 'Yea, yea I get you; all X-files and aliens and stuff.' He said scoffing.

Berry shot him a furtive, guilty, little glance.

Singh noticed. 'No way!' He whispered. 'Aliens?' He shook his unbelieving head. 'I don't believe it! Wow! Have you? I mean,' he pointed to the tranquilising knife on Berry's belt.

'Oh, no! God no.' Berry quickly answered, shaking his head. 'Never even seen one.'

He turned and looked seriously at Singh. 'I've heard the stories though, you can't be too careful.'

'Why? What do you mean?'

He leaned a little closer. 'They could be anywhere.' He whispered.

Singh's hackles rose and he shivered all the way down his back.

'Oh yea! Anyone, even you.' Berry continued. 'Why d'ya think we're going to all of this trouble to bring you in?'

Singh did think about it. 'But I'm not an alien am I?'

'You might say that. If I were an alien I think I would say that. You might be an alien and not even know it.'

Singh thought about that as well. 'So you could be one as well and not know it?'

'Could be.' Berry replied. 'But then again, I've passed all of the examinations which test for that, so I think I'm pretty safe.'

'Tests?'

'Yea, loads of tests; scans, examinations, samples - loads of samples. You name it, they've got a test for it.'

'Probing?'

Berry scoffed. 'That's the other side, mate, they're the fetish-freaks not us.'

The soldiers and their three captives sloshed on slowly through the unrelenting, sucking mire.

More than once Palmerson or Dixon had to stop and unplug a dislodged shoe from the mud and retie it back onto their squelching, slimed feet.

Singh on the other hand, didn't have that problem; he had both of his shoes and socks tucked away in the pockets of his jacket and had rolled his trousers up to the tops of his shins.

Another two hours passed by of walking through the swamped forest, but eventually it ended and a long valley spread out before them.

At the very bottom, some ten miles away, a row of lit up buildings could be seen.

Palmerson stood breathing heavily, looking at the buildings with something akin to miraculous relief on his face.

A trained, hardened veteran he may be, but he was still getting on a bit. His exercising these days was limited to lifting a glass and his workouts with the wondrous Crystal.

'I take it that's where were heading?' He asked Captain Hawkins, while he removed his shoes.

'Yes, sir, it is. Another ten miles and we're home.' The captain replied, smiling smugly.

Palmerson looked around for a vehicle. 'Didn't you think to leave a vehicle here for when you came back out?' He asked incredulously.

'We've been in there for almost two weeks,' Hawkins casually replied, 'the vehicles were needed elsewhere.'

Palmerson stood clashing his shoes together, bits of forest-swamp flying off in all directions. 'Well can't you radio down and get a bloody jeep up here or something, man?'

He was getting impatient, not least of all because he was well, well off his own trail and his socks were slimed to their hilts.

'No radios I'm afraid, sir; we're on *silent* exercise.'

'Of course you are.' Palmerson said bemused.

He slid his slimy feet into his wet shoes, grimacing as the mud in his socks squeezed itself between his toes.

His anger and exasperation rose even further when he watched bloody Singh wipe his feet clean on the grass and then put his pristine socks and shoes back on.

'Ready when you are, sir.' The smiling, young Mi6 agent said.

Chapter Twenty-One

A good sleep in a comfortable bed, and now a breakfast in an excellent dining room, serving excellent food? What more could a woman ask for?

Diane's phone pinged. She picked it up. Another sighting of Mathew Arnold. Well that went a long way to making the morning perfect.

She flicked the phone's screen and looked at the latest pictures of Mathew and Alison. They were inside a small cafe in the village of *Dry Drayton*.

She checked her own position on her phone map; she was twenty-five miles further north and that picture had been taken yesterday. So not too far away at all and there was no rush in getting down there.

She flicked back to the report.

The picture showed Mathew, Alison and a small gaggle of elderly women sitting around a long, wide table. Balls of wool of various sizes and colour were strewn across the top in front of them.

The caption beneath the picture read; *Dry Drayton Knitters welcome The Freedom Walker*.

Mathew and Alison were beaming, both of them holding up a big, cream bun for the camera to catch.

Crumbs from her croissant spilled onto her phone from her mouth.

She brushed them away and then swiped the screen to her email in-box. Edmund had sent her a message in the night.

Di, I've had a little tip from someone "inside" that someone high up is asking questions about Mathew Arnold. You may not be the only person looking for him now, be careful.
E

When Edmund said "inside" he meant someone at the houses of parliament.

Shit! Someone must have read her article and come to the *right* conclusion; that the story was actually *under*-played when one looked at the suicide element of the whole thing. *Shit! Shit! Shit!*

The croissant disappeared followed by a hefty mouthful of coffee.

Diane sat and chewed and thought about it. Oh, well. At least she had got a week ahead of them before anyone had noticed, but it was very significant attention if it was coming from someone in government.

Maybe it was the prime minister herself? If that was the case then you could bet your life that someone from the *service* would have been sent to *retrieve* Mathew.

The memory of the man-boy's words that night at the services paid her a visit and made her frown. *If they wanna stop 'im, all they'd 'av to do is send a car his way, if you know what I mean?*

She took another croissant from her plate and smeared a hefty dollop of blackberry jam across the flat bottom.

It was no good worrying over it, all she could do was follow the trail and build the story, the rest was up to Mathew and Alison. Especially Alison; if anyone could get Mathew to the doorstep of parliament, then Diane thought the young girl could do it.

She had that natural *mousy* instinct for staying out of trouble and surviving. And if they did happen to get caught, she thought the girl would just annoy the hell out of them anyway until they just let her go.

The second croissant disappeared and Diane wiped her mouth and fingers on her napkin.

Her phone pinged again, another message from Edmund, a text this time. *Go and look at the Freedom Walker website!*

She did as the text requested. The headline had changed: *Anonymous business-woman donates £200,000 to homeless charities through The Freedom Walker website.*

Diane blinked hard and read it again. *Two-hundred grand!*

She hadn't looked at the donation section, hadn't even noticed there *was* a donation section if she were to be honest.

The figure on the page made her skin prickle and she almost fell off her chair. £316,873 had been donated so far! Oh wait; £316,893 - someone had just donated twenty quid.

What the hell!? How was something so big remaining so quiet? The money figures alone were substantial enough to raise questions in certain accounting offices.

Steaming coffee sat in its tiny, two-cup, glass percolator, slowly bubbling and brewing unnoticed on the table in front of her.

It was the Swede, Lars Forsberg. He must be running the money through his own accounts. Shielding it from outside scrutiny whilst still actively flaunting how much had been raised. Clever.

She brought the latest picture back up on her screen.

Oblivious, the pair of them. What would they do though if they knew just how much of the world had its eye on them? As tempted as the journalist inside her was to go and ask that very question and find out, Diane held herself back.

If you were to ask her why she did that she wouldn't be able to answer, all she knew was it didn't feel *right*.

She sat back in her chair, sipping her coffee, and looked out at the world through the dining-room window.

The sky was still blue and the land rolled away in its patchwork-blanket way of usual browns and greens, birds were still just birds flying across the fens and fields. And when tomorrow came they still would be wouldn't they?

Her unease increased, which in turn made her unease increase even further because she *never* felt uneasy.

Her *curse* was her intuition, the very reason she was a journalist in the first place; wherever it pointed her she would always follow, even if it did sometimes get her into trouble.

But nothing compared to this novel feeling of that somehow everything she was now involved with was *personal*, that she was just as much a part of it as... As? As everyone.

She shivered.

People from all around the globe were following Mathew's progress and showing their support for his march. The old adage of *if only everyone would get together and do something* sprang to mind.

Everyone *was* doing something, but doing it very quietly and with only one representative; Mathew. And he, himself, didn't even bloody know it really.

She scoffed, her unease lifted when she thought of Mathew's ignorant bliss - she hated that clichéd term but it really did fit the picture. The man was so honest and innocent that he simply couldn't comprehend the enormity of the *torch* he was bearing.

Yes, he had told her he knew he was carrying a burden for more than just himself, he mentioned his friend Derek more than once and others whom he knew back on the estate where he had lived.

He'd talked about homelessness and the poor, the *robots* who threatened people and the unnecessary need for food-banks - he had been vehement in his deliverance when talking about food-banks. But everything he spoke of, his entire understanding, was all very *local*, he had no notion that what he was actually saying applied to almost every, single human-being on the planet. And without even knowing what he had done, he'd given them all access to his story.

She scoffed again and then raised her cup in a silent toast to Mathew.

It was a very brave-hearted thing he was doing, even if he didn't know he was doing it. Quietly brave.

* * *

Some miles to the south.

'Oh! God! I can't! Just leave it in! Oh! God!' Mathew wailed. 'Is it bleeding? I can't look! Oh! God, I think its bleeding. Oh! Oh! No! Leave it! Get away from it. Oh! God!'

'Well 'ow can I 'av a look if I can't touch it, y' wally?' Alison snapped.

'I think I might be sick. I hate the sight of blood. Is it bleeding? Don't touch it!'

'F' God's sake!' She huffed. 'A' y' gunna walk t' London wi' that stuck in ya arm then?' She tartly asked and folded her arms.

'Oh! I'm not going to London now, you'll have to go and get some help.' He replied, his breath shaky and his face paling. 'I'll need a tetanus, might need surgery to get it out.' His faced actually managed to pale even further as he thought about being on the operating table. 'Oh! I think I'm going to be sick.'

Alison just rolled her eyes and then did what she was best at and *nipped* in and pulled the barbed-wire out with a swift tug, quickly nipping back out of the way again once it was free

Mathew's wailing increased.

He held his arm as far away from his face as he could, keeping his watery eyes firmly upward and away from the *devastating* injury.

'It's bleeding isn't it? Oh! No! Is it bad? Oh! God! Will I need stitches?'

Alison pulled a rag from her pocket and gently wrapped it over the two, small, round punctures in his forearm, not even bothering to tie it.

'There,' she said, tutting, 'all done. We can ge' on now, eh?'

She stood with her arms folded and her eyebrows raised in question. 'Or does it need a *magic kiss* as well?'

Mathew turned his head to look at what she had done. 'B-b-but it was stuck *right* in!' He insisted. 'It-it was really deep, Alison, d-don't you think it would be best if a doctor took a look at it?'

She couldn't take it anymore.

With her face screwed up in a tight-lipped, angry frown, she stepped forward again and whipped the rag away and then spitefully pressed the two punctures quite firmly. 'Yorra big puff o' wind!'

'OW!' He danced around holding his arm to his chest now. 'What did you do that for you-you-'

''Orrible cow?' Alison sarcastically suggested.

'*H*orrible,' he repeated, emphasising the *h*. '*H*orrible cow. Yes, that'll do.' He rubbed at his wounds. 'Oh! They don't half hurt.'

Alison turned away disgusted and began the ritual of bringing the *camp* down, muttering under her breath. 'Big wuss.'

Mathew ambled over to her side, still rubbing his arm. 'I don't suppose you've got a plaster or something have you?'

'Av go' a very sharp knife if tha'll 'elp?' She quickly replied, throwing him a sharper look.

Mathew huffed. 'Oh, you are mean.'

'An' you're as soft as a mornin' pat.' She stood up. 'I thought you wer' an engineer on t' railway?'

'I was, thirty-seven years.'

'Well ya must 'av 'it ya thumb wi' an 'ammer at least once! *How* old are ya?'

Mathew stood up straight and raised his chin defensively.

'I'm a very careful and conscientious worker.' He said proudly. 'But if you must know; I *have* hit my thumb with a hammer.'

'So what's all t' fuss then? Ya 'it y' thumb an' then y' get on wi' it don' ya?'

'I had to go and lie down in the infirmary for the afternoon because I fainted.'

He looked at his boots. 'My dad had to come and pick me up once he'd finished work.'

Alison's eyes and mouth were agape but she didn't know what to say; his dad had picked him up from work because of a *boo-boo*. Like school.

'I cried in the car-park.'

His toe scraped aimlessly at the dirt beneath his boot. 'And then I fainted again when I caught my thumb on the car-door.'

There was a strange noise waiting to come out of Alison's throat but she wasn't sure if it was a laugh or a cry, or a word or ten. 'I-I-what? A' ya f' real?'

He nodded and didn't meet her gaze. 'Unfortunately yes.' He replied. 'I was very careful after that though.' He said and looked up and smiled. 'Bought some gloves.'

Alison stammered. 'But-but you wer' gunna 'av a go at Rag!' She said. ''Ow can you do tha' an' blood meks y' faint?' She threw her hands up in submission.

'Being squeamish doesn't mean I can't still be brave does it?'

'Wha' if summert 'appened t' me an' I wer' bleedin'?'

'Oh! You'd die.' Mathew nodded solemnly. 'I'd faint and you'd die. Guarantee it.'

'Well tha's jus' charmin' tha' is innit?' She turned away disgusted.

'Well, are you likely to hurt yourself badly?' He innocently asked.

She turned back around, throwing his coat to him but keeping a hold onto his walking staff.

She looked at him levelly. 'I'll give you *hurt badly* in a minute.'

Mathew put on his coat and then gently took his staff, looking down into Alison's small face. 'I wouldn't really let you bleed to death you know?'

She could see he meant it and nodded and scoffed.

'I'd probably be sick on you though, while I tended to your wounds.' He sniffed and tried to look casual.

Alison laughed and grimaced at the same time. 'Great. I'll 'av t' mek sure I don' cut me 'ed then.'

She led them out of the small wood and made for the next set of fields.

Both of them were wearing new, woollen scarves which were fluttering in the breeze behind them as they walked along; *donations* from the *Dry Drayton Knitters*.

Chapter Twenty-Two

What Edith Morris couldn't tell you about wool wasn't worth knowing, and if you ever wanted your *quilts* handed to you on a plate then just ask old *Edie* for a *knit-off*. If you dare.

Her legend whispered that there were one or two who *had* dared and now lived in another part of the country, their shame too much for the knitters of Dry Drayton.

It was no wonder she was the head *Needle* in the *Dry Drayton Knitting Club*. People came from miles around to sample her *woollen-wisdom* and listen to her tales, the latest of which was the day *The Freedom Walker* had paid them a visit.

That lovely, young reporter had listened to her and the others for almost two hours, a very nice young woman who was clearly sympathetic to Mathew's cause. Unlike the two, suited men who were talking to them now.

They'd only been in five minutes before they'd started being all *manly* and *authoritative*. Well one of them at least, the other, the younger man, seemed to want to get to the cake-counter more than he wanted to show his identification.

The older of the two seemed to frown patronisingly quite a lot when he was taking in the twelve women and thirty odd balls of wool, not to mention the several piles of knitting-patterns and jars full of knitting-needles strewn in front of them.

He walked his self-impressive suit up to the tables and stood looking down at them all as though he were overseeing a sweatshop gang.

And that just did it for Edith Morris, that did.

He wanted to ask them *some questions* regarding Mathew Arnold's visit, but Edith was having none of it until she had some *help to ball her yarn*.

Palmerson tried to divert. 'I'm sorry, as much as we would like-'

'Nonsense,' Edith crooned, cutting him off. 'There's always time for a good *ball-up*, very relaxing and clears the mind does getting nice big, tight *balls*.'

She held a yellow ball of wool up for them to see. 'We're all good at *balling* here.'

Palmerson sighed and then nodded at Dixon.

'W-what? Me?'

The older man just raised his eyebrow; that was an order, laddie, we need information and I need to stop her from saying *balls*.

Dixon paused and then his shoulders sagged, defeated. He sat down by Edith's side and held his arms out.

Edith smiled warmly at him and threw a gathering of lime-green yarn over his dutifully waiting forearms.

Palmerson looked around for somewhere to sit, but ended up resigning himself to sit in the only other available chair; between two very round, middle-aged ladies.

They were both knitting away furiously. Or rather their hands were knitting away furiously, while the women themselves were chatting and seemed completely oblivious to what was going on right under their noses. It was like they had little, sentient creatures hanging out of their sleeves who were tirelessly working away unattended.

The older man tried to make himself comfortable between the two, soft bodies of the women on either side of him.

They gave him warm, pudgy smiles which raised his comfort levels not at all.

He cleared his throat behind his hand. 'So, um, Mathew Arnold?' He said.

'Who?' Edith replied, her hands a whirly blur as she wound off the wool from Dixon's arms.

'The Freedom Walker?' Palmerson continued.

'Oh! Yes! He was in here. Lovely man.' Edith said, nodding and wool-winding.

'Did he-'

'Tried his hand at a spot of knitting as well.' She continued, completely ignoring Palmerson. She chuckled and shook her head. 'Oh! That was funny!'

'Yes, I bet it was. Did he happen to-' Palmerson tried again.

'It was like watching a child trying to tie his shoelaces.' She laughed even louder.

Palmerson opened his mouth again but didn't even manage to get a syllable to his lips this time.

'Earned him one of Shirley and Ethel's buns though. Not that they need them themselves, mind you.' She continued laughing.

The two, large ladies sitting on either side of Palmerson both grinned at him again.

'We don't eat them ourselves anyway.' Shirley said.

'Well not often, maybe the occasional *crumb* or two.' Ethel amended.

'Occasionally.' Shirley underlined.

Palmerson looked from one smiling face to the other and just blinked. 'Occasionally.' He muttered, his thought not staying where it should have.

With a mental shake of his head to *wake up man*, he turned his attention back to Edith.

She was just feeding another load of wool onto Dixon's waiting arms.

He was busy chatting with a lady on the other side of him, who was explaining the art of recovering a dropped stitch. He looked to be genuinely fascinated.

'Well, Mrs Morris,' Palmerson began. Again. 'Can you rem-'

'Call me Edith, please, and yes, I *can* remember, I'm not *that* old you know.'

All of the ladies erupted into a cackling laugh of various tones and pitches.

Palmerson politely chuckled along with them.

Dixon was laughing like he'd been coming to sit here for years.

'Do you remember where he said he would be heading next?' Palmerson managed to quickly say.

Edith looked up, a thoughtful look on her face and her hands never ceasing their whirling-balling. 'Didn't he say he was going to York Minster?'

'York?' Palmerson repeated, puzzled.

'I thought he said they were going to someone's house?' The women sitting with Dixon said.

'Might have been, Geraldine, might have been.' Edith answered. 'A house in York maybe?'

'That's right,' another voice piped up, 'a mister somebody-or-other wasn't it?'

'Mr Pine!' Yet another voice called out from further along the table.

'Yes!' Edith said, nodding, satisfied. 'That's it.'

She turned to Palmerson. 'They were going to Mr Pine's house in York Minster.' She said.

He tiredly pinched the space between his eyes. 'They're going to see the prime minister at the houses of parliament.' He returned, his voice still polite if not a little strained.

'Are they?' Edith's eyes opened wide and her mouth made a perfect O shape. 'Well fancy that!'

She turned to the other ladies. 'They're going to see the prime minister after they've been to York to see Mr Pine!'

While the *Dry Drayton Knitters* were happily giving Palmerson absolutely nothing, Singh, who had been left to watch the cars and keep his eye on the road, decided to nip into the local newsagents and buy himself another cornetto.

As the door swung closed behind him, Diane Jones stepped out of the phone box she had secreted herself in and popped into the shop herself.

Eight or so miles on her way out of Dry Drayton, Diane had passed three, black vehicles going the opposite way.

Her natural journalistic instincts told her that they were definitely *not* farm-cars, and so she had turned around and followed them back to the village.

Her hackles had risen when she saw the three men who had exited the vehicles; if they weren't the very embodiment of the acronym MiB then she didn't know what was.

Two of them had gone straight into the cafe while the third had been told to wait in the car.

She had slipped into the telephone box to get a better view, but then the young man in the car had decided to go into the shop.

Seeing an opportunity, she'd opened the top two buttons of her blouse, put on a fresh line of lipstick, pinched her cheeks, and finally ruffled her hair to get that windswept-tart look.

And now she was standing behind him in the freezer-aisle of the little shop watching him delving around in a chest-freezer.

She waited until he had brought his head back out and then barged into the back of him, sending him straight back in with a clatter, thud and an *oof!*

'Oh! I'm so sorry!' She said, standing back and holding her hands up to her mouth in horror. 'I tripped.'

Singh stood up and brushed himself down and then stood stupidly with his mouth open staring at the small - very pretty - distraught - beautiful in fact - dark-haired angel in front of him.

'Um. That's okay, accidents happen.' He managed to say. 'I once slipped on another man's vomit in the training yard and my weapon went off and I shot the drill sergeant in the calf.' He told her, trying to make her feel better.

She did feel better; that had been *much* easier than she had thought it was going to be. She thought she would have had to pull out all the stops to just get *that* little bit of information; that he was, indeed, a serviceman. Didn't really matter *which* service, the tip she'd had from Edmund said enough.

The bit about slipping on another man's vomit made her grimace well enough though.

'Oh, don't worry; he was okay,' Singh quickly added, mistaking her look for one of concern. 'It was just a flesh wound.'

Diane held her hands to her chest dramatically. 'Oh! Thank God, for that.' She said and stepped closer. 'Were you in the army then?'

Diane Jones didn't particularly like men in uniform, but the windswept-*angel* she was at the moment absolutely loved them.

'Oh, yea.' Singh replied, while his ego offered itself up for a good, old polishing. 'My dad was a Gurkha, but I went into the paras. *He who dares, wins* and all that.' He said, shrugging and trying to be cool and modest. And tough and mysterious.

'Oh! How exciting!' Diane the angel said, her eyes wide and wondering. 'What brings you to the village shop?'

She moved closer and leaned in. 'Is there a conspiracy going on in Drayton?' She whispered.

Singh's pupils widened at the angel's sudden proximity and the smell of her perfume, and he began to speak and didn't shut up until he'd told her everything. *Everything.*

She left him at the counter, moonily paying for his ice-cream, and made her way quickly back to her car. She smiled to herself when she noticed the other two were still *tied up* in the cafe.

Turning the car around, she drove back along the road again, humming to herself happily.

So these guys *were* from the prime minister, sent to bring Mathew straight to her. A clever move; from a *socio*-political viewpoint she could present herself as the saving *matriarch* of the country by being seen listening to Mathew and then helping him, use him as a token for the world to see. And failing that they could just *hide* him away somewhere anyway.

Although she hadn't planned on trying to actually track Mathew down until he was much closer to London, she now thought she should try and get to him as quickly as possible.

The men behind her were trained to track people, what chance did she have of finding them then? Mind you, *they* hadn't had any new leads either and it looked like they were using the same system of news as she was to plan their own moves.

'Well, Mister Arnold, it looks like you've drawn attention from the very top.'

From a journalists point of view that wasn't such a bad thing; it added meat to the story. But she wanted the playing field to remain fair, or at least as fair as it had been so far. How could she help with that?

Maybe it was time to write a bigger story now. Maybe that was the answer. Maybe it was time to write about what Mathew Arnold, *The Freedom Walker*, was really doing, what message he was really conveying to the *masters*.

It felt too soon for that though, she felt that when the time came for that level she would know it.

So maybe she should write another, small article, something using the information she had gathered so far. Something *quaint* but with a little mystery.

She began to laugh as she drove along. Her window was down and the wind really was sweeping through her hair as she laughed. The windswept-angel knew exactly what she should write.

Chapter Twenty-Three

It was quite chilly today. The camp had cooled down quickly in the night and Alison had to rekindle the fire while it was still dark; a sure sign that autumn was finally blowing in with winter on its heels.

Mathew's bones felt cold. His skin was clammy and his chest ached stubbornly. He marched along with his head bent forward, looking at the trampled grass he was following; the wake of Alison's light steps.

They had been walking for a few hours, mostly in silence. Alison had kept her eye on him as best as she could, but they really needed to find a place to make an early camp, somewhere near to a village or town so she could use the shops and chemist.

She tried not to think about it too much, but she had seen him rubbing his chest and she thought he was looking paler than usual, a little waxy.

At the moment they were moving through a huge tract of *middle-of-nowhere*, nothing but rolling, green hills and scattered, woody copses to be seen in all directions for miles around.

She turned around to check on his progress. ''Ow y' feelin', Mathew?'

He looked up and smiled weakly. 'I'm okay, I'm just really tired today.'

She felt a pang of guilt at keeping him moving, but she had no other choice; it was impossible to make a camp in the middle of a field.

'We'll 'av a break when we ge' over there.' She said, pointing to the low hedge which separated this field from the next. 'I reckon we can 'av a couple of hours there. Y' can 'av *forty-winks*, as me Nan used t' say.'

'I think my Nan might have said that as well.' He answered. 'Great Nan's think alike.' He chuckled and then coughed wheezily.

Alison took up her step at his side and draped his arm over her shoulder for extra support. ''Av y' go' any *Nasty* left?'

'Oh yes, about half the bottle still, I think.'

'We'll ge' ya under t' 'edge an' I'll ge' a brew goin'.' She told him. 'Y' can 'av a tot an' a kip while I sor' it out.'

Mathew squeezed her shoulder. 'You're a good girl, Alison.' He said, and smiled tiredly.

She patted the back of his hand and nodded humbly.

'I'd be done in miles and days ago if I hadn't had you by my side.' He continued.

'Yea, cos y' soft.' She teased, giggling.

She led him to the hedge and then took his walking-staff and bag while he settled himself.

'You know? Every time I do this,' he said, pointing to the ground and his surroundings, 'sitting under another hedge? It makes me think of Charlie Chaplin's tramp. All I need is a handkerchief tied to a stick and I'd be set.' He chuckled and made himself cough again.

'I don't kno' who tha' is.'

Mathew gasped. 'Really? You've never heard of Charlie Chaplin's *Little Tramp*?'

She shook her head. 'Is 'e on t' telly?' She asked while she made a shallow bed-down and pillow for Mathew.

'No, no, there were no televisions back in those days, just the *silver screen* as they called it.'

Alison scoffed. 'Am only fifteen, ya kno'? Am not three-'undred and fifty like you are! Blimey!' She began laughing.

'I'm not *that* old! Thank you very much, missy.'

He pulled the bottle of *Old Nasty* from his pocket. 'I thought everybody had heard of him, like John Wayne or, or-'

'Tommy Cooper?'

'Yes, or Tommy Cooper.'

Alison took the bottle from him and measured a double tot into his cup.

'I 'ant bin t' school since I wer' twelve.' She said, and handed him the cup. 'I think I've only bin tut cinema once in me life.'

Mathew gratefully took the drink and sat back against the hedge. 'Can you remember what you went to see?'

She began cutting a hole into the earth with the *scary* bowie-knife. 'Benjamin Button. I can't remember t' proper name o' title, bu' ya can't forget a name like *Benjamin Button*, can ya?' She laughed.

'I've never heard of it.'

'It's about a man who's born old an' grows up, bu' gets younger until he becomes a baby an' dies.'

Mathew blinked and then took a swig of his drink. 'A man is born old and grows up getting younger and then eventually becomes a baby and dies?' He repeated, trying to get the pieces in his head to fit the story and make some kind of sense.

'Yea.' She answered, her breathing ragged as she sawed a circular sod out of the ground. 'I liked it. I wer' only little but I remember it.'

She wiped her brow and blew her fringe out of her eyes.

Grabbing the sod with both hands, she began tugging at it until it came out of the ground. She left it to one side and then carried on digging the fire-pit out.

'I feel like 'im sometimes,' she said, 'Benjamin Button.'

'What? Like you're going to turn into a baby?'

She laughed again. 'No, wally. I just feel like am young on t' outside an' really old on t' inside sometimes.' She didn't sound bitter when she said that.

Mathew just watched her, his admiration and respect for her continually rising. She had said the very thing he was angry at the world about; she was growing up and missing out on her childhood, and she just took it all in her stride. By all rights it was *she* who should be angry, but she simply wasn't, it was in her nature to be *no-nonsense*, and to be angry would simply be nonsense.

'It's like I blinked,' she carried on, 'an' suddenly I wa' grown up an' then I blinked again an' I wer' old.'

She chuckled to herself but frowned at the same time.

Mathew noticed. Sadly, she wasn't completely oblivious to the things she had missed and was still missing out on.

She cleaned the knife in the long grass and then returned it to its sheath.

The hole was now twelve inches in diameter and five or six inches deep. All she needed now was the fuel.

She moved closer to Mathew and began picking the dry twigs and long, brittle thorns from around the *cave* which she had pressed into the hedge for him to take his nap in.

He lent a hand from his seat and between them they filled the hole to the very top with the very driest kindling.

'Do you regret not going to school?' He asked her.

She shook her head. 'No' really; "*If ya wer' born to regret things, y' first word would 'av bin* sorry."' She said and smiled. 'Me dad wer' always sayin' tha' when 'e wer' in trouble wi' me mam.'

Mathew nodded and chuckled. 'My father used to just run and hide in his shed when he was in trouble. He was afraid of nothing but my mother; by God she could put you in your place when she was angry.'

'What did 'e do, y' dad?'

'He was a secondary-school teacher, taught maths for nearly forty-five years.'

'An' wha' about y' mam?'

'She was a secretary,' Mathew answered, 'at the same school as my father. He taught the pupils and she taught *him*.'

Alison began piling some of the bigger sticks into a small, tapered bonfire.

'Di'nt y' 'av any brothers or sisters?' She asked while she worked away at the fire.

'No, no, just me.'

'Well tha' 'splains a lot.'

She sat back on her haunches and laughed when she saw the look on his face.

'What do you mean?' He asked innocently.

'You 'ant 'ad anyone to play out wi' 'av ya? In t' mud an' woods an' tha'.' She said sweetly. 'S'why y' scared o' cows.' She then added and laughed again.

'And quite right too! I've seen my fair share of westerns; cows are ferocious, charging beasts in all of them!'

He threw down the last of his *Nasty* and then coughed. 'Ferocious, charging beasts!' He repeated, wheezing somewhat.

Alison sat and giggled. 'Our cows don' charge like tha', y' daft 'ed.'

'Well you could have fooled me after I saw you *talk* to one.' Mathew said, indignantly. '*He* obviously didn't know that he was one of *our* cows, did he?'

The young girl flopped back holding her sides and laughed until she was a lovely tint of red.

The memory of Mathew running away as fast as he could, and the look of complete terror on his face, was threatening to make her sick.

'I don't know what *you're* laughing at,' he huffed, 'you swallowed eel-slime.'

And then he broke out laughing himself as he remembered the look of shock on Alison's face when she tried to rinse her mouth out with Merylin's brew.

They lay like laughing idiots in the grass for a while, but eventually Alison sat back up and wiped her eyes as the last of her giggles subsided into heavy breathing.

Mathew joined her a moment later.

'Oh, dear. If I keep laughing like that I'll never get to London.' He said. 'I must admit though, I feel much better, not tired at all now.'

Before Alison could reply another voice spoke.

'That would be all of fresh air; good for your lungs and your heart.'

They spun around to be confronted by the twin barrels of a really big gun being held by a really small woman. Standing behind her was the reason they hadn't heard anyone approach; a dapple-grey horse.

Mathew gulped.

Alison cocked her head.

'A' ya gunna shoot us?' She asked.

The middle-aged woman looked them both up and down and studied them, frowning as if in deep thought. 'Hmm.' She eventually muttered. 'I'm not sure.'

Mathew visibly paled while Alison grinned.

The woman flicked her gaze to the small girl, she was *in charge* then. Wonders never cease.

She lowered the shotgun heavily and sighed, relieved that the weight was off her arms. The blooming thing was almost as tall as she was and weighed the same as a small donkey, she always said.

'Well you haven't come to plough my top fields,' she looked between them both, 'so what are you doing sitting up here?'

She noticed the small, unlit fire and the two cups waiting by the side of it. 'Travellers are you?'

Mathew nodded quickly and then slowly stood up, trying his damnedest to not groan too much.

'We didn't mean to bother anyone.' He said, standing as though he were addressing a teacher in assembly or something.

The woman could clearly see Mathew was genuinely frightened. Probably because it was the first time he had come face-to-face with a shotgun.

Alison, on the other hand, didn't seem bothered at all by it.

'That's quite alright, don't worry,' the woman said, addressing Mathew directly. She raised the gun. 'It's not even loaded.'

He sagged and sighed heavily, smiling with genuine relief.

She pointed to the unlit fire. 'Got enough for one more?' She asked, meaning a cup of tea.

Both Mathew and Alison were thrown by that, especially Alison, who had received more than her fair share of being *moved on*. Someone actually asking to sit with them was quite novel.

'The's always enough tea t' go round.' Alison said. 'Av y' go' a cup?'

The woman went back to her horse and re-holstered the shotgun before opening one of the saddlebags to pull out a blue, tin cup.

She walked back to them and handed the cup to a smiling Alison. 'Thank you. I'm Cecily.'

'I'm Alison.'

'Mathew.' Mathew said, holding his hand out for her to shake. 'Sorry for barging through your fields.' He added sheepishly.

Cecily just laughed. 'It was the very distinct *lack* of barging which made me curious to come and have a look at you for myself.'

Mathew gave her a questioning look.

'I saw you enter from the road back up there,' she said, nodding behind her. 'Any normal *trespasser* would have jumped the gate or left it open, left a mess or damage - need I go on? But you two made an effort to leave everything as it was and not only that, you didn't go crashing across the fields either, you walked their perimeters.'

She shrugged her shoulders. 'I had to see for myself what sort of *thugs* you were before I set the dogs on you.'

The three of them sat down around the now built fire.

Alison lit it and then poured water into the tiny, tin teapot, adding a teabag lastly. Once the flames had died down and the thorns and twigs were glowing, she put the pot onto boil.

Cecily watched. 'You're from *the land* aren't you?' She asked Alison.

'Yea, me mam an' dad 'ad a farm in Yorkshire.' She replied without looking up.

The older woman didn't press any further, she knew how the land and farming could mould you to its own shape, making you as hard as the hills and as changeable as the seasons. She could see that the land had played a big part in healing whatever the young girl had been wounded by.

'I could tell; you go to a lot of trouble to make a cup of tea.' Cecily said, keeping the mood light. 'Only someone from Yorkshire does that.'

'You have that right.' Mathew put in. 'She's a blooming marvel is young Alison, tea is only the half of it, I can tell you.'

Alison scoffed. 'Don' listen to 'im, 'e zagerates a lot.'

'*Exag*gerates.' Mathew corrected. 'And I do not!'

He turned back to Cecily. 'Do you know, she actually rescued me from a thug!? A *big* thug at that!'

His eyes were wide and serious, full of the wonder that he first felt when he saw Alison standing there in the glow of the street-lights.

'She didn't just scare him off either,' he breathlessly continued, 'oh! No! She gave him a really good thumping and knocked him out!'

He turned back to Alison and held both of his hands out, gesturing at her. 'Look at the size of her! She's tiny!'

'Oh give over, y' wally.' Alison said, rolling her eyes and tutting. 'I only clouted 'im a couple o' times.'

She quickly turned to Cecily. 'I only clouted 'im a couple o' times.' She repeated, shaking her head, rolling her eyes and generally trying to play the whole thing down.

It didn't work, Cecily's expression said she was immensely impressed. 'That was a very brave thing that you did.'

'Exactly what I said.' Mathew blurted.

He folded his arms and just looked at Alison with an *I-told-you-so* look on his face.

'Very brave.' Cecily continued.

'And she stood in front of seven men who were fighting, to stop them from getting at me.'

The look on Mathew's face was now one of triumph; *I don't exaggerate!*

Cecily frowned, that was a little hard to swallow she had to admit, but then again, the size of the girl on the outside may have been tiny, but when looking into her eyes one could see the girl was actually very big.

'I can see there is an interesting story behind the two of you.' She said to them both. 'I think we might have to finish this conversation in the comfort of my kitchen. What do you say?'

Mathew and Alison looked at one another and then back to Cecily.

'I say that would be extraordinarily kind of you and we graciously accept.' Mathew answered.

'Good, that's settled then' Cecily said. 'Cup of field-tea first though.' She added, nodding at the boiling teapot.

Chapter Twenty-Four

Ah. His corridor again. From outer office to inner sanctum, the corridor of power, of secrets, of inside-knowledge. And todays special; the corridor of fear.

Oh! God! Why did he have to be the one to bring her the paper? Why couldn't he just be dead!?

She was bound to blame him of course, *bound* to!

Crispin Wells stood with his hand hovering over the door-handle, while his other was poised shakily over a panel ready to knock.

Come on Crispin, deep breath, count to ten.

He knocked lightly on the door.

'*Come.*'

He took another, deeper breath, and then walked in, crisply closing the door behind him.

Without a word he walked up to the prime minister's large, wooden desk and held the newspaper out for her. 'Um.' He began.

'Oh, God.' The prime minister muttered.

Crispin was about as tactful as a brain haemorrhage at Christmas when delivering bad news.

She snatched the paper. 'What is it now?'

'Bad.' Was all he said.

He watched as she read the circled article, her face slowly changing colour from pasty-pink to infuriated-red, while his own face drained to taught paleness in perfect compliment.

Her eyes flickered up to meet his. Forget daggers and all that, she was firing nuclear-fuelled laser-beams.

'Aliens, Crispin?' She quietly, dangerously said.

He flinched involuntarily. 'Yes, Prime Minister.'

'Do you see that wooden block at the front of my desk with my name on it?' She asked, her voice unchanging.

'Um. Yes, Prime Minister?'

'I want to pick it up and throw it at your stupid head.'

As menacing as the words themselves were, it was the actual delivery which sent a cold shiver of dread down poor Crispin's back, settling itself at the base of his spine and then threatening to make a noisy, wet appearance at any moment. His total sphincter-control that day had been truly inspiring.

'I won't, of course,' she continued, 'but I want to, Crispin, I really want to.'

She read the article again. '"I spoke with agents from the prime ministers office."' She quoted. 'Whom is she speaking of? Please tell me it's not Palmerson.'

'I have no idea at the moment, Prime Minister, but I can assure you-'

'I don't want assurances, Crispin,' she icily spat, cutting him short. 'I want Mathew Arnold standing right where you are, but instead I get,' she turned her hard eyes back to the paper. '"The agent told me they were looking for the Freedom Walker on secret D.O.D land, where, and I quote, *they deal with extra-terrestrial threats.*"' The prime minister looked up again.

Crispin wilted a little more; he knew what the next line in the article was but held on bravely anyway.

The prime minister knew it as well and quoted it without looking. '"When I asked if he thought the Freedom Walker was an alien, the spokesperson replied; *could be, who knows? Anyone could be one and not even know it.*"'

The prime minister's eyes flickered for a moment to the wooden nameplate at the front of her desk and then settled back on Crispin's pale face. 'I want him found, Crispin, and I want Palmerson in here tomorrow morning.'

'Yes, Prime Minister.'

'And I want a news-cleanup sorted out, pronto; this bloody Jones woman needs to be *checked*.'

Crispin didn't speak or move.

The prime minister sighed and rubbed at her temples. 'What is it, Crispin?'

'I don't think we should change the approach of this story just now.' He said, not meeting her gaze.

'And so we should just let Arnold and a riot march right up to parliament instead, should we?'

'It is that very thing which I am thinking; I think if we change it and draw any kind of *political* attention to it now we will arm the opposition and possibly fuel any of those, um, *rioters*.' He did look at her now.

She knew he was right, the *other* sides would surely jump all over it and make it much bigger than she could deal with. Fan the flames of the fire-starter. Damn them. Damn *them* and damn *him*. And bloody, bad-news Crispin.

'Fine,' she eventually said, 'what do you suggest?'

'It may be as simple as sending a quiet message to the police to keep a look out and to have Palmerson and his men continue with their search.'

He clasped his hands in front of himself. 'After all, we only have Diane Jones writing anything anyway and she doesn't seem to want to draw too much attention. Makes sense to use that to our advantage.'

She sighed heavily, as heavily as she thought the nameplate would feel in her hand.

'Very well. See to it.' She said and waved for him to leave.

He turned and made for the door, walking quietly across the wooden floor and then gingerly turning the handle.

'And Crispin?'

He stopped with the door halfway open. 'Yes, Prime Minister?'

'Have a good think about how heavy the nameplate would have been if I *had* thrown it at you, hm?'

He dropped his gaze and quietly stepped outside into his corridor.

As the door clicked shut behind him *something* heavy thudded into the panels and then clattered to the floor inside the room.

Crispin squeaked and clutched at his fluttering chest, running all the way back to his own, safe, little office.

* * *

Meanwhile, in another pub up north.

'Not a bad steak at all.' Palmerson said and tapped his stomach.

He wiped his mouth on his napkin and then threw it on the table next to the map.

There were a few more stains here and there on the cartographic landscape, including mud from their bog march and a small ketchup hill from the chippy.

Both Dixon and Singh were still finishing their lunch, but Palmerson carried on anyway.

'After our rather *interesting* talk with the ladies of Dry Drayton, I believe our man has gone into the *wild* again.'

He pointed at a place on the map. 'They must have come out here when we went through here.' He said, pointing to a place where Mathew and Alison had never set foot within twenty miles of before. 'I'd bet my life on it. That would explain why we were picked up by the D.O.D and they weren't.'

He sat back smugly and picked up his double whiskey and dry ginger. He sipped at it while he watched the other two working out which way Mathew and Alison would have gone, assuming Palmerson was correct.

'Come on, lads. You must be able to see the obvious now that I've pointed out where they must have come out.' His smug superiority washed over himself with the warmth of the whiskey in his cheeks.

Singh leaned over and pointed with his mushy-pea covered fork at a place a few miles back along the way they had come.

'How about doubling back to cover their tracks, somewhere around here?'

He left a green stain for Palmerson to check out.

The older man scoffed. 'Don't be daft, Singh, use your head, lad; that would take them almost straight back to us and *that*.'

He tapped the map over the motorway. 'They're avoiding the main roads remember?'

Dixon pushed his plate to one side and leaned over to have a look for himself. 'I know it probably sounds as daft as what Singh suggested, sir, but they could actually be right here, where we are now.'

He pointed to a place roughly where they were, unknowingly planting his finger right on top of the field where Mathew and Alison and Cecily had just the previous day been sitting drinking tea.

Palmerson scoffed even louder. 'They're not *shit-wits*, Dixon! Good grief, man. Only the thickest of the thick would come down this way.' He shook his head sadly and sighed.

He leaned over and pointed a pudgy finger to another place on the map, some forty miles to the east of them. 'This is all farm and woodland, and this forest may look like it's going back toward the north, but if you look at its edge you will see it is almost exactly straight and leads to this point.'

He slid his finger along the edge of the tree-line and then stopped, giving them both his *master's* look. 'It's quite obvious when you look a little more closely isn't it?'

Dixon and Singh both nodded slowly, both of them not comprehending at all and being unable to fathom any of Palmerson's reasoning whatsoever. But neither wanting to look stupid.

'Yea.' They murmured in unison. 'Obvious.'

Palmerson dropped his glass back to the table. 'Got to keep your eye on the ball when dealing with these people, boys, put yourself in *their* shoes, think like an amateur.'

He nodded at his empty glass. 'Whose round is it then?'

* * *

Less than four miles up the road from the pub Palmerson, Dixon and Singh were dining in, Mathew, Alison and Cecily were sitting on the small porch at the back of Cecily's farm-cottage eating their own lunch.

They had returned to her kitchen as she had suggested the day before, sitting down to another pot of tea while Mathew told his story.

Cecily was quite *old-school* and didn't have a computer or the Internet in her house, and so hadn't heard anything about *The Freedom Walker*. But Mathew's story had moved her in the very same way it had moved - was still moving - people from all over the world.

She had insisted that they stay the night at least and rest before they went on with what would be the last leg of the journey.

Sitting as they were now, around the small table, no one would ever have guessed that it was the same Mathew and Alison from yesterday who were eating lunch. They looked like any, normal country-family enjoying a peaceful lunch in the fresh air.

The clothes they were wearing came from either Cecily's own wardrobe or her husband's who had passed away some years earlier.

Mathew had on a white shirt, with blue jumper over the top, and beige, corduroy trousers on his legs.

While Alison wore a button-up shirt, with bluebell patterning, and a thick, woollen cardigan. On her legs were a pair of *skinny* jeans; skinny on Cecily, but just right on the tiny Alison.

As soon as they both had accepted Cecily's offer of a real bed for the night, she had immediately set about running baths and swapping clothes and filling washing machines (she had two) and slippering feet (yes, she had slippers for both of them, even if Alison's *were* two-sizes too big and had enormous, pink, fluffy pompoms stuck to the front.)

Grooming himself properly had been nothing short of a delight for Mathew, he felt - and looked - like a new man when he stepped out of the bathroom thirty minutes after he had entered.

Alison, on the other hand, didn't come out for about two hours.

Cecily had peeked inside and found the girl pruning in tepid water, fast asleep.

Alison sat now and munched on the croutons from her homemade, tomato and watercress soup, while her feet swung under her chair with the pompoms swinging along *fluffily* with them.

She looked up. 'Me mam an' me Nan both used t' mek soup like this,' she said, still holding her spoon in the bowl. 'It want tomato though, we med pumpkin an' apple.'

Her eyes filled with tears as she spoke but she didn't move or change her expression. 'An' me an' me dad used t' c'llect pumpkins from m' little bi o' garden,' and then the tears spilled down her face and her voice began to break, but she didn't stop.

'Our Dale allus brought t' apples back from t' orchard whenever 'e saw me an' dad diggin' up me pumpkins.' She sobbed. 'I 'ad me own, little pumpkin-trowel tha' me dad med f' me cos I couldn' use t' big knife, it wer' too long f' me.'

She cried and cried, tears which had been dammed for far too long.

'I 'ad a red wheelbarro' an' I put me pumpkins in there an' pushed it up tut steps, an then Dale 'elped me carry it up, but 'e allus shoved 'is apples in wi' m' pumpkins an' med me push 'em all in t' 'ouse.'

'Me Nan'd be waitin' forrus an' she'd 'elp me get me wellies off while mam unloaded me wheelbarro' and took it all in t' kitchen.'

Alison's tears continued to flood and her chest heaved as she sobbed and spoke.

'Me dad an' Dale would disappear when t' cookin' started, but it wer' my job to ge' all t' seeds out o' pumpkins after me mam 'ad cut 'em in 'alf fo' me. I loved t' feel o' them seeds.

'I loved me mam an' me dad, an' Dale an' me nan, an' now I can't mek pumpkin an' apple soup anymore, cos I can't do it by me self.'

Her little head slowly dropped forward and her face screwed tightly up as the pain she had been carrying for years raged unchecked through her shuddering, piteous sobbing.

Chapter Twenty-Five

The door was left open a crack, Alison lay sleeping on the bed.

'Poor thing. She cried herself to sleep.' Cecily said, taking up a chair back in the living room.

Mathew sat in the opposite chair, a small coffee-table sat between them with their tea on top. 'It's a terrible shame what she's had to go through.' He nodded slowly. 'She's a wonderful, young girl, you know? Caring and brave and as clever as they come.'

'Did she really fight off an attacker?' Cecily asked, picking up her cup.

'Oh! Yes! She certainly did.' He answered, his eyes wide and serious. 'Beat him with my walking staff until he fell bum-up on the road, she did.'

She laughed. 'And she said that you then went to help him?'

'I did. It's one thing to knock him out, but quite another to just leave him without knowing if he was seriously hurt or not.'

Mathew sniffed and rubbed his nose, just the way Alison sometimes did. 'As it happened he *was* alright; he started to come round while I was checking him! I've never run so fast in my life!'

Cecily laughed again. 'I bet you did!' She chuckled. 'But it was still very decent of you to make sure he wasn't injured, there are many who wouldn't have done that. Especially for a homeless person who had just attacked them.'

He nodded, agreeing. 'I know. It's a sad thing to say but it's the truth.'

He sat forward and put his cup back on the table. 'People are becoming as cold and as uncaring as the machines they are taking orders from.'

'Sounds all a bit *conspiracy-theory*, don't you think?' She asked, dropping her own cup back on the table and then standing up. 'The machines doing all of the controlling thing I mean.'

'But it's a truth, Cecily, they really *are* controlling things, but they have been programmed by humans to do it. It's quite ironic really.'

She opened a small cupboard and pulled out a bottle of sherry. 'I haven't had an afternoon-sherry for years' She winked as she returned to her seat.

Mathew held his finger up. 'I have something which I would like you to try if we're going to have afternoon tipples.' His eyes twinkled mischievously. 'It's not sherry mind you.'

He left the room, returning a moment later carrying Jolly's *gift*.

'A homeless man is offering me a drink from a suspiciously unmarked, brown bottle?' Cecily scoffed drily. 'Well they do say you only live once.'

'Yes. Yes they do say that, which is incorrect;' Mathew replied as he unscrewed the bottle. 'You only *die* once, you live every day.'

'Ha! Very good! I like that.'

She held her glass out and Mathew poured her a shot.

'It looks a little bit like wee.' She said as she brought the glass to her nose. She sniffed. 'I can't really smell anything.'

Mathew just sat and watched, fascinated. Should he warn her to take just a sip? Had *he* had any warning? Had *he* taken just a sip?

'How should I drink it?'

'Just throw it back.' He said and raised his own glass.

She did as she was told and swallowed the lot in one go.

Three or four minutes later.

'Are-are you alright, Cecily?' Mathew asked, genuine concern in his voice.

Cecily sat down again. She had stood up and sat down again eight times now in an attempt to catch her wheezing breath. Her face was taught and a little blue.

'Dear, God in heaven!' She rasped. 'Never mind *knock your block off*; that stuff knocked *everything* off! *Bloody hell!*'

Mathew sat back, a swell of relief washing over him.

'Wherever did you get that from and is there any more?' She asked hoarsely.

More? He chuckled. 'A fine lady called Merylin, brews it, she's a good friend of Alison's.'

'It's probably the best *hooch* I have ever had, and I've tried a few; my husband was always brewing *winter-tonics*.'

Mathew raised his own glass, his drink still untouched. 'I'll drink to that.'

He did as Cecily had done and swallowed the whole lot in one go and then went through the usual *recovery* motions while Cecily sat and watched, wide-eyed and grinning.

He shuddered and dropped his glass back onto the table. 'It hits all the spots at once that stuff, doesn't it?'

Cecily just laughed.

'You said your husband used to make stuff like this?' He asked.

'Yes, Mark, He had his own little *chemistry* lab in one of the sheds for the stuff.'

'Merylin was a chemist in her *old* life, so I believe.'

'Well, Mark *did* have a degree in chemical biology.' She told him. 'Looks like great *chemical* minds think alike.'

'Did he? What did he do for a living?'

'Oh, he was a farmer through and through, don't get me wrong, getting his degree was really about the farm; we have a lot of chemicals coming through here.'

She leaned over and poured them both a small sherry. 'Hooch *and* sherry!' She raised an eyebrow. 'On a Sunday afternoon as well.'

Mathew picked up his glass. 'What happened to your husband, if you don't mind me asking?'

She sat back with her sherry in her hand. 'Sadly, he developed Parkinson's disease, it was quite abrupt.'

'I'm sorry to hear that.'

Cecily gave Mathew a weak smile and then took a sip of her drink.

'I lost Mary seven years ago now. One minute she was just getting old like me and the next minute she was gone.' Mathew mused, frowning a little.

The suddenness of his dear friend and wife passing away still puzzled him.

'How did she die?' Cecily asked.

'Pneumonia,' he replied, 'brought on by complications caused by shingles they said.'

He sipped his own drink and stared into the empty space in front of him, remembering the day he had come home and closed the door behind him. The first day he had closed the door alone.

Cecily knew that look, she didn't need to ask, she could see he was doing what she had been doing for the past six years; wondering how it all had changed so suddenly.

'What do you think will become of Alison.' She asked, changing the subject.

Mathew looked up. 'I honestly can't say,' he shrugged a little. 'But I would be inclined to think that she will be okay wherever she ends up.'

'And what about you?'

'What about me?'

'You say that about Alison as though you already plan to not be in her future.' She raised her eyebrows at him. 'Or you don't plan to have a future yourself, is that it?'

He didn't know what to say. She was right though, he hadn't really planned any further than the steps of parliament. But that *was* the plan wasn't it? To sit down and just finish off this life right there. He had been tired when he had set off, he was *still* tired, but something had changed now hadn't it?

'I hadn't really thought about that.' He lied.

Cecily knew nothing of his Facebook statement, but she could see he was holding something back. 'I don't believe that for a minute,' she said. 'I might be a little drunk, but I'm not stupid; you mean to sit down and go on hunger-strike or something don't you?'

Mathew fidgeted uncomfortably. 'Well, no, not exactly. I mean I was just going to sit down and go to sleep or something.' He looked at her innocently. 'You know? Peacefully and without any trouble.'

Cecily stared at him and then a bubble of laughter suddenly escaped her lips. 'Peacefully and without any trouble?' She repeated. 'I'm sorry.' She said and laughed again. 'I know you mean well, but when you say it like that-,' she couldn't help it and just let it all come out.

Mathew just sat and watched.

'Oh! Dear.' She wiped at her eyes, 'I haven't laughed like that for years.' She said, still giggling a little. 'And what a horrid thing to be laughing about really.'

It was Mathew's turn to chuckle. 'I've been laughing since I set off. Before that I'd almost forgotten what it felt like.'

'The irony is awful isn't it?'

'Tell me about it.' Mathew replied. 'I was at my lowest point in my entire life when I set out. It felt like I hadn't smiled for years. Then as soon as I began it all dropped away and I was actually happy.' He threw his arms up in the air. 'I'm *still* blooming happy. Typical.'

'And now you've still got to go and kill yourself on the steps of parliament.' Cecily tutted sarcastically. 'Bummer.'

Mathew did his double-blink thing and then sniffed. 'You're as dark as Alison. You'd get on well you two.' He laughed.

She sipped her drink, her head cocking to one side ever so slightly and then she frowned.

'Something wrong?' Mathew asked.

She shook her head. 'No, no. Well, yes; there's a girl in there who could do wonders in life and isn't getting the opportunities.'

'My feelings exactly.'

Cecily opened her mouth to speak but hesitated. She was wise enough to think things through thoroughly. Especially serious things and more especially after a drink.

Mathew just watched her, unconsciously urging the words to come out, his own mouth twitching at the corners in anticipation.

Finally she sighed heavily and took on a more serious look. 'When you have done what you are going to do, I can see no reason at all why the two of you shouldn't be happy,' she said, 'you could come and stay here. I have plenty of room, Alison would be as free as she is now except safer, and you'll be dead in a few years anyway so…' She shrugged, trailing off. 'Might as well have a comfortable bed.'

Mathew scoffed and tutted. 'Blooming dark, the pair of you.'

He sat forward and picked up the bottle of *Old Nasty* in one hand and the sherry in the other. He looked at them both, studying them equally.

Finally he put the bottle of *Old Nasty* back on the table and poured them both another small sherry. 'I can only speak for myself you understand? But I think we would be idiots of the highest order if we refused.' He raised his glass. 'But I'm seventy-seven, so there'll be no farming.'

'Are you?' She said, surprised.

'Yes. How old did you think I was?'

'Well Alison told me you were three-hundred and fifty.'

'Cheeky dimple. *Ooo three-'undred an' fifty.*' He mimicked Alison. '*Ya three-'undred an' fifty an' y' soft.*'

The pair of them giggled stupidly.

In the other room, Alison lay on the bed wide-awake and smiling.

Wha' a cheek. I don' sound like tha'!

She had heard most of their conversation. Her heart had actually hammered when she had heard Cecily's suggestion.

She really did feel safe here, Cecily was quite *different*. Different in the same way that she, herself was. *Dark* Mathew called it. It made her smile.

Could she start something here, in this place? Maybe. As Mathew said, they would be idiots to not take up an offer like that, if trying meant failing then she would just get back on the road. But she didn't think it would be like that. Not here, not with Mathew *and* Cecily around.

She rolled over onto her back and stretched out on the bed, looking up at the white, painted ceiling.

There was room up there for a poster. Teenagers had posters on the ceiling didn't they?

Her hands found the quilted cover she was laying on. She stroked it, feeling the soft pads of each section, and then she grabbed a handful and dragged it over her head, burying her face in it and breathing it in deeply. This was what *home* smelled like, what it felt like when you buried yourself in it.

She threw the cover back again and sat up on the edge of the bed. She'd best go and have a talk with Mathew and Cecily then.

Chapter Twenty-Six

The humming was fine, but when Singh began actually singing the words, Palmerson found his trigger finger itching.

'*He marched them up to the top of the hill,*
And he marched them-'

'I'm going to shoot you, Singh, I swear to God, I will do it if you don't bloody shut your cake-hole!'

Palmerson didn't even bother to turn around, *couldn't* be bothered to turn around; walking up and down these damn hills was beginning to wear him down.

'Sorry, sir.' Singh quietly said. 'Walking song, that's all.'

Dixon looked over to his partner and smirked, pointing at him childishly for *getting into trouble.*

Singh put his hand in his pocket to retrieve something and then brought it out with his middle finger raised and offered it to Dixon.

Dixon grabbed his belly and silently mimed his forced laughter and then a split-second after that he disappeared downward with a yell, his foot finding the exposed root which his eyes - and the rest of him, particularly his chin - were wishing they had spotted first.

Singh loved it and laughed properly then, hoping that Dixon's fall had been broken by a nice, evening-cooled cow-pat.

Palmerson stopped in his tracks and sighed before turning around.

'You know? I might shoot *both* of you. No one would ever know. I'd just say the target overpowered me and took my weapon.' He mused casually.

'Sorry, sir,' Dixon said, 'I tripped on a root.'

'I don't *care*, lad!' Palmerson voiced, fed up. 'We're tracking our targets and you two are bringing all the noise which a night-forest *doesn't* have with you, you *pillocks*!'

Dixon stood up and brushed himself down, standing almost to attention.

Singh did the same, standing with his chest out and shoulders back a little, mentally noting that unfortunately there was no cow-pat in sight.

'Now,' Palmerson said, his tone dropping. 'Get your stupid heads in the *game* and let's get our *man*, eh?'

They both nodded.

'Good.'

He gave them one, last, hard stare and then turned back and began the hike to the top of this hill again.

The trio had covered almost fourteen miles since they had dumped the cars.

Palmerson had shown them the point that they had to reach, which by his reckoning should be just about at the top of this last hill they were hoisting themselves up.

The hill was half-in, half-out of a forested area, he was certain they would be only a few yards inside the trees somewhere. *You see, lads, they will instinctively make for the higher ground, thinking that it will help them in some way, but they aren't guerrillas, are they? No, they are just silly protesters who think that guerrilla-rules apply to them. Think like an amateur, lads, think like an amateur.*

Palmerson stopped. 'Right, we'll go in from here. Keep your torches on the ground and spread out.'

He pointed to the left. 'Singh, you go down that way, and Dixon,' he pointed to the right, 'you go in that way.'

'What about you, sir?' Singh asked innocently.

Palmerson stared and stared, but it was no use, Singh was still standing there no matter how hard he used the Jedi *force-choke* on him.

'I'll be going down the bloody middle, won't I?' He replied, his voice even lower than before, menacing almost.

Singh pulled his mouth into a tight, sheepish smile and nodded once in acknowledgement. He wordlessly pointed to the left and then made his way to his point of entry.

Palmerson watched him go, trying the *force-choke* just one, more time.

'I'll, um, go this way then, sir.' Dixon said, and slunk off quickly to the right.

'I still might bloody shoot 'em.' Palmerson muttered to himself.

He walked into the forest shaking his head and mumbling things under his breath about *stupidity* and *fools* and *a quick bullet to the head and who would know?* And other, similar musings.

The woody-floor was damp and the smell was of wet earth and musty trees. A light mist was slowly rising from the ground.

The three of them walked silently for almost ten minutes, checking in by flashing their torches up in Palmerson's direction.

Singh stopped and flashed his torch twice, the signal for *contact*.

Good man. Palmerson thought. *Here we go.*

He gathered the other two to him. 'What did you see?' He whispered to Singh.

The three of them were crouched on their haunches in a tight huddle, Palmerson's torch lighting them up from below.

'Nothing, sir, but I heard a female voice.' Singh whispered back.

'Could you hear what she was saying?'

'Um. I think she said something like, *pull 'em*. I'm not sure, sir, it came from further in.'

Palmerson thought for a moment. 'Right, stick together, we'll move forward until we have a clear visual of the situation and then move in from there.' He nodded once and then walked along slowly.

A few minutes later and they all heard voices this time.

Palmerson held his hand up for them to be quiet and then stepped forward again.

Several things happened at once then.

A woman groaned and then shouted *slap it!* Two male voices laughed and another said *oh yea!* And a very big torch was switched on and aimed right in their direction.

'Oh! Three more.' A man cheerfully called out. 'Come on fellas.'

A different female voice giggled and said, *it tickles*.

The three agents looked at one another but no one said anything.

'Come on, we don't bite.' The man said, beaming almost as brightly as his torchlight.

They walked slowly into the circle of several men and women, some of whom had either breasts showing or were standing about with their flaccid willies hanging out of their trousers.

Singh's eyes were popping out of his head while Dixon smirked salaciously and Palmerson just rubbed at his nose-bridge.

'Oh, let's 'av a look at it.' A large, bare-breasted woman said, looking directly at Palmerson.

Singh and Dixon turned and also looked at him.

He in turn looked back at the pair of them. 'Are you bloody mad!? I'm not-.' He stopped short and turned to the crowd, doing his best to avoid the eyes - and breasts - of the woman who had made the request. It was quite easy to avoid her eyes.

'Look, we're not here for-for-' He gestured to them all, the situation, everything. 'For whatever this is. We were expecting to find someone else.'

'Dela.' A man standing further back said.

He stepped forward into the light, his penis swinging left to right as he walked. He placed a foot on the bumper of the car beside him and leaned his arm on his raised knee.

The trio of agents stood and looked into the man's eyes. Hard and steady - rock-steady - gazes which were heroically defying the eye-pulling gravity of his pendulum penis.

'W-what?' Palmerson asked, shocked.

'You were coming to have a look at Dela, want ya?' The man said. 'Legendary is Dela.'

'Um. Well, actually no, we were-'

'Sally-Anne.' The woman said, sidling up to the man with his leg up. 'They were comin' for that bitch Sally-Anne, I bet ya.' She scoffed and folded her arms beneath her prodigious breasts.

Singh couldn't help himself and looked.

She noticed. 'How about you lover-boy?' She said, sliding her eyes up and down him. 'Let's 'av a look?'

Singh blushed and grinned stupidly. 'Um. Thank you.' He said, because he simply had absolutely no idea what else *to* say.

Palmerson and Dixon both turned and gave him questioning looks: *Thank you?*

'So if you aren't up 'ere for Dela or Sally-Anne, then who are you here for?' The man asked.

'I can't reveal that, official business,' Palmerson answered and turned back to resume his hard eye-contact. 'But-'

And then all hell broke loose as two sets of headlights were simultaneously switched on and a voice shouted; 'This is the police! Stay where you are, you are all under arrest!'

Instead of the expected rush and hurry of running feet, the crowd groaned and rolled their eyes, remaining where they were while they just *put themselves away* ready to be *nicked*.

Dixon pointed to the headlights and what was illuminated right in front of them. 'Why did we walk all the way up that hill when there's a road right there?'

Palmerson wanted to slap him. Actually he wanted to shoot him, or anyone for that matter. First bloody doggers and now a road which clearly *wasn't* on the map.

He was in no mood for the local *nit-wit* constabulary.

The two police-cars had two men each inside, they all ran up now and *surrounded* the party.

'Right! You're all nicked!' One of them said. 'Just stay where you are until-'

'I'll not be staying anywhere,' Palmerson said, cutting the officer short. 'I have important business which can't wait, so if you'll excuse us?' He finished, almost growling.

'Stop!' The young police officer called out professionally, his hand automatically resting on the *tazer* on his hip.

Palmerson whirled around on him, his frustration and anger coming to a boiling point.

The young copper instantly caught a glimpse of Palmerson's holstered pistol. 'He's got a gun!' He shouted.

Suddenly three tazers, from three different launchers, found three different parts of Palmerson's body while a thick line of pepper-spray found his face.

He stood on the spot for a few seconds, making a strange, abrupt *ah* sound followed immediately by a fart.

Ah! Thrrt! Ah! Thrrrt! And then he crumpled to the ground, vibrating and moaning while a dark stain spread quickly across his crotch.

'Oh shit!' Dixon groaned.

He snapped it together with a mental slap to his own face and stepped forward. 'Stop it, for God's sake! We're Mi6, we're here on government business.'

'Yea, and I'm an Avenger.' One of the officers said. 'Don't you move!'

Dixon and Singh both pulled out their identification wallets and flicked them open.

The first police officer had a look. 'Oh. Shit.' He muttered, repeating Dixon's sentiment.

'Switch 'em off! Switch 'em off!' He shouted out urgently, fumbling with the knobs on his hand-piece.

The other two did the same, and then withdrew the hooks from Palmerson's twitching body.

The officers all looked at each other. The crowd of doggers all looked at Palmerson. Dixon and Singh looked at their feet.

It was only a minute or so before Palmerson was *with it* enough to groggily sit up. His shoulders ticked and his head flicked to the side of its own accord.

'Y-you f-f-f-f-. Y-you *idiots*!' He said, ticking and twitching at each word.

His eyes were streaming and the beginnings of a red swell could just be seen around the edges. Oddly, he resembled *Count Dracula* as played by Christopher Lee. Well apart from the staining on his crotch, he did.

The officers didn't say anything, but the officer who seemed to be in charge leaned down and took Palmerson's arm.

He nodded at one of the others to come and help him, and between them they dragged the unfortunate, twitching man back onto his feet.

Palmerson bucked and ticked their hands off once he was up and stood there trembling, trying his damnedest to give the officer a hard, cold stare.

The muscles in his face, however, had other ideas and just wouldn't express anything coherent at all, while his eyes were quickly swelling closed.

'I'm sorry, sir,' the officer in charge said, 'but you *are* carrying a pistol; it's not something we are really used to seeing round here.'

Palmerson continued to try and glare. He could feel one eye bulging, but other than that he felt his face was just a puzzled mess.

'So you guys are Mi6 agents then?' It was the woman who asked.

'Yea.' Singh answered her.

'Oh! Go on, give us a look? It'll be like James Bond.'

'You can knock that off as well, Daisy.' The officer said and pointed a finger at the robust woman, raising his eyebrows.

She tutted and rolled her eyes.

'Y-you kn-know h-her?' Palmerson asked, his pelvis thrusting forward uncontrollably.

'Yea, she's married to my brother.' The officer replied and took a casual step away from Palmerson's pelvis.

'Your brother!?' Singh said, frowning. 'What would he say if he knew!?' He asked, unbelieving.

'What would you say if you knew, Pat?' The officer turned to the crowd.

The man who had previously had his leg up on the car bumper, Mr. *Pendulum*, scoffed. 'I'd say you were a spoil-sport for not letting our Daisy have a look, Nev.'

The officer turned back to the agents. 'That's what he'd say.'

Palmerson tried to figure out *what* the hell was happening and *where* the hell he had ended up.

His finger itched; he was sure shooting something would help provide an answer or two, bring a little order back into his world.

Instead he just said; 'I think I want to go back to the car now, you don't happen to have a spare pair of trousers do you?'

Chapter Twenty-Seven

Mathew and Alison had remained with Cecily for another two days, which was good for more than just reasons of resting. For one thing, it meant that the people who were looking for him, whom he had absolutely no knowledge of, were scrambling around in the dark, and for another it gave *the cause*, which Mathew also was completely unaware of, another couple of days to swell its ranks.

But it was time to go on with it now and Cecily had just driven them out of the village and back onto their road.

Oh, they'd argued, all three of them, about just driving there and being done with it.

Mathew and Alison both knew that as easy as that sounded it would haunt them knowing that they hadn't seen it through though, particularly Mathew.

In the end, Cecily had come round to seeing it their way, but insisted she drive them past her fields and back to the road they had been heading for when she had found them.

The three of them stood by her Range-Rover, Mathew and Alison both back in their usual *road-garb*. Their clothes were washed and cleaned, Mathew's Belstaff looked brand-new.

'I won't say *goodbye*,' Cecily said, giving them both a firm look. 'Instead, I'll just say *good-luck* and *safe-journey* and other such drivel.'

They both grinned.

'Thank you, Cecily.' Mathew said. 'We'll be fine and I'm sure we won't be *that* long, but I hope you will keep an eye out for us.'

Alison stepped closer and held her closed hand out.

Cecily opened her own palm beneath and Alison dropped a small, St. Christopher pendant on a slim chain into her hand.

'Tha' wer' m' Nans,' she looked up into Cecily's eyes, 'I'm a bi' lost wi' out it, so I'd like you t' look after it till I ge' back.'

The older woman didn't know what to say, the gesture was as deep as they come.

She delved inside her jumper-top and removed a chain from around her own neck, holding up another St. Christopher, this one a little bigger. 'And this belonged to my father and means a lot to me,' she said, 'I want it back, young lady.'

Mathew watched them both, there was something distinctly *right* about what was happening in front of his eyes.

The moment slowed down and swelled as it gathered up; they were bathed in a bright light, poised with hands held out, each giving and receiving.

The small, upturned face of Alison, her serious eyes meeting the gaze of Cecily's as she bent forward a little, painted a picture of something in Mathew's mind, but he didn't know exactly what it was. All he could sense was that it felt like a preview into something *better*.

And then with an audible *rrriip*, everything gathered back into the present and Mathew was listening to Alison asking him if he was alright.

'What!? Oh, yes. Yes I'm fine.' *Well that was different! What just happened?*

'Y' wer' on another planet by th' looks o' ya.'

'Have you been drinking your *hooch* while our backs have been turned?' Cecily asked, grinning broadly.

'Ha! No,' he laughed, 'I was just thinking, that's all.'

He looked away sheepishly, he didn't like goodbyes either, awkward things they were. 'We'd better get off then.' He muttered and pointed his staff to the way ahead.

He turned back. 'You lead the way.' He then said to Alison.

She looked up brightly and saluted and then turned to Cecily. 'See y' soon, Cecily, an' thanks.'

Cecily smiled back. 'You're welcome, love, I...' She paused and sighed. 'Just get back safely, eh?'

Alison nodded. 'We will.' And then turned to Mathew and the road. 'C'mon then, le's ge' on wi' it.'

They set off, turning and waving until they were out of sight and Cecily had driven back the other way.

Mathew walked with the strangely slowed-down image of Alison and Cecily exchanging their tokens firmly fixed in his head, puzzling it over; that had never happened before. Whatever *that* was.

'Y' quiet.' Alison noted, breaking the silence.

'Aren't I always quiet?'

'No' really.' She replied and wrinkled her nose at him.

He sniffed and wiped the end of his own nose, the way she sometimes did, and then looked ahead passively. 'I'll try to make more noise from now on then, shall I?'

* * *

The irony of Mathew's words that day would forever be lost on the world, no history books would remember that particular exchange.

Which was a pity really because almost to the hour of him saying those words to Alison, a university student in Dijon, France, called Rupert Gasiley, had decided - just for the hell of it - to try and make a mathematical model which would predict the day and time, to the hour, that *The Freedom Walker* would arrive at parliament.

All a bit of *mathematical* fun until he had published his findings on his Facebook page.

The Freedom Walker website had a small team of site-administrators who were constantly gleaning data from all over the Internet in their tireless search for news and sightings of Mathew.

One of those *admins* had come across Rupert's interesting experiment and had published it on the main page.

Now, that alone wasn't enough for what happened next. No, it was the very first entry in the comments-box attached to the article for the public to use for discussion which was the *pebble on the pond.*

Mrs. Velda Grosche, had innocently written: *"If everyone went to their governments at the same time that Mr. Arnold did, we could all hold our hands up and shout, NO! I'M THE FREEDOM WALKER! :)"*

Within twelve hours of that message going up, thousands of minds had all made the very same *sound*; *"Hmm."* Which often preceded the words; *"I wonder."*

Fate was having a ball!

* * *

Night and the darkness had a helping hand tonight in the thick, dark clouds which were covering the entire sky. The sun had tried its hardest all day to come out but had slid away unseen.

Debden wasn't too far away, so Alison had taken them westward across the lands and away from the RAF town instead.

'Will no' mek it inta town, it'll rain in a bi'.' She'd said.

'It's getting chilly as well.'

'A kno' a place abou' four miles tha' way. Some old RAF 'owses.'

They had walked the four miles and just as Alison had said, there were rows and rows of empty, post-war, prefabs lining empty, weed-crazed roads. It was like something from a ghost story.

'It wer' 'Amish 'oo told me abou' this place when I first come down t' London.'

Mathew had been quietly stunned. So many houses, all those roads and pavements. Empty. Why were they empty? So much could be done with all of these houses, so much good.

They walked down a long, lonely street, lined with tidy rows of houses all with their *eye-windows* sadly looking out at them, unlit and lifeless.

'You say Hamish told you of this place?'

'Yea, when I firs' met 'im.'

Mathew thought about it. 'So you weren't with Merylin and the others for long?'

'I've known 'em for abou' a year. I wer' jus' passin' through, like you wer'.'

He nodded. 'I see. And then you went to London after meeting them all.' It wasn't a question.

'Yea. Even though the' all tried t' talk me owt of it.'

Mathew chuckled. 'Well, you ended up back up there with them so I'm guessing they were right?'

'The' wer',' she answered, and laughed, 'I 'ad t' see f' mesen though. Wish I 'ant bothered.'

'*Myself.*' Mathew said.

'*Myself,*' she repeated, 'I had to see for *myself.*' She piped, her face taking on that universal, *raised-eyebrow-long-nose* look of imitated *poshness*.

'You know, if you talked like that in your normal voice you'd be good enough to read the news?'

'The *news*!' She scoffed. 'Oo thee 'eck would wan' t' read the flippin' news!? All tha' doom an' gloom, I bet most of 'em a' depressed an' suicidal!'

She straightened up and held an invisible microphone up to her mouth. 'Good evening,' she began, her English perfect and her voice almost completely normal. 'This is Alison Scrimpletop reporting from a deserted, RAF, housing estate. I'm joined by Mathew Tickletwit,' she held her mic out. 'Could you tell us, Mathew, about what it is we are seeing here today?'

Mathew had a face as round as his eyes and mouth; what a completely different person Alison had become just by sounding her *p's* and *q's.*

'You're completely mad.' He answered and smiled.

'As you can see,' she said, taking her mic back and talking to the *camera* rolling along in front of them. 'The only inhabitant of this lonely town is almost certainly senile and probably Hoovers the lawn in just his underpants.'

Mathew choked and wheezed, laughing.

'And it leaves this reporter with a saddening feeling that she will be opening her vodka this evening and washing down half-a-dozen horse tranquilisers before bed.'

Mathew slapped his thigh as they walked - which was fast becoming a little more like a stagger than a real walk.

'This is Alison Scrimpletop, for Gloom O'clock news, wishing you all goodnight and that I was dead.' She finished.

It was no good, Mathew had to stop; he couldn't breathe, laugh *and* walk at the same time, not with any semblance of coordination he couldn't anyway. 'That's one of the funniest things I've ever heard!' He wheezed. 'You should be on the telly.'

'Y-you'll b-b-both end up on *C-crimestoppers* if you g-g-get any l-louder.'

Mathew's laughter was snapped away by his greedily, beating heart and the filling of his lungs as he gasped - squeaked almost.

The pair of them whirled around to face a tall, security-guard, a young man in his late-twenties.

He held his hands up and stayed his ground. 'D-d-don't w-worry, I'm not here to k-k-kick you off.' He stuttered. 'It's m-my job to c-c-come up here and ch-ch-ch-,' his face screwed up as he struggled to get the word out. 'To make sure it's empty.' He quickly finished.

Mathew and Alison looked at one another guiltily.

'It-it-it's okay,' the guard said, his head twitching with the word. 'I f-find a lot of homeless p-p-people up here. As long as they're n-not setting f-f-fire to the p-place, I k-keep my m-mouth sh-shut.'

Alison was impressed and nodded her head.

'Well that's very decent of you, young man.' Mathew spoke, equally impressed. 'My name's Mathew, and this is Alison.'

'G-george.' He replied and then took a small step closer, peering at them both in the quickly fading light. 'M-M-Mathew Arnold? The F-F-Freedom W-Walker?'

Mathew scoffed. 'Apparently so.'

He turned to Alison. 'What's your flipping name then? How come I get a super-hero name and you can remain anonymous?'

The guard called George, stepped right up to Mathew now, his face beaming and his hand held out.

'It-it-it-' he tried. He stopped and took a deep breath, his eyes flickering at the same time. 'It-it's s-such an honour!' He finally managed to get out.

Mathew took his hand and shook it, flushing with embarrassment.

Alison smirked and then blushed madly herself when George side-stepped to her and stooped down, offering the same hand.

'It-it's an honour t-to m-m-meet *b-both* of y-you.' He said. 'Y-y-you're m-much s-s-smaller than in-in-in your photos.' He cheekily added.

His radio suddenly crackled and then a male voice *scratched* out. '*Base to G-man. Come in.*'

He flushed as his *nickname* blared out from the box on his hip. He pulled it out and smiled awkwardly at Mathew and Alison. 'G-G-man here, g-g-g-go ahead.'

There was a short pause and then the radio crackled again. '*Be a dear and nip into Neptune's and get us a bag o' chips on ya way back will ya, flower?*'

'W-w-will d-do.' He returned, his blush now positively glowing.

There was another short pause, then; '*Ya didn't use my handle, G-man, is everything okay? We said that if we don't use our handles we know that there's trouble; is there trouble, G-man?*' The voice asked.

George the security-guard laughed weakly and gave Mathew and Alison a sheepish look, then quickly turned away and spoke into the radio. 'If I w-w-was in t-t-trouble, what w-would the p-p-point be in asking m-me?'

'*So you're in trouble then?*'

'N-no, I'm f-f-fine.'

'*But you didn't use my handle?*'

'Sorry, I f-f-forgot.' George lied.

There was yet another pause and then the voice said; '*How do I know you're not just saying that?*'

'Why w-would I j-just say that if I w-w-wasn't!?' He almost hissed.

'*Maybe you said it under duress, a gun to the head or something?*'

George gave Mathew and Alison another sheepish look and smile.

They just stood and blinked, both of them wondering if *base* and George weren't married or something.

'I'm f-f-fine! F-for G-g-god's sake, I f-f-forgot!'

The radio clicked and a static-sigh crackled through. '*Okay, I'll let it go this time, G-man, but we have to talk about what we do if you forget to use my handle again. And don't forget me chips.*'

'R-r-roger. I w-won't f-f-forget.'

And then quickly ended with a rush of unintelligible syllables which were meant to be the other guy's handle.

'*What?*'

'I s-s-said-' and the very same, strangely misshapen and rushed syllables were ejected.

'*I'm not getting that, G-man. Please repeat. Over.*'

'I said; *George's Glitter-pony.*' The words came out perfectly. Perfectly and with plenty of volume.

'*Thanks, G-man, that really hits the* Spot. *Over and out.*'

If he had blushed any harder he would have bled from his eyes.

He turned around and faced Mathew and Alison again.

They were both trying their utmost to be polite and not laugh.

'Th-th-that w-was b-b-b-'

'Glitter-pony. We kno'.' Alison finished for him, her face bright and unnaturally cheery-cheerful.

Mathew wheezed quietly by her side and studied his walking boots; he hadn't noticed Cecily had cleaned these as well.

Chapter Twenty-Eight

The very last house, at the furthest edge of the empty, RAF housing-estate, had the only glow coming from the windows for miles around.

A coal-fire crackled and popped in a proper fireplace and there were several comfortable seats and even a carpet.

'We d-d-did all th-th-this.' George told them as they sat and drank his *flask* tea. 'Th-th-th-there's p-p-plenty of c-c-coal and th-the w-w-water works in-in-in the k-kitchen.'

'Why'd y' do it?' Alison asked. 'A place y' can come an' ge' away from it all forra bit?'

George shook his head. 'N-n-no.' His mouth dropped at the corners. 'I f-f-found th-three homeless p-p-people sh-sh-sheltering in one of th-the houses b-b-back n-near the entrance. F-f-four years ago n-now. It w-w-were C-C-Christmas Eve. All th-th-three of th-them were s-s-suffering f-f-from hy-hy-hy-' he struggled, his head twitching as it snagged on the word.

'Hypothermia?' Mathew suggested.

George nodded quickly, drawing his breath in sharply. 'I m-m-managed to g-get them to ho-ho-hospital, b-b-but one of them d-d-didn't m-m-ma-,' his head dropped and he sighed. He couldn't say it, even now.

He looked up again and his eyes were shining. 'Th-th-that should n-n-n-never have happened.' He said. 'Th-th-that old w-w-woman shouldn't have d-d-died l-like that. N-n-not at C-Christmas, n-n-not at any t-time.'

Mathew and Alison both met his gaze, silently agreeing with him.

He stood up and walked to a box beneath the window.

Opening it, he pulled out a red, woollen blanket for them to see. 'Th-th-there's p-plenty of b-b-blankets.' He told them. 'Th-they're used b-but clean; w-w-we wash th-them once a m-month.'

'I 'ant bin on t' road as long as some 'av,' Alison said to him as he came back and joined them, 'bu' I can tell ya tha' thes no' many people 'oo would do wha' your doin'.'

Mathew nodded. 'I haven't been on the road at all really and I can say the same thing, George; we could do with more of these places and people like you.'

George smiled and looked down, embarrassed. 'W-w-we've done another th-th-three of th-these, me and D-D-D-'

'Glitter-pony?' Alison chimed.

'D-D-Darren, but y-yea,' George laughed, 'Glitter-p-p-pony.'

'Three more?' Mathew was even more impressed. 'Do they get used often?'

'W-w-winter m-mostly. S-six or s-s-seven is the m-m-most I've ever s-seen in here.'

Mathew scanned the room. 'Remarkable.' He muttered. 'You and your partner - he is your partner I take it, Darren?' He asked, facing George again.

George nodded.

'You two are providing three of the four, basic needs for safe living; warmth, shelter and water.' Mathew continued. 'Amazing generosity, young man.'

George blushed again and smiled, pointing through to the kitchen. 'W-w-we p-put a f-f-f-few tins of s-soup and c-c-c-canned f-f-fruit in the c-cupboards as well.'

Mathew just shook his head in astonishment. 'I should have guessed really.' He said. 'What makes you do it though? I mean, you've told us about the three homeless people you found, but it can't be just about that,' he gestured around the room, 'all this.'

George shrugged. 'W-why are y-y-you going to p-p-p-parliament?'

He turned and pointed out of the front window. 'All th-that out th-there b-b-b-belongs to the g-g-government and it's b-being left to r-rot while human-b-beings are f-f-f-freezing to d-death in shop-d-d-doorways.'

'Th-there isn't a s-s-single person on this p-planet that can t-t-tell me that's r-right. I know w-w-what's r-right, and empty h-h-houses while th-th-there's p-people living on th-the streets isn't.'

Alison stood up and crossed to where George was sitting. Bending over, she wrapped her arms tightly around his neck. 'Yer a 'ero t' those people, George, a proper 'ero.' She said and then stood back. 'In t' olden days, where Mathew comes from,'

'Eh? What? Oi!'

She cutely wrinkled her nose up at him and then turned back to George. 'You'd a bin med a knight, you an' Sir Glitter-pony, f' what y' doin'.'

She sat back down.

George laughed. 'S-sir Gl-itter-p-pony? He'll l-l-love that.'

He sat with them for another hour and talked, telling them about his life and listening to them about theirs, but it was soon fully dark and he had to go back out on the round.

'W-will y-you be here in the m-m-morning?' He asked.

Mathew looked to Alison.

She just shrugged. 'Will probly be mekin a move when t' sun's come fully up.'

George shuffled his feet uncomfortably and smiled his sheepish smile.

Alison's head cocked to one side and she frowned as she watched him. 'Y wan' t' come back wi' Glitter-pony an' ge' a selfie don' ya?'

He scoffed. 'Ha. N-n-no of c-course n-not,' he said, shaking his head and chuckling feebly, not meeting anyone's gaze. 'N-no, no,' he continued and then, 'unless th-that w-w-would b-be okay?' He looked at them both hopefully. 'W-w-we'd b-bring b-b-breakfast. G-G-G-Glitt- I m-mean, D-D-Darren w-would love to m-meet you.'

Alison didn't notice, but George had been looking specifically at *her* when he had said that.

She folded her arms. 'I knew it.'

Mathew stood up creakily. 'That's very kind of you. Again.'

'G-great! I'll see y-y-you in the m-morning.' He held his hand out.

Mathew took it and shook. 'Goodnight, George, and thank you.'

'Nigh' George. Thanks.' Alison said and raised her hand.

He left them with a smile, closing the front door behind him and then jogging off back down the road and to his waiting van.

'I bet 'e f'gets his chips.'

Morning came. They had both slept comfortably using the cushions from the chairs as mattresses laid out in front of the glowing fire.

They spent ten minutes putting everything back in order and stoking the fire back up for tea.

No sooner was the water boiling, they both heard voices drifting up the path outside. One of them was George's, who seemed to have all but lost his stutter.

'Just another m-minute, D, patience. Patience.' He was saying.

'I can't believe you dragged me all the way out here, this early, on my day off for a bacon sarni.' The *camp* voice accompanying him replied.

The front door opened and a huge man walked in. He stopped dead in his tracks when he saw the room wasn't empty.

He was a little taller than George, but much more *built up*. His huge, tight muscles bulged through his equally tight clothing.

And then his eyes fell on Alison and he gasped, clutching at his chest.

'OH! EM! GEE!' He blurted. 'It's *you*, it's really you.' He sucked his breath in, his lips trembling. 'Oh. My. God!' There were actual tears in his eyes.

Alison looked terrified.

Mathew looked at her and grinned, satisfied. *Ha!*

The big man, who was no doubt Glitter-pony, rushed up to Alison and stooped down, gathering her up in a bear-hug embrace. 'Oh. YOU are my HERO!'

Alison was crushed between his muscles. 'Fanks.' Her smothered, tiny, faraway voice answered. Not that anyone heard.

She felt herself being whirled around.

'And you? Come here!' Darren said and wrapped an arm around George's neck, pulling him forward. He kissed him on the cheek with a heavy *smack*. 'How did you keep quiet all night about that? No wonder you forgot me chips.'

He released George and then bent down, plopping Alison back on her feet.

She took a deep breath and blew the fringe out of her eyes. 'You mus' b' Glitter-pony, then?' She said.

He clutched his chest again and the corners of his mouth drooped suddenly and he did cry then. 'Oh! You called me by my *special* name. That means so much to me.' His voice was cracked as he spoke. 'Thank you.' He squeaked.

He turned to George. 'She called me by my *special* name.'

George put his arm around him and looked at Mathew and Alison. 'You'll have to bear with us; Darren's on hormone treatment to combat the effect of s-steroids.'

Darren sniffed. 'I am, I am.' He confirmed, nodding and sniffing again.

Both Mathew and Alison were silently relieved to hear that; for one, alarming moment it had felt like they had fallen into a psycho-movie, and the psycho was a huge, bulking, testosterone-filled hulk with muscles in his spit.

Alison changed the subject. 'Wha' 'appened t' ya stutter?' She asked George, taking a seat and drinking her tea.

He just looked at Darren. 'He did.'

Darren sniffed and wiped his eyes. 'Oh shurrup, ya big puff.' And then hugged him.

He turned to Mathew then. 'I'm sorry, I didn't even say hello.' He held out his hand. 'Darren.' He said, 'it's an honour, it really is.'

'Mathew,' Mathew replied and shook Darren's hand. 'But I suspect you already know that.'

'Oh, yes, I think everyone knows Mathew Arnold, *The Freedom Walker*, by now.'

Mathew scoffed. 'I don't know *that* many people.' He said and looked at Darren and George. He could see they weren't humouring him. 'Really?' He then asked, his brow rising into a questioning frown.

'Well yea! Hello!' Darren said, rolling his eyes. 'You have a website with-' He paused while he flipped open his phone and swiped at the screen. 'Just over eight million visitors.'

'Eh?' Mathew grunted.

Darren looked at George.

George just shrugged and curled his lip.

The big man turned back to Mathew and Alison. 'Your website?'

Neither of them responded with anything more than another look at each other and another shrug of the shoulders.

'You don't know about the website?' Darren asked, folding his arms and looking at them as though they were in trouble.

'Um. No.' Mathew replied.

'Or the fund whose total is now up to-' He swiped his phone some more. 'Four and a half million?'

Mathew slumped to the chair behind him, loudly, while Alison leaped to her feet and dropped her cup.

'*Four million quid!*' She shouted.

Mathew echoed the same words, but very quietly.

'Oh! Good, Lord.' He said. 'Whatever is happening?'

''Oo's gettin all t' money?' Alison asked Darren.

He shifted weight from foot to foot uncomfortably. 'You really didn't know?' He asked, shaking his head.

'No, we dint. 'Oo's gettin' t' money?' She asked again.

'It's not going to any charity that we know of, the fund is for *World* homelessness.'

Alison's face took on a look of thunder. 'If a charity ge's tha' money, t' 'omeless won't see a penny of it!'

Mathew, George and Darren, all gave Alison a puzzled look.

'Th-that's a bit cynical isn't it?' George said.

She stared at him, at all of them. They could see she was clearly furious about something.

'Is it?' She answered darkly. 'Well le' me ask you a question; 'ow long 'av these *charities*,' she almost spat the word, 'bin goin?'

The three of them exchanged looks between themselves, hoping for an answer.

Mathew spoke. 'Most charities have been going for years, Alison,' he replied, 'hundreds, some of them, they're well-established.'

'Exactly!' She shouted, looking at each of them in turn as though the answer were obvious - which in reality it was. 'If a charity 'as bin goin' f' so long, then it's no' *workin'*, is it!? It's no' curin' t' problems tha' it sez it will!'

Her voice lowered. 'The' no' charities. The' businesses! Successful, long-standin' businesses 'oos resource is misery an' conflick.

'If y' put all t' charities t'gether an' added up all t' money the'd raised, it would 'av solved every, single social-problem aroun' t' world and 'av enough spare t' feed t' greedy fat-cats. But no, the' 'av t' 'av it all.'

Darren looked at her proudly and clutched his beefy chest, the tears threatening to make an appearance again. 'I knew I was right about you.'

He held his large hand out, snapping his fingers for Alison to take it.

She held his hand while he squeezed hers gently.

'From the first moment I saw a picture of you,' he carried on, 'I could see you were a *giant* - I actually said the words didn't I?' He said, turning to George.

George nodded. 'You did.' He answered, and then to Alison; 'He did.'

'A *giant*, Alison.' Darren carried on. 'Just listening to you speak just then,' he stood back and clutched his heart again. 'A *giant*.' He repeated.

Mathew sniffed and sat quietly, staring stunned into the empty space in front of him. 'Mary and I gave to charities for years. I never would have thought of it like that.'

'You an' everyone else *up 'ere*.' Alison said, meaning everyone who lived in a house. 'Why *would* ya question it? You wer' bein' distracted wi' yer own worries tha' hav' bin created f' ya. Ya dint 'av *time* t' ask other questions, Mathew. All part o' t' plan.'

She didn't sound condescending, on the contrary, she actually sounded more like she was teaching a class.

She sat back down and poured herself more tea, calming herself back down.

'It does make you feel a bit s-stupid though, doesn't it?' George said.

'People can be *really* stupid.' Mathew added and held his cup out to Alison.

George and Darren took up chairs and allowed Alison to pour them a cup of tea each.

'It-it's that stupid side of us that they exploit.' George said.

Alison nodded. 'Yea. Sometimes t' problem's righ' on t' end o' ya nose but y' jus' don' see it, an' the' 'no tha', the' use tha' against ya.'

'It's almost as if we have given over our consciences to a business!' Mathew suddenly surmised. 'The same way we've given away the control of our food and shelter and common-blooming-sense.'

George and Darren nodded vehemently, agreeing.

'Now y' seein' it.' Alison nodded. 'More tea?'

Chapter Twenty-Nine

That was the fourth police-car she had seen in the last ten minutes. And in Debden of all places. It could only mean one thing; the hunt for *The Freedom Walker* was intensifying.

The most recent *selfie*, taken by two, Debden-based security-guards, could be the only reason the police were patrolling in and out of the small town.

Diane leaned against the bonnet of her car and flicked through her messages on her phone. She was waiting for a reply from Edmund. It began vibrating and ringing in her hand. The man himself.

'Hello?'

'*Right, I can't be bothered to fingers-and-thumb all of this in a text so listen. You were right; a quietly placed bulletin went out to the police force, two days ago. I don't know what the content was, but going by what you've told me I think we can assume it was telling them to look for Mathew Arnold.*'

'I knew it!' She snapped. 'What about the security firm, did you get an address?'

'*I did, I'll email it to you when I hang up.*'

'Okay. Thanks, Edmund.'

'*One other thing, Diane; I have a gut feeling that now Arnold is as close as he is, the powers that be will have to think about using* their *media-outlets to begin a counter-offensive, if you know what I mean?*'

She frowned and thought about what Edmund was implying. 'What do you suggest?'

She heard him sigh and then say; '*I think it's about time our little newspaper made the leap into television reporting.*'

She waited for the punchline. It didn't come. 'You're serious?'

'*Yes, absolutely. If the* big-boys *get in there first they'll destroy and discredit the whole story in the evening-news and it'll be done and dusted by the following morning's breakfast-show.*'

He was right, but what could *they* do? 'As much as I agree and see your point, Edmund, I can't see how we can do it.'

'*You leave that to me.*' He said cryptically. '*So you wouldn't be against taking on a cameraman and presenting this thing?*'

'Well no, of course not, but-'

'*Good, that's all I wanted to hear from you.*'

For a rare moment, Diane Jones was at a loss for words.

Eventually she spoke. 'Okay. Okay, let's do this, but *why*, Edmund? Where has cautious, *fasten-all-your-seat-belts-and-don't-sleep-in-you-car*, Edmund gone?'

He sighed again, she could almost hear his mind trying to put the answer into words she would understand.

'*I'm terrified, Diane.*' Was all he could think of.

'Oh, Edmund-' she soothed.

'*I'm serious.*' He said, cutting her off. '*Something is about to happen and for once in my life I have no idea what it might be, only that it terrifies me.*'

They both remained respectfully silent for a moment, Diane wondering what it was that Edmund had *sensed*. She knew him well, she had often thought that his intuition bordered on the *uncanny* sometimes.

She slowly released her breath and spoke. 'I'm not sure what it is that's got you so *on edge*, Edmund, but I trust you.'

'*Thanks,*' he sounded tired. '*I'm not really certain I trust myself, but thanks, Jones. Keep your phone handy; I've a few calls to make and then I'll get back to you with a cameraman and a plan.*'

'Okay, I'll speak to you later. And, Edmund? Go and stand in the *lavender* room and have a coffee. It'll clear your mind.'

He scoffed and then laughed. '*That bloody colour. I made a right old pig's-ear with that one didn't I?*'

'You did. It's horrendous, but it does have that subtle ability to *blast* all thoughts straight from ones head with its screaming, auroral phosphorescence, so you might as well use it for the one thing it is good for.'

Edmund guffawed loudly. '*Screaming, auroral phosphorescence!?*'

Diane smiled to herself. 'I'll see you later, Edmund, don't forget to mail the address of the security firm.'

'*I'll do it now,*' he answered, still laughing, '*see you later.*'

She could hear him chuckling as he hung up, still muttering s*creaming, auroral phosphorescence* and then laughing again.

A minute later and her phone chimed in her hand; the address from Edmund.

The place wasn't far from where she was now.

* * *

His back was still aching, bruised and holed from the *tazering*. The skin around his eyes itched and was driving him mad as it flaked away leaving a thin, red welt. He looked like a well-fed heroin-addict.

Palmerson smoked his cigarette, his back pressed up against the wall of the porta-cabin office of *Debden Security* as he stood and waited.

They'd been here for half-an-hour and there was still no sign of anyone opening up. The van they could see in the *selfie* was nowhere in sight either.

Dixon sat in Palmerson's big, four-wheel drive. He had his head resting back and his eyes closed.

Singh, on the other hand, was in Debden, sitting in his own car at the crossroads, watching for any sign of the security-van.

Or to be more precise; at that very moment he was walking back from the small bakery on the high-street, a steaming cheese and onion slice in his hand. And around his mouth and chin. And down the front of his neat, black suit, left knee and a little bit of melted cheese on the left shoelace.

The wind had picked up a little today and every bite of the cheese-slice sent a *puff* of pastry flying off behind him, while any of the heavier stuff inside the slice not making it into his mouth, paid homage to the fine cloth of his suit.

He walked along happily smiling and content - as he usually was when eating.

And that's just how Diane Jones found him when he almost bumped into her as she was climbing back into her car.

'Oh! Sorry! I-' Singh began.

He stopped when he saw it was his *windswept-angel*. 'It's you!'

Little bits of flaked–pastry fluttered magically around his face in the wind as he broke out into a stupid grin.

'Hello again, fancy seeing *you* here.' Diane replied, quickly recovering from her shock.

She leaned closer and spoke in a lowered tone. 'You're not after *aliens* down here are you?'

She made sure her eyes were nice and round and shiny and in his face.

The cheese-slice made a hasty disappearance into his pocket while the rest of it, still around his face and on his clothing, remained exactly where it was, unnoticed. Well, unnoticed by himself at least.

He smiled radiantly through pastry-caked lips. 'No, no, not aliens, but we're still looking for *The Freedom Walker*.'

It was his turn to lower his voice. 'He's been here.' He said, giving her a knowing look and tapping the side his nose.

Diane looked astonished. 'No!' She breathed.

Singh nodded. 'Yea. We're hot on his trail as we speak.' He cast his *trained* eye around his immediate area as though *The Freedom Walker* could make an appearance at any time. It came to rest on Diane again. 'What are you doing here anyway?' He asked.

'Oh, work.' She replied, casually gesturing behind her.

'Oh, right, you work here?'

'Um, no.' Diane answered, evading as best as she could.

She wouldn't lie, it was part of being a *good* journalist to be able to tell the truth and still get what you want, but she wouldn't volunteer the information either if she could help it.

'Oh, I see.' He said. He didn't. 'No, I don't.' He laughed.

'I'm here on business for my job.' Then before he could ask any further questions, she indicated the small cafe across from where they were standing. 'And I was just about to grab a late breakfast and a coffee.'

She looked right at him, not exactly *fluttering her eyelashes* at him, but a more *professional* version of something similar.

He darted his eyes from cafe to Diane and back again several times.

'Um.' Was she asking him to join her or was she telling him goodbye? He was crap in these situations.

Luckily for him, Diane saw his uncertainty - which she thought was warm and cute and endearing, something she quite liked about him if she were to be honest.

'If you're not in a hurry to capture *The Freedom Walker* you could join me?'

He grinned and then laughed. 'We're not going to *capture* him, not like that anyway, the poor fella's done nothing wrong. I think the people *up there*,' he pointed up, 'just want to help him that's all.'

His naiveté added another warming mark in his favour, not to mention referring to Mathew Arnold as *poor fella*.

She linked her arm through his. 'So you have time for a coffee then?'

And for the second time in a week, Agent Singh happily sang his heart out for his *windswept-angel*.

Palmerson, on the other hand, was anything *but* happy. The bloody security-firm's office was still closed and no one had been in or out of the yard since they had been there. Two bloody hours now.

He threw the most recent cigarette butt onto the ground in front of him and crushed it spitefully beneath his shoe, as if to blame the butt for everything.

It lay there, sadly broken, alongside the other fallen *butt* comrades, a small graveyard of them.

Turning to face the car and the still-snoozing Dixon, Palmerson placed two fingers between his lips and whistled loudly.

Dixon sat bolt-upright and blinked rapidly, looking around dazed.

'Get yourself out of whatever dirty, little dream you were having, lad, and come over here.'

The yawning Mi6 agent climbed out of the car and walked briskly to where Palmerson stood.

'Sir?'

'I'm getting ruddy sick of waiting here; go and have a talk with the local *piggies* and see if you can get some info on these clowns.' Palmerson said, thumbing over his shoulder and indicating the porta-cabin. 'See if they have a home address for any of them or something.'

'Right away, sir.' Dixon replied and made for his car.

'And, Dixon?'

'Sir?' He answered, stopping and turning around.

'Don't fall asleep at the wheel, lad.' Palmerson drawled sarcastically.

Dixon meekly nodded. 'No, sir.' And trotted on to his car.

Once he had gone, Palmerson walked back to his own vehicle and opened the door. He leaned inside and retrieved a packet of mints, taking one and popping it in his mouth. He threw the packet back on the seat and closed the door.

'Can I help you?' A *mincy*, male voice said.

Palmerson whirled around and his mint zipped back and straight down his throat, lodging perfectly in his windpipe.

His eyes bulged, not least because of the enormous man standing in front of him.

The man's pink, tie-dyed shirt looked like it had come from the body of a werewolf victim; there was more skin showing than was being covered, and the skin which *was* covered was bulging with that much muscle that it stretched the shirt to *skintight* anyway.

Darren - Glitter-pony - took a helpless step back and looked on in horror as the man in front of him began changing colour. And what was wrong with his eyes!?

'Do you need help?' He asked shyly, unconsciously clutching at his own throat.

Palmerson gagged, pointing to his back, and tried to *mime* that he needed it hitting because he was choking.

Miming that you are choking when you actually *are* choking can be very confusing, not to mention quite funny to watch if you are *that* way inclined.

Fortunately for Palmerson, Darren wasn't *that* way inclined, nor was he thick, and quickly grasped the situation.

'OH-EM-GEE! You're choking aren't you?'

He rushed around the back of the now almost blue Palmerson, and wrapped his huge arms around the choking man's podgy waist.

He thrust into Palmerson's back and pulled his abdomen at the same time, then relaxed a little allowing Palmerson's body to drop forward before he heaved and thrust again.

On the third *heave-and-thrust*, Dixon walked back into the yard.

He'd spotted the very van they were looking for parked in a side-ally which ran all the way up to the top of this high-fenced yard. There was a small side-gate standing open where the van was, so he had left his car on the main road and then walked back to the gate.

For one, brief moment Dixon's eyes met the bulging, red eyes of his commander, but his feet had seen enough and without breaking stride, turned him about-face and marched him back out to the car and out of sight.

He slumped into the driver's seat and scanned the blank sky through the windscreen, purposely avoiding the rear-view mirror where his eyes were waiting to beg him to gouge them out.

It was a lovely, cool day, he thought, *almost like a bummer morning than an autumn afternoon.*

Back in the yard, Palmerson wheezed at every pounding his stomach and backside was given, but the damn mint remained firmly fixed. He could feel it burning *mintily* in his windpipe.

And then Singh had turned into the yard in his car, followed by another, smaller car being driven by a young woman. She was holding her phone up he could see.

Darren was getting more and more worried that the Heimlich wasn't having any effect and began thrusting and pulling even harder and faster. '*Come on! Come on, you little bugger!*' He snarled.

Heave-thrust-heave-thrust.

'*Come on!*'

Heave-thrust.

'*Come!*'

Heave.

'*On!*'

Thrust-*POP!*

The mint flew several feet across the small yard, coming to rest at the feet of Diane Jones, mobile phone still in hand.

Chapter Thirty

Diane had managed to *escape* unexposed when Palmerson had finally gathered himself up and told her, in no subtle way, that this was an *official* matter and that she had better not have been filming.

He'd whipped his ID out, flashing his pistol at the same time, trying - unsuccessfully - to regain the control and show them *just who was boss!*

Dev - he'd told her to call him Dev instead of agent Singh - bless him, had stepped in and saved her.

'She was just lost, sir. I told her to follow me here and we would point her in the right direction. As a good agent of the crown would be expected to do. Sir.'

Well, what could Palmerson do or say to that?

She drove her car down the road and pulled off a hundred yards along, parking out of sight to wait.

She didn't have to wait more than half-an-hour before the black, four-wheel drive pulled out and disappeared over the hill in the other direction.

She didn't know for certain, but she sort of felt that the man called Palmerson was behind the wheel by the *angry* sort of way it growled away.

The other two followed a few seconds later and then Diane drove back to the yard.

She pulled up outside the office and the walked to the open door.

The big man who had saved Palmerson from his minty death sat behind a desk, wiping his eyes as though he had just been crying.

'Um. Are you okay?' She enquired gently.

His big, wet blue eyes looked up sharply.

'Oh! I'm absolutely *fabulous*!' He said sarcastically, almost shouting the word *fabulous*. 'Why wouldn't I be? I mean I've only saved a fat, zombie-eyed stranger from choking to death, who turns out to be *Ghengis*-bloody-*Hitler*!'

He sniffed and then sobbed. 'He called me a *pooh-pushing deviant* and a *brown-beard jockey*! I mean-,' he threw his arms up helplessly, 'what is wrong with people?'

He sighed shakily and then sat up straight, abruptly composed. 'Can I help you?'

Diane walked to the desk and sat in the chair where Palmerson had previously been abusing Darren from.

'I'm a reporter.' She said and held out her hand. 'Diane Jones.'

Darren hesitated for a moment and then gently took Diane's fingertips and shook them once. 'Darren.'

He sat back and closed himself off by folding his arms. She could see he didn't trust her.

'Weren't you lost?' He asked her.

'Um. No. I'm following a story.'

His suspicion deepened. 'About the Freedom Walker?'

'Yes.'

His chin stiffened. 'I'm not saying anything.' He said and turned a cheek. 'I'll say to you what I said to *them*,' he looked back at her, the most stubborn look on his face she had ever seen anyone give. 'We gave them a lift to the motorway and that's it.'

He looked away again, raising his nose.

Well she knew *that* was a lie for a start; Alison wouldn't have taken them anywhere *near* the main roads let alone the motorway.

'And they believed you?' She asked, fully understanding where this big, soft lug of a man was coming from.

He cast a worried glance at her. 'Why wouldn't they? It's the truth.'

'No it isn't, but we'll come back to that.' She quickly answered. 'Are you *certain* that they were convinced they had gone to the motorway?'

'Wha-,' he scoffed, and then looked impeccably innocent, 'of course, I-I mean why woul-'

Diane held her hand up to stop him from lying again. 'The reason I know you are lying - and I don't blame you, Mister-?'

He pouted a little at being caught out. 'Just Darren.'

She smiled. 'I don't blame you, Mister *Just Darren*, for trying to help Mathew Arnold, but I know for a fact that Alison would not, in a million-years, use the main roads.'

She sat back and folded her own arms now, allowing that to sink in.

'Hmm.' He hummed, thinking. 'What if she had us take them there and then *doubled-back* instead?'

He raised his eyebrow and folded his arms again; fifteen love, your serve.

'Again, I doubt Alison would add all those unnecessary miles to Mathew's journey. Do you?'

As much as she tried, she couldn't quite keep all of the *sing-song* smarm from her tone. Fifteen all.

A second of thought passed. 'Unless they planned to *cross* over the motorway and go down the other side?' He said as though he were making a very, careful chess-move. Thirty fifteen.

She gave him her best, winning smile. 'And Alison, most definitely wouldn't take them into the heart of the country and the very place where most of the major roads meet up.' She paused, just for a little effect. 'Cameras everywhere, you see?' Game, set and match.

Darren blinked a half-dozen times and then threw his racket down; *you CANNOT be serious*!?

'Fine!' He huffed. 'But your first words; *I'm a reporter*, made my mind up; I'm not saying anything.' He huffed again. 'Especially to a *hack* who will probably just use that poor man to get a fast *thrill* headline.'

He sat up straight and wagged his finger at her. 'And you leave that young girl out of it!' He warned passionately. 'She's a *giant* she is, a bloody *giant*!'

Diane just looked on, unfazed. 'I agree.'

The angry expression, the wagging finger and the moving mouth, all stopped and paused. 'Eh?'

'I said I agree; they are both giants in their own right and need all the help they can get.'

Darren dropped his hands heavily to the desktop and shook his head.

'But your a *reporter*,' he said, the word coming out like a dirty-word, 'reporters don't *help* the victims, they make money off 'em!'

She took a deep breath and counted to ten.

'I know it's a very prominent view that all reporters are *hacks* and in it only for the *thrill-scoop*, but we're really not, not the majority.

'The big media companies employ *those* sort, and because they are so big it becomes the only thing that everyone sees.'

She sat back and relaxed. 'Most of us believe in the stories we chase, most of us want the stories to be heard because they have meaning and because they have a right to be heard.'

She opened her phone and swiped the screen a few times before handing it to him. 'Most of us *know* right from wrong.'

Darren took the phone and read the article she had written for the globe.

'That's the only written article in any newspaper so far, but that's all going to change very soon.' She told him.

He looked up, alarmed. 'Why? What do you mean?' He handed her phone back.

'It won't be long before the mainstream papers and television companies make an appearance, and when they do they will *not* be helping Mathew or his cause.'

Darren looked genuinely worried. 'What will they do.' He asked, unconsciously clutching his chest as was his wont.

Diane stood up and walked around the desk and took the coffee-pot from the shelf, filling it as she spoke.

'They will stop him from reaching parliament.' She said. 'Then they will make his whole message into something quaint and cute and eccentric.'

She switched the pot on and returned to her seat. 'And finally they will forget about him and make everyone else forget as well.'

Darren looked from her to the coffee-pot and back again. 'And you have some kind of plan that involves us having a cuppa?'

'Yes.' She laughed. 'As a matter of fact I do have a plan.' She cocked her head to one side and frowned a little. 'Are you going to talk to me now?'

Again, he looked from her to the boiling coffee-pot and back. 'As long as you say nice things about Alison and mention that she's a real giant?'

He raised his eyebrows and looked at her seriously, pointing with his finger at the *deal*.

'I had no intention of doing otherwise, I promise you. In fact, I was going to ask you if I could quote you as calling her a giant.'

He pursed his lips for a second, thinking, and then finally nodded. 'Okay,' he answered and stood up, 'what do you want to know?'

He turned to the shelf and took two mugs.

'Well, you could start by telling me where they went?'

* * *

It was still a little damp from the night rains, the tall grass had dried out in the breeze at its tips, but the ground was still springy and damp at the roots.

George and Darren had taken Mathew and Alison to the other side of the A120, clearing the busy road by some five miles before dropping them off by a gate in a hedge.

As usual, the travellers were plied with parting hugs, handshakes and gifts. And a few tears from Darren.

'I really like those two.' Alison said, striding skilfully through the leg-grabbing tussocks. 'The' understan' a bi' better 'an most.'

'Better than.' Mathew said, automatically now.

'Better than.' Alison repeated, equally automatically.

'Yes, they do.' He placed a hand on her shoulder as they walked. 'But I don't think there are many others like yourself who understand it all.'

She looked up and scoffed. 'Oh shurrup. Y'll b' cryin' like Glitter-pony next.'

He smiled to himself. He knew she was being humble and modest, but the very fact that *she* didn't know she was being humble and modest was truly uplifting.

'Did you see his face when you were talking to us all?' He began chuckling. 'He looked like he was hanging on every word of a bedtime story.'

Alison didn't say anything, she just nodded.

She still felt a little uncomfortable at being called a *giant*. Oh, she knew what he meant by that alright, what she was uncomfortable with was that there was someone out *there* who thought of her like that; she hadn't been around for long enough for a start, she was only fifteen.

It was all down to that blooming website. How many more were looking at her like that?

'Am not an 'ero.' She suddenly said.

Mathew just gave her a serious, raised-eyebrow look. 'Oh, aren't you?' He said. 'What are you then?'

Her mouth opened but no words came out.

'Well that's a first.' Mathew teased. 'Cat got your tongue?'

She shook her head, flustered. 'Well 'ow am I suppose' t' answer tha'?' She threw her arms up and scoffed. 'Wha' a you?' She countered.

He leaned down and smiled right into her face. 'I'm a soft, old man who needs a hero to help him make it to London.' He answered smugly.

She stared at him for a moment, resisting the urge to flick the end of his silly, smirking nose, then tutted loudly and turned away again.

'Wha' you need is an 'ed doctor an' a big mallet.'

Mathew chuckled and followed a step behind. 'You can be proud of yourself, Alison; you might not be a hero the way you see a hero, but believe me, you are a hero.'

He heard her scoff again.

She flicked her head round to look at him. 'Dunt that' website botha ya?' She manoeuvred.

'Yes, as a matter of fact it does a little' he answered, 'I mean what do they all expect of me?'

'Exackly! Tha's 'ow I feel when y' call me an 'ero.'

He understood. 'Yes.' He nodded thoughtfully. 'Yes, I see your point when you say it like that.'

'It's easier bein' an' 'ero when no one knows 'oo you ar', but as soon as people start t' see ya like one,' she shook her head and flapped her arms again in submission. 'I don' kno'.'

He laughed again. 'You know, every time you say things like that you sound wiser and more *heroic*?'

She turned around and stopped in front of him, looking straight up at him. 'I could jus' lead y' into a bog, y' know?'

'Oh, I know you could,' he continued laughing happily, 'and then you would *heroically* rescue me, I know.'

178

With an overly-loud sigh, Alison turned away again and began walking.

'I can' win, can I?'

'No, you can't.'

'Oh, shurrup.'

'*You* shurrup.'

Chapter Thirty-One

Sundown came on with a chill breeze, they'd been making a slow march along the canal for half the day.

'Are we still walking along the canal? It looks a bit different along here.' Mathew asked, turning to Alison walking at his side.

'No, we passed t' lock a couple o' 'ours ago.' She answered.

'Did we?' He sounded surprised.

'Yea, we're on t' river Roding now.'

Mathew was always impressed by the things that Alison knew, her knowledge of the countryside and its *laws*, but he was particularly impressed by her knowledge of the rivers and their names.

'How do you know the names of all these rivers? I've never heard of the Roding until now.'

She shrugged. 'I jus' remember things.' She said, 'but along most rivers ar' signs tellin' ya its name.' She pointed ahead to a concrete bridge with concrete steps running up the side, spanning the river. 'The'll b' a sign at top o' them steps.'

Mathew squinted as though she herself could actually see it.

'Y'll no' see it unless y' go up t' steps.'

'Right. And that's what you do to find out the names of rivers and canals.' He wasn't asking her, more telling himself.

She laughed. 'Yea. If I end up somewhere tha' I don' kno', I jus' look forra bridge and read 't signs. The's allus bridges over t' canals an' rivers somewhere.'

An overhanging willow-branch made them both duck underneath.

When Mathew stood up again he heard Alison squeal in delight.

'Oh! Look! It's a puffball! The's no' many left this time o' year, and t' ones that ar', ar' allus full. Watch.'

And as she prodded the brown and ruddy-red, puffball mushroom with her booted toe, Mathew felt, rather than heard or saw, a light-bulb flash behind his eyes and then everything slowed down as it had done before with Cecily.

It felt like he was in an eternal, peaceful heartbeat.

The whole of the left side of the scene was blurred and ghostly-white, but the sun going down on the right flared through the languidly rising spores to be reflected back into the smiling face of Alison. Her wispy hair caught an unfelt breeze and flowed like it was being pulled through hot, golden honey.

The gold deepened and the sky bruised suddenly and then, *rrriip*, the moments rushed forward again, only this time everything felt wrong at once.

His view for a start, had gone from vertical to horizontal, the sky and clouds were suddenly in the wrong place and even his *weight* was in the wrong place.

Then his focus returned as he saw Alison's terrified face looking down at him. He was on his back. How the devil had he got there? There was something *dimensional* going on there, flipping heck!

'Mathew? Mathew?' She was calling.

'W-what happened?'

He remained where he was and looked up at her, puzzled.

'Y' jus' dropped. I mean like y' body wer' suddenly empty or summert.' Her eyes were as round as they had probably ever been.

She couldn't have said it any better than that; it looked as though everything had switched off at once and his body had dropped straight down, crumpling at the knees and then falling sideways.

'I thought' y' died or summert!'

'Something.'

'Something.'

'Well I'm not dead, but that was the strangest thing, I can tell you that.'

He slowly sat up, Alison hooking him under one arm and helping him rise.

'I don't feel ill though. I think I just fainted.'

He wasn't lying, he felt pretty okay, just *spaced out* at suddenly finding himself on the ground like that.

She gave him a dubious look. 'Fainted?'

'Well what else could it have been?'

He looked at her seriously, as though challenging her to say he had a brain-tumour or something, because that was the only reason he was being so flippant about it; he was afraid there was something horribly wrong with his head and it was easier to just have fainted.

'Well 'ow should I kno'!? Ya might 'av a brain-tumour f'r all I kno'. Blimey!'

He sniffed and stiffened his bottom lip. 'Well thanks for that terrifying thought.'

'Don' look at me like tha'! You asked. I mean it might no' be a tumour; it might be Parkinson's or owd age, or mebe it wer' a stroke or the's a blood-clot or summert.' She said and then quickly amended; 'something.'

'Or I might have just fainted.' He added.

She shrugged. "Oo kno's.' And smiled.

'I don't know what's more scary; the list of things wrong with my head or the *matter of fact* way you say it. If you're trying to scare me into going to the hospital, it's working!'

'Good. But we don' need an' 'ospital; the's a doctors abou' six-mile down 'ere.' She said.

It was his turn to look at her dubiously. 'If you wanted me to go and see a doctor you could have asked first before planting terrifying thoughts in my head.'

'Best t' mek sure y'll go by mekkin y' scared enough.'

'Dark.' He muttered and reached for his staff. 'Blooming dark.'

Alison helped him to his feet and then brushed him down.

'The's a pump-'ouse abou' two or three-miles between 'ere an' t' doctors. I don' like pump-'ouses really cos the' cold an' noisy, but we can 'av one night there an' then go see doctor *whoever* in t' mornin'.'

She stood in front of him and looked up into his pale face. 'A' y' sure y' feel okay?' She gently asked him.

'Strangely - and I'm being honest - I feel no different at all, just a bit *freaked out,* as you would say.'

He pulled the bottle of *Nasty* from his pocket and shook it for her to see. 'But I think I'll sort *that* out with some of Merylin's medicine.'

Alison sniggered. 'It's probly tha' stuff tha's givin' y' tumours.'

She took his arm and led him back onto the trail.

They walked the few miles more to the pump-house. The green, metal door was closed and padlocked.

A yellow sign in the middle, which should have read *Keep Out!*, had been turned into a speech-bubble coming from the mouth of a spray-can painted alien riding in a flying-saucer and pointing to the stars.

Mathew laughed and pointed. '*Keeping Outer-Space!* Very clever.'

They both stood and admired it, the artist had gone to a lot of trouble to render the galaxy and alien in high detail and then had gone on to make the whole thing resemble a 50's comic-book cell. The speech-bubble had been blended perfectly with the yellow colour of the sign and the altered words were indistinguishable.

'There really are some very talented people about aren't there?' Mathew stated, cocking his head over to the other side to appreciate another angle. People often did that very same thing when standing in front of a Monet or Degas.

'Yep.' Alison replied and stepped forward with a two-pronged bit of steel.

She fiddled with the padlock while Mathew stood behind, her wide-eyed accomplice.

The padlock clicked and popped open, Alison removed it and then opened the door, gesturing for Mathew to step inside. 'Afta you.'

He delved into his satchel and pulled out Derek's wind-up torch, flicking the switch and then stepping inside.

Alison followed and closed the door behind them.

The machinery wasn't too loud at all and actually looked like it had recently been serviced. There were several piles of rough-cloth sacks strewn around the main pump; bags which had held spare parts no doubt.

'Well tha's a bonus.' Alison said and pointed at the sacks. 'We can sleep on those, the'll mek loadsa diffrence.'

She opened the door again. 'I'll b' back in a few minutes.' And then gave him a ponderous look. 'Y'll still b' alive when I ge' back, won' ya?'

He returned her look with a blank stare. 'Well that depends whether I die from laughing or not, doesn't it?' He smiled sarcastically.

She just laughed and walked back outside, leaving the door ajar.

Mathew looked around, shuffling on the spot and sniffing. The pump-house wasn't that much different than the one he had found on the first night.

He propped his staff up against the wall and dropped his bag into the corner, then began *sweeping* the dry leaves into the edges with his feet.

Once he had the space cleared, he piled the leaves up to one side for Alison's kindling and then began working on getting the sacks laid out for them to sit on.

He slid his back down the wall and slowly lowered himself to sit, raising his knees and resting his arms across the top.

How close were they now? Time had, had no meaning to his journey once he had started, he'd been quite happy just being on the move, making headway at any speed. But now?

He rubbed at his face, his skin felt *less*, or *faraway* might have been a better way to put it. He didn't know, it just felt like that what he was touching and what he was touching *with* were not wholly connecting no matter how hard he pressed. Something had changed.

His memory of Alison and Cecily exchanging their parting-returning gifts, and of just Alison pressing the puffball, were incredibly vivid and stark, not like memories at all, but more like a picture he had just a split-second ago looked at.

As much as he marvelled at their complete perfection, right down to the soporific slow-motion and wispy softness thrown around the edges, he was still terrified by them. They meant something. Like his altered skin they were a message to get a move on and time now had some meaning.

'I'm actually still going.' He said aloud and looked to the ceiling.

He hadn't talked to Mary since that first day. 'Did you hear that, love? I'm still going.' He dropped his gaze and chuckled, adding; 'and I still haven't had to drink toilet-water.'

He had a sudden yearning then, to see Mary again, and his heart ached in his chest. 'We did have it quite good didn't we, love?' He sniffled. 'I mean we had the chance to love each other, didn't we? There are many that don't ever get that, do they?

'Then there's another sort, love; there are those that don't even get the chance to show how much they *can* love, how much they *can* care and be sincere and brave.' His eyes filled with tears which rolled down his cheeks, across skin which could barely feel them.

'I've been meeting them everywhere, Mary.' He sniffled again and wiped his nose on his handkerchief.

'Alison's like that,' he continued. 'Brave and sincere and honest, she's like a little fairy-thing on the outside,' he chuckled, 'you'd have liked her. But on the inside she's like a *giant*, as Glitter-pony puts it.'

He sighed and then blew his nose. 'A giant.' He mumbled, nodding slowly and staring at nothing.

'I'm afraid, Mary.' He quietly spoke. 'I-I'm afraid of failing; what if I die before I get there and it all becomes dust for nothing? I can't let her down, none of them really, but especially Alison. I see a hopeful future when I look at that girl, I really do. And did I tell you she *clonked* a big bully on the head and rescued me?'

He produced the infamous bottle from the depths of his coat pocket and took a swig straight from it. His eyes never flinched, they just stared ahead at something only he could see or imagine, as the liquid assaulted his lips, tongue and throat.

'Yes, she's done that and much more besides.' He carried on, and took another sip of *Nasty*. 'But something's coming now, Mary, and I-I think it might be coming for me.'

The double-shot of *Old Nasty* - triple if you count the one straight after his *faint* - really hit his emotional spots all at once.

His face went from blank and thoughtful into a full-crumpled sob of near despair in the blink of an eye. 'And she's had so much pain already, that poor girl.'

And then after a deep, shuddering sigh his face relaxed again. 'I will make it.' He said quietly, then shook his fist at nothing. 'By God, I will!' Loudly.

He slumped back again, his legs dropped and straightened out and his hands, still clutching the bottle, slumped to his stomach. 'I'll probably need a sleep first.'

He looked at the bottle. ''Elp y' sheep.' He couldn't stop himself from saying it out loud and then laughed wheezily. Then hiccoughed and burped which made him giggle again.

All the while he had slowly but surely been slipping further and further down the wall until just his head and shoulders were resting awkwardly up against it.

And then Alison walked in. She had a small pile of dry sticks in her arms.

She stood and looked him up and down, head to toe and then back to eyes. ''Av y' bin cryin'?' She asked, noting the still-wet streaks on his cheeks.

'Eh? What? No. You?' He said, casually gesturing at nothing.

He held the bottle out. 'I hate this stuff, do you want some?'

Chapter Thirty-Two

Motorways are amazing things, creatures of habit, for creatures they really are when they get going. Their habit lies in the times of day and year, and one can watch them evolve through the seasons even as they flow along.

Watching from the air, one is given a better understanding of this creature, and usually one would be in the air alone.

But not today. Today the pilots of the six, news helicopters from the six, major news-groups, were not having the easiest of days doing what had been asked of them; follow the motorways and look for Mathew Arnold.

All of this happened because of Darren - Glitter-pony - telling Palmerson that they had dropped Mathew and Alison off there. And Palmerson had actually believed him and so had *phoned home*. The rest was academic (the frantic phone-calls and encrypted emails etc, etc.)

And exactly as Diane Jones had predicted, these news stations were setting the stage for their first *assault* on *The Freedom Walker's* march.

Already they had spoken of the *poor, lost man with a grudge and a message.*

Another had said that Mathew Arnold needed all the help he could get to get his life back in place, get his pension sorted out and every other thing which Mathew was marching for, making the whole piece come across as though it was a silly fault of the system and it was a mistake which was happening only to him. *Aw, bless him.*

And the public would believe every word that they lapped up.

All of that was going through Diane Jones' mind as she sat in the waiting area of Stanstead Airport.

Their secret weapon - a televised broadcast of their own - had actually been put in place, and amazingly quickly too.

Edmund had made a single phone call to Lars Forsberg, the website sponsor in Sweden, and told him with a single paragraph what he would like to do and why.

That phone call had lasted a total of just under two minutes.

The next one, Forsberg to a Canadian contact, lasted four minutes, and one hour later, George Hamil, freelance, wildlife photographer and camera operator was on a plane to London.

And there he was now.

Diane stood up and waved at the tall, very well muscled and tanned, blond-haired, blue-eyed, well muscled - did I say that already? How can I see *all* that from here anyway?

The tall, ruddy *Norseman* ignored her and walked the other way. Her eyes sadly followed like a pair of left-behind puppies.

A smaller woman walked over to her, carrying a large, black shoulder-bag. 'Diane Jones?' She asked.

'Um. George Hamil?' Diane asked, looking the woman up and down.

'Georgina Hamil, yes. My friends call me, George.'

She smirked and pointed at the retreating *Herculean* specimen. 'You were hoping that was me weren't you?'

They both turned to take a good long - longing - look.

'Yea.' Diane said, a little too dreamily.

'Me too,' George returned, 'me too.'

The man turned a corner and both women turned back to face each other.

'So, Georgina Hamil, welcome to England,' Diane held her hand out. 'Coffee first? And I'll fill you in with what we'll be doing'

George took Diane's hand and shook it. 'Good to be here,' she answered, her accent Canadian-thick. 'Call me George, and coffee sounds great.'

As the two women entered the coffee-shop, the devil himself walked out of the gentleman's lavatory and took the causeway to the next passenger-pickup lounge.

Palmerson's contact stood ominously on his own; a tall, slender, Rwandan Tutsi. Not that you would know his tribe unless you could read his scarring.

The other passengers seemed to keep a *certain*, respectable distance away from him, flowing around him like he had an invisible barrier surrounding him.

Palmerson walked over. 'Glad you came, Elias.'

Elias nodded once. 'Mithter Palmerthon.' He said in his well-educated, baritone lisp.

'Did you have time to read my report on the flight?'

'Yeth, thir, it shouldn't be a problem.'

'Good man. There's a car outside, I've set up a *boo* in a motel a few miles north.' Palmerson told him as he led him away.

'A *boo*? A trap, you mean?'

'What?' Palmerson asked, looking at him with an annoyed frown on his head.

'A *boo;* it thoundth like a trap.'

'Base of operations, lad.'

'Ith it an acronym you uthe in your fortheth over here?'

Palmerson flushed. Why was this always happening to him; being surrounded by questioning underlings, stupid apprentices and cack-handed lackeys? Eh? Why him, eh?

And now bloody Elias the tracker - and he *was the* absolute best at what he did, without a doubt - who had almost driven Palmerson mad back in the days of the Rwandan disaster, with his constant questioning lisp and an attitude to boot. He felt like they were picking up exactly from where they had left off.

Why couldn't he just be back comfortably in bloody London, damn it! Gods! He was only up the road, he could almost smell Crystal and her wonderful parlour.

'No, it isn't, it's one of mine.' He managed to say, quite civilly and without any thought of his pistol.

'Oh, I thee.' Elias said and nodded. 'Quaint. Do you have an acronym for trap?'

Palmerson whirled, but quietly, carefully spoke as he brought them both to an abrupt halt, smiling strangely.

'No. No, I don't have an acronym for trap, Elias, I really don't.' He stared wildly for a few seconds more, scanning the big Rwandan's face, and unconsciously licking his lips before turning away and carrying on toward the exit.

Elias followed at his shoulder, wondering if Palmerson had been overdoing it lately.

'I thee.' He casually thaid.

* * *

Meanwhile, in a doctor's-surgery waiting-room.

Mathew stood out like a sore thumb, sitting there with his head bowed and staff in hand, waif in tow.

His head was bowed because it didn't feel like it belonged to him today, it felt like it belonged to mister *Hurty* or mister *Stabby-throb*, depending on how he was sat. Currently it belonged to mister *Hurty*.

He'd only had three more tots before falling asleep. He'd woken up in the morning with the strangest sensation that he didn't belong where he currently was, he felt he should be somewhere else, anywhere but in that body, in that pump-house. And then he had sat up and the mother of all head-pains sped up his spine and into his brain.

It was so painful and throbbing that it made him feel sick. Then he wanted to cry because he didn't want to be sick, and then he was sick. He didn't cry however, even though he wanted to.

Then Alison had patted him on the back and pointed to the bits of apple in his sick. 'Don' y' wan' tha'?'

And so he was sick again, only there was nothing left to sick out and all he ended up doing was retching and groaning to the heaving strains of his empty stomach. And *then* he cried.

'Mathew Arnold?' A woman's voice called.

Everyone's gaze in the waiting-room turned to Mathew and Alison.

The pair of them stood up, Mathew shakily on legs which were still carrying the awful memory of his sicking.

The doctor stood in the doorway, holding the door open and smiling his well-practised welcome.

He eyed them both up as they passed. 'So it's true then; The Freedom Walker has come to my surgery.'

'How did you guess?' Mathew asked. 'I can't be the only Mathew Arnold on the planet.'

The doctor pointed to Mathew's staff. 'A dead giveaway,' and smiled. 'You can leave it over there.' He then said and pointed to the corner.

He turned to Alison and looked down into her frowning face. 'Could you wait outside?'

'Yea, I could,' she replied and sat down on the chair at the foot of the examination-table.

Mathew smiled but said nothing.

The doctor, however, wasn't used to having his authority usurped by a child. 'What if I ask him to remove his trousers?' He said sternly.

Alison thought about it for a moment. 'I'd 'av t' remind y' tha' 'e's come in because ov 'is 'ed,' she eventually said, 'and no' because 'e needs y' t' look at 'is willy.'

She shrugged and smiled, friendly. 'An' then I'd probly clonk ya on t' 'ed wi' 'is stick.'

Mathew laughed and then quickly shut up.

The doctor turned to him and frowned. 'Did she just say she was going to hit me on the head with your walking-staff?'

Mathew nodded and smiled. 'Oh, yes,' he replied, laughing again, 'but she means well, doctor, and it's fine by me if she stays. I have to concur though, that I *probly* won't be removing my trousers.'

The doctor just sighed and closed the door.

He turned and looked at Alison for a moment, pursing his lips slightly, then simply thought better of whatever it was he was going to say and went back to Mathew. 'If you could remove your coat and jumper please, and then sit on the bed.'

Mathew did as he was told.

The doctor took his arm and felt his pulse, looking at his watch as he did so.

'So, what's this problem with your head?' He asked as he finished counting. 'Roll up your sleeve please.'

Mathew rolled his sleeve up and over his elbow. 'I'm not sure really, doctor, I fainted yesterday.'

The doctor attached a blood pressure strap to his arm and began pumping. 'What happened exactly?'

'I'm not sure,' he repeated, shrugging, 'one minute I was standing there watching Alison pressing a puffball mushroom, and the next I was on my back looking at the sky.'

'Did you feel nauseous or have a headache at the time?' He asked, placing his stethoscopes in his ears and then listening to Mathew's heartbeat again.

Mathew shook his head. 'No. No, I felt fine. I felt fine when I came to as well, funnily enough, just surprised and a bit shocked to have everything change so suddenly like that.'

The doctor stood back and removed his stethoscope. He took a pen-torch from his pocket and looked into Mathew's eyes one by one, flicking the beam up and down while holding the lids open. 'And you didn't feel poorly you say?'

'No, not at all.'

The doctor put the torch away and pulled out his otoscope. He pulled Mathew's ear gently and then took a look inside. 'Have you had any ringing in the ears, or sudden popping sounds? Clicks and irritating itches, that sort of thing?'

Mathew shook his head again. 'Can't say that I have.'

The doctor stood back and sighed. 'You're fine physically, your blood-pressure is a smidgen low, but you have walked quite a few miles and you are how old?'

'Seventy-seven.'

'You can put your jumper back on now. Come and sit over by the desk.' He gestured to the chair and then sat down in his own seat.

Mathew dressed and sat down. 'So, am I going to *kick the bucket*, doctor?'

'Not today, Mister Arnold,' he scoffed. 'You are, as I said, physically fit and healthy, but without the proper tests though, I can't tell you why you fainted. It could be because you are fatigued, and it would be easy to just pass it off as that.'

Mathew looked to Alison. She just looked back, her face hard-set, but she didn't say anything.

'But it could be something else?' He asked, turning back to the doctor.

'Yes,' he replied, 'yes it could, and as a doctor I would advise you to have a proper examination at a hospital.'

Both Mathew and Alison opened their mouths to speak at the same time, but the doctor held his hand up and stopped them.

'I know you will probably refuse,' he said, 'and the next move would be for me to remind you that I have taken my Hippocratic oath and to allow you to leave would put me in danger of breaking the *do no harm* part, and then you would say *but you will harm me if you force me to conform*, then I say I can't force you but I can section you, and then,' he pointed to Alison, 'she would hit me on the head with your staff and you would both just leave.'

Mathew looked back to Alison again.

'I would an' all.' She promised, nodding seriously.

The doctor chuckled. 'So we can save ourselves from all of that unpleasantness and I'll say no more.'

'Um.' Mathew began sheepishly. 'Thank you?'

The doctor chuckled again. 'Don't thank me, thank her; I can see she is a young lady of peculiar talents, one of which seems to be hitting people on the head.'

He turned back to Mathew and looked at him seriously. 'I can't say I am happy about what you are doing however, particularly the *suicide* bit, as a doctor is smarts right up against my ethics.'

Mathew looked away, feeling ashamed.

'But I do understand, Mister Arnold,' he continued, gently. 'I deal with hopelessness every, single day. I see everything you wrote about in the eyes of my young patients, my old patients, they are all cowed by their lives and it must stop.'

He rubbed his face and suddenly looked just like any other, tired human-being. 'I don't have a cure for hopelessness, Mister Arnold, and I'm tired of patching up the same wounds over and over again. It must stop.'

Alison's face was grim, she had mistook this doctor to be just another one of *them*, but he actually looked wracked with enough guilt to make him suicidal.

He sat up and sighed, the doctor was back. 'Apologies.'

'No need.' Mathew replied. 'You're right; it must stop. For her.' He pointed to Alison. 'For everyone like her now and for all of those heading the same way; it must stop.'

The doctor nodded slowly, thoughtfully. 'Then I would advise you get there as quickly as you can.'

He leaned closer. 'At your age there is more chance that what you experienced may well get worse - if it *is* age related you understand?' He said. 'And I *really* am struggling not to allow you to leave, that's how concerned I am and how serious I want you to take me.'

Alison stood up and came over to stand by Mathew's chair. 'Don' worry, 'e'll b' goin' straigh' to 'ospital as soon as 'e's bin t' parliament, won' ya, Mathew?' She sniffed and wiped the end of her nose.

Mathew took her hand and squeezed it. Her *bullying* optimism wasn't lost on him. 'I will, I promise.'

Chapter Thirty-Three

Palmerson walked around the table with the huge map laid out on it, held down at the corners by a hotel bible, a wine bottle and two shoes.

Elias walked around as well, a full half-table away from Palmerson.

The two men occasionally stopped and stooped forward to look at a particularly interesting area of the map, sometimes even sticking a pin in.

Dixon and Singh stood back and leaned against the wall of their current *boo* - a quickly converted double-room at the *Quicky-Inn* they were staying at - and sipped at their orange juices, watching their superiors circling the table.

It was like watching two men chasing each other really, really slowly and without much intent on catching the other up; a strange game of *tag* whose rules were laterally understood.

Elias stopped again and bent forward to pull one of Palmerson's red pins from the map and place it at the edge.

Palmerson missed a step and then took two, huffy steps onward again.

Elias placed another pin of his own, a yellow one, moved on and then removed two more of Palmerson's red pins.

This strange game went on for around twenty minutes before Elias stopped and stepped back. 'I think that jutht about coverth it.'

Palmerson stood by his side, Dixon and Singh coming up behind.

They all studied the map. There were seven yellow pins and a single red pin left, a small pile of removed red pins lay at the edge of the map.

They could hear Palmerson breathing heavily.

Elias pointed to two of his yellow pins. 'I think thith ith the line they will follow.'

Palmerson snorted. 'But that's nowhere near the motorway.'

'They won't uthe a motorway.' Elias responded unemotionally.

'But the security company said they'd dropped them off there.' Palmerson shook his head and scoffed.

'They lied.'

'What? Why? What would *their* objective be?' He asked, frustrated now.

'Becauthe they liked him more than you.' Elias shrugged. 'I don't know, but the entire motorway hath been covered for the patht two dayth and no thighting. Not a thingle thing.'

Palmerson looked flabbergasted. 'What do you mean they liked *him* more than me?' He looked to Dixon and Singh. 'What did he mean they like him more than me?'

The other two just squirmed and studied the carpet.

'I'm jutht thaying that they naturally thaw the law ath the enemy, tho to thpeak.' Elias said.

Palmerson huffed and scoffed, he didn't like the thought of being *played* as much as he didn't like all of his pins being removed.

He stepped closer to the map again and took a good, long, hypocritical look at the two yellow pins which Elias had indicated, searching for any obvious flaws in their positioning.

He straightened up again, slowly shaking his head and smiling that sarcastic smile of his. 'There's nothing there for miles around really, just fields. They're *beggars* on the road, *tramps* looking for scraps. They won't bother with fields, lad.' It was the best he could do.

Dixon's phone chimed. 'Um, sir? I think you might want to see this.' He said, carefully handing Palmerson his phone and then quietly taking a step back.

The three of them waited while he read about the latest sighting of *The Freedom Walker*, watching, quietly worried, at the quickly changing colour of his face.

He leaned over and looked at the map, then back at the phone and then up at them.

'Great bloody Canfield!?' He managed to bluster.

Elias took the phone and then did as Palmerson had done, checked the map against the information he could see. Great Canfield was two miles north of the two yellow pins he had placed.

He handed the phone back to Palmerson, saying nothing and trying his very best to be humble.

'Well look at that,' Singh said, truly impressed, 'it's right next to the two pins you pointed out.' He gave Elias a smile of respectful admiration. 'Almost in the dead centre as well!'

Palmerson shuffled around and gave Singh the coldest, blank stare which that particular hotel-room had ever witnessed.

The young agent laughed nervously and pointed behind himself. 'I-I'll go have the cars brought round then.' He said and walked straight through the bathroom door, closing it behind himself, only to reopen it a second later and then, without a single misstep or look at the others, walked out of the *proper* door.

Three pairs of eyes blinked for a moment, watching for the door to reopen. When it didn't they turned back to each other.

'Right,' Palmerson said, ignoring the glaring map and bloody pins and taking command again. 'Dixon, get on the phone to the local constabularies round there, get them patched in to us and tell them to alert us as soon as they spot Mathew Arnold.'

'Right away, sir.' Dixon replied and began dialling.

'And tell them not to approach them, they're just to watch and make sure they have eyes on them until we get there.'

At the first mention of contacting the local police, Elias had inwardly shaken his head; they would fail if they used the police. Mathew Arnold wasn't the sort to be able to evade capture for long, but the girl was.

Elias had taken one look at Alison in the videos and knew he was up against something more than just a protest march; she was more than capable of looking after herself and the old man.

To Elias' Tutsi, tracker's mind he could clearly see he was up against the land itself when he looked at the girl. Palmerson would never see that, not on his home-country's soil.

And so Elias said nothing; at least he was still getting paid he supposed.

* * *

Back in London, the prime minister had just finished watching the very first broadcast (webcast if you were to be absolutely accurate) of *The London Globe's* new, news pod-cast presented by Diane Jones. And she looked good doing it too, splashed across the main page of *The Freedom Walker* website, courtesy of Lars Forsberg.

Crispin was hiding in the hallway, his eyes red and wet.

'*I'LL KILL HER! I SWEAR,*' he could hear the prime minister's, thunderous voice shouting through the door, '*I'LL HAVE HER EXECUTED FOR TREASON!*'

Something large and heavy smashed against a wall.

'*And WHO is this inside-INFORMANT!?*'

Crash!

'*And Aliens? IDIOTS!*'

Thud!

'*She's turning him into a bloody living martyr! AAAGH!*'

Crash! Thud! Smash!

It went quiet for a moment. *Just* a moment.

'*CRISPIN!?*'

Poor Crispin cringed and sniffled.

'*CRISPIN!? GET IN HERE!*'

He straightened himself out as best as he could and took a deep breath before opening the door and entering her *lair*.

Everything he had imagined to have happened in the room had actually happened and more besides.

The furniture was upside down and thrown out of place. Papers and documents, files and even the discarded stuff from the bin was scattered across everything.

The bookshelves were almost bare, the books being at all points of the compass and nowhere near where they had once, peacefully, serenely resided.

The prime minister stood in the middle of the room, hair askew and bedraggled, skin aglow with the sheen of lady-perspiration, but most alarming was she was only wearing one shoe.

The other lay with its heel firmly stuck into the wooden panelling by the door. As though she had thrown it as he had scuttled away when the fury had begun, Crispin was thinking.

He gulped. 'Prime Minister?' He managed to say without squeaking too much.

She limped comically over to him, rising on one high-heeled foot and then dropping again on her other.

She stopped in front of him and slowly raised herself onto her high-heel, bringing her nose up to his.

'*Wh*ere,' she began, - the letter *H* in the word blasting into terrified Crispin's nostrils; a furious, fiery breath. 'Is Palmerson?' She actually growled her agent's name through gritted teeth. 'And if you say you don't know, Crispin, I'll punch you so damned hard in your kidneys that they *will* roll out of your trousers.'

The poor man's heart was ready to just leave him standing there to face the kidney-punching and hide itself in the corridor.

He knew she could do what she said she would, her fourteen years in the Royal Navy hadn't been spent in a row-boat in the Maldives; she was a trained Royal Marine and had seen two major conflicts at close range. Plus she was uncannily strong for her rather small size.

'I-I-, he-he-, I mean-' Crispin gulped. 'He-he's on his way to the latest sighting.' He gasped. 'With a tracker.' He quickly added, hoping that the addition of a tracker would somehow make it all seem much better. It didn't.

'A tracker?' She said, coldly. 'A bloody tracker!'

Crispin's kidneys throbbed helplessly.

'I want Mathew Arnold on *my* television stations, on *my* news casts. Do you understand, Crispin?'

He nodded frantically.

'And I want *their* pathetic, little station taking off the air. Do you understand that as well?'

There was no forgiveness in the way she said that, only the cold promise of imminent pain and possible disfigurement.

Crispin's face crumpled. He didn't want to cry but he just couldn't help himself; he had to tell her something she wouldn't like and she was so incredibly, dangerously close to him, nose almost touching in fact.

'Are you crying, Crispin?' She asked, the coldness still more than apparent, particularly at this distance.

'Yes.' He squeaked.

'Well stop it.' She demanded.

'I'm trying.' He sniffled.

'Why are you crying?'

'Because you can't shut their broadcast down.'

'Oh! Can't I?' She answered, as though she had a secret weapon which could shut anything down at any time, anywhere. She didn't, but she sounded like it.

'No. It's coming from a website out of our country's broadcasting laws.' He was still sniffling and his words were squeaked and rushed.

He watched as she breathed in and out deeply, staring into his eyes.

'I feel a *stabbing* coming on, Crispin.' She said, breathy calm.

'Oh! God!'

'Get out!' She barked.

He didn't have to be told twice and leaped a foot in the air at the order, rushing for the door as quickly as his feet would carry him. Which for him was pretty, damned quick.

'And get *our* media right into Mathew Arnold's face, Crispin, or I'll be sticking things into *yours*!' She shouted as he opened the door.

He almost flew out of the doorway, getting halfway along the corridor before the door had even closed properly.

The paintings lining the hallway walls all seemed to follow him with their eyes as he galloped past. *Run, Crispin, run!*

* * *

The cause of most if not all of the troubles of the poor, hounded Crispin, sat with her rump on the bonnet of her parked car while George the photographer squatted down behind a wall.

The road they were parked on was in the middle of nowhere particularly interesting. Exactly where they wanted to be.

'I can see woods from here.' George's voice called out from beyond the wall.

Diane stepped right up to the grey stone and peered into the distance, looking at the small wood George was talking about, while George herself was peeing away silently below her.

'It's getting late, it's going to be dark soon.' Diane said, looking down. 'I think that is a pretty good place.'

Yea,' George agreed, looking up. 'If they are definitely coming anywhere down this way, they'll see that.'

'What do you think?' Diane asked as she handed over the roll of toilet-paper. 'Should we go in and wait for them or wait out here until it's dark?'

George took the paper. 'Thanks. If we can hide the car behind one of these walls and hedges, I think taking a *recce* isn't such a bad idea.'

She stood back up and pulled up her jeans. 'They've met you, you said?'

'Yes.'

'That might be our ticket to getting close to them, or rather them getting close to us.'

Diane helped her climb back over the wall. 'You mean set up a camp in there and wait for them to find us?'

George shrugged. 'Why not? Beats the hell out of scaring them when we sneak up on them.'

Diane was actually quite impressed with that way of thinking. If they came this way and Alison led them into the woods, she would definitely spy them out and would want to know why they were there.

'I think you might be right,' she said, beaming, 'are you any good at making a campfire then?'

Chapter Thirty-Four

George had indeed been more than able to build a smokeless campfire, and she and Diane were sitting around it sipping tea from tin-cups which she carried in her camera backpack.

Not that *Alison* knew they were George's, or that they had come from her backpack, or even who she was. But she knew Diane Jones.

What were they doing there? Around a pretty good campfire as well.

She stayed motionless, squatting on her haunches and peering through the bushes she was hidden behind.

Mathew was a few yards back waiting for her to come back and tell him it was safe.

He stood by the tree she had left him at and continued sniffing the air. He still couldn't smell any blooming fire.

He squinted into the dark, she was coming back.

'It's tha' reporter woman.' She told him quietly once she was back in front of him.

'Diane Jones? Really? What the heck is she doing out here?' He hissed.

'I don' kno' but she's wi' someone, another woman. The'v med a really good fire an' all.'

Mathew's brows knitted and he looked at the ground in thought. 'They must be waiting for us.' He eventually said. 'There's no other explanation.'

He looked up. 'Might as well see what they want and have a cup of their tea.'

Alison did her own thinking; she thought Mathew was right, she'd thought the same thing as soon as she had seen who had made a fire, but there was a much bigger picture they had now found out; the world was watching.

'A'rite,' she said, 'but if the's owt fishy goin' on we get away from 'em quietly.'

'Fishy?' Mathew's face took on that innocent school-boy look.

'Yea, fishy.' She hooked her arm through his. 'The's summert-something much bigger 'appening now, int the'? People a' still people, an' when the's four million quid chucked in people can do stupid, people things.'

He smiled down at her and then nodded. 'But you don't give a damn about the money do you?'

She began leading him through the quickly darkening wood. 'Y' kno' tha' sayin'; devils greatest trick is mekin' y' not b'lieve in 'im?'

'Yes?'

'Well tha's exactly wha' money does, 'cept other way round.'

Mathew was confused. 'But money *is* real, I should know, I haven't got any of it.'

She shook her head. 'No, tha's th' illusion, y' see? Tha' money *is* real? When all it is, is a way t' mek things seem like the' 'av a cost, an' all t' best stuff is expensive an' rare an' out o' reach from most folk, when really the's enough.

'Th' real truth is; the things tha' ar' well expensive and out o' reach y' don't need anyway. Why'd y' need gold in y' ears an' diamonds on y' fingers? Daft.'

She shook her head and chuckled sadly for the lost souls who were ensnared in that material world.

They were still chatting when they stepped into the circle of Diane and George's campfire light.

Both women turned to watch them enter.

'You rang?' Mathew joked, looking at Diane.

She sniggered. 'Hello again, Mister Arnold-' she quickly noted his raised eyebrow, 'Mathew. This is Georgina Hamil, she's a photographer and cameraman-woman-' she stumbled, 'whatever.' She finished, waving her hand dismissively.

George nodded at them both and just smiled.

'Come and join us?' Diane then asked and patted the ground by her side.

Mathew took up the place she had indicated and Alison sat at his other side.

'It's probably a stupid question, but,' Mathew began, sniffing and rubbing his nose. 'But what are you doing here exactly?'

He held his hand up before she could speak. 'I know you are here for *me*, but what I mean is; what are you doing? In all of this, everything that is going on.'

'Ah!' She pursed her lips a little. 'You've found out about the website haven't you? And the fund. Yes, Darren did say-'

'Y' kno' Glitter-pony?' Alison asked, unable to stop herself from butting in.

'Um. I'm not sure who Glitter-pony is, but if he's big, strong and gay then I would have to say yes.'

''Ow did y' ge' t' see th-' She stopped mid-sentence, realisation spreading across her reddening cheeks. 'Bloomin' selfies! Y' followed 'em and then the' told you wher' the' dropped us off dint the'?'

She scoffed. 'Bloomin' selfies.' She repeated.

George cleared her throat and held a finger up. 'Sorry, but *what* the *hell* did she just say?' She asked Diane. 'I can understand you, and I can understand you' she continued, pointing to Mathew, 'but you?' She gave Alison an astonished stare. 'You're speaking *alien*.'

Alison suddenly understood Jolly very well. 'A' ya a yank?'

George blinked and pointed at her. 'See! Did you hear that? *Alien!*'

What George had heard, came to her ears as *eyeyay ankh*. 'It's like ancient Sanskrit or something.' She said and shook her head. 'What is that?'

'Yorkshire.' Mathew told her.

'*Yor ksha*.' George repeated. 'Now it sounds Klingon.'

Mathew and Diane laughed. Alison just scowled.

'York*shire*.' He emphasised.

'Right, York*shire*.' She repeated again. 'So you're a *Hobbit* then?' She turned to Alison.

Alison wasn't impressed. 'If I'm an 'obbit, then 'e's really Gandalf an' you two ar' those other two twits 'oo go wi' 'em.' She fired back. 'Jus' wha' a y' doin' 'ere?'

George looked at Diane. 'I heard the words *Gandalf* and *twit*, the rest was a lot of angry sounds. Am I in trouble?'

'Yes.' Diane answered and patted her gently on the arm.

Alison rolled her eyes. 'Gordon-bloomin'-Bennett!' She snorted. 'Well at least I kno' y' no' 'ere t' ge' in us way or owt, cos if y' were y' would 'av at least med a plan an' go' someone better 'an illiritat camera-*bag* 'ere.'

George turned to Diane for the translation.

'She's confident that we aren't here to harass them.' She said.

George smiled, relieved. 'Great.' She said and turned to Alison with a loaded high-five.

Alison gave her a hard stare, leaving the raised palm hanging, then flicked her gaze to Diane and gave her the remainder of it before turning to Mathew, the stare still in place but not really aimed at him.

'Translate.' She said firmly.

Mathew didn't really know it wasn't aimed at him though.

He leaned forward quickly and looked directly at George. 'She referred to you as an *illiterate camera-bag*.' He dutifully translated and then sat straight back, looked into the fire and became *invisible*.

The blond Canadian didn't move or speak and then quite suddenly she began laughing. 'Camera-*bag*!' She howled. 'I Love it!'

Alison's mouthed turned up at the corners a little then, the woman had a good sense of humour at least. Even if she couldn't *hear* properly.

'Now that we all trust one another,' Diane began, 'perhaps I can fill you in with the latest developments at *The Globe*?' She said. 'I think you'll like what I have to say.'

Mathew nodded and was about to say *yes*, when Alison butted in again.

'No' till we've go' a cuppa in ar' 'ands.'

Diane laughed, George picked up the boiling pot.

'I understood that,' she beamed, 'tea-up!' And failed miserably to imitate Alison's accent.

* * *

Somewhere further west right at that moment, Palmerson was also failing miserably. At keeping his mind straight and cool.

Just as Elias had silently predicted, as soon as the police had been told to patrol the areas where *The Freedom Walker* was expected to turn up, everything had gone silent.

Whether the girl had read the signs or not she had now disappeared into the land with Mathew Arnold. And Palmerson was just getting the gist of that. Especially after his latest discovery, the one which he was pacing up and down because of now.

Elias, Singh and Dixon were standing at the furthest point away from Palmerson as they could get, which wasn't very far at all really because they were in such a tiny room.

'I want them, Dixon,' Palmerson growled as he prowled. 'I want them and then I want to watch them being shot.'

He stopped for brief second to look at Dixon. 'Make a note of that.' And then carried on pacing.

Dixon began searching his pockets for a notepad and pencil which he knew he didn't have, just going through the motions.

'Make sure you get the whole post as well.' Palmerson continued. 'All of it. I'll show them they can't pull the wool over my eyes and get away with it.'

Dixon swapped his search for his nonexistent notebook to pulling out his phone. He went back to *The Freedom Walker* website and searched for the post which had led them to here.

'It's-it's not here, sir. It looks like it's been deleted.' Dixon said, gulping at the end of the sentence.

Elias folded his arms and waited. He could have told them that as soon as they had spotted this *post*.

The simple fact that it was stating Mathew Arnold had been seen forty miles away should have rang alarm bells in Palmerson's mind, but no, he was so hell-bent on getting the job done now that his stupid pride was fast becoming his hubris. The deleted post was merely confirmation to what Elias had already known.

Palmerson stood rooted to the spot and stared at himself in the two-way mirror of the interview room they were borrowing from the local CID.

Twice! He was thinking.

His eyes flickered to Dixon's. 'Deleted?'

'Yes, sir.'

He looked back at himself. '*He* deleted it, didn't he. It was *him*, wasn't it?' He was asking himself. 'Yes. Bloody gay-hulk and his barrelling Heimlich.' He muttered.

Dixon blushed, Singh smirked and Elias didn't have a clue what he was talking about.

'Are you alright, Palmerthon, thir?'

Palmerson slowly rubbed at his chin and checked his hair. 'No, Elias, I'm not alright.' He answered as he steadily fixed his collar and tie. 'I've been dragged through knee-deep mud and sent to the brig, I've had a huge member dangled in my face and was electrocuted until I soiled myself,' he continued, still gussying himself up in front of the mirror. 'I've sat through a barrage of knitting puns from a little, old lady with a testicular mindset which bordered on carnal, and I've been dry-humped by a man whose arms are larger than my legs.'

He pressed down his lapels and then turned around to face them.

'Don't forget the pepper-spray, sir.' Singh pointed out sincerely.

Palmerson scowled for all of half a second and then smiled, pointing at Agent Singh. 'Yes, thank you, Singh; and I've been pepper-sprayed.'

He walked around the table in the centre of the room to take up a place directly in front of them and then looked straight at Elias again. 'And now I've been deliberately fed false information which has me forty-odd miles away from where we should probably be.'

He smiled again. It was a little unnerving. 'So, to answer your question, Elias, no, I am not alright, I am very, very far away from being alright.'

He stood back and held his hands out as though he were presenting a *new* him. 'But I will be.' He said. 'Because I'm going to shoot them.' He beamed broadly. 'Yes, I am. I'm going to have them shot and I am going to shoot them as well. So you see? It will be alright anyway.'

He ended by taking a strange, little noddy-bow, like an orchestra conductor, and then turned to the table and pointed at it. 'Get a map on there, Dixon,' he commanded, 'get your pins out, Elias, and get the coffee, Singh.' He stood with his fists planted on his hips.

The two agents and tracker just stared at the back of his head and then looked at each other with a mixture of fear and questioning-puzzlement. Mainly fear though.

Chapter Thirty-Five

Claustrophobic stall-walls and the over-powering smell of disinfectant made Singh's terror feel skin-deep. *He'll shoot me! Oh! God. He will, I just know it.*

He sat on the closed toilet-lid and watched the streaming video from Diane Jones' news-report.

His heart sank to depths he didn't know he had when he heard his own words being repeated back to him. But it wasn't just that alone which had him on the edge of the toilet, legs drumming and the fingernails of his left hand stuffed into his mouth. No, it was the latest report where his *windswept-angel* was standing *with* Mathew Arnold and the girl. Chatting!

He'll probably empty the whole clip into me and reload and do it again. Oh! God!

Before he could torture his mind any further the outer door opened and Dixon called out. 'Are you ready or what? The old man's getting ready to shoot something.'

Oh! God! 'Won't be a second.' His voice sounded strained. Because it was.

'You're not still squeezing one out! Oh, that's just great! Thanks for that, mate.'

Singh heard the door close and he sagged back against the porcelain cistern.

What the hell was he going to do? It was only a matter of time before Palmerson saw the newscast and recognised Diane Jones as the woman he had brought back with him to the security offices.

So what? A cocksure, little voice said.

He thought about it for a second. Well they still couldn't pin the leaks on him personally could they? It could have been any one or all three of them.

Yea. As long as there is that element of doubt, keeping quiet is the sensible thing to do.

He stood up and straightened himself out before confidently smiling and walking out to the others. He'd just act normal.

And so they began the forty mile drive back to where they had begun.

The plan was simple; after making another, slow circuit of another map - which entailed exactly the same procedure as last time, including the removal of several of Palmerson's pins - after all that, they were now split into two teams: Palmerson and Dixon in one car and heading to one location, and Singh and Elias behind them in the other car, but heading to a different location a few miles further east.

'So, you worked with Palmerson in the Rwandan crisis?' Singh asked.

'Yeth,' Elias replied, his baritone voice filling the car. 'He'th not an eathy man to get on with. Thticky, thtuborn and thtupid thometimeth'

Singh scoffed. 'You can say that again.'

In the other car, Palmerson was behind the wheel. 'It should work much better now, lad, eh? Just the two *real* agents, eh?'

'Yes, sir.' Dixon said unhappily, wishing he was in the other car. Why couldn't *he* be an idiot like Singh?

Palmerson didn't notice, his eyes seemed to blaze out through the windscreen at the road ahead, his thoughts along with them.

Blazed in a glazed sort of way, Dixon thought, like someone who was sleepwalking on drugs after a night of heavy drinking and glue-sniffing.

'Have a look at the latest report, lad; we might have to make a route change on the fly.' Palmerson said quickly. Not exactly *urgently* but close.

Dixon did as he was told and flicked through to the website on his mobile.

The tinny voice of Diane Jones came out crisply for both of them to hear, only Palmerson couldn't see who it was who was talking yet.

'*...and as you can plainly see, Mister Arnold is alive and well and in fact very human,*' she was saying.

'What's that?' Palmerson asked. 'Have they found him? The copter-crews? Why wasn't I informed?'

Dixon's eyes were frighteningly close to dropping down his cheeks on saggy stalks. *OH! SHHIIIT!* Because he *could* see who was talking.

'*Mathew has given Globe-news permission to come along with him for a few days and report live on this unique and ultimately historical event.*' Jones continued.

Palmerson almost choked. 'There's a news-crew with him? Who the hell is it? Why haven't they reported it to me that they found him, damn it?'

'*...sheer number of visitors to the site and the vast figure of almost six-million Euro's in donations, has made the world turn its eye...*'

The words trailed off in Palmerson's mind as he *did* choke then *and* swerved, dragging the vehicle over to the hard-shoulder to come to a gravel-crunching halt.

'*...so instead of staying on an-*' Singh's life-story was cut short as he saw his commander's car swerve over to the left and brake sharply.

He drove past and then pulled over a few yards ahead, keeping his eye on the rear-view mirror. 'What are they up to?' He muttered.

'New information maybe?' Elias suggested.

Oh! God! Singh's mind yelped.

Then Palmerson's door flew open and the man himself leaped out. He whirled around and looked right into Singh's terrified eyes through the mirror.

'Oh! God!' The yelp was audible that time.

'YOU!' Palmerson yelled, pointing at him now.

He hadn't just watched the latest newscast, he'd watched a couple of others as well. Including a video of himself being almost sexually *Heimliched*.

'These cars are bullet-proof aren't they?' Singh asked and pressed his door-lock down.

'What have you done?' Elias asked him.

'I've told a reporter everything.' He looked helplessly into Elias' face. 'Everything.'

'Oh! God.' Was all Elias could mutter.

Palmerson came hurtling over to Singh's side of the car, his hand clearly resting on his holstered gun. 'Open the door, Singh, I'm going to shoot you. I am.' He tried the handle. 'Open the bloody door so I can shoot you!' He shouted. Then leaned closer, composing himself ever so slightly. 'If you get out now, lad, I'll only shoot you in the leg, I promise.' He couldn't say fairer than that could he? 'Tell him I'll only shoot him in the leg, Elias.'

'He'll only shoot you in the leg.' Elias repeated.

'Um.'

Elias leaned around Singh to look at Palmerson. 'He thaid, *um*.'

Palmerson hammered his fist on the glass. 'Open the damned door, Singh. I'm going to bloody shoot you if it's the last thing I do!'

He stood back and licked his lips, eyes wide and a little bit red. 'Right! That's it. I warned you!'

He pulled his pistol from the holster and aimed it right at Singh's position.

Dixon's door flew open next and *he* came hurtling like a bat out of hell toward Palmerson.

Palmerson let of a shot. It hit the glass and ricocheted off with a loud *crack-sptang!*

And then Dixon collided with his boss, bringing him down before he could fire off another round.

Singh hadn't moved a muscle, he just sat there and stared at the spot where the bullet had struck the glass. 'Bullet-proof then.' He nodded. 'That's good.'

* * *

'It's all abou' o'nin' things innit?' Alison was saying to Diane. 'Everyone has been told the'v go' t' o'n things so tha's wha' the' do; the' try an' o'n it all. Daft. Really, really daft.'

Diane walked by her side while George walked slightly ahead with her camera clicking away. She had a digital video-camera strung round her neck as well.

Mathew strode along by Alison's other side, setting the pace for everyone else.

'I would have to agree,' he said, 'but there was a time when I wouldn't have. Until I ended up here, in the very place we should be but are made to feel we should fear instead, it wasn't until then that I could see very clearly what this *ownership* thing was really about, and I agree with Alison, it's just daft and laughable when you can see it.'

'When you say *the very place we should be*, do you mean homeless and living outside?' Diane queried.

'No, of course not.' Mathew and Alison both laughed. 'I mean *free*.'

'Right,' Diane said, 'I see.'

Alison scoffed. 'No y' don', no' really, but you ar' tryin' and tha' means summ- something.'

She pointed to the sky. 'D'ya see tha'?'

Diane looked up.

George carried on clicking away.

'What are you looking at?' Our intrepid reporter asked, expecting to see a flock of birds or a jet-stream or something, a rhetorical remark coming her way about *flying free* and *soaring* etc, etc. 'I can't see anything.'

'Exackly! Cos y' no' lookin' at t' bloomin' biggest picture of all; the's a sky above y' 'ead an' y' wer' lookin' f' summer- something spectackeler.'

She shook her head but she didn't scorn, she just smiled. 'Bein' free is like t' sky; it's so obvious tha' y' don' see it so y' think y' mus' b' free already cos y're a bit 'appy an' y'av go' a bit o' money.' She winked. 'An' wha' 'appens then? Y'av go' t' give all y' money t' someone else so y' can keep bein' *free*. But y' no',' she wagged her finger. 'Cos y' can' see t' sky.'

Diane stopped in her tracks and frowned. She muttered 'giant' under her breath, thinking back to her conversation with Darren.

She hadn't given any credit at all to the real meaning, she had just thought he meant she was bigger than she looked and could handle herself - which she could and Diane agreed with - but that's not what he means is it?

Mathew stood by her side and watched her. He knew exactly what was happening. 'It's like listening to Yorkshire Ghandi, isn't it?' He said, grinning.

Alison ignored him and looked at Diane. 'Did y' jus' call me a gian'?'

Diane snapped to. 'Um, I was just thinking back to Darren.'

Alison shook her head and threw her arms up in the air. 'Flippin'-Nora! I give up, I really do!' She said, and turned away and began walking on again, muttering and gesturing. 'Can' say flippin' owt round some people!' She grumbled. 'S'not my fault I can see b'for they do, is it? Blimey! Am only bloomin' fifteen!'

George carried on taking photographs, turning her lens to Diane and snapping away.

'*Flippin'-Nora,*' she mimicked, and clicked, 'the look on your face is quite something.'

Mathew chuckled at the Canadian's imitation of Alison's words, he prided himself on his own efforts.

The three of them walked on behind Alison, who was still quietly grumbling.

'*Yorkshire Ghandi?*' Diane laughed.

Her laugh was genuine, but she was still no less *stunned*, if that was the right word for it.

It may have at first seemed that Alison was just being a *teen*, her ego flapping around all over the place and spouting rhetoric. But that would mean that there should be an easy, *adult* argument which one could fire back. Only there wasn't. Alison was absolutely right; she was continually paying for her place in the world, like *life-rent*, with no other choice but to step onto this *treadmill* and walk until she eventually stepped off again.

'She doesn't really understand what she is.' Mathew said, chuckling. 'All the things which we say are *good* qualities in a person are just normal qualities in Alison, you see?'

'She refuses to be labelled, I know that much.' Diane answered. 'Her character I mean. But I think you're right; she normalises the things that we see as-,' she paused while she thought of the right word.

Mathew chuckled again. 'I know how you feel; it's difficult to put into words properly, I know. But I think you're not seeing the sky again.'

Diane frowned.

'It's not that she normalises anything that we see,' he explained, 'she normalises the things which we *don't* see.'

Diane nodded then. 'Yes, that's a little easier to understand.'

'Y' kno' I can still 'ear ya?' Alison called back without turning around.

They both grinned.

And then Alison spun round on her heels and stopped.

Mathew and Diane flinched, both thinking she was about to give them a mouthful, but her eyes were looking behind them and up into the sky.

She just stood and stared for a few seconds then pointed to the base of the hedge. 'Ge' under ther'!'

'Wh-what? Why?' Mathew and Diane asked together. Then they heard it, a distant engine and the fast *chop-chop-chop* of a helicopter.

'It's a helicopter.' George then confirmed.

'The's two! Ge' under t' 'edge, qwik!'

The four of them scrambled to the high hedge and then rolled underneath the lowest twigs and brush, pressing themselves back as far as they could.

A helicopter was bad enough, but two helicopters was sure sign that they were now making their *sweeps* further afield and the only thing they could be *sweeping* for was *The Freedom Walker*.

'That's a news-crew.' Diane told them as the first helicopter flew past a few fields away. 'They're definitely looking for you two.'

The second copter came hurtling almost directly over them. 'That's a news chopper as well.' She said. 'It looks like the big guns have been loosed.'

Chapter Thirty-Six

An hour and a bit after diving under the bushes, Alison gave them the *all clear* and they had rolled out stiff and kind of *bedsore* as George put it. But until Alison couldn't hear the helicopters any longer she had kept them still. Which was quite the while seeing as she had great hearing.

They had continued through these fields until the land had rolled away and then stopped at a long, quiet road. The day had worn on enough.

'Righ'. Wiv go' t' be a bi' careful through 'ere.' She told them all.

'Why? Where are we?' Mathew asked, looking around with wide eyes for policemen or shotgun-wielding farmers, or worst of all, cows.

He always was the first to ask a question when sentences with words like *careful* or *danger* or *maiming-screaming-death* were in there somewhere.

'Wi no' far from London, we'r in *posh-land* now.' Alison told them, as though that was explanation enough.

Diane scanned her phone to see where they were.

'Posh-land?' Mathew repeated.

'Yea. A lot o' money's 'ere,' she answered, 'everyone o'ns everything, so y'av go' t' be careful crossin' t' fields. Best t' stay on t' road forra bit.'

'Ah, yes, I see where we are.' She looked up to Alison. 'Warley. You're right, there is a lot of money up here.'

'A kno'. Will see some ov it in a minute.'

They came out from beneath the thin line of trees they had been following for the past hour.

Alison led them down the far, right-hand hedge and to what looked like a gate a quarter of a mile away.

She pointed to her left. 'Keep y' eye on them trees.'

The three of them dutifully looked. There was a group of tall oaks clustering at the back of a large house.

As the view changed and the trees slid away they saw what Alison meant when she had said they would see some of the money in a minute.

George whistled, impressed. 'That is one big swimming-pool.'

'Blimey!' Mathew gasped. 'In a glass building!'

'Keep lookin'.' Alison said, unimpressed.

They kept looking and the trees moved a little further back, revealing an open, grassy space.

'Oh, my Lord.' Mathew gasped even louder. 'A helicopter in your backyard? Who has a helico-'

'Keep lookin'.'

'Oh, give over.' Mathew huffed, but kept looking.

The small, two-man helicopter slid away with the trees, the grass rolled back to come up to a single-storey building with a low, grey roof.

The entire front of the building was made from glass, and sitting behind the glass were an assortment of sixteen, different sports-cars (Mathew counted them.)

He stopped walking and stared and rubbed his eyes and stared some more. 'I haven't even had two bicycles let alone sixteen cars.' He muttered, shocked. 'What is the point of all those-those-,'

'Toys?' Diane offered.

Alison touched a finger to her nose and pointed at her then.

'But-but that's just so-so-,' he struggled again, frowning and stammering.

'*Gross?*' Diane offered, again.

'Yes. Yes, that's it; it's so damned *gross!*'

'An' tha's why we've go' t' ge' outta 'is fields, cos 'e'll shoot us probly.'

Alison smiled broadly at them all, made sure they were all following and then carried on to the gate and the road.

Once they were back with tarmac under foot they walked on down and toward the village proper.

George had her video-camera up to her eye, filming the surrounding landscape while Diane made herself presentable for the evening's broadcast.

Mathew and Alison walked side by side in front.

'The's a good place t' make a fire abou' five or six miles out o' t' village.' She told him.

When he didn't answer she looked up at him. 'Did y' 'ear wha' a said?'

'Uh, what?'

He had been miles away on thoughts of sports-cars, helicopters and huge swimming-pools.

'I said; the's a good place t' mek a camp abou' five miles past t' village.'

'Oh, right. Sorry. I was thinking about all of those *things*.' He said, flicking a gesture behind him.

She rolled her eyes. 'Don' bother, y'll only drive ya' sen mad wi' frustration.'

'Yourself.'

'You will drive *yourself* mad.' She replied, perfectly and without any sarcasm. She threw him a sly glance and smiled.

He noticed and returned the smile with a wink. *Sauce.*

Both of them could hear Diane talking into the camera behind them.

They both ignored her - as promised. She had asked them to just carry on as if George and herself weren't there until she asked either of them a direct question.

Which she had just intended to do, until they had both stopped and were stood looking ahead down the road.

'That doesn't look, um, helpful.' Mathew remarked.

They all stood and stared at the parked police car at the main crossroads, at least one officer in the car itself.

'I can only see one ov 'em.' Alison said darkly. 'Back up before 'e sees us. The's usually at least two of 'em.'

They began turning around, but too late it seemed; the blue-lights lit up and then flashed like blue, sparkling strobes. The siren came next and then the car pulled out from its spot and careered straight across the junction and out of sight.

They all turned to each other.

'Well that was a stroke of good luck.' Diane stood and stared and just blinked rapidly, astonished.

'Or bad,' Mathew answered, 'depends on which way you look at it.' He said. 'Whatever the emergency was it's because someone else is in trouble.' He shrugged.

And then they heard what they thought might be that very trouble; gunshots, repeated gunshots.

'What the blooming devil is going on?'

Mathew stared off into the direction the sound was coming from, far over the rooftops of the village they were walking up to. And then a streak of fire shot skyward and exploded into a crimson flower, showering its star-drop petals back down to the earth with a final, crackling hiss and pop.

'Fireworks!?' It was Diane and George. They both laughed. 'Some kids have got their hands on some good rockets there.'

George filmed away.

'A stroke of luck it is then.' Mathew grinned like a big kid and watched, excited, as more fireworks were let off.

'It's no' kids,' Alison said and then tugged on their coats to get them to look at her. 'It's no' kids, it's forrus.'

'Who's *Forruz*?' George asked, the name sounding like a sinister, Turkish mobster or something.

'She means *it is for us*, meaning the fireworks.' Mathew told her. 'Why do you say that?' He then asked Alison.

'Jus' trus' me and let's get a move on.' She answered firmly and then pointed down the hill.

They got their move on and almost jogged to the bottom. George took up the rear with her video camera to record it all, and then nipped to the front and filmed some more.

They reached the crossroads and the spot where the police car had been waiting.

The fireworks hadn't let up the entire time, but once they had crossed the road and were on the way back out, the skies had returned to their usual, blue silence.

Diane took up her role as television-presenter again, looking straight into the camera as she walked slightly in front of Mathew and Alison, the crossroads still clearly in view.

'Just a few moments ago,' she began, 'a police vehicle which had just been parked at the crossroads you see behind us, was called away on another emergency, giving us the opportunity to cross without detection.

'The emergency then revealed itself as an out-of season fireworks display which erupted over the rooftops of this sleepy, little village.

'As fun as it was to watch the sudden, colourful exhibition, this reporter can tell you now that the *emergency* for the police was no coincidence. According to Alison, this was staged for our benefit and with the sole purpose of clearing the road of the police so we could cross.'

She turned and stood next to Alison, while George took up another angle.

'What made you so sure that the fireworks were for us, Alison?' She asked.

Without looking at Diane or the camera, she pointed ahead. 'Cos o' them.'

Diane and the camera spun round and looked down the road.

There was a church on this side of the road and a small park opposite with a white, transit van parked at the entrance. *Hodson's Upholstery* was emblazoned along the side and back doors.

But most alarmingly, standing in the church doorway were two, large men, and across the street, sitting on one of the park benches, were another two men, both bulky and a little bit scary, thought Mathew.

'Um. Should-should we just stay here and wait for the police to come back?' He suggested. 'I feel like I'm in the middle of a kidnapping.'

Alison didn't stop walking or even slow down, but her face became very hard and her eyes were everywhere at once... Nippy was here.

As they approached the church, one of the men in the doorway stepped out and stood in the path waiting for them.

Alison took Mathew's staff from him and sped up a touch so she could be well in front of him.

All this was dutifully being caught on video camera and being broadcast live (well almost, it did have to go through a security filter to actually stop it from being hacked into and stopped, and that took several minutes, *but hey*! As George said.)

'What's she doing!?' Diane kind of squealed.

'Am tekkin Mathew t' London, tha's wha' am doin'.'She answered for him.

Diane was looking a little flustered for a second and the pulled herself together. 'As you can see now, new events are just unfolding in front of us,' she said into the camera. 'We seem to be heading for a confrontation of some sort. All around us and bearing witness, the unbelievable vista of the landscape under a lowering sun is the setting for something even more unbelievable.

'Dotted around us are, what I can only describe as, soldiers.' She pointed to the men who were sitting on the bench and the two at the church.

George turned the camera onto both pairs.

'And bringing up *our* front is just one, single, solitary girl.'

The camera studied on Alison then, determination and relentless focus set in her face and movements.

She held the staff casually in both hands and firmly planted her feet into the pavement as she walked.

'It seems that these men have deliberately created a *diversion* for reasons we don't yet know, but it would seem we are about to find out.' Diane continued.

Alison stopped with ten yards between her and the big man in front; if he was going to make *a move* then he would have the task of closing the gap.

'Do you really mean to take me on with a stick, girl?' He said. Funnily though, he didn't actually sound mean. 'There's four of us.'

Alison didn't show anything, she just looked at all of them again and then settled her eyes back on the one in front of her. 'I migh' no' ge' them, but al ge' you.'

She planted the staff really firmly by her boot and stood straight. 'An' it'll 'urt an' all. Y' might even lose an eye.' She promised.

The man continued to stare. There was no anger or stinging scorn in his look though. It was something else.

He walked slowly up to her, palms held out so she could see he meant no harm, then stopped in front of her and planted his hands on his hips and looked down into her small, fearless face.

'Hamish was right;' he said, 'you are *bloody terrifying*.'

All the breaths which had been held behind her were expelled at once. Mathew just laughed.

''Amish? 'Ow'd y' kno' 'Amish?' She asked, her suspicions lessened but not gone.

'There's not a lot of time to tell you all of that here, the police will be back on vigil in a few minutes. But Hamish did tell me to tell you my, err, the-the, err, name he gave me.' The man said uncomfortably. Suddenly he didn't look so big anymore.

'Yea?' Alison pushed.

'Um. *Maj-major-disaster skittle-butt.*' He quickly said, blushing and looking down. The name wasn't the problem, it was the story behind it, and anyone who had heard the name knew the story.

Alison squealed and dropped the staff to the ground and then took a running jump right at the big man, wrapping her arms around him.

Very quietly, mainly because she was squeezing into him so hard, she was heard to say; 'You saved 'Amish's life! An' he's told me tha' story, an' when he did, I said I would giv' you an 'ug if ever I met ya, cos 'Amish is one o' t' best people in this world.'

The ex-soldier stood a little stiffly at being hugged so genuinely by someone who he had never met and who, just a minute ago, was going to give him a kicking.

'He is that, love,' he answered, and then returned her embrace, 'he is that.'

Chapter Thirty-Seven

Captain Henry Dixon, the man who had rescued *The Freedom Walker*.

Well that wouldn't come out for years yet, but the man himself sat in the back of his mate's transit van and told Alison how he knew Hamish, and why he and his three comrades were there and, the burning question on Diane Jones' lips, why they had done what they had.

'He calls me once a month.' He told them. 'Part of our bargain, you see?'

'Yea, 'e told me 'bout callin' ya.' Alison nodded.

'What was the bargain, Mister Dixon?' Diane asked, still in reporter mode and with George stood filming quietly in the middle of the van.

Her balance was supernatural as she stood there swaying and dipping and bobbing, the camera appearing to simply, somehow, float in the same spot in front of her.

The retired-serviceman dropped his gaze and frowned. There was a moment of silent respect for wherever the man's thoughts were carrying him.

He looked back up. 'I did save his life; I dragged him out of a house when he was injured. Yes, I did that.' He remembered. 'But what Hamish did for me can't ever be repaid; he didn't only save my life from death,' he looked at them all one at a time, 'he saved my life from *life*; a dead soul is just that, dead, but a *living* soul which is dead...' He trailed off for a moment.

'I came home and I couldn't cope.' He said unashamedly. 'I'd had that company for years, all of them, my lads, my good and honourable brothers who I had to lead and protect and order into the thickest of the shit.'

His jaw clenched and unclenched as he spoke, then slowly it relaxed. 'And slowly they disappeared, one by one; Fallon, Hamed, Carmichel, Regis, Torbin, Khan, Benson, Hewitt, Davis. Almost half of us.' He continued grimly.

'Then one day someone was finally happy and said, *right chaps, I think we've broken it enough, well done, well done.*' He mimicked. 'And we came home and I couldn't cope.

'I was in a *game* when I walked down my street, through town, anywhere I went. It was so surreal to be in built-up areas, only the experience can explain it to you, not words.'

He sat back. 'My family took the brunt of it. They were three, strange people to me when I got back. I couldn't reattach to them, my nerves were shot and my emotions were frayed into going AWOL.

'I slept in the garage for three months, on the floor, a toolbox for a pillow. I didn't want comfort, I couldn't handle it, I needed to stay on the edge all the time.

'I'd go for long walks into the countryside, get under the canopy of trees. Slowly I started to go there more and more and stay for longer before going home again, until one day I didn't come back. It was Hamish who came in and rescued me.

'I was in there for more than a month before he found me, and then he stayed with me for another month until we came back out. And I haven't looked back since.'

He sat up straight again. 'And if it wasn't for him you would have ended up in the *wrong* hands, so you could say he's rescued you lot as well.'

Mathew raised a finger. 'How did he exactly do that? I mean how did you know to wait for us there?'

Henry nodded to Alison. 'He knew Nippy would bring you one of two ways. I've got another three lads a few miles over to the east, but this way made more sense.'

'Could you tell us why you are helping Mathew and Alison to evade detection?' Diane asked.

'Hamish asked.' He shrugged. 'If he thinks it's important, then it's important. Besides,' he gave Alison a friendly pat on the shoulder, 'he said he'd set her on me if I didn't.'

The van began to slow down and then it turned sharply to the right, driving along for another few minutes before stopping.

'Looks like we're here.' Henry said.

He opened the back doors and jumped down.

George and Diane came next, followed by Mathew who was being helped by Alison.

They had stopped at the top of a long, dirt road, which was splitting two, huge fields down the middle. Both fields ran all the way up to a wooded area at the back, the place they had stopped.

Henry took Mathew's arm as he climbed out of the van.

'Hamish said that when he first met you he could see a stubbornness in you that would keep you on the road. I've got to say, Mathew, I totally agree; I can see you're bloody knackered, man, and yet here you are.'

Mathew slowly climbed to the ground and stood up straight. 'I don't know if I should thank you for that or set Alison on you.'

Henry just laughed and took his arm leading him around to the other side of the van.

'I've read the reports now,' he said, 'and what it is you're doing, but you don't strike me as the *unhappy-suicide* sort at all, in fact I would say it's quite the opposite.'

'Yes, you've got that right, but when I first set off, that very first day,' he paused and thought back 'Well. Let's just say I wasn't very happy and the final straw had been drawn.'

'And now?' Henry asked.

Mathew scoffed. 'I haven't felt so happy and alive since before my wife passed away.'

He then went on to tell Henry about the similar conversation he'd had with Cecily and the offer she had made them.

'Ah, yes, *having a future*,' Henry nodded, 'that would do it. So what are you going to do?'

'We'r' goin' back,' Alison firmly answered before Mathew could reply. 'Ar'n we?'

Mathew smiled his warmest smile; she really was a marvel. 'Yes we are,' he said and pulled her closer. 'We're going back.'

Henry led them through a gap in the trees and then out into the open again. A small, white cottage stood in the centre of a perfectly round grove.

'This belongs to Jonathon and his wife,' Henry told them, pointing to the man who had been driving the van.

Jonathon gave them a wave but stayed back where he was.

'It's private and protected,' Henry carried on, 'you can have a good rest here and know that no one,' he looked at them both keenly, a promise in his eyes. 'And I mean *no one* will come here to disturb you.'

Mathew was puzzled by how he had said that, then took note of the other men who had escorted them here and were now standing back waiting. Like soldiers.

The reason they hadn't all gone *selfie*-mad was because they were - for want of a better description - on duty.

He gazed at them, they gazed back. 'I-I don't know what to say,' he said to them all and Henry. 'I don't really know what's happening *out there*,' he gestured with his hand to everything over the trees, 'or why, for that matter. It all seems to have bloomed into something else now.'

George moved in with her camera as Mathew addressed the men who had all given up there current lives to step back into their old roles as shields and protectors. Alison held his hand.

'I suppose I could just say *thank you*, couldn't I?' Mathew continued. 'But-but that would make it all about *me*, and it's not about me, I don't think it ever really was.

'Something needs to be said and I have found myself being the one who is going to say it, but you,' he pointed at them, 'all of you, and all of the other people I have met on my journey and all of those I haven't met, it's *your* voice as much as it is mine.

'I'm not a hero like you.' He then said. 'I'm scared of cows, for goodness sake.'

Alison affirmed that with a nod.

The men chuckled.

'But I'm not a coward either, I'm just soft, as Alison points out to me often enough.'

They all laughed then.

'A person can only be pushed so far,' he carried on, 'before something breaks in them, and I think that we are all being pushed too far now. Something needs to be said.'

He blinked and then just stood there looking a little embarrassed; speeches weren't really his *thing*.

The man called Jonathon spoke. 'You're right about one thing; you're not a hero like us; you're a hero like *you*. It's a personal thing, you understand?'

The others all murmured their agreements and nodded.

Mathew once again found himself not knowing what to say. Then he laughed. 'It's all a bit bonkers really, isn't it?' He carried on laughing. 'I mean, I'm a seventy-seven year old, ex-railway engineer walking to London from Doncaster, I have the tiniest bodyguard in the world, the prime minister is looking for me and four soldiers are going to keep guard while I have a kip!' He continued to laugh and threw his arms up. 'You couldn't make this stuff up could you!?'

This was one of the rare occasions when George's camera wobbled because she laughed along with everyone else. It was absurd when you heard it said like that.

Henry clapped him on the shoulder. 'Come on, let me show you where you'll be sleeping.' He offered. 'The lads are going to set up and then we'll get some food on.'

He led Mathew and Alison to the front door of the cottage, while Diane hung back with George and finished the evening broadcast.

George turned her camera onto the three other men who were now retreating to the van again.

'Another day's adventure for *The Freedom Walker* draws to a close,' Diane said and turned to the camera, 'and his *guard* are now leaving to set up position somewhere out of sight to continue their watch.'

She paused, allowing the van to be seen departing back through the trees

'Being a witness to this remarkable story as it has been unfolding can only be described as something of an historical privilege.

'The world has its eyes firmly fixed on us now and I think the feelings of everyone, both near and far, who have some connection to Mathew Arnold's quest for justice by way of their own daily, suffering, can be summed up by the actions of the men who have now stepped up to the plate to lend their assistance.

'These retired soldiers, with their own, horrifying experiences and stories from the wars overseas, have answered the call of one of their own, a man who has himself been homeless for more than five years and whom Mathew has met and spent some time with.'

She took a deep breath and paused again, the reporter disappearing as Diane came to the surface.

'I don't think I need to tell you anymore, do I?'

She sounded like she was talking to someone right in front of her, someone whom she knew intimately.

'The seriousness of what is actually happening is more than apparent now I would think. It doesn't matter what *they* think or try to get us to believe; Mathew Arnold is right.' She calmly said, almost matter-of-fact. '*He* knows he is right, *we* know he is right and most importantly, *you* know he is right; our rights as human-beings are being horrifyingly abused in every quarter of our existence now, everything from food, water and shelter to birth, marriage and death is now being held in the greedy, corrupted and deceitful hands of *others*, and it *must* be said out loud and then stopped.'

She straightened herself out again and smiled.

'The news you will soon see on your TV screens will, no doubt, be told very differently than how I have just said it, but you will know the difference won't you?' She asked. 'This is Diane Jones, for *Globe News*, saying goodnight and think freely.'

Chapter Thirty-Eight

An after-glow of fire remained in Mathew's mind when he opened his eyes again.

Alison had curled up on the rug and fallen asleep almost immediately after they had eaten and Henry had left.

Mathew had taken to the chair and sat thinking for awhile. And then it had happened again.

Alison's face was bathed in the orange glow of the fire as Mathew watched her sleeping.

A splitting log had cracked and popped loudly, sending a million fireflies straight up the chimney, and then it had all smokily frozen.

The detail was vivid, every spark was sharply outlined and the flames were deep and pulsing, while Alison's small fairy-face was radiating a pale, warm light.

He wasn't afraid, he was fully aware of what was happening and simply relished the moment until he knew it would all gather back up and bring him up to the present.

He sat and sighed and then smiled to himself. It was okay.

* * *

The prime minister stood at her window in her chambers, arms clasped behind her back.

She stared out into the midnight sky and wistfully wished that *she* could shoot someone and make it all just go away. Preferably Palmerson and his little squad of *pillocks*!

Only an hour ago the police-commissioner had demanded to know why Mi6 were discharging weapons at the side of a busy, main road. *Demanded!*

She couldn't see the stars tonight, the outer-reaches were hidden by a slow, gliding blanket of dark, concealing cloud.

Why couldn't she find him? One man for God's sake, why wasn't he being brought in? How could someone as old and as slow as *The Freedom Walker* not get picked up by *hers* but was being seen by everyone bloody else!?

Even the live reports didn't provide any clue to his actual whereabouts, that bloody Jones woman had made sure of that.

There was some small hope though; the firework distraction which Jones had reported on had been called in by the local police, so they at least now knew the approximate location.

Her reflection in the glass caught her eye. 'Distraction.' She murmured. 'Coordinated distraction.'

She sighed and then turned away, walking over to the decanter of brandy on her desk. She poured herself a double and then took it to her seat.

The liquor warmed her throat and soothed her thoughts.

The timing had been perfect, far too precise, she had thought when first seeing the footage, but as it carried on and the camera revealed the four men and the waiting van – number-plate and markings all conveniently blurred out - she had shivered; she knew a soldier when she saw one.

It was getting very bad very quickly. The world had seen that whole report. The only thing missing which stopped it from looking like a coup was a painted flag and the presence of weapons. Thank God for small mercies.

She scoffed and then took another sip.

God. The one thing she was hoping Mathew Arnold would do was spout off a load of religious rhetoric, but he hadn't, not a single psalm's worth. She could have played one of many mental-health cards then, but no, he was all for homeless bloody soldiers and coffin-dodging pensioners.

It would have been nice if she could have brought him in quietly and then quickly get the job done, but now there was a reporter with him stealth was pretty much redundant.

So be it, let them see what they like; once *The Freedom Walker* was off the road everything else would be elementary *damage-control.*

Flooding the area with the police and media had been the only sensible thing to do, but it wasn't making great news on the national stations. It was beginning to look like everything Diane Jones had been saying was actually true and the mainstream media stations were in danger of unwittingly *scoring for the other team.*

Her brandy disappeared and she pushed the glass back on the desk. She stood and then walked around to the front.

Her shoes slipped off and then she undressed and changed into her sleeping garments; khaki sweatpants and matching vest.

Laying down on her sleeping mat in the middle of the rug, she folded her arms behind her head and lay staring at the ceiling.

They would have him in just a few hours. And if they didn't? Well, she would personally *kidney-punch* her way to him if she had to, so it would be better for everybody if they did.

* * *

'There.' Elias said and pointed through the dark to a tiny pinpoint of light.

'I see it.' Singh replied breathlessly.

He made a move to carry on but Elias pulled him back down to his haunches.

'Not yet, there'th guardth.'

Singh looked around. 'I can't see anyone, are you sure?'

'They wouldn't be much good ath guardth if they were eathily thpotted would they?'

Singh had another look, straining his eyes through the dark and squinting hard to get a point of focus. Apart from managing to look like he was straining for a pooh he saw absolutely nothing.

'They're not vithible.' Elias said.

'Then-then how do you know there are guards?'

The big tracker scoffed. 'I can thmell them.' He pointed to his left 'One there,' and then to the middle, 'two more there,' and then the far right, 'and one down there.'

Singh's mouth rose at the corner while he studied his large, lisping companion.

'My dad used to tell me a story about how he crept up on an enemy outpost in the pitch dark once.' He told Elias, that look of schoolboy amazement he was so good at doing masking his face. 'He said the only way he could find his targets was by smelling for them and then spending hours creeping up on them to *take them out.*'

Elias sniffed and nodded. 'A Gurkha you thay he wath? Thoundth egthactly like the thtorieth we have heard about them; fierth warriorth.'

'You've got that right; my dad had the medals to prove it too, but outside, at home, you would never have guessed what it was he did. He was such a gentleman and a true advocate of peace, even if it meant fighting for it.' Singh smiled sadly. 'He passed away two years ago, ninety-two he made it to.'

The big tracker clasped Singh by the shoulder. 'Then he'th thitting at the thame table ath my own father.'

They took that moment to remember their fathers and then Elias pointed to the west. 'Thirty-minuteth that way and then we will cut back in behind the firtht guard.'

'Roger that.' Singh replied and smiled. 'Lead on.'

* * *

223

Even though Elias didn't know for a fact that he was heading straight for the cottage where Mathew was sleeping, his trackers-sense had pointed him that way anyway, and he and Singh were definitely on the right track.

Whereas Palmerson - who had been relieved of his sidearm by Dixon until he had definitely *uncompromised* himself - was following his own intuition and might as well have been on another continent altogether he was that amiss.

'Right, lad, dawn's not far away.' Palmerson spoke as he pulled his sleeping-bag up to his chin. 'They'll be coming out right here, but you know these bloody *protesters*,' he said the word like it encompassed a whole, sedimentary section of the population who all fit neatly under its label. 'They'll be lazing away until lunchtime wishing they had Jeremy Kyle and can of *super-strength*, so might as well get some sleep.'

Dixon remained silent, not that Palmerson really noticed.

He was well and truly *pissed off* with the job today. Rugby-tackling his boss was bad enough - even if Palmerson *had* understood and forgiven him - but watching, helpless, as he then flashed his badge all over the place to the police who had arrived armed and ready to take on world-war three by the looks of them, had really driven something home; no one was free or safe if a badge of authority could clean away a serious crime and the perpetrator could just get back in his car and drive away. What was *that* about?

Since driving away from the police, with Palmerson at the wheel, Dixon had slowly come to the conclusion that he was nothing more than a Doberman; somehow his badge had become a dog-collar and he was being wielded by an authority which could bypass the very laws he was supposed to be upholding.

He didn't think for a minute that *The Freedom Walker* was about to come out here anytime soon. Or ever even.

Well at least Palmerson was miles away from anything, both literally and inside his head, God knows what would happen if he actually got his hands on Mathew Arnold.

Palmerson snorted and muttered and then snored deeply.

The old man was too long in the tooth for this job now, his perspective seemed to extend somewhere from the seventies; a relic of the *struggles* and countless *black-ops*.

Dixon sighed, breathing his frustrations out; Palmerson was as much a victim in this as Mathew Arnold was, or any of them for that matter.

If the world was being turned by slaves looked over by Dobermans, then it stood to reason that every, single person under the *rule* had no say in their own lives. Why was that and when did it begin?

Thinking about the trouble which *The Freedom Walker* was causing them all - was *going* to cause if he reached London - made him wonder if this wasn't all very carefully planned out. Not by a person, or even a group of people, no this was a plan which seemed to be just happening as everything transpired, but was so cleverly executed that only something *supernatural* could have planned it. Not ghosts or spirits or anything *mystical*, but a *super* nature event.

It was as if the way people had been pushed and shoved around, pressed, squashed, shaped and reshaped until they eventually fitted into the shape which *the Masters* had cut out for them, had made something in these people react in certain ways to certain events and happenings.

The shape of Mathew Arnold's journey was absurd, and yet there it was and it had happened because many, many other individuals and groups of people had somehow helped him along, opening before him like the parting sea and then closing tightly behind him so that his pursuers were either lost or drowned.

Nature had, had enough, her *keepers* were being herded and being prevented from carrying out their duties of care.

His eyes shone in the dark; what the hell am I thinking? Where did that come from?

He had shocked himself with such a radical and yet arguably sane theory, but it made him sound so, so, - he didn't want to think the word - *hippyish*.

He gulped. *I care about the world, of course I do,* he thought to himself, his eyes wide in the dark. *But I've just* cared *in a really strange way haven't I?*

Like a hippy you mean?

Yea.

Cool.

Who are you?

I think I'm your inner-hippy.

The dark wasn't helping his mind-opening thoughts at all, he was sure he could see through the canvas of the tent. His eyes seemed to pierce the blackness and then reach out between the treetops and see the stars and the galaxies beyond. They swirled languidly, a sparkle-pop of light pricking through and then quietly dulling away again.

For the first time in his life, young, Brian Dixon felt he was actually somewhere where he was supposed to be. Not *belong*, but more like a single player on a cosmic game-board - he would be damned if he was going to use the super-cliché of *chess-piece* - who could only be in this place at this time for whatever it was that was *going* to happen, *to* happen.

Was he scared? Well just like the thrill of his first ride on the *corkscrew roller-coaster* when he was eleven, he was bloody petrified!

Chapter Thirty-Nine

Piping brass cornets and the voice of Nat King Cole sang out through the radio in the cottage.

"There may be trouble ahead,
But while there's moonlight and music and love and romance,
Let's face the music and dance."

Mathew and Alison were going through their morning tea-routine and the straightening out of their sleeping spaces.

'I slep' righ' well.' Alison said as she folded the blankets she had been under.

'I know, I heard you.'

She sniggered. 'Eh? 'Ow can y' 'ear someone sl-' She stopped what she was doing and looked at him levelly. 'I *don'* flippin' snore!'

Mathew stirred the tea. 'Oh. Must have been a burst drain or something then.' He said and threw her a sly glance. 'Or a gurgling bog-pipe maybe.'

'I'll gurgle *your* bog-pipe in a minute!' She snapped and pointed at him. 'What does that even mean?'

'I don' kno' do a? I've only jus' woken up!'

Henry walked in from the outside and stood in the doorway to the living room.

'You were out like last summer's fashion when I checked in on you last night' He said. 'Someone snores like a rattling lands-'

A dark green and relatively heavy cushion whacked him in the face.

He blinked sharply. '-Or not.' He finished.

Mathew chuckled and handed the tall ex-soldier a cup of steaming tea. 'Good morning, Henry.'

Henry stooped to pick up the cushion and then took his tea. 'Thanks.'

He threw the cushion back on the chair and then sat in it. 'There's a lot of activity out there this morning.' He nodded through the bay-windows to the outside.

Both Mathew and Alison stopped what they were doing to listen.

'Started in the night.' Henry continued. 'There's law enforcement and media all over the place now.'

Alison sat down on the settee and stared off somewhere neither Mathew nor Henry could see.

'Ar' the' all in t' village?' She asked, not breaking her gaze.

'A heavy proportion of them yes, but there's police patrolling the roads further out as well. Maybe as far as ten miles out.'

Alison's face didn't change, she just nodded slowly, thoughtfully. 'So t' reporters an' tha' are all in t' village though?'

'Yes.' Henry replied and frowned. 'Why? What's up?'

She looked round at them both then. 'It means everyone's already watchin' village like hawks, dun'it?'

'Doesn't it.' Mathew put in.

'Doesn't it.' Alison dutifully repeated, not in the least bothered that she was being corrected.

Henry just studied her. What did it mean that the village was being watched? What good was that?

'They don't know you're aware of them.' He finally said and nodded. 'Clever. They are exposing themselves so blatantly that it can only because they don't know that you already *know* that they are looking for you.'

'Zackly.' She replied. 'An' the' watchin' roads an' not woods an' fields; we can easily ge' ou' if we go straigh' over t' fields at back o' t' 'ouse.' She nodded over her shoulder.

Henry sipped his tea and thought about it. 'That's good thinking, as long as you can stay unseen from the air.'

Alison nodded again. 'Yea, tha'll b' a bit more 'ard but nowt we can' 'andle.'

And there it was, Mathew thought, when he saw the expression on Henry's face suddenly change, that moment when the soldier didn't see a teenage girl anymore and found himself looking at Glitter-pony's *giant* instead.

Her words themselves should have come across as just bravado, or even just teenage ignorance, but it was the way she said them that pricked him very deeply; to Henry, she sounded like an old soldier who was only alive because he had gone to war saying he was already dead.

He continued to frown and study her, not being completely aware that one: he was being rude, and two: he was staring at a potential *pit-bull* who hadn't been awake for very long and even more seriously, hadn't had her cup of tea yet because Mathew was just sat staring at Henry with a big, silly smile on his face.

Alison leaned over the chair arm and looked right into Henry's, green eyes. 'A y' gunna ask m' forra selfie?' She quipped, pursing her lips tightly. 'Hm?' Like *Cruella D'baby-Jane*. The bedraggled hair wasn't helping the visage much either.

'Terrifying.' Henry quietly said, eyes pretty wide for a man as big as himself in front of this *lamb* of a girl. 'I'd have you on my squad any day.'

Alison's eyes hardened and her nostrils flared. 'Right,' she said sharply, 'Am gunna 'av a cuppa tea now,' the *clinking* of a stirring spoon immediately took up as Mathew caught the hint, 'an' then am gunna 'av a wee an' a wash.'

She paused and then said; 'Like a *normal* person. Right? Like someone 'oo does *normal* things an' is just,' she leaned a smidgen closer. '*Normal!*'

'Okay.' Henry nodded.

The tea appeared and broke the grip of the *pit-bull's* stare.

'Thank you.' She said and took a big slurp, emphasising that she was just drinking tea like every, other *normal* person did.

'It's a good job you're not called Abbie, really isn't it?' Mathew said.

Alison just looked at him over the edge of her cup but didn't ask why, just stared the question across.

'You would have been *Abbie*-normal, then.' He chuckled.

Alison's body and face, or anything at all for that matter, didn't move a single jot, but somehow her whole presence became harder and more *hitty*.

Mathew quickly picked up his cup. 'You wouldn't hit someone holding a boiling cup of tea now would you?'

'Yes. Yes a would, Mathew,' she said, wet-lipped and smiling strangely, 'a would do that.' She took another big, mental, slurp and spoke over the rim of her cup. 'A would.'

It took another thirty minutes for Mathew and Alison to get themselves ready for more walking.

They stood side by side in the front garden, with George and Diane rolling off their morning broadcast behind them.

Henry handed Mathew his bag. 'We've restocked your essentials, you'll be fine for three or four days.'

'Thank you, Henry,' Mathew returned. 'All of you.' He looked at the other men standing around the van.

They all nodded and smiled silently.

Henry turned to Alison then. 'Keep to your plan, stay in the top fields until you have to cross the road. And mind the skies.'

'We will, thanks 'Enry.' She said. Then she frowned and pointed. 'A' the' wi' you?'

Henry turned to look at the two men who were just now emerging from the trees at the front of the garden. 'No.' He answered darkly.

He threw a glance at the lads by the van. They all stepped up and stood waiting, and then Henry made to move out and meet the two strangers, but Alison beat him to it.

She pulled her hood up and grabbed Mathew's walking-staff, striding forward and planting herself in front of him just as she had done when Henry had first met them.

She didn't speak and just stared at them both with a look which said *you're about to walk into a brick wall.*

Elias stopped in his tracks at first sight of her, the look she had given him had been all the warning he had needed.

'Who'th that?' He asked Singh. 'What'th she thtaring at uth like that for?'

Elias knew a *look of curses* when he saw one. Or thought he did.

'Um.' Singh began.

He wasn't paying much attention now because his *windswept-angel* was standing right there and blushing furiously at him through her smile.

Alison took another step forward and peered right at poor Elias then. 'Wot's wrong wi' y' tongue,' she asked, 'an' wots all tha' on y' face?' Her arm raised and she pointed it in circles at the scarring on Elias' cheeks.

He took a frightened step back; the little creature had just cursed him, he was sure of it. What his ears had heard and his eyes had seen had been translated as: *Wossron wear tung! Anwossaltha onyafays!* Accompanied by a gesture with her hand.

'D-did she juth curth me!?' His eyes were enormous and afraid.

Everyone stopped their thoughts at the same time and looked from Alison to her *victim* and back again, blinking away a Morse-code of astonished puzzlement.

Alison shook her head and tipped the staff toward Elias. 'A dint curse ya, y' wally! 'Ow does tha' even work!?'

Adinkussya ywali! Owduztha eevenwerk! And she'd pointed her staff at him that time.

Elias took another step back and to the side, keeping Singh in front of him.

A moment of weird silence followed then, weird because everyone had just witnessed a little girl routing a very tall - not to mention very capable - *warrior* with her stare and staff.

Diane cleared her throat. 'Dev?'

Singh smiled and raised his hand. 'Hi.'

'Um, who's that with you?' She asked, pointing at the frightened man hiding behind him.

'This is Elias, he's a tracker.' He replied moonily.

Alison looked gob-smacked! 'A tracker!? Forrus? Tha's mental!'

'What'th she thaying now?' Elias asked.

'I-I'm not sure. I think she's wondering why there is a tracker looking for them.'

Mathew had heard enough. 'Just who the devil are you?' He asked as he walked up to Alison's side.

Diane quickly trotted over to both of them before it got out of control (and whether she would admit it or not; because she didn't like the thought of Dev getting hurt.)

'That's, um, Dev, he's the agent I've told you about.' She told them.

Dev raised his hand again and sheepishly smiled. 'Hello.' And then he held his finger up, calling for a pause.

He turned around to face Elias. 'I'm really sorry, Elias, I really like you.' He said, a small look of shame in his eyes, and then he flashed his palm out and grabbed Elias by the cuff, pulling the man forward to throw him off balance ready to be pinned.

Elias was cheetah-fast and went with the motion instead of trying to keep his balance.

He countered by twisting his hand quickly over the top of Dev's own wrist and then using the forward motion to spin himself underneath Dev's arm, attempting to twist it at the shoulder and then lock it behind his back.

The agent immediately flexed his thighs at the knees and loaded them with force and then sprang, cartwheel fashion, over the top again, using Elias' grip as a spinning point.

He landed on his feet, each man still gripping the others wrist.

Dev threw a low kick then to Elias' ankles, sweeping the leg and trying to bring the bigger man down onto his back, but Elias was as highly-trained as his opponent was and flipped his heels over his head using Dev's attack to throw himself into a back flip.

Dev narrowly avoided the flipping heels as Elias whipped over and back onto his feet again.

Both men still had a hold on each other.

Everyone else stood watching agape at every gob.

Elias took up the initiative next and tried to use his extra height and weight to Judo-throw his opponent over his shoulder.

Dev reacted by leaping again, this time bringing his legs straight up and straightening himself out upside-down, he then twisted to the side so he could grab Elias' head between his knees.

Elias was already on the forward foot and so when Dev applied his downward force - aided by a healthy dose of gravity - the tall tracker went flying head over heels with the clinging Dev still attached.

They thumped to the grass.

Dev immediately began pulling Elias' holding arm down toward himself while at the same time he pushed his knees up to apply pressure to the man's chin and throat, effectively cutting of his air supply.

Relaxing his body entirely for just a second, Elias then punched the back of the choking legs with his free hand.

The sudden lull in tension and then the powerful punch had been enough to free Elias' head and the choke-hold he was under.

He raised himself into a sitting position and reached out to grab Dev by the lapels.

Dev slapped his hand away expertly and then brought his foot up to crack at Elias' chin.

Elias slapped the foot away and reached out again for Dev's lapels.

Snatch SLAP!

Kick SLAP! And so on and so forth.

No one in that group had ever seen anything like the display of speeding, martial-arts that they had just witnessed. And that was saying something, because seven of them had been to bloody war!

But they were now sitting on their arses and were actually slapping each other like children in the playground sandpit.

Kick SLAP!

Alison marched over to the pair of them.

Snatch SLAP!

'Will you two idjats jus' stoppit! Wha' ar' you doin'!?'

SLAP! SLAP! Slap…sla.

They slowly stopped and looked up at her.

'What did she jutht thay?'

'I'm not sure, I think she wants to know what we're doing.' Dev answered, and then turned to Alison. 'I'm here to help you.' He said hopefully. 'There's a lot of police and-'

'Wait a minute,' Elias put in, 'I'm here to help them ath well.'

Dev smiled like that schoolboy. 'Really? Why?'

Elias shrugged. 'Why do think? Becauth of Palmerthon.'

'Me too.'

The pair of them held onto each other but as comrades now.

They stood up and brushed each other down and then shook hands warmly and then embraced.

Alison blew her fringe from her eyes and shook her head, bewildered. 'A y' gunna 'splain wha' y' doin' or am a gunna use Mathew's stick on ya?'

'Explain.' Mathew said.

'Explain.' She repeated.

Elias looked to Dev again. 'Do you know what language she'th thpeaking?'

Mathew chuckled. 'It's Yorkshire.'

Elias looked at the small girl who, by the way, was still looking very unimpressed with them all and had begun to scowl again.

'Are they all ath fierth ath you in Yor Ksha?'

Alison's scowl lifted and was replaced by eyebrow-raising disdain.

She handed Mathew his staff back and walked off toward the trees where Elias and Dev had appeared from.

'I'll b' sittin' in t' *sane* part o' t' world when y' ready t' ge' off again.'

Chapter Forty

Palmerson and Dixon paced. Palmerson because he was getting impatient and Dixon because he was making sure his boss didn't walk straight off the edge of the gravel-pit they had ended up at.

They had just had news from Elias that morning, a set of coordinates and message that *The Freedom Walker* was close to that area. An hour they had been waiting now.

Palmerson had steadily built a wall of cigarette butts along the track he was blazing back and forth.

Dixon kept an uneasy eye on him, but something other than his boss' mental state was also bothering him; what the hell were they doing here?

They had been miles away from the original path, the path which Mathew Arnold and the girl had clearly been on when Palmerson had decided to split up and follow his own nose.

And now Elias had sent them even deeper into the country with the promise that they were on the right track and he would be making his way right to them.

Something stank and it wasn't his boss' smokes.

Palmerson stopped his pacing and stood looking down into the gravel-pit, squinting to get a better view of something.

Dixon followed his gaze.

'Do you see that, lad?' Palmerson asked.

As much as he really wanted to say he couldn't see anything, Dixon nodded as two people clearly walked between the gap of the entrance to this huge hole in the earth, walking casually from behind one mound and then across a short, gated path to disappear behind another.

Palmerson clapped him on the shoulder and giggled. 'In we go then.' He said, and pointed over the edge and down the slope.

Without waiting for Dixon to reply he slipped his legs over the edge of the pit and began sliding, slowly at first, down the dry, dusty scree. Plumes of yellow and brown rock-dust began to follow him as he slid.

Dixon just stood and watched, helpless, as Palmerson's speed increased. The smoky dust suddenly resembled something from a *Roadrunner* cartoon, and before long there was nothing to be seen of his boss at all. But he could hear him.

Noises like *oof* and *eek*, and *aah* and *ooh* were not so subtly mixed in with the sounds of the hushing scree, and every now and again an explosive puff of dust erupted upward as Palmerson slammed into the ground while he bounced, sending up little smoke-signal plumes of helplessness.

It felt like hours were passing, his boss was approaching the bottom very slowly it seemed, and Dixon cringed and gritted his teeth at every thump, bump and smoke-signal, wringing his hands in a silent prayer for it to just bloody stop!

Palmerson rolled and tumbled all the way to the bottom and then came to a sharp halt with a crunch and an '*Oh, thank God!*'

It went eerily silent for a few moments.

'A-are you alright, sir!?' Dixon called, aiming it at the big, yellowing cloud which had completely enveloped his boss.

Through the billowing thickness, Dixon watched as a form began to take shape, the bright sunshine filtered through the dust-cloud and created a Palmerson-shaped, staggering shadow.

The shadow stepped out of the dust but remained almost as a shadow, just much lighter now.

It coughed and a small landslide fell from its head, then it spoke, small billowy-puffs coming from its gob. 'Are you just going to stand there all day, lad?' Palmerson called and placed his hands on his waiting hips.

Dixon didn't know what to do or say. The old man looked like he had just stepped out of a demolition job but didn't really seem to notice that simple fact.

There he was now look, pulling out his crushed cigarettes and lighting one up as though he had just had his dinner and a pint!

'I-I-um. I'll case the perimeter, sir, and meet you at the gate.' He shouted back. 'Just in case they slip up the other side before you get there.'

Palmerson pointed with his cigarette hand. 'Good thinking, lad, I was hoping you were going to say that.'

He turned away and waved behind him and then walked through the settling dust-cloud and quickly made a path to the gates.

Dixon began legging it around the edge of the deep pit and made his way to the road which the gate ended at and where Palmerson was headed.

He wasn't worried about his boss, but there were two people, somewhere down there, who he *was* worried about his boss meeting up with. Thank God he still had his confiscated pistol in his pocket.

Below, walking quickly, dragging a dusty cloud behind him, Palmerson zeroed in on the gate.

They would be somewhere beyond it, he was certain. Pity he didn't have his pistol though.

The gate wasn't locked when he tried it, so he pushed it open and strode into the road and followed it for a few yards until it opened out into a huge yard.

There were old buildings dotted all over the place; disused and abandoned offices and warehouses, two-storeys high, and a scattering of wooden sheds and shacks.

He made his way to the nearest building, offices with their windows painted out in white by the looks of it.

He stopped outside the open doorway and listened. It was eerily quiet. Then his eyes widened as he heard a quiet footfall coming from somewhere inside and above him.

Stealth was his game, he was trained for this, he lived for it.

He quietly stepped inside and walked down a corridor with empty rooms on either side. A staircase lay at the end of the hallway and a doorway led on into another long corridor beyond.

Scuffling feet and then full on running steps came down from above.

Palmerson used his target's noise to mask his own and made a quick dash for the stairs.

He stopped at the bottom and stood still, looking up and listening.

Another set of feet began running, this time coming from behind him in one of the upper corridors or rooms.

He placed his back against the wall, giving himself the widest view possible of the upper landing, and then began slowly creeping up, one ginger step at a time.

At almost exactly the same time his feet had reached the last step and he was looking left and right down another empty corridor, a whistle was suddenly blown and a dozen or more pairs of feet began stampeding simultaneously, the din coming from everywhere at once.

Palmerson pressed himself back against the wall in the shallow well of the stairs, blocking his view of the corridors to the left and right.

He stared straight ahead to a closed door in front and held his breath as a shadow appeared beneath the door before it was thrown open.

A small, black-clad figure, with a full-face combat-mask and red helmet on its head, appeared in the doorway and halted dead in its tracks, took an insanely deep breath and then screamed like a woman - which she was.
There was a zombie standing right there!

The stunned Palmerson raised his arms and opened his mouth to speak, and then cringed and looked on in complete disbelief - and a little horror - as she raised what looked like a small machine-gun and pointed it at him.

She pulled the trigger and hail of red paintballs splattered across Palmerson's torso causing him to take a shuddering step back and groan. Like said Zombie.

At the sound of the weapon being discharged, those numerous other pairs of feet which had all been running toward him suddenly turned and began legging it back again in retreat.

He narrowed his eyes and glared at the woman and then lunged out and ran toward her.

She screamed again, dropped her gun and ran back into the room and away down another corridor at the back.

Palmerson stopped at the door and picked the paint-weapon up.

He shook his head sadly and smiled madly, stroking the barrel clean of dust and inspecting the almost full hopper of red paintballs. *This is my rifle, there might be other rifles like it, but this one is mine.*

He set the fire-rate to single-shot and then laughed loudly.

Turning left he walked confidently down the corridor and began doing what he was very, very good at.

Dixon, meanwhile, was still running pell-mell along the outer edge of the gravel-pit, skidding his way down the sides as he approached the end of the rim before sliding down a shallow hill until he reached the bottom.

A tall, wire fence stood before him with an open gate in the middle.

He ran through and into the yard which Palmerson had entered by the gate from the pit itself, dramatically sliding to a halt in front of the large, painted sign which welcomed all visitors through here, the *proper* entrance.

'*The Garrison - Paintball for Elites.*' It proudly proclaimed.

'Oh, bugger.' Dixon's shoulders sagged and he sighed heavily. And then he cringed as the high-pitched, shrill scream of a woman came from the building at the end of the yard. *Looks like she's met the demolition man then.*

He trotted off toward the building, his heart not exactly heavy but trying its damnedest to drop into his stomach.

He reached the open door and stood as Palmerson had done, looking inside and listening.

He didn't have to listen for long before he heard the running feet of the people upstairs.

He stepped inside and called out. 'Hello?'

Pfft! Shplatt! 'Agh! Not in the face!' Someone shouted 'Who is tha-!'

Pfft! Pfft! Shpla-shplatt! 'It's gone in my mouth!'

A woman screamed again, Dixon wasn't sure if it was the same one or not. Then a man screamed.

Pfft! Pfft! Shplatt! Shplatt!

'Get be'ind 'im!' *Pfft!* 'Be'ind '*im* not me!' *Pf-pf-pfft!* 'Aagh!'

A charge began from the furthest part of the building, steadily growing louder and heading for the stairs.

'Oh, God!' Dixon mumbled and held his head in his hand. They were going to try and rush him. They didn't stand a chance.

With that very thought... *Pfft! Pf-pf-pf-pfft! Shplatt! Shp-shp-shp-shplatt!* 'I can't see!', 'It's in me hair!' and 'Aagh!'

Dixon stepped back outside, shaking his head, and stood leaning up against the wall next to the door.

His head dropped to his chest and he wondered if he should take up smoking *before* or *after* he'd lost his job and had been sent to the brig for the rest of his natural life! Knowing his luck he would wind up with Palmerson for a cell-mate.

Now, poor Dixon had no idea that Elias had been fibbing and so presumed that only he and Singh were now on their way, so he was more than a little alarmed when he heard the *whopping* of helicopter blades.

Pfft!

And they were flying right toward him, two of them.

Pfft! Pfft!

Well that was it then, that was the press or he wasn't and Mi6 agent. And might not be for much longer.

He straightened himself out and brushed himself down; might as well look presentable. It couldn't get any worse now could it?

And then it did.

The first of the red-paint covered, screaming women - or was that a man, Dixon still couldn't tell - came belting down the corridor and then out into the yard.

Steadily more feet began approaching and a few seconds later a steady stream of Palmerson's victims came running out, all adorned with the hall-mark head and multiple chest-shots that old man was so brilliantly trained to do, bless him.

Dixon was wondering if he should just shoot himself right there and then when the upstairs windows were shattered and a fair-sized wooden table came flying out.

He didn't move a muscle, he simply pursed his lips and waited patiently.

The helicopters were hovering overhead, their film-crews suicidally hanging themselves out of the doors to catch the story and action explosively unfolding below them.

The Paint-ball gunman was standing in the smashed-open window now, two paintball-guns in his hands, firing out at the helicopters with a Rambo-style snarl slashed across his yelling, dusty, pale face.

Palmerson was at home.

Chapter Forty-One

'It's very peaceful isn't it?' Mathew remarked.

It really was a calm and still afternoon.

'Might b' a storm comin'.'

Mathew looked around. The sky was clear and blue and empty. 'I'll take your word for it.'

Alison pointed to the hills surrounding them. 'It'll come o'er them. All t' air's stayin still an' gettin' warm, an' then all o' t' cold air from right, high up drops down on it and clouds start t' form and then it rains.'

Mathew looked up to see if he could see the cold air. 'How do you know all that?' He asked, genuinely intrigued.

'M' dad.' She answered, shrugging 'Farmin' meks y' keep y' eye on t' weather.'

They walked along side by side, almost another fifteen miles laying behind them now.

'I've go' an idea.' Alison said.

'Oh, yes? About what?'

'About 'ow we can ge' in t' London wi'out bein' spotted.'

'Without.'

'Without bein' spotted. The's a village down 'ere an' the's a bus tha' goes righ' to a bus-station in London.'

Mathew frowned. 'A bus? Really? Would that be wise?' He asked, and then added, 'are we really that close?'

'Yea, abou' twenny-five miles mebe.'

He stopped in his tracks. 'Are you serious?'

She stopped and turned around to face him. 'Yea. Why, wot's up?'

Mathew looked quite shocked and then he smiled broadly. 'I actually walked to London.' He said proudly.

Alison grinned then. 'Yea, you 'av.'

She took his hand and pulled him onward.

The sun was ahead, low and beckoning, while the narrow canal they had been following flowed along by their side, keeping them company with its slow, silky gurgle.

Autumn creatures watched them go by from their places in tree and hedge, hole and crevice, log, rock and pebble, nature's witness; the old man and the tiny girl who were twenty-five miles away from changing the world.

* * *

Training. She loved training. She loved training and money and telling people what to do.

The prime minister lunged and double-jabbed at the punchbag; *thwack-thwack!*

What she *didn't* like were those people who she had told what to do, not doing as they were told.

A roundhouse kick followed by a lunge-kick sent the bag hammering back. *Thwack! THUMP!*

Crispin didn't like that either, because when people didn't do as the prime minister had asked it was he who had to hold the punchbag.

That last kick had seen his feet leave the ground as he hung on and was swung backward.

He steadied himself and the sawdust-filled bag, and then sniffled.

'So, Crispin,' *thwack! Thwack!* Double-jab again. 'Our media has finally caught up with the Freedom Walker.'

Thwack! Kick! Head-punch, drop-kick. *Wham!Wham!* And a double-hammer knee to the guts.

'Oh! Wait.' She then said, sarcastically innocent. 'Not the Freedom Walker,' *thwack!Thwack!Thwack!* Flying-backhand, double-punch. *WHAM!* Jumping double-heel kick to the face. 'IT WAS PALMERSON! WHY WAS IT PALMERSON, CRISPIN!?' She yelled as she flipped herself back onto her feet.

The bag was swinging quite high now, Crispin firmly attached, clinging on with legs and clawed hands like a Koala infant on its mother's breast.

'I don't know, Prime Minister.' He sobbed.

As the bag came back toward her the prime minister darted out and hammered her elbow into it and brought it to an abrupt halt.

Crispin bounced to the ground, landing on his arse with a bump and a squeak.

She stood in front of him and began unwinding her knuckle-dressings, her jaw tightly clenched as she concentrated on the wrappings and not strapping Crispin to the *front* of the punchbag and having another twenty minutes.

She flicked her eyes up and looked at him. 'How is it going so wrong?' She asked. 'How can one little, old man and an even smaller girl get past all of us, hm?'

She didn't wait for him to answer. 'Why now? Of all the times it could have come to this, why actually right bloody now!?'

She stabbed a finger down at the ground, emphasising the *now*.

Crispin picked himself up and brushed himself down, wiped his eyes and blew his nose. 'I don't know, Prime-Minister, I can't even begin to see where it could have gone wrong.'

'It went wrong, Crispin, when I listened to *you* and kept Palmerson in the field after someone had *blabbed* to that bloody Jones woman.' She pointed at him.

He dropped his gaze. He heard her sigh then.

'Well until we know where Arnold is we can't do anything else can we?' She pointed out.

The cringing Crispin looked back up. 'I would suggest,' he began.

She gave him a look which said this had better be the suggestion to end all suggestions, the golden-fleece of suggestions, the very suggestion God himself would want to hear.

He coughed and cleared his throat and then continued. 'We could utilise the city camera network.'

She raised her eyebrow. 'I'm listening.'

'If we use the EARS we can monitor everything which approaches. They will have access to all of the cameras which are all around London.' He cleared his throat again. 'As long as they are switched on, that is.'

She frowned. 'Switched on? You mean using cameras attached to mobile devices which members of the public are using?'

He remained silent.

'Are you mad, Crispin?' She looked at him sternly. 'If it ever got out that we had the capability to do that we would have a countrywide riot on our hands.'

Crispin nodded. 'Yes it would be bad, but only if it were to be discovered that it was *we* who were doing it.'

She gave him another queer look; he actually sounded a little confident that time. 'Again; I'm listening.' She said, and began drying herself off.

Crispin went on to tell the prime minister about a *deft piece of software*, as he called it, which could do things like send emails and mobile text messages to anyone in the world and actually show up as coming from anyone they chose. Anyone at all including *The London Globe* or even Diane Jones herself.

She had thought about that. 'So if we do it,' she began, raising her eyes to the ceiling and thinking it through. 'And we were discovered, we could deflect the blame to someone we don't like, and if we *don't* get discovered, we've given ourselves an advantage.'

She began pacing as she dried her hair.

Crispin stood back and just watched as she thought about the implications.

'Okay, let's do it. You set it in motion, Crispin.'

'Yes, Prime Minister.'

'Now, what do we do about the broadcasts which have been going online?'

Crispin began pacing then, head bowed as he thought about the damage which had already been caused by Diane Jones and her newscast.

He stopped and looked up. The prime minister had removed her top and was stood drying her armpits, looking at him and waiting for his reply.

'I-I-um, I-I think once we h-have Mathew Arnold with us, I-I um,' he seemed to be addressing her bared breasts. 'W-we should be able to completely discredit the whole thing with-with our own titties. I mean boobs. News!'

She placed her hands on her hips and made no effort at all to cover herself up. 'My face is up here, Crispin.'

He quickly raised his large, round eyes.

'Anyway, I thought you were gay?' She asked.

Crispin looked even more shocked. 'What? I-I-what? Why?' He said. 'I-I'm not gay.'

'You could have fooled me, Crispin.' She said, still doing absolutely nothing at all to cover her breasts, or to show that she was even bothered that Crispin wasn't gay after all.

'Wh-what do you mean?' He asked. Probably one of *the* most difficult question his eyes had ever had to be part of.

'Well, you *look* gay for a start.'

He straightened himself up. 'I must say, that's a little homophobic, Prime Minister.' He replied a little snootily.

'Yes, maybe,' she answered, 'I don't care. Come here.'

'Wh-what? Why?'

'I'm going to kiss you and then I'm going to molest you, Crispin.'

Crispin's eyes widened again. 'W-what?' He squeaked.

'I said I'm going to kiss you and then I'm going to molest you. So come here.'

He blinked a half-dozen times and then a very tiny smile appeared at one corner of his mouth.

Crispin Wells strode onward to take up his duty as aide to the prime minister of Britain with pride.

And neither of them were the ever same people again after that.

* * *

A simple plan from a simple girl. No that wasn't right, Alison was anything *but* simple. Diane scratched her head and thought.

George sat opposite her at the table they were using. The roadside cafe had beckoned both of them with the words: *Bacon* and *All-day.*

A simple plan by a small, giant of a girl. Hmm. That nearly worked. She could make it work when they broadcast.

'Do you think your boyfriend and his buddy will be okay?' George asked.

She cut up her bacon and egg breakfast and dipped her sausage into the runny yolk.

'Hm? What? Oh. Yea, they'll be f-.' Diane looked up from her notepad. 'Oh. No. No, Dev's not my boyfriend.' She flushed as she spoke.

'Soon to be maybe?' George said and winked at her as she stuffed sausage into her mouth.

Diane's blush increased furiously as her eyes watched the sausage disappear. 'I-I don't know what you mean.' She coyly answered and then returned to her jottings.

George chuckled through her food. 'Yea, righ'.' She teased. 'Well you could have fooled me; the way you were both looking at each other - especially, *Dev,*' she said the word as salaciously as the single syllable would allow, and then *chcked* her tongue and winked. 'He looked ready to sweep you off to the nearest motel!'

Diane's pencil clattered to the tabletop. 'He did not!' Her face was scarlet by now.

George raised her cup but said nothing.

Diane smiled and then covered her face. 'He did didn't he?' She confessed and laughed. 'He is gorgeous though, isn't he?' She said, looking up like a moony twelve year-old.

'Yea, he is, and he's dead keen on you.' George raised her sausage again and pointed at her.

She bit into it again and then pointed back, narrowing her eyes a little this time. 'If he's ever found out, about talking to you I mean, doesn't that make it some kind of crime over here? Like treason or something?'

Diane thought about it. 'I don't think it's treason as such, I don't even think it's interfering with police business either.'

She pondered it again. 'He'll probably lose his job though.' She looked a little sad when she said that.

George scoffed. 'Who needs a job like *that*!? And with that other man they were talking about, Palmerson was it?'

'Yes.' She looked into space at nothing for a moment. 'I don't know.' She continued, looking back to George. 'He must have worked hard to get to where he is.'

She leaned closer and smiled widely. 'And did you see what he did when he was fighting Elias?'

Both of them giggled then.

What they had seen *both* men do had really knocked their respective socks off.

'Well I sure hope they both stay safe.' George said and carried on eating.

'I'm sure they will be, Alison has a remarkable mind, don't you think?' Diane remarked. 'When she told us of the next stage of the journey and what we all could do to help…' She trailed off.

'Mm. Yea. She's a clever girl that one, she'll do well no matter where she ends up, you can be sure of that.'

Diane sat back and sipped at her coffee. 'Do you think he can do it?'

'Huh?'

'Mathew. Do you think he can make it and do what he says he's going to do?'

The Canadian sat back and wiped her mouth on her napkin. She picked her coffee up. 'I think so, yea.' She took a sip and studied Diane. 'Do you?'

Diane thought back to that first day she had accidentally bumped into him, boobs out and knickers in her pocket. She wouldn't have thought it then, but after that first meeting? 'I think so too.' She said. 'But I don't want him to.'

It was George's turn to think back to Mathew.

She had been staggeringly unimpressed at first glance. But after she had spent more than a day with the pair of them, watching and listening to them as they just went about their quest with an air of regularity, she realised that Mathew Arnold was exactly what he said he was.

He had no social facade, he didn't need it, and that was a very unique and strange thing to comprehend when one had spent their whole lives constantly lifting and lowering a multitude of masks just to be able to function in so-called *civilised* society.

'I don't know what I feel about that if I am to be completely truthful, but I do know this; the world needs that man and girl to be right where they are. And the millions of people who are watching him know that.'

She raised her cup in toast. 'All of them know that, Diane.'

Chapter Forty-Two

It was Dev's turn to drive and Elias' turn to eat and drink.

'What do you call thith again?' Elias asked, holding his paper-wrapped pasty up for Dev to see.

'Cornish pasty.'

'Cornish pathty.' He repeated and took another bite, *mm'ing* as he chewed. 'Nithe.'

He opened the road-map and drew a line with his finger. 'Nextht thtop ith about five mileth away.'

'I'll talk to him thith-this time.' Dev replied and cringed inwardly. He cast Elias a hasty, apologetic glance. Maybe he hadn't heard him properly.

'I heard that.' Elias said.

'Sorry.'

And then he laughed. 'Don't worry about it. It happenth all the time back home.'

Dev relaxed. Apart from Elias being a Tutsi and ferocious with it if he wanted to be, Dev liked the man immensely

'I don't want to pry, but I've heard some stories about the wars - the Rwandan wars.' He began. 'Are you a victim of all of that?'

He looked over to Elias, who had his eyes straight ahead and a face which looked to be carved from the purest onyx.

The big man took a deep breath. 'Yeth. It wath at the very beginning of the uprithing,' he looked at Dev, 'before they thtarted cutting off armth.'

He turned away again and frowned out into the world. 'They came through my village and *educated* all of the males under the age of thirteen by hammering penthilth into their ea'th, tho they couldn't be *educated* by the government fortheth.'

He looked back to Dev. 'And if they thought we had already been educated they cut out our tongueth tho we couldn't thpread it.'

Dev gulped. 'I-I'm sorry that you had to endure that, Elias. I-I don't know what to say.'

'You don't have to thay a thing, my friend; what we are doing now ith all the payment needed. Maybe even for all of the crimeth of the world.'

A pub loomed up in front of them, the next stop.

Dev brought the car into the car-park and killed the engine. 'Do you really believe that? I mean *I* do, for some strange reason I believe that.'

'Yeth I believe that. There ith thomething very powerful about Mathew Arnold and the girl.' Elias replied. 'If you athk me what it ith I couldn't tell you, but it'th in the very air, in the earth; thomething ith happening all around the world, we can all feel it becauthe we are all feeling it at the thame time. A thtrange connection.'

The younger man sat and pondered that. Then nodded. 'A strange connection.' He repeated.

Of course, Dev was thinking of Diane Jones right then, but it was a poignant moment. And just a little bit *treacley-pink-fluffy*.

This stop was the last, from here they had to make the final call to Lars Forsberg and make a new false report.

'Quite brilliant when you think about it.' Dev said, while he dialled Lars' number on his mobile.

'Yeth, she'th a very athtute girl. And a bit frightening ath well.' Elias gave Dev a serious, wide-eyed look when he said that.

'It'th a good plan though,' he continued. 'I can't thee anyone getting near them now. Not before they reach their goal anyway.' Elias answered.

Dev opened his mouth to speak but his call was answered almost immediately. 'Hello, Mister Forsberg? We're here.' He said and paused while he listened. 'Yes, that's the one.' And paused again. 'Um, hang on a minute and I'll have a look.'

He got out of the car and looked up at the sign for the pub. 'It's called *The Travellers Inn*.' Pause. 'Right, give us a few minutes to get the orders in and I'll send pictures straight away.' Pause. 'You too. A pleasure to work with you, Mister Forsberg, goodbye.'

He walked back to Elias. 'He said we should order lunch and eat at this place, take a picture over the top of the food and make sure to catch an empty spot in front.'

Elias got out of the car. 'Well, ath nithe ath the pathty wath, I thtill have room for more.' He patted his stomach and grinned.

The pair of them marched off together, this unlikely duo of Mi6 agent and Tutsi tracker.

Above their heads the Universe smiled down and nodded its approval; a tiny blue rock was suddenly at the very centre of everything, and it was all because of one old man and a little girl and the people they had deeply touched as they had encountered them on their journey.

* * *

The world had become increasingly quiet over the past five days, the buzz and usual noise and clatter was at an all time low as people everywhere watched this strange story unfolding on their Internet screens.

246

Mainstream media, worldwide, had seen their ratings plummet, while *The Freedom Walker* website had more than ten million followers now, and three times that in visits to the website.

And if the number could have been accurately counted, half the population of this entire planet were now whispering to each other, sending the messages far out into even the most remote of places.

If only the powers that be had simply kept quiet about it, if only they hadn't all sent their own - owned - journalists out to simply try and play it down or even maybe get a good old *smear* on Mathew. If only they had taken this *silly old man* more seriously. If only.

* * *

Lars Forsberg paced his small, private room at the back of his large, studio-office. This was his *think-tank* and it had a member of one; him.

It was getting very warm now, the heat of the world was bearing down on him, business-peers shouting out their frustrations and consternations at him, threatening him with disassociation. Even the bank was getting involved now. Not that it surprised him; it was the banks who had the most to lose. And they *were* going to lose, he could feel that now. They could feel it.

Five, false sightings had kept most if not all of the heat from Mathew and the girl Alison, but it wouldn't be long before someone, somewhere managed to *switch them off* and close the stream down for good.

Owning your own satellites went a long way to keeping it up and running, making it as difficult as possibly could be for any would-be saboteurs, but they were running out of *firewalls* now.

His team had thwarted over twenty-eight thousand attempts by unknown - ha! Unknown? Really? Ha! - hackers who had tried to access *The Freedom Walker* servers and take control. Twenty-eight thousand was an unprecedented number of attacks and only went to show just how frightened the *masters* really were.

He sipped at his water and stared at the only adornment in this room; a poster-size photograph of the Universe as seen by the Hubble telescope.

This was his connection to Mathew Arnold; just human-beings under the same stars and in the same Universe, uniquely.

He shivered. So much blood had been spilled in this unfathomable Universe, right here on this planet in fact. It was time for the flow to be staunched and then healed. But would it first have to be wounded even further? Like removing a gangrenous limb.

His head dropped and his gaze fell sadly. The rivers of blood he had seen already, the pain and suffering he had witnessed and chronicled, all of it he had borne in silent rage, filed away but never forgotten. His horrifying motivator.

There had never been an opportunity to present everything and then say; *look! This is happening. We must end it now.*

There were papers and documents and articles and newsreels full of the very same horrifying motivators, presented with alarm and by wide-eyed, serious professors, clergymen, doctors, philanthropist, archaeologists, humanitarians and even soldiers and the victims themselves, and it all amounted to nothing more than a *show*, a morbidly attractive *story* for the public to feel outraged about while they sat in the false-comfort of their own lives.

But the day and age of the terrorist-governments and their private wars and their greed was all on the verge now. The question was; what was awaiting us on the other side of that precipice?

The wall behind him slowly began to glow with a subtle green light; someone had entered his office.

He took another sip of water and then left his *think-tank*, the lights dousing themselves when the door closed behind him.

'Everyone has left now, Mister Forsberg.' It was Bianca, his personal assistant.

'Thank you, Bianca, you can-.'

'If it's alright with you, I'd rather stay here, sir.' She said, standing up a little stiffly.

At sixty years-old, Bianca was still the most solid foundation which Lars Forsberg had with him.

'Then you're off duty.' He wouldn't bother arguing with her, he didn't stand a chance and he knew she'd probably ignore him anyway.

She looked at her watch. 'I am. I hadn't seen the time.' She smiled and let her official position retire for the night.

'Right, I'll make us both a stiff drink and then you and I, Lars, are going to sit it out together, up here.' She said.

She crossed the room and opened the door into the small kitchen and then turned around. 'I've taken the liberty of having mattresses brought up.'

'What about Carl?' He asked, Carl being her husband.

'He's on his way and he's bringing some friends.'

'Friends?'

'Don't treat me like an idiot, Lars; I saw security leave and I know why they have left.'

The company who provided their security was owned by one of the *masters*.

'An oversight we shall have to correct when this is all over.' She added.

He smiled. 'Thank you, Bianca. How many more are coming?'

He raised his drink to his lips and took a mouthful.

'There will be thirty men here in about an hour.'

And then immediately spluttered it out again. 'Thirty!? Did you say thirty?'

She smiled as broadly as he had ever seen her smile before. And she was smiling because she had never seen her boss lose his composure before, let alone slop his drink all over his shirt, shoes, carpet and desk.

Priceless, absolutely priceless.

* * *

Mathew lay with his eyes open but unseeing.

Alison sat by his side and watched him, holding his hand tightly.

The campfire was high and warm in front of them while everything around them faded away into that insignificant shadow-world. Nothing outside the ring of firelight could encroach, but everything watched and listened and held Mathew's hand as tightly as Alison did.

The soft ground beneath him embraced him and held him in place, *his* place, and it connected him to the Universe in its own, unique way.

His mind was at ease. It was nice here. It was neither light nor dark, this place, it was something in between but not grey. A new colour perhaps.

I can feel everything. That's strange. Am I dreaming, I wonder. I wonder.

And then there is that; there it is again, that black-violet mote which is both darker and brighter than everything else. What is that? And now there are two of them and then twenty and a million and then none again.

I wonder.

An ocean is swelling, I can feel that, hear it without my ears.

Oh, bugger! I'm dead aren't I? That's what this is.

No. No, that's not it, I'm alive, I can feel myself in exactly the same way I can feel the ocean. Well it was worth a shot I suppose. Maybe I'm not all dead, maybe I'm only half-dead.

No, I was half-dead before I stepped out. Hm. Still, it's very pleasant here, I could stay here if this were *the place we go afterward. Mary would love it here.*

I'm here, love, if you can hear me. Still on the road and still toilet-water free.

The earth gave a subtle shift beneath his prone body and his eyes slowly began to un-glaze.

Oh! I think I'm off again. Blooming typical.

And there's that mote again. I wonder.

I wonder if that's Mary.

Chapter Forty-Three

As soon as she saw them walking down the road toward her, she knew who they were; Mathew Arnold, *The Freedom Walker*, and the little bodyguard Alison.

Senna French whipped out her mobile and swiped open the camera, and stood waiting for the pair of them to pass.

She raised her hand to wave at the smiling pair, her thumb hovering over the *capture* button on the screen, and then she just froze.

Mathew gave her a big smile and hearty hello, waving as he did so; a normal, cheery old man. And then she had seen Alison's face and the stare she was giving her.

Alison shook her head and wagged her finger and then pointed up at the sky and finished by putting her finger on her lips and *shushing* quietly.

Senna French took a minute to let the cryptic hand signals and blazing glare add up and then she smiled and nodded and pressed the capture button. The camera flashed.

Mathew reached out with his free hand and pulled Alison back to his side by the collar.

'What are we called?' He said and laughed.

'Eh?'

'*Freedom Walker*, remember? She's free to do as she pleases.'

He pulled Alison close and hugged her to his side gratefully. 'You're such a good friend and carer, Alison, uncommonly brave and loving and very understanding with your brand of wisdom.' He said and then released her.

He turned to look down into her face but she wasn't there, she was off and pelting it across the road to the young woman with her mobile.

He threw his arms out and gave in.

Alison would be damned if a stupid cow with a mobile phone would jeopardise her plan. And besides that, she had totally gone and done the opposite on purpose so she couldn't give a damn about them anyway.

'Oi!' She shouted as she came to a halt right under the woman's nose. 'Why wou'd y' do tha' when I asked y' no' to, eh? A y' tryin' t' ge' pleece on us?'

The woman blinked rapidly. 'Wotcha say, lav?'

'Eh?' Alison said and blinked herself then.

'A sed wotcha say, lav? You awite?'

'Eh? Wot a y' sayin'? A y' postin' tha' now? Cos pleece'll come righ' 'ere y' kno?'

'Ey?'

'A sed pleec'll come.'

'Wotcha sayin', lav? I can see your marf movin and ya geddin' ahngry an' awl.'

'Wha'?'

And that was how Mathew finally found them when he walked back up the road; frowning at one another and saying *wha'? Eh? Ay?*

'Just stop, will you?' He stood his staff by his foot and leaned heavily on it. 'Now, let me translate. Alison is saying if you post that image of us the police are likely to come and pick me up, and therefore not allowing me to get into London.'

The woman rolled her eyes. 'Right, ah see, lav. Weww you're in lack, lav becau-'

'Well.' Mathew said.

'Pardon?' The woman said.

'We*LL* I'm in luck.' He emphasised and then smiled nicely.

Alison looked at the woman. 'Yea, 'ee does tha'.' She winked.

'We*LL* your in lack cos I 'aven't posted anyfing yet.' Senna carefully said.

Mathew continued to just look at her, his smile still nice. Very nice.

'Anything yet.' She then added sheepishly.

Alison's grin threatened to catch the breeze and whip her off her feet if she wasn't careful.

'Well thank goodness for that.' Mathew said. 'What's your name , young lady?'

'Senna French.' She answered.

Mathew held out his hand. 'Thank you, Senna, and it is a pleasure to meet you. Would you like a *selfie*?'

Senna beamed almost as widely as Alison had been doing. Only now *she* was rolling her eyes and tutting. *Bloomin' selfies!*

Once Senna had a photograph of all three of them safely on her phone, they had left with the promise from her that she would only post it once she knew for certain that they had reached their goal.

'What a nice young lady that was.' Mathew had said.

They were just walking past the first of the houses along this short road leading into a fair-sized hamlet.

'Yea.' Alison nodded and agreed. 'She could do wi' some English lessons though.'

'Ha!' Mathew guffawed.

'Oh! Shurrup.' She huffed, but laughed anyway.

She had found herself doing that a lot with Mathew along this journey. It somehow felt okay. It was going to be okay.

'The's a caffy down 'ere.' She told him and pointed to the crossroads they were heading for.

'Cafe.'

'Cafe.' She dutifully repeated and then without a pause said, 'a y' bloomin' sure y' wanta a teacher or summert? In y' past life mebe?'

Mathew laughed again.

'Y' kno'? One o' them *irritatin*, Victorian teachers tha' y' jus' wanta 'igh five in t' face wi' a deckchair?'

He loved it by now and his sides were telling him so. 'Oh, that's mean.'

They turned the corner and there was the cafe *and* the bus-stop a few yards ahead along the road.

'We'll be in London soon.' Alison said, crisply.

Mathew shot her a fast look and then shook his head. 'You blooming catch me out with that every time.' He gave her a friendly nudge. 'You're like a little posh fairy when you talk like that.' And then patted her gently on the head.

'Gerroff, y' wally.' She batted his hand off. 'I'll give *you* posh fairy in a minute!'

Mathew laughed all the way to the doorway of the cafe. 'I still don't know what that means.'

'Oh! Shurrup.'

They walked through the wooden door and into the cafe, still talking and ribbing each other.

The bell *dinked* and then they both stopped dead in their tracks and stared at the broad backs of the two uniformed policemen sitting at the counter.

Coffee and doughnuts. Mathew instantly thought for some, American reason. *Doughnuts though*. It had been awhile since he'd had a doughnut.

Alison started to back him up slowly, but Mathew was pulling the other way.

He gave her a warm smile and just shook his head and then led her to the nearest table.

They sat down.

'I think I'm going to have a doughnut or four.' He said. 'And do you know? I really fancy a cup of coffee instead of tea.'

Alison just looked completely gob-smacked. 'A we really doin' this?' She hissed.

'Doing what?'

She looked around her and then settled her eyes on the policemen for a moment and then just looked back at Mathew again. Her eyes were trying to tell him - slap him actually - that *this* was what she meant. 'This!' She emphasised with sharply raised eyebrows.

'Um.' He began, and then scanned the room himself, his own eyes settling on the open display of cakes beneath the counter. 'Well I don't know what your doing, but I'm having some doughnuts and coffee.'

What could she say to that? Her mouth opened ready to deliver an automatic retort, but her brain had nothing it could think of for her open gob to actually say. So she didn't and just snapped it shut. 'Right. Coffee and doughnuts then.' She just stood straight up and marched up to the counter.

Three minutes later and she was back with seven different doughnuts and a pot of coffee for two. And the coppers hadn't even looked at her; heads down as they were and busily demolishing their mounds of mashed potato and peas and pie.

Mathew poured the coffee, eyed up the doughnuts and chuckled for no reason at all.

'Oh! Shurrup.'

'You *shurrup*. Pass me that disgusting yellow-iced thing at the back would you please?'

Alison carefully picked up the requested lemon-cream and icing-sugar doughnut and leaned over to hand it to him.

He reached out just as her hand glided away again and speedily found her own mouth instead, which incredibly made almost half of the doughnut disappear with one, single bite.

She leaned over again and held out the rest, her cheeks bulging like gerbils pouches. The pressure was actually squeezing little bits of mashed doughnut and cream out from the corners of her mouth there was that much stuffed in there. 'Wan' shum?'

Well the little devil! Not to be outdone, Mathew snatched the remainder of the doughnut and shoved the lot into his own mouth, chewing it spitefully and never taking his eyes from hers. '*Fang oo, ishk wovwy*!' He almost actually said.

Alison snorted and a little cream shot out from the corner of her mouth and landed on the side of the coffee pot with a perfect *splat!*

Mathew made a gurgling guffaw with his mouth wide open and then almost choked on the creamy, yellow mess which was quickly finding his tonsils.

And the policemen *still* didn't turn around and have a look at them; refilled plates in front of the both of them and a coffee on the house at their sides.

Only then did Mathew notice the old man who was serving them.

He was watching Mathew and Alison intently, and the look on his face said he was doing his damnedest to remain calm and not freak out, because sitting right there is *The Freedom Walker* and *right* in front of him are a couple of local coppers - good lads, honest to a pinch - and the amount of mashed potato they could devour was actually an unknown, so could they please, for God's sake, *keep bloody quiet!*

'I think we should be quiet.' Mathew said quietly.

Alison gulped down the last of her doughnut. 'Why?'

Mathew nodded to the old man. 'Because we're scaring him into giving free food away I think.' He answered.

She turned and studied the old man for a moment and then smiled weakly, nodded once and turned back to Mathew again. 'Yea, y' right.'

She picked up another doughnut. 'Wondered why 'ee dint charge me fo' these.' She said and took a bite. "E dint look like 'e reco'nised me.'

She turned around again and held the doughnut up, mouthing the words *thank you.*

The old man just somehow went even paler. Was he clenching his jaw as well?

And then the thing which the old man was clearly trying to avoid dodged his attempts skilfully - as is often the wont of fate the fickle - and a deep voice said; 'Well, 'Arry. If ya gonna rob a bank, today would be the day to do it; we'd never catcha.' One of the policemen said.

They both pushed back their seats and stood up, the pair of them going through the usual *standing-up-after-stuffing-up* routine of back stretching, shoulder squeezing, stomach tapping and plenty of *oh'ing* and *ah'ing.*

'Right, see ya on Sunday mornin' then, 'Arry.'

'Ta-ra, 'Arry, give ya best to, Madge, mate.'

'Take care, lads.'

The policemen turned and walked down the small aisle of chairs and tables, both of them nodding and smiling a friendly, community-bobby acknowledgement as they passed granddad and granddaughter enjoying doughnuts. And then walked straight out of the door.

Mathew and Alison, and particularly Harry, watched with exactly the same expression on their puddled faces as the pair of burly coppers turned left and walked past the window and then out of sight.

'Cor! Blimey!' Harry wheezed, holding his chest and looking like he'd just seen Elvis himself. Harry was a mad Elvis fan, so, so, mad. 'I fought me *spare-part* was gonna burst!'

'Eh?' Alison said.

'Pardon?' Mathew followed.

'I said-' Harry *slammed the invisible piano lid* in front of him and shook his head. 'Neva mind.'

He limped over to them and pulled up a seat at the table. 'I caan't beelieve yaw in *my* gaff!' He laughed.

'And I can't believe that you knew we wouldn't want to be spotted by the law.' Mathew returned. 'Why did you do that?' He then asked and picked up another doughnut. 'Thank you for these as well, very kind of you.'

'Yaw wewcome.' Harry replied and smiled. 'Yew deserve more than I could eva giv ya.'

He poured himself a coffee. 'The world's gone maad aint it?' He said. 'And then yew cam along and BOOM!' He chuckled.

'Boom?' Mathew asked, but chuckled as well. *Boom?*

'Yea! Boom, mate. The world's watchin' ya, Mista Arnuwd, miwyons ov peopuw. Miwyons.'

There were actual tears in Harry's eyes as he spoke.

Mathew reached out and grasped old Harry's hand, giving him that *Freedom Walker* smile which he didn't even know he had. 'Mathew.' He said kindly. 'My friends call me Mathew.'

Harry sniffed and wiped his eye. 'Yev got a lowed on ya plate, Mafyew, but there's a lowda peopuw be'ind ya as wew, rememba that. Ya not alown.'

Alison had been sitting and nibbling the *corners* of a doughnut, fascinated by the words that Harry was saying.

She turned to Mathew. 'Can you un'erstand 'im then?'

Before Mathew could answer, a shadow appeared at the window. It was one of the policemen.

He looked at them all shrewdly, then cast his eye to Mathew's staff and then back again.

They all just sat frozen in whatever pose they had been in when he had first appeared.

'Uh! Oh!' Mathew managed to murmur.

The burly copper frowned. Then looked to the right. Then back again. He nodded almost imperceptibly at Mathew and Alison. 'Bas ta Landan cams in fifteen minutes.' He said and then grinned at them broadly before walking back the way he had come.

Harry broke the dazed spell by laughing. ''E's a good laad, thatun.'

So it seems as if Mathew and Alison had been stroked by lady-luck herself then.

They toasted each other and Harry, and finished their coffee (free refill provided) and a particularly nasty looking doughnut which looked like it may have come from the side of a small boat.

But luck isn't all one-sided you know? No, it often likes to fall on *snake-eyes* when tumbling for those double-sixes.

The tiny red light of the security camera which Harry had over the counter and till blinked slowly. Slowly enough so they didn't notice it at all while it languidly spied on them.

Chapter Forty-Four

Rumbling wheels and the thrum of the dull, diesel engine had seen Mathew drop his chin to his breast, but it was Alison's elbow which woke him up.

'Eh! What?'

The bus journey had been really quite unspectacular, with the only passengers being Mathew and Alison and two old dears sitting at the back.

Wheels hissed as the bus screeched to a halt and the driver unlocked his cab-door, unseating himself and then walking straight up to *The Freedom Walker*.

He actually touched his peak before he spoke. 'There's a roadblock been set up down this road.'

The two women at the back came forward then.

Mathew and Alison just sat silently for a moment and watched.

'Did you say there's a roadblock?' One of the old dears asked.

'Yea, about four-mile down 'ere.'

'Well he can't get out right here!' The other lady said.

'Don't I know it!?' The driver answered.

Mathew's and Alison's heads were turning back and forth as they listened.

'What if we swapped clothes?' The first lady suggested.

The driver thought about it then shook his head. 'What good would it do if you and Ethel swapped clothes?'

'Not *us*, you fool of a man. With *them*?' She pointed at Mathew and Alison.

Everyone looked at them, weighing, measuring, sizing; like undertakers in the fashion business instead of dead-bodies.

'Nah! He'll never get into your clothes, Sheila.'

'Not *my* clothes, you *dingleberry*!' She shouted and rolled her eyes at Ethel, who tutted and rolled them back again.

'*He* would have *your* clothes on, and *she* would have mine.'

Everyone thought for a moment. Alison wasn't particularly keen on the idea of wearing this intrepid old woman's clothes. Not for a million pounds. Ever.

Mathew raised his finger. 'If I might make an observation?'

They turned and looked at him.

'I can't drive a bus.' He stated.

The driver and the two old ladies paused for a second and then *ahhh'ed* simultaneously.

'Wha' abou' in there?' Alison said and pointed to a small, closed door behind the driver's seat.

Mathew nudged her. 'How would both of us fit in there!?'

'We don' need both of us t' fit in there d' we? Jus' you.'

The two ladies, Sheila and Ethel, nodded in sincere approval at each other and then beamed their respectfully radiant smiles right at Alison. *Clever girl, this one.*

The driver opened the small door-cum-hatch and pulled his jacket out. And then his work-bag and training-shoes for when he got back on his bicycle. And some magazines about bicycles. And after dumping all that in the well of his driving-cab he pulled out a fold-up bicycle and handed it to Sheila.

'Plenty of standing room now.' He said and gestured with his hand for Mathew to inspect.

He stood up and had a look. 'Well so there is.' He beamed and stepped inside.

He peered out at them. 'I suppose I should say-'

'Oh, jus' ge' in an' shu' bloomin' door.'

After everyone except Mathew had taken their seats - Alison making hers with Sheila and Ethel now - the bus set off again.

Five minutes later and it was stopping at the roadblock. The driver opened the doors and waited for the policeman to climb on board.

He stepped up onto the floor and scanned the passengers, nodded at them, smiled politely and then turned to the driver. 'Anyone got off before you reached us?' He asked.

The driver shook his head. 'No. Just those three from the village.' He replied and nodded over his shoulder.

The young copper turned back to the three sitting on the rear seats. 'Could I ask you your names please?'

'Sheila.'

'Ethel.'

'Alis-' she stumbled and recovered almost immediately, 'nippy.'

The policeman frowned. 'I'm sorry? Did you say Alisnippy?'

'It's Yorkshire.' Alison said, perfectly forming her words as though she had been born under the *Bow-Bells* themselves.

She shrugged and smiled apologetically.

The policeman relaxed immediately and nodded back. *Oh, right, that explains it.*

He gave the driver a nod. 'Thank you, sir.' And then climbed back down to the pavement.

He waved to the officers who were manning the small, wooden barriers. 'Okay.' He called.

Two of the five men present picked up the barriers and moved off to the side with them.

'All yours, sir.' The policeman gestured to the open barrier.

The doors hissed closed and the bus pulled away and that was that. What was all the fuss about?

The driver pulled over again a few miles further down the road and then for the third time that day he made an unscheduled stop, this one to let Mathew out of his *cubby-hole*.

An hour later and they were entering the fringes of the big city itself. And things suddenly began to look wrong from that moment on.

There was a massive police presence everywhere for a start. It was almost like they were cordoning off for a dignitary or something. Which they were - sort of.

The traffic still flowed along and the people on the pavements were still going about their business, but they all had a look about them, like they were all waiting for something to happen to them over their shoulders and behind their backs. Which it was.

'Cor! Blimey!' The driver called back to them. 'Someone don't want you getting through do they?'

Mathew lowered himself in his seat and turned away from the exposing window.

He gave Alison a frightened look. 'It's all getting blooming silly now.'

She took his hand in both of hers and squeezed it. 'It's bin bloomin' silly since y' 'ad a figh' wi' Rag.'

He relaxed then. Just the reminder of his fiery-dwarf made him feel much safer.

She looked at him, looked into him would be a better way of saying it. 'We 'ant go' this far t' jus' ge' caugh' now. I don' kno' 'ow will get y' t' parli'ment, bu' will do it some'ow.'

He believed her. 'I believe you.'

The journey continued slowly. The traffic helped to conceal Mathew in his seat; lanes and lanes of it moving steadily in one direction or another. Mostly another.

The driver skilfully found his way through the moving lanes of vehicles, keeping inside the middle-lanes and away from the pedestrians.

None of the stops were his anyway; he was heading in completely the wrong direction for his route.

And so the *snake-eyes* popped up again. Not a sighting of Mathew this time, but because a vigilant bobby had noticed that the destination on the front of the bus didn't match the direction it was travelling.

Could have been nothing, but today, PC Brian Hurd - and the rest of the coppers in the briefing-room this morning - had been told to be *extra* vigilant and report *anything* out of the ordinary. And so he did.

And that's why, minutes later, a small squadron of helicopters began to arrive. Well okay, three helicopters. And even more alarmingly; the policemen and women on the paths were suddenly listening at their radios and looking around for-

'That's not good,' the driver murmured, 'they're looking for something and I'm sure it's not love.'

He snatched up his radio and began yammering things into it which Mathew and Alison didn't understand and the ladies at the back couldn't hear.

'Thrilling!' Sheila beamed and clasped her arms about her self, screwing her face up tightly in satisfaction. 'It's like James Bond: *On the Busses.*' She chortled.

'*On Her Majesty's Public Transport!*' Ethel said.

They both cackled and nudged each other.

'The' lovin' it them two arn' the'?' Alison grinned.

She thought both of them reminded her of her nan in a strange sort of way; a bit here and another bit over there.

'We're goin' to take a detour.' The driver called back to them all.

Mathew just waved and didn't care less; he was quite happy to just *let it all happen.* 'Righto.' He called back.

The detour started almost immediately - and quite abruptly and unexpectedly harsh on the old shoulders if you were sitting against the widow-side on the left. Which is where Mathew, of course, was sitting.

Alison, being on his right, helped the wall in its attempt to crush his ribs by being flung into him and adding her own weight to his. She was fine though, she was fine.

'Oof! Blimey!' Mathew gasped.

'I'm fine,' Alison said. 'I'm fine.' And dragged herself back up.

Sheila and Ethel both gave a chuckling *whee* when the bus suddenly turned right.

The speed had picked up a bit now, Mathew noticed. The buildings were quickly zipping past.

'Getting a bit exciting isn't it?' He was smiling but wide-eyed.

The daylight suddenly disappeared as they then entered a long tunnel system.

They both sat back up and looked out again. There were no pedestrians or police down here. But there *was* a lot of traffic and they were passing it at quite an alarming pace, but the alarm they should really have felt was replaced by *jaw-drop-eye-pop* amazement.

Of the four lanes they were travelling along, two of them had an inordinately large number of busses travelling at a much slower speed, effectively keeping the fast lane open for them.

But if that wasn't enough, they watched as busses from behind them came out of their rear-positions and speedily burn right up to the back of them, while ahead a new line of busses fast approached and *their* driver expertly pulled his speed down to come in behind and follow them.

'They've all got the same destination showing.' Mathew noted, blinking stupidly. 'Parliament.'

'Blimey.' Alison quietly muttered, her own eyes still popping out of her head; they were travelling in a wall made of bus bricks.

From the air, every crew - news or otherwise - reported the same thing; the bus which was carrying *The Freedom Walker* had entered the Thames Blackwall tunnel.

They then had raced off to the other side and sat hovering in their designated airspace and readied their cameras and microphones-on-jackets, waiting for the *Freedom Bus* - yes someone actually said that - to re-emerge.

There they ar! - Was the most common first words that any of those crew said. In fact the next words were pretty much the same all round as well: *Around thirty to forty busses have just emerged from the tunnel.* Reported as professionally as their tight faces would possibly allow. And one journalist even said: *My God! It's full of busses!*

The *pack* of busses moved slowly through the traffic, most of which just decided it wasn't worth whatever trouble was coming up behind them in the form of a thick, diesel-spewing wall of public-transport, and just turned off or pulled over at the very first opportunity.

'Blimey!' Both Mathew and Alison chorused this time.

And then somehow, strangely and weirdly magical, all of the engines roared at the same time and all of the horns of them burst forth at once. A mighty blast of some titanic harbinger, a herald to everything before it; *The Freedom Walker* has arrived.

The horns died down and the engines changed back to all of their unique sounds again as each driver now veered off down this way and that, across that road and this other one over there and there and there, until they were all now heading for parliament, but from everywhere at once.

Sheila and Ethel were well and truly impressed by now. 'Blimey!' They chorused, mimicking Mathew and Alison but meaning it nonetheless.

It was exactly three in the afternoon when the brigade of busses began their puzzling and maze-like charge through the streets of London.

Foolishly the media in the air were actually helping the bus-drivers to find the strangest possible routes to their final destinations, simply because they were telling the other road users below what was happening, not thinking for a second that they would actually *want* Mathew to reach his goal.

As news of this final charge began to reach the haggard and almost hostage-held servers of Lars Forsberg back in Sweden, the reports coming from the microphone of Diane Jones and the camera of George couldn't have begun any sooner.

Actual bullets had been fired at the main entrance door-lock of the building he and his personal assistant, her husband and another thirty-seven men - not thirty as she had previously thought - were making a stand.

No bullets had been fired at any people, and the armed police were refusing to go through unarmed civilians no matter *who* gave the order. So instead they were enjoying a classic *standoff*.

At precisely three-forty GMT, the world who had been watching everything so far had seen enough, and suddenly a silent signal was sounded somewhere. A sound which no one actually heard, whispered around the globe as nothing more than a phantom and a thought of an echo of something.

And the people began to move at the same time.

Chapter Forty-Five

She was back at the window, looking down at the streets below. What was she looking at today? On the surface nothing seemed to be any different, but beneath? Beneath there was a *feeling*, that's the only way she could put it; the people milling around in the streets were simply moving with a different *feeling*, and Eliza could subtly sense it from up there in her chambers.

The fuse had reached her doorstep then? Lit by her *fire-starter*, Mathew Arnold, *The Freedom Walker*.

She sighed heavily, resigned; even she could feel the world changing now. It wasn't just the reports she was getting from around the political globe, the messages from ministers of other countries - allied or not - all saying the same thing; there was something *wrong* with their *slaves* and it was *her* fault it was happening. Yes she could feel it.

Crispin sat in her large chair and flicked through some of Eliza's reports. (Yes he called her Eliza, now.)

'Wouldn't it be much better if it all just disappeared?' Eliza muttered.

Crispin looked up. 'I'm sorry? I missed that.'

She turned around to face him. 'I said; wouldn't it be better if it all just disappeared?'

He looked at her serious face, questioning it with his own frown.

She walked over to where he was sitting behind her desk and plopped herself into his lap, wrapping her arms around his neck. 'Let's leave, Crispin, you and I, right now, and not look back.'

His heart jolted in his chest. 'Seriously?'

'Yes, seriously.' She responded with a kiss for his nose. 'Can't you feel that out there? It's too big to resist and, quite frankly, I'm beginning to wonder how I have be so blind to it for most of my life.'

Crispin gave her a reassuring squeeze to let her know she wasn't alone in her feelings about the changing world. Both out there and in here, in their own hearts and minds.

'They're not the people I know anymore, Crispin,' she said, gesturing to the outside world, 'they're the people who *should* have been there all along, aren't they?

'I've been so blinded by *the job*, both back in the navy and here in parliament, that I have become an *overlord* rather than a prime minister, and *my* masters have been pulling my strings for far too long now.

'I didn't know who I was meant to be until all of this happened. And you. Especially you.' She kissed him again, on the mouth this time.

He responded by kissing her back and then holding onto her for his very life.

Crispin Wells wasn't a particularly strong man physically, he was a little wiry and soft in places, but he did his damnedest to lift himself and Eliza from the chair and throw her back onto the desktop, hastily scrabbling the paperwork and clutter away.

Pens, pencils and all adornments including name-plates and pawns set under small, glass domes were brushed out of sight.

And for the very last time in that office, but the very first time for them as just free, loving human-beings, Crispin and Eliza made love, right there on the desktop, before leaving quietly by the *back door*, and were never seen or heard from again.

But I will tell you this; they were together for a long time and were very, very happy, and the people they touched were all left feeling very, very happy too.

A story for another time, perhaps.

* * *

Well, no one was answering their sodding phones now, not anyone with any authority anyway. His mum had managed to get through to him though, *no* problem.

Dixon slumped back in his seat again for the seventh or eighth time in the past four or five minutes.

Even Dev had switched his phone off. And Palmerson? Where the hell had *he* gone? *How* had he gone? They'd had him locked in a cell for Christ's sake!

He needed orders. He couldn't just sit in this roadside cafe all day. But he knew, he just *bloody* knew, that if he went north he was bound to be wrong and should have gone south, and if he went left he should have gone right. Damn it!

His phone rang. It was an unknown number showing on his screen. Bugger it; talking to a *stranger* was better than talking to no one.

'Hello?'

'*Hello, mate. Where are you?*' Dev said.

'Singhy!' He barked, stunned. 'Where am I? Where am *I*? Where the hell are you, agent Singh?'

He paused and then quickly added; 'No, don't tell me because I'll come straight to wherever you are and shoot you myself!'

Dev laughed. '*Okay, mate, I probably deserve that.*' He said, then his laughter stopped abruptly. '*You* do *still have Palmerson's weapon, don't you?*' He sounded a little worried.

Dixon scoffed 'Yes, I've still got it and I'm going to bloody use it on you if you don't tell me what the hell is happening. And you *do* know that the old man has gone missing, don't you?'

'*Mathew Arnold?*'

'Yes.'

'*Oh, no, you see he's fine, he's coming rig-.*'

'What do mean; *he's fine*? What are you doing, agent Singh?' He asked sarcastically, but his voice still lowering as he spoke.

Dev paused and sighed. 'Well I think I'm probably not agent Singh anymore, mate, just Dev now.'

It was Dixon's turn to pause and think. 'Why were you calling me, Dev?' He said, not a hint of agent Dixon being present, just the man who had gone through much of his training with Devram Singh, his friend.

'*Well, mate, I was going to ask for your help.*'

He paused again. '*Things are changing, Rob, I don't know what's going to happen, mate, I really don't, but something's changing and I want to make sure I'm on the right side when it does.*'

Robert Dixon swallowed hard; he had only ever heard Dev speak like that when they had been in the conflicts together overseas. Hearing him talking like that here, on their home-soil, somehow made it even more *real*.

'Okay, Dev, I'm listening.'

* * *

'We need to be set up here. What do you think?' Diane asked George.

She nodded. 'Yea. This is great. I can use the steps and the barriers if I need to get higher when it gets crowded.'

'I don't think the crowds are going to be a problem to be honest.' Diane remarked. 'As strange as it sounds; somehow I don't feel this is going to turn into a full-scale riot.'

The Canadian looked around, people were still moving back and forth, doing whatever it was they were supposed to be doing, but she could feel their held breaths as well. A strange feeling.

'Maybe.' She thought aloud. 'You know? It reminds me of a creature-feature I did about hyenas once.' She blew her fringe as she opened the legs of her tripod out.

'I had to go deep out into the desert in Africa and set up a cage-camp across a well known path where herds of antelope crossed year in year out.

'Wherever antelope are you can bet your life there will be lions following and hyenas behind *them*.

'The antelope came and then the lions, but not the hyenas. I'd waited days for them and then they made a no-show. *Jilted under the acacia trees.*' She laughed.

'I packed up once the lions had gone and took my camp further along the route they had been following, and lo and behold! There they were, all twenty-six of this big *cackle* - did you know a hyena group was called a cackle?'

Diane shook her head. 'No, I didn't, but it makes sense.' She laughed.

'So I get as close as I can to try and figure out what they were all doing up there,' George continued, screwing the video-camera onto the tripods camera-bracket. 'Just sitting around on the ground and not following a good food source as they should have been.

'Once I had my tower up and my cameras out I saw what they were sitting around; an old bull-elephant who had laid down to die. He was huge and he was still breathing when I found them.

'I'd never seen hyenas do that before. Usually they were very vocal around a food source and yammered and fought with each other constantly, but these guys were just laying under the shades of the scrubby trees and waiting.

'There was something very respectful about that.'

She stared off at the memory for a moment.

'How long did it take for the elephant to die?' Diane asked.

'That's one of the strangest parts of all; he died in the night. I was woken by the hyenas chattering and cackling. When I had a look through my night lenses I saw the bull had stopped breathing, but not one of the hyenas went anywhere near the body until the sun had risen. They knew he had died, because they were heralding it with their shouting, but didn't go near him.'

They both stood and looked at one another, the meaning of how George's story connected with what was going on right now wasn't lost on either of them. They didn't say anything though. Nothing needed to be said.

Once the equipment was set up and they had run their tests, Diane and George sat on the bench directly in front of the houses of parliament and waited, eating sandwiches and drinking cardboard-cup coffee.

They didn't have to wait very long.

The first engine noises of the busses heading for parliament came to both of them at the same time.

'Here we go.' George said and swilled her coffee down and stuffed the last of her sandwich in her mouth. 'Whef wohw.' *Let's roll*, in sandwich-talk.

Seven busses emerged from three, different roads, while another eight or nine were coming up behind them.

They began to drive along the road in front of parliament just as thirty-odd police officers spilled out of the same roads charging after them.

None of the busses stopped. Instead they drove straight on and back out again, passing more busses coming from the opposite direction and making *their* way into the road at the front of parliament.

Busses and police officers continued to pass Diane and George by, Diane frantically tried to keep the piece she was delivering as professionally presented as she possibly could, but the sheer enormity of what was happening and the sudden appearance of busses and police had thrown her for six.

'And more busses are spilling from the roads and crossing the traffic and going right past us as we speak - as I speak - and the police are *ejecting* themselves out of the roads and simply can't keep up and neither can I!'

Anyone watching the footage which George was filming would never have known that she was almost hysterical with laughter; not because she was *that* good at keeping a steady camera, but because it was on a tripod and she was crumpled up behind it.

'I can only describe it as coordinated, bus-driving mayhem. But which bus is our mayhem-causing hero riding in, causing all of this mayhem and madness.' She ran out of breath.

So did George.

Diane stood wide-eyed, looking shocked, and mentally kicked herself. *I said mayhem three times!*

The whole street was fast filling up with the public as well now, all watching and murmuring to one another, but on the whole remaining strangely quiet.

The busses continued, the police continued - somewhat hampered now because of the sheer number of public - and Diane's broadcast continued.

But there was no sign that any of the busses were going to stop. Until one suddenly did without warning.

The bus screeched to a sudden halt right next to Diane and George.

The police suddenly made similar screeching noises with their boots as they skidded and then reversed direction, sprinting as fast as they could to the bus.

Within twenty seconds it had been surrounded.

A policeman stepped up to the doors and frantically knocked - hammered at one point.

The doors hissed open and Sheila and Ethel stepped carefully down to the ground, holding their hands out for the policeman to help them. Which he did.

'Just the man I need.' Sheila said and patted his hand on her arm. 'Could you give us directions to *Madam Tussuad's* please, young man?'

Chapter Forty-Six

It was really *stinky* down here, Mathew was thinking. The air was greasy and thick from the belching extractor-fans, and everything, including the said extractors, had an oily tarnish to it.

They had *jumped* their bus almost as soon as they had turned the first corner back out onto the streets from the tunnel.

It was an easy job to just stay still for ten minutes while the busses sucked everything in behind them before the set off again, following slowly.

Once again it had been Alison's idea to let the busses go ahead and create a distraction while she and Mathew took their time to get through the almost empty streets and on to their goal.

She had insisted that they stay away from the main-roads as much as possible to avoid any or all CCTV cameras which they were bound to run into at some point.

That's why they were now slinking along a small – four foot-wide kind of small - alleyway, the steps to parliament being not too far away now.

'When it's really cold,' Alison said, turning her head behind her to talk to him, 'people come down 'ere t' stay warm. The's loadsa these little alleys. Most o' t' big cities 'av alleys like these.'

'That's awful really.' He said. 'How does anyone even *exist* down here?'

'Tha's just it, innit? Tha's all y' *can* do down ere; exist. Just.'

'Isn't it.'

'*Isn*'t it.'

They walked onward and as though the walls had been listening and needed to be vindicated, the haggard-stained form of a tired-looking, old man appeared ahead.

He shuffled along with his grimy head bent forward and his eyes pinned to the ground in front of him. God knows how long he had been living down here.

His clothes were spotted and splattered with all the different stains which this stewing back-world could provide. He looked as though he were carrying the world on his ragged, tired shoulders.

Mathew's heart bled for the man.

He continued to shuffle toward them.

Alison pulled Mathew over to one side so the man could go past unhindered.

He slowly hobbled up to them and without a look walked on past.

They watched his back right up until the point he suddenly stopped dead in his tracks and whirled around. Then they were looking into his wide, mad eyes.

'You!' Palmerson shouted, and pointed at Mathew.

Alison snatched the staff from Mathew's hands and then took up her usual position in front of him.

Palmerson glared at her. 'And YOU!!'

Alison tensed and glowered. 'Don' even think abou' comin' one step closer.' She felt Mathew's hand gently holding her shoulder.

'I'm sorry,' he said, 'but I don't know who you are. My name's Mathew.'

Palmerson flushed and the words caught in his throat, almost gagging him as they fought to get out. 'I know who you are! I've been bloody looking for you for *days*!' He emphasised *days* with a vicious stab of his finger.

'Um.' Was all Mathew could think of at the moment.

'Why?' Alison asked, knowing, as usual, exactly what to say.

'Why!?' Palmerson squeaked. 'WHY!?' He then screeched.

His eyes were threatening to leap out and attack them of their own accord while his arms were propelling his hands into a questioning dance of jerking, little spasms.

He froze again, this time with his eyes bulging and arms still thrown out during his frenzied gesturing. Then he blinked and relaxed all at once.

'I don't know. I really don't.' He finally said, sounding thoroughly beaten down. 'Because I was told to.' He finished.

Mathew didn't know what to say, so instead he opened his jacket and pulled out the last of Merylin's *Old Nasty*.

He unscrewed the cap and offered the bottle to Palmerson. 'I'm sorry.' He said. What else *could* he say really?

Palmerson took a couple of unsteady steps forward and took the bottle.

He looked at the pair of them, studying them as though he were seeing them for the first time in his life and with a new and clear perspective.

He had a look and a sniff at the bottle then. 'Is it safe to drink this? I can't really smell anything.'

Mathew chuckled. 'No, the word *safe* isn't amongst any word I would ever come across to describe that stuff. It is the very anti-thesis of safe.' And then he laughed whole-heartedly and genuinely.

Palmerson actually liked him. It was also refreshing to just hear the plain, old truth about things for once.

'Bottoms up then.' He said with a shrug, and raised the bottle to his mouth.

Before Mathew could tell him not to take a whole swig, Palmerson took a whole swig.

Alison covered her grinning mouth and stared on, waiting for the inevitable entertainment which was to follow.

Mathew grimaced and sucked his teeth.

The Mi6 agent lowered the bottle and his eyes went perfectly round and glazed for a few seconds before he smacked his lips. 'By God! That is *amazing*!'

Mathew and Alison stood looking on, obediently being amazed.

'You-you like that?' Mathew asked him.

'It's not bad,' he replied smiling. Genuinely smiling and not insanely in any way at all. 'Not bad at all. Where did you get it?' he asked, and offered the bottle back.

Mathew raised his hands. 'You keep it,' he said and passed Palmerson the top. 'An extraordinary lady called Merylin, brews it. Back up in Lincoln.'

Palmerson screwed the bottle-top back on and stowed it all away in his pocket.

He stood up straight and brushed himself down. 'So, which way are you going?'

Alison pointed back down the way Palmerson had come from. 'Parliament.' She said.

'Ah, yes, of course.' He nodded his head and sighed heavily. 'Well, good luck then.' He held his hand out to Mathew.

He took it. 'Thank you.' He replied warmly. 'You too.'

Palmerson turned to Alison and did the same. 'You're a clever little girl,' he said and winked, 'shame *you* weren't the prime minister, eh?'

Alison grinned and then laughed. She took Palmerson's hand and shook it. 'Thanks.' She blushed.

He gave them one last look and then shook his head, scoffing and wondering at all of the madness that had been. And for what? *Ha!*

He turned away, his step much more buoyed than it had been when they had first set eyes on him.

Crystal? Here I come, love. And as an afterthought; *I must get this stuff in my pocket to a lab so I can make some more.*

They watched him go until he disappeared around the bend at the end.

'Y' kno' 'oo tha' wer' don' ya?' Alison asked, turning to lead Mathew along again.

'No. Do you?'

'Tha' wer' tha' fella called Palmerson. 'Im we heard abou' from those agents.'

Mathew spluttered. 'Really!? The *mad-psycho-MiB*, as Diane called him, who shot at his own agent!?' He whistled. 'Blimey!'

Alison laughed. 'Yea; blimey. Word o' t' day that.'

'He didn't look as bad or as mad I thought he would be.'

'No' afta Merylin's brew 'e wan'.' She laughed again.

The end of the alleyway came into sight at the next turn. People were flickering past the narrow entrance, going to and fro but none of them even looking down here.

They crept up to the end and then casually stepped out onto the pavement and joined the flow of people going their way.

It wasn't long before someone whispered and then pointed and then everyone began to look. But none of them pressed in on them or rushed at them with their mobiles out. In fact they seemed to be walking around them, keeping a thick wall of people between them and the road beyond. A bit like what the busses had been doing only they were bricks in a wall of people now. Hadn't that always been the case?

The mass of people swelled as it walked the last few hundred yards to parliament.

Alison pulled Mathew close to her and then held onto his sleeve. She led him across the road, the swell of people all making the path clear for them.

The police were just dealing with Sheila and Ethel when Mathew and Alison walked calmly up behind everything and stepped straight for the main entrance to the houses of parliament themselves. And not a single police officer saw them until it was too late.

The crowd had stopped at the bottom of the steps and stayed quietly put while Mathew was led by Alison up to the top of the first steps.

Even when a group of armed police officers ran from the building and lined up in front of Mathew and Alison to block their path, the crowd remained silent and didn't move a single muscle.

Mathew stopped and looked up at the officer directly in front of him, a tall, bulky man wearing all the equipment to stop - or start - a small rebellion.

Mathew smiled up into his stern, square-jaw face. 'Hello.' He said. 'I've come to see the prime minister, I think she's expecting me.'

The officer sighed. 'I'm very sorry, sir, the prime minister isn't available.' He reported professionally.

'I see.' Mathew then said and looked at his boots. They'd seen him come all this way.

He looked back up and smiled again. 'Thank you. If you could get a message to her that I am here I would be most grateful.'

The officer didn't return Mathew's smile. 'I will leave a message. Anything else, sir?'

'No. No, that's everything thank you, officer. I'll wait outside.' And he turned away to walk back down the steps.

Although he didn't know the exact figure - no one did at the time - Mathew was faced with nine thousand, one hundred and sixty-three faces, all of whom were looking at him.

Almost ten thousand people were standing in the streets, on the road, on the walls, in the buildings, on the roofs, down the alleyways and every minute saw some more arriving to try and squeeze into the party. And most disconcerting of all - especially from the police's point of view - no one was making a sound.

There was none of the usual chanting and shouting, jeering and cheering; they were all just watching and waiting and being supportively quiet.

Mathew's jaw dropped when he saw everyone gathered behind him like that.

'Don' say *blimey*.' Alison said and took his hand.

'I'll try not to.' He muttered. 'Come on then. Let's have a seat.'

They walked back down the steps, passing Diane and George at the bottom.

Diane was speaking into the camera but gave them both a fleeting glance and a hidden *thumbs up* as they walked by.

The police on the streets didn't know what they were supposed to do now. They had been told to report any sightings and just hold Mathew Arnold until someone came and took him off their hands. But they were here now and no one was doing any kind of *taking into hands* so far.

The silent sea of people moved and swayed and allowed Mathew and Alison to make the last few steps to the wooden bench across the road from the parliament buildings.

The police tried to make a cordon around the area but gave up when they saw with their own eyes just how many people were now present.

They did the only thing they could then, they moved and swayed with the crowd and allowed Mathew to pass.

Mathew sat down heavily and propped his staff by his side. He leaned back and fixed his eyes on the monstrous building in front of him. *Here we go then. Here we blooming go again.*

He'd faced this dragon on its own terms when living back in his old life, it was time for *it* to face him on his terms now.

Alison sat by his side. 'Y' ready then?'

He gave her a reassuring smile. 'Yes, I'm ready,' he replied, 'I think everyone's ready now, Alison.'

Chapter Forty-Seven

The Three Days of Waiting.

Day one.

Government buildings all around the world were now seeing the same thing which was happening at the UK parliament building.

Thousands of people were marching into their capitals and setting up camp.

No one was making any kind of demand, no one was preaching, shouting, propagating, instigating or recruiting for the cause; they were all sitting around quietly.

Men, women and children of all ages, all cultural backgrounds, all faiths and all beliefs were sitting together in peace and with only one thought in common; wait quietly for The Freedom Walker to be heard.

Surrounding Mathew and Alison now were over twenty thousand citizens, spread out across the whole of London from their point on the bench.

The night had been okay and they had both slept quite comfortably; blankets and pillows had found their way to them from within the vast network of people, and warm food and hot tea seemed to be never far away.

Inside parliament the serenity of the outside was being beautifully balanced by the chaotic running and frantic shouting of members of the leading party as they scoured every inch for their beloved leader. And where the hell was Crispin bloody Wells!?

The deputy-prime minister was hiding in the lavatory. Everyone knew he was hiding in the lavatory because he had told them that was where he was going to hide.

The deputy-prime minister's aide, however, had a mind to get a boost in his career and began issuing a few orders on his bosses behalf. One of which was; get Mathew Arnold off that bench and into a cell for vagrancy.

Stupid, stupid little man, but let's go and see how that went.

The sun had been up for about an hour, Mathew and Alison had been handed baby-wipes to clean themselves with, and someone had cooked them a bacon and egg breakfast with tea.

They had just finished eating when four policemen marched up to them.

Alison was on her feet in a flash and stood by the staff, glaring daggers and other missiles at the four, big coppers coming toward them.

They stopped in front of Mathew, who just looked up at them in surprise. 'Good morning.'

'I have to ask you to come with us please, sir.' One of them said.

'Oh, yes? And why might that be?' Mathew asked, wiping his mouth and readying himself to stand.

'You're under arrest for vagrancy and you will have to accompany us back to the station.' The policeman answered.

Mathew sank back to his seat. 'Vagrancy? Really?' He scoffed. 'I've been victimised out of my home by them,' he jabbed a finger at the dragon behind them, 'and now they're calling me a vagrant.' He chuckled. 'Ironic really isn't it?'

The policeman sniffed and cleared his throat. 'Yes, sir, it is, but I'm afraid I still have to ask you to come with us.' He finished sternly.

He leaned forward to take Mathew by his collar and lift him from the bench.

Alison snapped in front of him and barred his hand with her body and the staff which she was holding across it.

Ten thousand people stood up.

'Don't you dare touch that man!' Alison shouted, clearly and as precisely as she had ever spoken. 'How dare you!? Is that how your mam and your dad brought you up? To intimidate and bully weaker people?' She berated. 'You should be ashamed of yourself! And you and you, all of you?' She then said, pointing at the other officers standing there. 'Is that how your mam and dad brought you up? To be bullies!? No, they didn't and they would be ashamed to see what you are doing here today! Ashamed.'

She lowered her staff and presented Mathew to them. 'If you are a bully and you don't know any better then you come and take him. But be warned; Mathew has a lot of friends.'

Ten thousand pairs of eyes blinked a silent confirmation of that.

'That man is doing this for you, and for you,' Alison continued, pointing at the officers again, 'and you and me and all of them,' she gestured all around her. 'He's doing it for everything that is good in this world. What does that say about them in there when they ask you to come and drag him away? Whose side are they on? Not yours or mine I can tell you.'

She plopped the staff back where it had been resting and then sat back down next to Mathew, taking his hand and holding onto it tightly. He could feel her trembling.

The policeman nodded slowly and then took a step back. 'Come away lads,' he said, 'it's not a vagrant, it's just a tourist, let's get back to it.'

The others nodded subtly to Mathew and then walked away with their team-leader.

The deputy-prime minister was called up before his peers to answer the horrible questions which were now being posed and the answers to which he didn't have a clue about.

His aide on the other hand had made a hasty retreat back to his apartments in Brighton where he would say he had been all along and hadn't managed to get into London at all that day. Wouldn't have made any difference anyway really.

And that was pretty much the highlight of day one.

The prime minister hadn't made an appearance and Mathew and Alison were set for another night on the bench. But it was quite a comfortable bench and he still had his waterproof bed on his back.

* * *

Day two.

Morning had passed very quietly, the breakfasts finding Mathew and Alison as soon as they had woken up.

Mathew had spent most of the morning reading from the book which Hamish had given him. He read aloud to Alison and any who could hear.

"'She opened the tin and pulled out one of the black and white photos in the shaky grasp of her right hand. It showed a handsome, smiling young man in American G.I. uniform standing next to a large, canvas, kit-bag; it was Edward. He had given her the photograph a week after they had met and she had returned the sentiment by giving him a photograph of herself, which Edward took with him to his grave.

Other photographs in the tin were, for the most part, of Sylvia, usually with someone unfamiliar to Rose standing in the frame also, or of places Sylvia had been that Rose didn't recognise.'"

He stopped and looked over to his right. Something was coming.

The heads in the crowd turned to follow Mathew's gaze.

A group of tall men were marching through the crowd, chanting anti-government slogans and waving their hands around trying to rile the crowd.

From the alleyway directly opposite where they were currently pushing through, seventeen men stepped out and formed a line in front of them.

Alison's eyes widened when she saw the backs of two of them and then heard Hamish's voice.

'Now then lads.' He said and held his hands up in front of him.

The seven, hoodie-wearing men stopped and formed up menacingly in front of Hamish and Puddle and Henry, and the other ex-soldiers who were all standing their ground with them.

'You're not coming through, lads, and that's final. No one here wants to fight or protest.' Hamish said and gestured to the people behind him.

He pointed at the leader of these men. 'And I know a soldier when I see one, lad.'

He stood back and folded his arms across his chest, giving each of them an appraising stare. 'What are you doing?' He asked simply, honestly. 'Look around you, what do you think all this is?'

The hoodies were looking at one another uncomfortably now.

'Yea. That's right;' Hamish carried on. 'You've been sent to fight a war that doesn't have the same rules as you have been trained to deal with, lads. This isn't a war that needs fighting with guts and guns; this is a war that needs fighting with little heroes, the heroes we are supposed to protect with our guts and guns, lads, not to throw ourselves at them because someone thinks they are in the way.'

He stepped forward and stood to attention. He flipped back his lapel and showed them his platoon pin. The other lads around him did the same; all showing different pins.

'Real soldiers only become heroes when we protect the small ones.'

One of the hoodies stepped forward and peered closely at Puddle.

Puddle dropped his gaze and looked a little embarrassed.

'Graham Sykes? Psycho? Is that you, mate?'

Puddle didn't speak, but he nodded.

Hamish turned to him. 'I bloody knew you were an army man, Pud. I knew it.'

'We all thought you were dead, mate! How did ya get out?' The hoodie asked.

Puddle looked up. 'I crawled out and then they caught me.'

The hoodie dropped his eyes. 'I'm sorry, sir. We heard nothing except you'd been killed.'

'You don't have to call me sir anymore, Kevin.' Probably the longest sentence he had ever said as far as Hamish was concerned.

The hoodie called Kevin, nodded. 'I do; you're still my captain whether you're in with us or not. You got us all out, sir, that's enough for me.' He said, and then stepped over to Puddle's side and faced off with the rest of the hoodies.

Hamish elbowed Puddle. *Captain*! He mouthed. *Wicked*! And held out his hand for a five-slap.

Puddle sniffed and looked down his nose and then lightly tapped Hamish's fingers and actually smiled.

Hamish wondered if the world really was going the right way after all.

The other hoodies shuffled their feet and then two of them nudged each other and walked over to where Kevin was stood.

'If we're gonna lose us jobs might as well be on this side and suppin' tea.' One of them said and shrugged.

Hamish gave the remaining four a look. 'What's it to be, lads? Captain Puddle and his merry band, or are you going back to the dog-handlers?'

The remainers shook their heads; they were army through and through, orders were orders.

After giving the three lads who had crossed over a wry look they turned away and walked back the way they had come, the crowd opening to let them through and then closing silently behind them once they had passed.

'If you start calling me captain Puddle you'll wake up one morning to find your lips have been super-glued together.' Puddle said, leaning down so only Hamish could hear him.

He gave a tiny salute. 'Yes, captain Psycho, sir!' He answered just as quietly.

'And if you call me that you'll wake up to find your lips have disappeared entirely.' Puddle promised and smiled again.

'Ya look good when ya smile, Pud.' A tiny voice spoke up from behind.

They both spun around to see Nippy standing there.

Puddle picked her up and hugged her to his chest, his beard finding her eyes and mouth. 'I knew you'd stick it to them, wee lass, I just knew you'd get Mathew here.'

He dropped her back to the ground and then just stood and laughed like a bear.

Hamish and Alison just watched on, smiling amazed.

'Amazing.' Hamish couldn't help but say it.

'Yea. 'E does tha' dunt 'e?' Alison said.

'Who?'

She pointed to the bench. 'Mathew.'

Hamish looked. 'Aye, I suppose you're right there, Nippy. We've been following for three days. Off in the distance, proper reconnaissance like.' He sniffed and rubbed his nose.

'Oh, shurrup y' daft 'ed.' Alison said and gave him a thump and then a big hug.

He let her go. 'We've got to get back into position, lass, but Merylin sends a message for you; she said she'll see her little dove very soon.'

Alison sniffed and wiped at her eye. 'Thanks 'Amish.'

Hamish took her head in his hands and stooped and kissed her forehead. 'Stick with him, Ali, we've got your back.'

He released her and turned back to the others. 'Right, we all know the plan and the setup, except for you three who don't, but apart from that.' He beamed at them all and held his hands out but said nothing else.

Henry cleared his throat just before Puddle did.

'Was there an instruction or order in any of that?' Henry asked.

'No, course not, this isn't the bleedin' army is it!?' Hamish winked at them and laughed his gleeful laugh.

Chapter Forty-Eight

Day three.

Mainstream news had killed most of the stories of *The Freedom Walker* now and were no longer reporting anything. But it was far too late for television to make a difference to anything for a change.

Diane and George hadn't slept for the whole of the time Mathew had been seated on the bench, snatching only a few hours, turn by turn, after he had gone to sleep.

The views and news had still been reached everywhere though, and the first of the violent clashes happened that morning in Sweden.

It wasn't a direct consequence of any particular act by either the public or the police themselves, but because of a sibling rivalry.

Nineteen year-old Nikita Anderson, had been standing with the people outside Sweden's government buildings when she had spotted her older brother dressed in jeans and soccer-top and a baseball cap on his head. Her brother was supposed to be overseas on a mission in the gulf.

When she realised he was being used as a saboteur and agitator for the government, she immediately called him out and stood in front of him on live, Internet-television and began a fight with him.

It all got a little out of hand quite quickly and soon the whole crowd were pulling the other agitators off the brother and sister, and then some of the uniformed police jumped in and started pulling everyone off everybody else - including police officers off other police officers and the likes - while they themselves were being pulled off their targets by- oh who cares? They were fighting. In Sweden.

France had a similar scene unfolding after agitators were spotted and confronted by the crowd.

Unlike the others, these French chaps were carrying clubs and had masked their faces. But as usual, a few sticks didn't overcome the twenty or so thousand peaceful, French citizens standing around them. Not this time.

Many of the African nations were not as peaceful. Oh, they were peaceful alright, just not quiet with it.

Practically everybody was dancing or singing, even the police and most of the dignitaries and government officials themselves. It was even reported that one certain president of a certain nation - no one would say who or where at the time (it was Zaire) - had thrown his gates open and said; *"I feel freedom walking through our country today! Let us dance and be free!"* And they did. All of them, and it was loud.

American and Russian citizens were focused so intently on beating the other at keeping quiet that the land itself began to smile as everything took a day or three off to just be still and sit in quiet reflection.

We could travel around the world and the same tales were being told in several different languages and one unique one; human.

Mathew had woken in the night, his head was pounding. He wondered if he'd laid wrong and had trapped a nerve or something.

He rubbed at his throbbing scalp with both hands and just stared up into the clear, night sky.

The stars were bright and flaring. He imagined each throb being a breath from the resting people all around him.

I wonder what would have happened if it had rained? He smiled to himself at the thought. Unusual weather for September.

A bright streak flashed across his vision. And then another and then two more.

He smiled again, Mary loved those. They'd had more than a few romantic nights sitting in their deck-chairs in the back garden, just star-gazing and holding hands.

He asked her once if she still wished upon a star, and she had told him that you can only get one wish from a star and she'd already had hers.

He smiled again at what his stupid face must have looked like when she had turned and just looked at him, saying absolutely nothing and squeezing his hand with all of the meaning she needed.

He closed his eyes again. And then what felt like a blink later he opened them again and it was almost daylight.

He rubbed at his face and stretched. Well at least his headache had gone. He felt tired though. Tired and *thin*. Not thin in the sense of being underweight, but thin as stretched too far, stretched to almost transparent.

Alison stirred below him. She'd placed her bed beneath the bench and slept directly beneath him, head to toe.

'Y' 'wake.' She muttered, still half asleep.

'No.'

'Good. Me eva.'

'Either.'

'Ei-' yawn 'ther.'

Mathew swung his legs over the edge of the bench and sat with his head hanging down and his arms on his knees.

He pushed his back down and eased out the bench still imprinted there. Damn that felt good.

He straightened himself up and stared his morning greeting to the building across the road.

It sat there staring back at him coldly through its hundred-eye windows. *Morning you sly buggers, I'm still here and I have something for you.*

He dipped his hand into his pocket and pulled out the crumpled teabag he had carried with him all the way from its tin back in Doncaster.

The things this brew could tell of if it was dunked right now and drunk. It would be like one of Mary's secret wines or Merylin's brews or Cecily's hooch.

It would tell all the tales of the whole journey, giving you the courage with each sip to take the next step and listen to some more, until finally it had nothing else to say and someone else would have to get out another teabag and brew another story.

The sun began to show over the edge of parliament now, finger-streaks of bright light flared over the top, making the whole thing even more ominous and darker than it already was in the morning twilight.

Sleeping people began to stir, just as they had been for the past three days, usually as soon as Mathew had risen with the sun.

Others, like Hamish, Puddle, Henry and the lads, and others still in the form of police officers who were quietly standing by for Mathew if he should need them, all had been vigilant all through the night, sharing the shift of sleeping and watching like the professionals they were.

Dixon and Singh stood together in the alleyway behind Diane and George, marking their own patch and watching for any more agitators. And Diane, plenty of watching and smiling at Diane.

Mathew sat back, clutching the teabag and watching the sun climbing over the house of *tricks*. It was a good feeling to see the light burning it away the higher the sun rose.

The first tip-edge of its fiery rim poked a blazing eye-flash over the middle of the high roofs.

Alison came and sat by Mathew's side. She picked his arm up and placed herself underneath it, leaning into him and just watching the sun rise as well.

Breakfast smells began to float along the ranks of people; the usual bacon and frying egg smell, and toasting bread and strong coffee. Here, outside parliament, as thousands of people lived for a few days amongst one another, strangers for the most part. Strangers who were being anything but strange, for some very, strange reason.

Fire lashed and shimmered across the parliament roofs now, showing its pure-light dominance over every dark thing, even those hidden, crawling, leeching things which hid away under its crenelated cover.

And it made Mathew smile as his mind flashed hotly with it; *I beat you.* And then he gave Alison one, last hug.

So that's what it's been all about then? Blimey.

And slowly began to close down and die.

Well that wasn't so bad now was it? I actually made it! I did everything I set out to do, everything I said I was going to do, I can't ask for more than that can I?

I actually made it, Mary? Do you hear me? I made it and I am one-hundred percent toilet-water free! Ha! How about that then?

I hope Alison will be okay. I'm sure she will, she's surrounded by the best people, and I know she will go back to Cecily, even if it's just to get her Saint Christopher back.

Well blimey! That's Merylin over there! And Peach and Jolly. How the heck have they got all the way down here? Well I'm not complaining, I'm glad. That will make it much better for Alison.

I know she knows I've died. I can see it in her eyes. And there goes the teabag, straight to the ground. I think everyone will know now then.

I beat them. WE beat them. Me, Alison and every single other person down there and not down there.

Well that just tops it all; Glitter-pony making a path through the people like he's swimming through snow, and Darren following quickly in his massive wake. Marvellous. Perfect in fact.

And there goes the crowd, they've seen the teabag and Alison's crying face then. Poor girl, I wish it hadn't had to have been like this, but I don't think there was any other way really. But I'm sorry. For what it's worth, I'm sorry, dear Alison.

But good grief! How are the windows still intact with the noise of that roaring crowd? How?

The parliament building and all of the people inside will be shaking now I would think. I'm sure we are finally being heard. Ha! Well thank goodness for that.

So that's *what* The Freedom Walker *was meant to be then, I get it now. I hate it when I don't know what the point is.*

Don't I, Mary? Hate it when I don't get the point?

Well, I suppose I'd better go and see what I'm supposed to do next then. There's always something to do next *isn't there?*

Blimey!

Epilogue

Fifty-years later.

There were butterflies on the flowers today and flitting around the hedges and lawns at the front of the tall, glass building.

The wooded hills all around were alive with the sound of life, big and small.

Life thrived in most parts of the world now. Nature had found an ally in the humans after all.

The abundance and freedom that nature was allowed, had seen the planet flourish on almost every single technical and educational level that a human could achieve.

Wars were no longer studied or revered, they were remembered as lessons, severe lessons for all sentient beings to study.

That wasn't to say that everyone was now completely pacifistic, on the contrary, it was widely believed now and accepted that human-beings were not alone in the Universe and by extension it went without saying that we would still one day, maybe, have to defend ourselves.

But war and militarisation were a distant memory and only a memory which one would find in the history books now. The proper history books.

The world government had seen changes made to the planet which had never before even been heard of in the public domain.

Secret energy sources and other technologies were unwrapped and made public for the first time. And for the first time ever currency of all kinds were dropped as resources were suddenly no longer scarce.

It hadn't all been easy and straight forward though. The world had bled and had been made to pay a high price for the peace which had followed The Freedom Walker's protest.

But it had worked out in the end. Perfectly.

The butterflies lifted at the sound of the laughing children coming up the pathway. Their school-shuttle sat humming on its repulser drive and waited until the last child had disembarked.

The class of eight year-olds walked and chatted happily, smiling and giggling and pointing at things as they passed.

They stopped in front of a large, bronze statue and gathered around its base, looking up with wide, wondering eyes.

A little boy leaned forward and stroked the teabag which had been perfectly rendered by the artist.

A life-size Mathew and Alison were sitting side by side, holding hands. Mathew looked to be asleep while Alison stared up into his face and wept. The teabag was between Mathew's boots.

The teacher crouched down and read the plaque aloud for them (not that he needed to, they were all well into their advanced English by now, but it did save all of them from having to crowd around.)

'"Mathew Arnold, The Freedom Walker,' he read, '"and Alison Minting, also known as Nippy. They looked the dragon in the eye and beat it for all of us."'

The glass door opened and small, smartly dressed lady in her sixties stepped out. She walked quickly and excitedly down the shallow slope and rushed up to them all.

'Oh! Good morning, my little doves,' she beamed and then laughed. 'Welcome to the Freedom Walker Memorial Centre.'

She leaned forward and looked each child in the eye. 'It's wonderful to have you here.' She told them. 'My name's Alison, let me tell you a story about my best-friend Mathew.'

ABOUT THE AUTHOR

Well, if you really want to know about me, then read on.

M G Atkinson lives in the Cathedral city of Lincoln on the East-coast of England.

His writing-life began back in the days of his childhood, but his author life only began in 2014.

When asked; "What do you write?"

Atkinson replies; "Things unique and inspired."

He is inspired by the great writers, whose names simply do not need to be listed; they are the greats.

The English language has developed and evolved for hundreds of years but the meaning of prose, the deeper understanding of the written word, is all founded upon those great writers who paved the way.

Atkinson brings all of the old-word beauty and reveals it in his modern-world prose.

His belief in words and how to use them makes him think of them as playthings, hence his favourite saying: *Words are toys; play with them and build novels.*

Printed in Poland
by Amazon Fulfillment
Poland Sp. z o.o., Wrocław

54325833R00166